The Makings of a Fatherless Child

Chandler Alexander

Printed in the United States of America

ISBN: 978-0692398296

House of Cotton Publishing
Itta Bena, MS 38941

Dedication

This book is dedicated to my family, friends and close friend whose life prematurely came to a sudden end. This is our story. Until we meet again, rest on.

Imagine living in a world

Imagine living in a world where you are born to fail.

Where dreams are shattered by outward forces before they are realized and allowed to set sail.

Imagine living in a world where wolves are dressed in the best of religious attire

Where those who have courage to live without consent are condemned, judged, and called a sinning liar.

Imagine living in a world where poverty and despair signifies a reason to be gratified

Where hope and perseverance is of a different language; and being poor, ignorant and uneducated equates to being inwardly satisfied.

Imagine living in a world where the guidance of a father is unknown and lies solely on the lips of a struggling mother

Where the emotions of life are exaggerated, promises are broken, and the thought of reason never explained; causing the perpetual cycle of fatherless children to suffer

Imagine living in a world where the makings of a man lives within the essence of his eyes

Where the barrenness of his soul is concealed by dark blackened frames of cowardliness influence, embodying the lack of courage to achieve and chase after life, and of course dreams, the ultimate self-fulfilling-prize.

Imagine living in a world where the souls and minds of the young die way too soon

Where trying to go against the odds perceives you as being a negative castaway, an uppity chicken, and a "greater than thou," money laundering fool

Imagine living in a world where this kind of life is a reality.

Well look about yourself, open your eyes and mind, because this is the world that surrounds both you and me.

-Shake

Prelude

It's been ten minutes since the guards escorted me to the main interrogation room just outside of Zone 13.

Before I left my cell, six guards made sure that I was fully secured in hand and foot shackles. For some reason, for my daily one-hour recess time, six guards watched me carefully with semi-automatic rifles in hand ready for me to even think about doing anything outside of my daily exercise routine.

The system branded me as an imminent threat and danger to society, or as the prosecutor stated "A text book psychopath". They can say what they want about me but those who really know me, know who I am. To me, personally, I am hero and a man who did what he had to do to survive, to teach, and to redeem peace for others.

My lawyer reached out to me three days ago telling me that a young writer, who heard my story somewhere, wanted to write a book about my life.

Baby Sister wouldn't had believe this if I told her. Just knowing somebody wanted to write about me would have brought joy to her life.

"How you doing Mr. River. My name is Mark Wilbert," Mark said entering the room and extending his hand for a shake.

"I am good Mark and you," I responded extending my hand to meet his.

"I am well. I am very excited about working with you and hearing your story," Mark said.

"Well good. I am excited to tell it to you," I said. "How did you hear about me,"

"I remember reading the details of your case in the Delta Chronicles back in Mississippi," Mark said.

"Are you from the Delta," I asked.

"I am. I am from Inverness," Mark said.

"Down there by Belzoni," I asked.

"Yes sir," Mark responded.

"Now I know I am in a good place now. A delta boy interviewing a delta boy, can't go wrong with that," I said with pride. The Mississippi Delta was the place where I was born. A place that made me who I am.

We both laughed.

Mark sat down and gathered his materials from his brief case, put the recording device on the table and pressed record.

"So let's get started," Mark implied.

"Ok," I said.

"This is Mark Wibert here with Mr. Amel River on March," Mark said but I quickly cut him off.

"I don't want this to be dated" I requested.

Mark looked at me with confusion.

"I just don't," I insisted.

Mark nodded to say he understood, still with a "why" look on his face. But he respected my wishes and continued.

"So tell me Mr. River, how did you become one of the most influential individuals of our time," Mark asked.

I chuckled, "Lawd have mercy. Most influential, ain't that something".

I paused for a second to stop blushing from what Mark had just said about me.

"Well, let's see," I said looking into the sky, trying to find the right place to start telling my story.

Mark opened his notepad, pen in hand, and the session began.

Chapter 1

I remember the spring of my thirteenth year of existence like it was yesterday.

I remember how the spring wind swept across the old white wooden house with whispers of the past and chills of the future. It was a beautiful Saturday morning in the small Mississippi Delta town of Bear Ridge. I remember how the little birds were chirping in the plum trees with grace, how the wooded trees green leaves matched the blueness of the sky just right, and how the mixed smell of fresh cut grass and sewage filled the air, from people mowing their yards and taking a shit that flowed to the back of our house, down a hill, and into the lake.

I slowly awoke to the sound of my mother, Baby Sister, warming up my favorite breakfast, the leftovers from the night before. Food always tasted that much better to me when it had set in the refrigerator and marinated in its own flavor overnight. The aroma from the pig feet, collard greens, and sweet hot water corn bread would have made the most disciplined vegan mouth water.

"Boy, get on in here and get you something to eat," Baby Sister yelled to me from the kitchen. Baby Sister usually called me "boy" or "mane" except for when I was in serious trouble, then my name was back to being Amel, only in a more severe tone.

I laid in bed as I usually did each morning, trying to gather my thoughts about what possibilities the day could bring. Before I rose, I threw the covers to the right side of where I laid. Then I sat up straight in the bed, wiping cold from my left eye first, then my right eye. I placed both feet on the floor, making sure my socks were pulled tight on my feet, yarned out loud, put on my house shoes, standing up to stretch.

"Today gotta be a good day," I said with a smirk.

The phone rung on Baby Sister dresser, I answered.

"Hello," I asked.

"What's up," the caller said.

"Who this," I asked.

"This Sea'Sea fool, who else," My home girl Sea'Sea said.

I rolled my eyes and gritted my teeth. "What I tell you bout calling me when I first wake up," I said in a low angry tone.

"How I pose to know you just woke up. Come on now," Sea'Sea screamed.

"Cause I wake up every day at the same time," I said. "Imma call you back this evening aight,"

"Don't worry bout it. You too fucking stupid for me," Sea'Sea said as she hung up the phone in my face. I will get to who Sea'Sea is later.

I hung up the phone, shook my head and journeyed towards the kitchen. "Stupid ass, just fucked up my whole day, just watch,"

I slowly entered the kitchen, finding Baby Sister slumped over the sink in her old white night gown that was torn at the belly; with a black du-rag wrapped tightly around her head to keep her rollers in place; cooking, drinking a beer, mumbling words to herself and doing the dishes all simultaneously. I noticed she was dripping wet from sweat, due to the lack of an air conditioned unit being in the old white wooden house we resided in. Baby Sister had moved me and Melo into the house from another wooden house, only the current house had running water and an inside sewage system. In summer months, the wooden house was filled with smothering heat, evident by the old wooden floors that sweated like pigs and the fan that occupied the front room window that acted more as an oven than a cooling mechanism. In the winter months, each bedroom had its own individual electric heater and each bed had its own electric heater blanket for warmth. The old wooden windows were covered with plastic to keep out unwanted cold breezes that gracefully sipped through any rotten wood cracks it could find. The old wooden floors resembled walking on ice due to its coldness. Watching television, washing dishes and doing laundry were done in full winter attire. In any given season of the year, roaches, rats, spiders, and ants were common critters living amongst me and my family. Though many things needed to be improved within our home, Baby Sister felt proud to call the place her own and had big dreams for it.

"What up Baby Sister," I said.

"Hey Boy," Baby Sister quickly replied as she wiped sweat from her face with her forearm. "Sit down and eat you something. You know you got to get out there and mow that yard before it gets too hot. People die of heat strokes every day and you ain't gone be one of them,"

I nodded my head as to say yes ma'am. I respected Baby Sister for all that she was. She was small in stature, but she could rip a person's soul out of their body with the words that came from her mouth. Nobody messed with Baby Sister and everybody around town knew that she was a lady that was meant to be left alone, or else serious consequences could follow. Everybody knew my mother, Augusta River, by her nick name "Baby Sister". Often when we went out to make groceries, people would come up to her and say "You must be Bunny Sue daughter cuz you look, curse, and fight just like her". I knew Baby Sister had a tough exterior but I also knew she had a sensitive side because of the way she interacted with little babies, especially my little nephew Javion, my sister Melo's baby.

"What that noise is," Baby Sister said with a certain irritation in her voice as she heard something thumbing in the back yard of the house.

"Here comes the bullshit. I keep telling Sea'Sea not to call me in the morning, just fuck up my whole day every single time," I thought as I dropped my head. I knew that today was going to be like the rest of days when things were out of order, filled with drama.

As Baby Sister briskly walked over to the torn back screen door, she saw her car unattended and running, with the radio blasting.

"I know that bitch didn't leave my car on. I bet my motherfucking battery done ran down," Baby Sister said out loud to herself. I could hear the anger in her voice. I knew that trouble was about to show its face yet again.

As Baby Sister stormed her way through the house to my fifteen year old sister, Melo River, room, I watched in fear of what was going to happen next. These types of situations were frequent in Baby Sister's house. Baby Sister usually lost her temper over the simplest things while Melo rebelled against her with immense cleverness and attitude. I often felt caught in the middle of the fighting because I loved both Baby Sister and Melo dearly. I feared for them both and often locked the door of the room I shared with Baby Sister, usually several times before I fell asleep, just in case Melo decided she wanted to try something dangerous in the midnight hours.

"Why the fuck my car out there running and you in here sleep," Baby Sister screamed with rage as she entered Melo's room.

"What you talking bout," Melo said awakening from her sleep, surprised to see Baby Sister so upset so early. Her upset time was usually around 5pm not 10am. Melo had mistakenly fell asleep while washing Baby

Sister's car in the back yard trying to put Javion back to sleep after I told her he was woke and was crying for her.

"You heard what the fuck I said, why the fuck my car outside running and you in here sleep. You don't pay no bills around this motherfucker so how the fuck do I pose to go to work if my car stop running. Stupid bitch," Baby Sister screamed.

"Ain't nobody stupid," Melo responded quickly with a slight rebellious tone. I had told Melo many of times not to say anything to Baby Sister while she was angry. We both knew Baby Sister seemed to hate every aspect of her life on most days, including us. I desperately wanted Melo to understand how to deal with Baby Sister's anger instead of reacting to it.

"Who the fuck you thank you talking to like that. You what the fuck I call you bitch. And say another word and watch I knock the teeth out yo motherfucking mouth," Baby Sister screamed now pointing her finger in Melo's face.

I feared for both of them, for I knew that both of them were in search of finding something. Perhaps they both were on the search to find happiness. To Melo, I knew that her happiness was found in having nice things such as clothes, shoes, and jewelry, something Baby Sister couldn't provide or afford. To Baby Sister, I assumed that her happiness was found in the relationship she had with her own mother, something she had lost at the tender age of 16.

"Didn't I say ain't nobody stupid," Melo responded again, this time looking at Baby Sister in the eyes while saying her words with strong conviction. The room fell to a dead silence for a few seconds as Baby Sister looked at Melo with an ice cold stare.

"Ok, bitch you thank I'm playing witcha don't you," Baby Sister screamed reaching for the television remote on top of Melo clothing chest.

I watched with distress through the peep hole of the Melo's bedroom door. I started to feel guilty about what was transpiring due to the fact that I told Melo to come and put Javion back to sleep, something that I could have done myself but was too busy thinking about getting back to my own sleep.

In the mist of my guilt trip, I spotted my one and a half year old nephew climbing out the bed and running to Baby Sister, but Baby Sister didn't notice Javion because her mind was set on Melo.

As soon as Baby Sister grabbed the remote from the clothing dresser, she threw it at Melo head and charged at her like a raging bull in the same motion, unintentionally knocking Javion to the floor.

The remote hit Melo in the forehead, sending her into a complete daze. By the time Melo understood what was happening, Baby Sister was on her striking her like a punching bag in the face as Javion little body laid face down on the floor.

"I told you Bitch, I told you didn't I? You talk too fucking much. You just like yo stupid ass daddy. Stupid and foolish, nobody can't tell you nothing. Stupid bitch," Baby Sister screamed, now on top of Melo, choking her. Melo refused to fight back out of respect for Baby Sister.

Javion started to cry loudly as I watched Melo and Baby Sister fight. It was a cry that represented deep fear, not a cry from a child that had been knocked to the ground. I quickly opened the door and grabbed Javion.

Even at the age of thirteen, I was a good uncle to Javion. I fed him, kept him, changed him, and intentionally saved him from seeing the daily boxing matches that I wished I didn't witness myself. I felt that he was too young to be tainted with such anger and violence, I wanted him pure for as long as I could protect him from real life.

"It's ok Champ, its ok. Shhhhhhhhhhhh. Shhhhhhhhhhhh," I said to Javion as I tried to calm him down. "It's ok Buddy, its ok," I said again as I quickly walked out of the room as the boxing match between Baby Sister and Melo continued.

I had a great attachment to Javion. I deeply admired his innocence and worry free nature that all babies had. Melo had given birth to Javion when she was only 14 years old, but I didn't care about that. Melo had been my mother and father ever since I could remember.

"And you tell that motherfucker Stoney that if I see him around my house one more time, I am going to put a bullet dead in his ass, you hear me. You not going to get another baby on me, you can bet yo ass on that. And you need to take yo ass to that health department and get checked out. Seems like you fucking with a different boy every week. Fast ass, pussy hotter than the fucking sun," Baby Sister screamed walking out of Melo's room, slamming the door.

"Damn no wonder these people scared of her, this motherfucker crazy," I thought silently as me and Javion listened from the living room.

As I walked onto the front porch with Javion attached to my hip, I sought comfort in the things that took me away from all the drama, my imagination and thoughts. I often imagined and thought about the day when I would become a man and have my own family.

"One day, you will be proud to have known me Javion. You, Baby Sister, and Melo will be proud one day, you hear me Champ," I said looking at the smile on Javion face while we both stood before the front porch door, admiring the beauty of the country that surrounded us.

Melo and I had different fathers that were absent from our lives. It seemed like when other people were about to celebrate their sweet 16, Melo was getting ready to celebrate her introduction to being a real woman.

"Give me my motherfucking baby Shake," Melo said as she stormed out of the front screen door, making her way onto the porch. "That bitch in there talking bout not getting another baby. Hell, I wouldn't have a

16

baby if her ass would be a fucking momma and take care of us like a momma should. I gotta fuck these niggas in order for me, you, and Javion can eat. Those shoes and clothes on yo feet and back, I bought that. Those pig feet you ate this morning, I bought that. Hell I am 15 and doing more than she is doing. Because she fucked up she want everybody else around her to be fucked up just like her. Crazy bitch, get on my fucking nerves,", she continued while grabbing Javion from me and bursting out of the front porch door. I knew that she was upset by the water that was filling up in her eyes, something she tried to hide from me by keeping her head down. But I noticed it anyway. She always kept from crying in those situations. She wanted to show her strength and prove to Baby Sister that she couldn't be broken by sticks or stones.

As Melo was getting into her 1987 Ford Pinto, the car that she had paid for with her waitress salary at Cabbie Chicken and sexual favors, Baby Sister stormed out of the house wanting to say her parting words to Melo before the drama subsided for the day.

"And if you thank for one motherfucking minute that that motherfucker got yo best interest at heart, you got something else coming. That motherfucker don't love you or that baby. Just look at you, always running to him and his family. They don't give a rats ass bout you or that baby. You will see one day that life ain't no fantasy and that so called love you got with that motherfucker is bullshit. You will see, with yo stupid ass. Can't nobody tell you shit though, that's what wrong witcha now," Baby Sister screamed from the front porch at Melo.

"It ain't bout love Baby Sister, it's bout survival," Melo screamed back with her voice cracking.

I sat down on one of the white plastic chairs that were on the porch. I watched as Baby Sister stormed back into the house and as Melo loaded Javion into his little car seat. As she was about to get into her car, I seen her wipe her eyes due to the tears that flowed from them. I hated to see Melo hurt like that.

"Everything gone be aight Melo, just trust me. A better day coming. One day, all you will be proud of me and I will be proud of you," I said as I looked down and stared at the ground for a second. "Take care of that boy Javion aight Melo cuz that Pinto you driving gone break down any second. Look how it smoking and how loud it is. Yall be careful," I thought as I watched Melo slowly speed off.

A few minutes passed as I sat on the porch reflecting on what had just transpired. Although I didn't show it, seeing Baby Sister and Melo fight impacted my life more than they could ever understand. Seeing them fight scared me and made me afraid for my life and theirs. Emotionally, it tore me to pieces.

"Amel," Baby Sister yelled to me from inside of the house. "Bring yo ass in this kitchen right motherfucking now,"

"Fuck, I forgot to take out that trash," I thought as my heart dropped to my knees. I knew that Baby Sister called me by my real name only when I was in serious trouble. I jumped up quickly. I didn't want to get on Baby Sister bad side.

"I did take out that trash last night, I wonder what I done did now. Man I hope it ain't nothing bad though," I said with a confused look. I knew I didn't do anything wrong, but I was still scared to face Baby Sister.

As I entered the kitchen, I found Baby Sister sitting at the kitchen table hulling field peas. She sat in silence until I came close enough to where she could look at me in my eyes.

"Don't you be no fool for nobody, you hear me. Always thank for yoself and don't let nobody steer you wrong. And leave them little fast ass girls alone until you ready for them. Leave them babies where they at cuz you can't take care of nan one," Baby Sister said, looking at me in the eyes.

She stopped hulling her peas and looked out of the torn back screen door. Her demeanor instantly changed from being hard to being a bit softer, like she had somehow transformed into another person which happened quite often. It was like she felt bad for what had happened earlier with Melo and felt a reason to explain and rectify her actions.

"I'm doing the best I can with yall, the best way I know how. I know I can't get yall the best of thangs, but I am trying my best Amel. I just want yall to be good folk and strong minded. When I be hard on yall, I be preparing yall for life and this evil world. Cuz in this world, you have to be strong, and ain't nobody going to give you nothing or give two cents bout you. That's why I be so hard on yall. That's why boy," Baby Sister said to me, still looking out of the door in almost a daze. "Don't you be a fool for nobody, you hear me. Nobody,"

She snapped out of her daze and looked up at me standing next to her.

"My dream is for you to grow up and be a respectable man, a man that work hard, a man that take care of his family, a man that make sure his family live a good life. I want you to be a good man you hear me. Not no hoe out here fucking every bitch you see," Baby Sister said. Baby Sister knew that she could mold me into being a good man, far from the no good men that she had been hurt by in her own past. She knew that she could mold me into being the man that she always wanted: hardworking, respectful, and not full of bullshit. She promised herself the day I was born that she would make it her life duty to teach me all she could about being a man, her way.

I nodded to Baby Sister like to say yes ma'am. I always listened to what Baby Sister had to tell me out of respect for her. I knew that she meant well and had a good heart, but sometimes she struggled tremendously trying to show it.

I left the kitchen and made my way to the room that me and Baby Sister shared. I grabbed my black notebook from the dresser that often captured my feelings.

I searched for a pen in the drawers of the kitchen and found one. I stepped out of the torn back screen door and sat on the steps where twenty or so cats usually resided. I looked into the sky and took a deep breath.

I wrote:

Confusion

Only God knows the depths of a young soul that understands life before it is meant to be understood

When good seems to be evil and evil seems to be good

Broken, stupid, alone and confused

Am I all that you think of me or Am I all that of a fool

Oh God bless me and my family in the times of pure despair

When no one seems happy and no one seems to care.

Sometimes I want to go far, far away and run

But I only stay for the sake of my nephew, for he needs me, my little Champ Javion.

All will be greater in due time, but will that time come soon enough.

Please bless us all with patience God, when times get too tough.

-Shake
--

I finished my poem and sat quietly on the steps. I knew that at that moment most kids my age were outside playing while I sat there on the back steps of my house deep in mature thoughts, trying to search for peace within my family household. As I stood up, I let out a big sigh, trying to rid myself of any negative energy that I might have had from Baby Sister and Melo altercation. I then started to think back on the day Baby Sister found out that Melo was pregnant and how upset she was. I remembered Baby Sister telling Melo that she had to get out before the baby was born because she could not afford to feed another mouth. But things changed once she saw Javion's sweet face for the first time, accepting him wholeheartedly into our family and treating him like her own. It was times like those that constantly reminded me of the good Baby Sister had in her buried underneath all the anger.

I entered the house and made my way to the bathroom, locking the door behind me to secure my needed privacy.

"Who is you and what you got to offer this world," I asked myself as I stared in the little mirror that hovered over the bathroom sink, looking at myself trying to uncover peace and hope within my own eyes, the same peace and hope that I saw in Javion's eyes. The mirror was like a dairy to me, a place where I could vent and recite my poems and short stories. It was a place where I talked to my future self.

I stood still for a second as I heard footsteps coming towards the bathroom. The old wooden floors in the house always squeaked and shook when people walked on them.

"He coming today? Didn't he tell you that he was gone take me fishing," I asked Baby Sister as she passed the bathroom door. It was these moments that I got excited about. Just the thought of my father spending time with me made me smile. I watched from a distance as my friend's fathers took out time with them, taking them hunting and fishing, sharing those man moments with them. I wanted that so badly from my own father.

"He said he was coming. We will have to wait and see. You know he got circumstances. He might not be able to come," Baby Sister said. She never explained what kind of circumstances my father had, she only explained that those circumstances were the reason why my father couldn't fulfill 99.9 percent of the promises that he made to me. Out of my thirteen years of living, my father only fulfilled one promise, taking me to buy a jungle juice when I was five. I remembered that day like the back of my hand and wanted that one moment of excitement back.

"And don't be in there all sad and shit. He mean well. He a good man when he want to be. He just got circumstances, just like the rest of us. You will learn bout circumstances when you get older and then you will understand," Baby Sister said. It was something about Baby Sister when she spoke of my father that brought about a certain calmness and peace in her. Baby Sister always told me with confidence and conviction how good of a man my father was, never saying one bad thing about him, which confused me. I often thought "How can a man be so good if he never around and always got something else to do,"

I rolled my eyes. I knew that making a promise had succumbed to merely being a placeholder that gave hope to a young boy in search of quality time with his father. It was no longer something to be valued and upheld.

I hovered over the bathroom sink leaning slightly forward to get my face closer to the mirror. Both of my hands gripped the sink tightly with anger. I stood there with my head down as the tears flowed from my eyes. I knew my father wasn't coming. My feelings were hurt again, something that had become normal but still had the same hurting affect on my heart.

I then lifted my head up and faced myself in the mirror, this time my face two inches from it. I tried again to search for peace and hope in my eyes, only to find hurt and sadness in them in the mist of the flowing tears. I tried to search within my own soul for answers I knew my young eyes didn't possess. The only thing that I found, like countless other times before, was a reflection of a lost fatherless boy.

"I must not be good enough for him. He must be ashamed of me or something, but it's cool though. But I tell you one thing, I ain't gone disappoint my kids. Never in a million years. When I be a daddy, I will be the best daddy in the world, no matter what my circumstances is," I whispered with a sense of certainty in my voice. I knew deep within my heart and soul that being a good father to my future children wasn't a choice, it was my destiny.

Chapter 2

As the sun began to set and the tension level around Baby Sister's house began to settle, I found myself on the back door step once again thinking about Melo and Javion to the tunes of the crickets and frogs of the fast approaching sunset. Though I was concerned about their journey into the unknown, both mental and physically, I wished their travels well from afar. I desperately wanted them to be home with me so I could keep them out of harm's way and protect them.

As I was in the middle of a thought, I heard Melo car pull up in the front yard. I knew it was her by the sound of the old Ford Pinto she was driving. I smiled. My heart started to race with excitement as I ran to the front of the house to meet Melo and Javion first, before anyone else could. I wanted to be the first face they saw, to make things more comfortable for them entering Baby Sister's house.

"What's up Melo," I said with excitement and clearly out of breath from running.

"Hey Shake," Melo said to me as she pinched both of my jaws. Shake was a pet name she had given me as a toddler. I know seeing me always brought a smile to her face and made her day go a bit better. I was her baby before she had her own. The bond that we shared was indestructible.

"I am glad you came back, I was worried bout you driving that raggedy smoking car out there," I said to Melo smiling. I always said jokes intentionally to make her smile when she was down and out. "Yall had me worried though. I didn't know where you guys was or where yall went,"

"Don't do me," Melo said smiling as she walked into her room. I followed her like a cat clinging to its owner and sat on her bed. "But I just went up the road to calm myself down before I had to hurt somebody," she continued, cutting her eyes towards Baby Sisters room. We both smiled.

"Javion," Baby Sister yelled from her room. "Bring yo little sweet self in here so yo grandma can get some of that good suga of yos,"

When Javion heard Baby Sister voice, he jumped out of Melos arms and wobbled his way to Baby Sister's room. No matter how mad Melo and Baby Sister got at one another, the one thing that held true, Baby Sister worshipped the ground Javion walked on. The love Baby Sister had for Javion strangely manifested into a love we all felt and admired.

"You know Baby Sister just stressed out with her job and stuff, so don't worry bout what happened earlier. Thangs happen sometime that gets out of control," I said, trying to make peace between Melo and Baby Sister. "Just try not to say anythang next time and you will be good, ok Melo,".

Melo looked at me and smiled again. She knew that I was always trying to tell her how to handle tough situations, even though she was three years my senior. She knew I was coming from a good place with every spoken word.

Melo placed her purse on her dresser and sat on the bed beside me.

"Life is just so tough for me right now Shake. We too young to be struggling and living like this. I'm out here working jobs that pay no money, leaving me to have to turn tricks for money and stuff. I don't want to do that for the rest of my life. There gotta be a better life out there, you know," Melo said.

"It is a better life out there, I know it is because I dream bout it. We just got to wait on our time for thangs to change for us. But until then, stop talking back so much," I said with a smile. People always said I talked beyond my age, even as a little boy. I wanted to reiterate to Melo that talking back was only going to make our situation worse than it was.

The room fell into a deep silence.

"Shake," Melo said with a nervous tone looking down at the floor. It was obvious that she had a burden on her chest that she wanted to release.

"What's up Melo," I responded as I watched television.

"I want to tell you something that I ain't told nobody. So you can't tell nobody when I tell you, it's our secret aight," Melo said, still nervous.

"Aight," I replied.

Melo blew out a big sigh and rubbed both of her thighs with both of her hands simultaneously. She was nervous.

"What," I said to cut the silence.

Melo continued to hesitate.

"I got HIV," Melo replied with a cracking voice trying to hold the tears in. She knew that life had sentenced her to death at the age of 16.

"Oh ok. Where it at? You must want me to see it," I responded still watching television, showing my immaturity and ignorance towards the matter. My dumbass thought HIV was something that she had bought from a store, like a piece of paper or a writing pen.

"Shake, look at me," Melo silently screamed, irritated that I was so dismissive about her situation. "I'm sick,"

Then Melo started to cry.

I jumped up instantly to see why Melo had gotten so emotional all of a sudden.

"What's up Melo," I said as I hugged her with concern. "Who fucking witcha. Let me know who and watch me go holla at them right quick,"

The tears flowed down my face just as fast as they did Melo's face. When Melo heart hurt, my heart hurt. We were one in the same. She was all I had. Though I didn't know what HIV was at the time, I knew the impact that it had on Melo life due to the fact that she was crying real tears nonstop.

Melo pulled me closer and hugged me even tighter, trying to hold on to her safe haven that had always resided in me. To disappoint me meant failure to her life. She had two babies in her life, Javion and me, and she understood she wouldn't live to see neither of us grow up.

"I'm dying," Melo said with hurt in her heart as the tears continued to pour from her eyes, now even harder. "You my responsibility and I fucked that up,"

"What? You dying? What you mean," I said as I cried harder. The word dying matched with Melo name took a piece of my life away. I hugged her tightly.

Melo took a minute and gathered herself and placed my face in her hands. She looked into my eyes and kissed me on the forehead.

"Don't you make the same mistakes that I made or else life will do you like it's doing me. You hear me," Melo said with a serious tone looking me in my eyes. "Do you hear me I said,"

I nodded my head with tears still flowing down my face. Melo wiped both of my eyes as a mother would do her crying son.

"And don't be around here moping around. Yo sister gone be aight. But believe you me, these niggas gone pay for what they did to me. They gone pay Shake, believe that. There gone be lots of hurt souls round here. You just watch and see,"

I didn't understand what she meant by what she had said, the only thing I knew was Melo seemed determined to make people pay. To see the fire in Melo's eyes made me proud. I knew whatever Melo said she was going to do, she was going to do with full force.

--

A couple of hours passed. Peace was the mood in Baby Sister's house as a result of my conscious efforts to not let Baby Sister and Melo cross paths. If one needed something, I jumped to do it for them with the hopes of keeping them separated at all cost.

While everyone watched television in their own separate rooms, I found myself in the bathtub pondering about this HIV thing that Melo had. I wanted to ask Baby Sister about it, but thought twice for the sake of not starting an argument or another boxing match.

I wondered "What is it bout this HIV shit that made Melo cry like she did. It can't be that bad where she talking bout dying,"

I stared at the old shiny bathtub facet as tears started to stream down my face. I started to think about what life would be like without Melo. I started to feel that it was partly my fault that Melo had HIV, that I didn't protect her enough.

As I finished bathing and slid into my sleeping clothes, I found myself standing in front of the small mirror that hovered over the sink.

"Don't you even thank bout looking at me. You a fuck boy my boy. Melo thank she gone die cuz of you. You coulda done more for her. Naw but you do what you want to do though," I said silently

While in the middle of my self-induced rant, I heard Baby Sister pacing back and forth in front of the door breathing hard and mumbling to herself like she was in distress. I knew something was not right. I could feel Baby Sister anger through the door.

"Come on Melo. I thought I told you to just not to say nothing," I whispered exiting the bathroom.

"What's wrong Baby Sister," I asked Baby Sister as she quickly paced passed me mumbling to herself.

"I told that motherfucker good to stay away from my house, but he want to do what he want to do. I guess its fuck me then," Baby Sister said as she stopped pacing and walked into her bedroom to get her 38 revolver from her clothing dresser.

"Baby Sister, what happened," I asked with concern. I thought this was the end for Melo. My heart dropped to my knees.

"Shut.....the....fuck.....up......Amel. Please," Baby Sister responded as she gave me a look that silently told me to get the fuck out of the way. I knew she wasn't in her right mind so I just moved out of the way before she pointed that motherfucker at me.

Baby Sister made her way back to the front door, with her gun in hand, still mumbling and cursing to herself. I slowly followed her, like a fool, in fear as she approached the front door, hoping that her mission wasn't to go take out Melo. As she was about to burst out of the front door, I noticed one of Melo's guy friends, Stoney Edwards, at her bedroom window talking to her. Baby Sister had seen him two minutes earlier, but Stoney didn't know she had seen him.

"Stoney, didn't I tell yo motherfucking ass to stay away from my motherfucking house," Baby Sister screamed as she burst through the front door.

When Stoney heard her voice, he instantly panicked like he had heard the voice of death itself. Stoney feared Mrs. River, as he called Baby Sister, from his core. But his love for Melo couldn't keep him away.

"Stoney," Baby Sister screamed again as she dashed out of the front porch door.

Stoney slipped as he tried to run off. He quickly gathered himself and ran as fast as he could behind the house and into the darkness of the night.

Baby Sister followed in hot pursuit with her gun raised to the sky.

Pow. One shot went into the air. Pow. Pow. Pow. Three more shots went into the air.

As I followed behind Baby Sister as she fired her gun, for some reason something in me feared for Stoney. Even though Stoney was a good dude to me and Melo, at that moment Stoney was an enemy of Baby Sister, so he was an enemy of me too.

Pow. Pow. The last two shots were fired in the direction of the dirt that was left from Stoney ducking, diving, and dodging bullets that he thought were aimed at him.

I could hear Stoney running like a deer through the woods.

Me and Baby Sister stood there in the darkness of the night in an awkward silence after the last shots were fired at Stoney.

"Don't come around here no motherfucking more. You hear me Stoney. If you thank you bad then try me, I won't be so good to yo ass the next time. Next time, all the bullets gone be flying at yo motherfucking ass. I'm trying to save yo life you stupid motherfucker and you don't even know it," Baby Sister yelled into the darkness of the night. Although she felt disrespected by him, her motives weren't just about disrespect. I think she knew of Melo's condition and somewhat feared for the young man. "And I want you to tell that mamme of yos too. I'll put a bullet in her ass too,"

I stared at Baby Sister as my heart continued to beat like a drum. I was traumatized, couldn't move, couldn't say shit. It was that moment that instilled fear of Baby Sister into my mind, into my soul. I knew before that she didn't play, but I knew for sure then that she was stone cold crazy.

Baby Sister looked at me with her gun still smoking in her hand and caught me staring at her with fear in my eyes, not blinking at all like I was in a daze. "You want some of this too,"

"NO SIR," I said as I stood erect with my head to the sky, saluting Baby Sister like my toy army men did.

Baby Sister laughed. She knew I was scared out of my mind but she wanted to make a point to her family and others in the community that she was not going to be disrespected by anyone, especially in her own home.

"That's what I thought," Baby Sister said with a smile. Then her demeanor quickly turned serious. "Look at me. You respect others, you hear me. Don't expect nobody in this world to respect you if you don't know how to give it. That's just how thangs work in this world. Respect yo elders and yo peers, but especially yo elders, that's how you get yo blessings. You see what happened to Stoney just then, that's what happens when you disrespect somebody. Disrespect can land you in a heap of trouble but respect can save yo life. You understand,"

I nodded.

As we made our way to the front of the house, I started to fantasize about a particular type of life, one that consisted of me and Melo having an active father in our lives. I wondered if we had a father around, would Baby Sister be so miserable, unbalanced, and unstable. Even at thirteen, I understood that those kinds of thoughts were only reserved for wishful thinking. I knew all too well the difference between wishful thoughts and dreams. For the first, I knew I had no control over what a man did. For the later, I knew I controlled whether or not my dreams came true.

As we entered the house, I worried about what Baby Sister would do to Melo, but to my surprise she didn't say a word. I figured that she knew she had made her point loud and clear to us all, including Stoney. One thing that I knew for sure, from that day forward I would never cross Baby Sister in a wrong way, ever.

The following day, Melo took Javion to Belzoni to get some Crabbie Chicken and never came back.

Chapter 3

Two years passed. I was now fifteen and somehow found myself all along with Baby Sister. I was no longer the little boy everyone once knew. It seemed within one summer, my entire body had changed. My voice had gotten deeper. My body had filled out into a 5'8 174 pound, stocky, muscle bound frame. Baby Sister told me that my body type reminded her of my father, especially my big calf muscles.

All that I had ever known as a mother and father was gone along with my innocent and hopeful eyes. I desperately missed Melo and Javion. I felt lost without them, somewhat incomplete. People around town whispered that Melo was living with a motherfucker that constantly beat her every single day with no regards for her failing health or young son. Word was she had gotten hooked on heroin, causing her to become dependent on the nigga she was living with and lose sight of her dreams for a better life that she and I always talked about. I assumed she was hoeing fulltime for money, which scared me since I understood what HIV was now and how deadly it could be.

I knew that if Melo was having sex or sharing a needle with anyone, those people would also be sentenced to death like her. I knew that her life mission was to make people pay dearly for her terrible tribulation, hence rewarding them with the same fate. The local newspaper had recently run an article that reported there had been a tremendous rise in HIV cases in the Delta, mostly among married men and teenage boys. By reading the newspaper article, I knew Melo was responsible for a good chunk of the cases. My main concern was for Javion. I knew Javion was just a little baby and hoped that the nigga Melo was living with wasn't beating on my little Champ like he was beating on Melo.

As for Baby Sister, my relationship with her was slowly reaching the point of no return, like her and Melo relationship started to turn when she was 15 but worse. Baby Sister was starting to act erratic towards me for no reason, often throwing heavy and dangerous objects at my head, trying to stab me with knives, and even going to the extreme of putting an unloaded gun to my head and squeezing the trigger to hear it's emptiness. I often found myself in the bathroom in front of the same small mirror that hovered over the sink, searching for answers as to why Baby Sister treated her own children the way that she did. I knew that a change had to come soon, or else someone would end up badly hurt.

--

I arrived home from school and quickly began to clean the house and prepare dinner for me and Baby Sister. Regardless of her erratic behavior, I still felt obligated to care and be there for her. I still could see some good in her even in the mist of all the drama.

The night before, I had taken a pack of chicken wings out of the big white deep freezer to let them unthaw while I was at school. I wanted to try something different with the chicken wings instead of baking them like I usually did. I wanted to try out a recipe that I had seen on television that consisted of cooking the chicken with a pot of rice.

"Oh, what's up Baby Sister, I didn't even hear you walk into the house. You almost scared the daylights out of me," I said with a smirk and a look of uncertainty. I didn't know which Baby Sister I was going to be faced with.

"Hey Mane. I see you throwing down in here. That's my boy," Baby Sister said with a smile as she patted me on my back.

"Damn she good today. Thank God," I thought with a sense of relief.

"Just trying to make sure you have a good meal after a long day," I said while walking the fine line of being nice and guarded.

"There you go. Take care of yo momma then boy," Baby Sister responded with a chuckle.

As I observed Baby Sister, I leaned against the big white deep freezer as I crossed my arms and started to contemplate. I wanted to tell Baby Sister about my problem, but I feared that she would fly off the deep end like she usually did. But I chalked up the courage to tell her anyway.

"Baby Sister, I got a problem that needs solving," I said with hesitation.

"You too young to have problems boy," Baby Sister quickly responded.

I let out a big sigh to calm my nervousness.

"Baby Sister, I need clothes and shoes for school. All my clothes just too little and too old for me. My blue pants done turned grey and is flooding. My shoes talking. My coat is older than I don't know what. I am still wearing Melo old pink and purple jacket she gave me like 3 years ago. And plus it's getting cold now. Bad enough it's cold outside but it's even colder in this house," I said trying to put together a good argument.

In my heart, I was growing tired of wearing hand me downs and Melo clothes to school but I didn't have the courage to tell Baby Sister that.

"Thank God Melo dressed like a boy sometimes or else I would be all messed up. You ought to see me at school looking thrown away," I said as I started to sweep the kitchen floor. I felt myself getting emotional but I didn't know why.

"Where do I pose to get the motherfucking money from to buy you some clothes, huh? The sky I guess. Money don't grow on them damn trees out there. Hell I feed you and put a roof over your head, but naw that ain't enough for you. You know you starting to smell yo piss just a little too much around here and it starting to get on my motherfucking nerve," Baby Sister said with an attitude.

"Baby Sister, all I am saying is that I need clothes to wear to school, that's it. I don't even need all that name brand stuff. You can just take me to the dollar store and get some stuff. I will wear the bobos, but at least my feet won't be cold. I just need something to wear," I said looking for empathy from Baby Sister.

"I don't have the fucking money Amel, what more do you want me to say," Baby Sister said looking at me in my eyes.

"Didn't you and Mae just go to the boat in Greenville just yesterday? Where the rest of that money at," I quickly responded before I realized that I had talked too much.

"You wait just one fucking minute little nigga. It ain't none of yo motherfucking business where I went, where I am going, and what the fuck I did with my money. You hear me,"

I instantly fell quiet and sat back against the big white deep freezer and thought about my options, but I knew I didn't have any.

I started to shake my head from side to side. My breathing started to get heavy. Before I knew it, tears began to form in my eyes.

"I am tired of begging for thangs that I need," I yelled as I began to breathe even harder, trying my best not to break down into tears. "It's just not right Baby Sister, I am tired of people laughing at me when they see my clothes. I am tired of people making fun of this house we live in. I am just tired Baby Sister,"

"Now if you say another word bout that bullshit you talking, I am going to be on yo ass like white on rice. Just keep on and see what happens. Just try me if you want to," Baby Sister said. "And don't start all of that fucking crying. Boy sometimes I thank you got a slit between yo legs just like me how much you be crying. Only the strong survive in this world Amel, so those tears don't mean shit to me. Just keep on living and you will see,"

"I ain't got time for this bullshit. Shit, I am hungry," Baby Sister said as she grabbed a spoon from the table and tasted the rice, blowing the scope of rice first to smother the warmth.

She took two long bites, paused, and spit the rice on the floor. Baby Sister turned and looked at me with the same cold stare she had given Melo time and time again.

"This rice ain't done Amel," Baby Sister said, still looking at me with a cold stare and with her mouth open due to the disgust she tasted and felt.

"It's my first time trying to cook rice. I wanted to try it with the wings," I said.

"Then why in the fuck would you cook it," Baby Sister said in a rage.

My facial expression turned into confusion. What Baby Sister was saying didn't make sense to me.

Before I could say another word, Baby Sister threw the hot pot of rice at me, hitting me in the stomach and knocking the wind out of me. I kneeled down on one knee to catch my breath.

"Now eat all of it up and I mean all of it. I hope it burn yo motherfucking tongue off," Baby Sister said as she started to take off her belt.

I knew all too well what was going to happen next. This kind of behavior was becoming more and more prevalent with Baby Sister.

"I'm not eating that," I whispered, still kneeling down trying to catch my breath. The pot had burned my stomach and left a bruise.

"What you just say to me," Baby Sister quickly responded.

"I said I ain't going to eat no rice off no floor," I said looking under-eyed.

The first swing from Baby Sister belt landed across my head and face, leaving a mark under my eye from the buckle. She started to hit me on every place on my body. With every swing, it seemed to be a release for her anger not just towards me but towards life itself too.

I sat there trying to be strong and refusing to let tears flow from my eyes. As with Melo, I refused to let Baby Sister break me. My respect and pride for Baby Sister wouldn't let me physically hurt her even though I knew I could.

As her arm grew tired from the swinging, my body grew in bruises from the buckle and thick leather belt.

"Now get yo ass in there and take yo bath and get ready for school. And you wonder why yo damn daddy don't give a damn bout you, why he don't want to see you. That's right he don't want yo ass. That's why he don't come around. And I'm the one sitting my dumb ass up here lying trying to make yo ass feel good. But hey, can a motherfucker blame him. Just look at how you act. With how you act, I wouldn't want to be around yo ass either,"

"What you say," I said squinting my eyes trying to make sense of what Baby Sister had just said. I quickly jumped up from the floor to understand her better. I stood toe to toe and nose to nose with her.

"What you say," I reiterated in a low serious tone, now looking her in the eyes, repeatedly biting down on my jaw so my lower jaw bone could display my anger, almost daring Baby Sister to repeat what she just said.

"Oh I guess you bad now. Ok motherfucker, I said....," Baby Sister tried to respond. Before Baby Sister could get out her words, I grabbed her by the throat and slammed her against the refrigerator so hard that the items on top on the refrigerator fell off and the sound of items falling over from within could be heard.

I stood there, with my hand wrapped tightly around Baby Sister's neck, watching her try to fight my hands off of her neck, looking her in the eyes in silence.

"You don't thank I know that motherfucker don't love me, huh," I said with rage in my eyes as I squeezed her neck even tighter. The tears started to pour from my eyes. Baby Sister had finally broken me with words. I knew Baby Sister's love for me had long faded, but with my father I felt a sense of hope that love had a small chance to be there since he never expressed his dislike for me in person. With her words, Baby Sister had validated that my hope of being loved by my father would never happen, something I had known all along but didn't want to accept like I accepted Baby Sister. "You don't thank I know that huh," I continued as I felt myself beginning to feel even more overwhelmed by emotions.

"You don't love me either, Baby Sister," I said as I started to cry. "You ain't no better than that nigga. You don't care if I live or if I die Baby Sister, so what's the difference. At least that nigga had the courage to let it be known he didn't want me. I thank him for that. You tell him that when you see him,"

Then suddenly my crying stopped. My once aching heart had suddenly turned somewhat cold. My mind instantly started to change towards life. My eyes began to lose the ounce of glare they once had. My once loving ambition was now a distant memory.

"I am sorry for what I just did, but just know you don't have to worry bout me no more Baby Sister, I won't burden yo life no more. You free now," I said as I released Baby Sister. She dropped to the floor to catch her breath like someone that almost drowned.

I stood there to make sure she was ok as she caught her breath. Then Baby Sister unexpectedly leaped up from the floor.

"That's my baby. That's my baby. That's my baby. I can't hurt my baby. I can't," Baby Sister whispered to herself as she started to pace back and forth in front of the refrigerator.

I stood there and observed her.   I was trying to see what the verdict was from my action.

She continued to pace, coughing every five to six seconds.

Then something clicked in Baby Sister, like she was possessed by a demon or something.

"You motherfucker. Imma kill yo motherfucking ass," Baby Sister said as she dashed to her bedroom to retrieve her gun.

"You already have Baby Sister," I silently said as I quickly grabbed my backpack, unlocked the back door and fled from the house.

I vowed to never return, just like Melo did.

--

I made my way to the small bridge that hovered over the small lake behind everyone's house in Bear Ridge. It was a place where me and JoJo always hung out. It was our safe haven sort to speak. The bridge and the water provided us with peace and comfort, far from the chaos of our normal lives.

Joseph "JoJo," Collins Jr. and I had been friends ever since we were in pre-school at the Brazil Center in Itta Bena. His mother, Mae, and Baby Sister had been friends since they were in pre-school too. Mae and JoJo would often come over to Baby Sister's house so that Mae and Baby Sister could gossip about what was going on around the way. To me, JoJo was a good dude who was misunderstood by almost everyone. To those in the streets, JoJo was a rugged little nigga who was known for robbing, stealing, and drug dealing.

I sat quietly on the grey rocks below the bridge as I made rocks skip across the water. I was deep in thought about what my next move should be.

"Damn I need a ride to Itta Bena. I know Sea'Sea should be at home. I need a phone to make sure though," I thought.

I reached in my backpack and took out my notepad. I wanted to capture my thoughts and feelings with words.

I wrote:

Dear Future Self

A black eye filled with emotions of bearable pain

Pain tender to the touch, cut deep within my skin, cut deep within my soul

Some say its love, some say its life, but I refuse to hide behind that

I ain't gone never be a bitch when it comes to truth, constantly taking what they say real love is, what they say real life is

To be real, I ain't never felt no love, hell, I ain't never felt life before

But here I am, sitting here, face in hand, with no one else to blame

Alone again, on the phone again, searching....trying to find everything else except myself

Just maybe...Just maybe, if I was born in another life, situations and circumstances would be better, people would do for good and not for evil, the meaning of love would mean more, promises would be a man's bond

The truth is, I don't know whose I am and who I am...but is that my fault though?

Since a lil boy, I was thrown to the wolves to figure it out, fight it out, you know like a man, on my own like a blind man working through a world of darkness with no hope of light

I tell ya, sometimes this here life can get too confusing, sometimes too scary, sometimes too intimidating to even try to be something

But underneath the heavy touch of life is where the truth lies,

The deceit, the dishonesty, the ignorance, it's all there

It's a dark and lonely feeling that leaves so many bruises that it's hard to keep count sometimes

Look at me!! I know you see these eyes on me, staring at you. Now, this is real truth. Now, this is real love...Now, this is real life

But like a cub trying to be a lion in an unknown world, I will try to survive and avoid the vultures that are all around me, trying to prey and devour directionless souls, like me

The truth is, deep down. I know it's something out there for me worth chasing, worth loving, worth dying for

Dear Future self, be patience with me, for I know that I know nothing of love or of life, but I am trying

You will have that feeling of who you are and whose you are. That's the only thing that keeps me going. Chasing what I think that feeling feels like.

But the harsh reality for me, in this breath, is...that I know I will have to die first so you can have a chance to live. For then I will be the old you and you will be the new me.

But until then.....Patience my future friend....You will exist before you know it...

Forever yours,

-Shake

--

As I finished composing my poem, I saw JoJo walking on the bridge smoking a cigarette.

"Writing in that stupid ass pad again," JoJo said from the bridge.

"Fuck you nigga," I yelled.

"Nigga I knew you was gay," JoJo said with a chuckle as he leaned on the railing of the bridge. "You gone burn one with me though,"

"What you on," I responded.

"Dro," JoJo said.

"Dro my ass. More like bama," I said with a smile. "Nah, I'm bullshitting. Role one though,"

By the time JoJo made it to the bottom of the bridge, he had a blunt rolled and lit already smoking. He tapped me on the shoulder and held the blunt out. I grabbed the blunt and took three quick pulls off of it without exhaling the smoke. I held my breath for about twenty seconds with my jaws bloated like a balloon. I finally exhaled the smoke followed by two small coughs.

"Got damn my boy, where you be getting this shit from. I been wanting to ask you that for a minute now," I said as I repeated the same routine.

I passed the blunt to JoJo.

"Shiiddd, I get it from my uncle Bay. He leaves shit loads of dope laying around like it's nothing, so I take a little here and there. Bay a fool with pushing that shit though my boy. I'm thanking bout bringing a little something to school tomar. You gone fuck with me and get this money," JoJo said taking a long pull from the blunt.

"LIES," I said looking at JoJo smiling.

"That's on you if you don't believe a nigga. You bullshitting, I'm bout that bread partner," JoJo said taking another long pull from the blunt, passing it to me.

"Shid, I'm bout that bread too," I said.

"Bet, let's make this money then. So you gone fuck with me," JoJo asked.

"Yeah Imma fuck witcha nigga," I said.

JoJo stopped and looked at me to make sure I was for real or not.

"Now when you see the dope, don't bitch out," JoJo said.

"Ain't no bitch in me nigga, you know that," I said.

"We'll see," JoJo said.

JoJo blazed another blunt and started it in the rotation.

"Nigga what happened to yo eye," JoJo said as he pulled on the blunt. He saw the blackness under my eye and a couple bruises on my arm.

"Momma bullshitting," I said grabbing the blunt from JoJo. "Nigga what you talking bout, what happened to yo lip,"

"Daddy bullshitting," JoJo said. His lip was swollen, which explained the reason why he was at the bridge too.

"Exactly," I said chuckling. "Nigga I can't feel my face right now I'm so high,"

We both laughed.

"All shit, I knew I had to tell you something my boy," JoJo said.

"What's that," I asked with intrigue.

"You heard bout yo boy AJ," JoJo asked.

"Naw, what that boy do this time. He stay into some shit," I said pulling off the blunt. Adrian "AJ" Jackson was a good friend of mine since the 1st grade. He lived in the City with his grandmother and grandfather. Ever since I could remember, AJ constantly stayed in trouble. He was a big boy for his age. At 15, AJ stood 6 feet 2 and 195 pounds of solid muscle. People around town said he had some kind of demon in him because he was a ticking time bomb. Everyone was scared to death to cross his path.

"They say he shot his daddy in the head 6 times, point blank range with a 9. And check this shit out. " JoJo said. "They say he was smiling while he was shooting him. But you know how people talk around here, they just talk for the hell of it. But we know AJ and how he gets down," JoJo said. JoJo knew the dark side of AJ from the times they use to collect money for JoJo's uncle Bay. He knew that AJ had no conscious.

"He did this shit in the City. I thought that boy daddy was in prison or somewhere,"

"It happened right in the middle of The City. His daddy just got out the pen bout two months ago. AJ been living with his granddaddy and grandmomma in The City. They say his granddaddy told AJ to kill the nigga. And that's his son. Ain't that shit crazy,"

"Mane that shit too crazy. But you know that's how he got so fucked up. His daddy use to beat the living shit out of him. You remember when AJ use to come to school in the first and second grade with black eyes and all the teachers crying just looking at him. That shit was sad mane," I said reflecting on the days that AJ was beaten so badly by his father. "Didn't the nigga go to jail for killing AJ momma,"

"Yep," JoJo responded.

"See what I'm saying. I bet the nigga got out, ain't seen AJ in forever and tried to come out and whip his ass like he use to when AJ was 5. How you gone try to whip a 15 year old man, when you ain't seen him in 10 years," I said.

"So what you saying? That the nigga was right for doing it," JoJo asked.

"I just know that if I was in that position, with a nigga like his daddy, that beat children and shit, I don't know what I would do. I might squeeze the trigger too," I said.

"Now you know that yo scary ass ain't gone fight nobody, let alone pull a trigger on a gun," JoJo said.

"But you know what's so fucked up," I said looking at JoJo.

"What's that," JoJo asked.

"That nigga told me when we was little bitty niggas that he was going to kill his daddy because of all the stuff he was doing to him. And we was no more than 7 or 8 then,"

"You for real," JoJo asked.

"For real though. That's on everything I love," I replied.

"Damn. What all he say though. I mean back then when yall was talking," JoJo insisted.

I looked at JoJo with a smile.

"Look at yo ole wanna be thug ass trying to get the scoop on some shit. Nigga if I didn't know no better I thought you was pussy," I said while laughing.

JoJo laughed out loud. "Mane chill with the bullshit and tell me what cuz said,"

"I just told you he said he was going to kill his daddy,"

"Nah, I'm talking bout, like, what he said like for real. Like say what he said just like he said it then,"

"He said he was going to kill his daddy one day. Just like that. Nothing more than that," I said. "And he said that with his arm in a sling,"

I looked off into the water.

"Mane, I know I might be wrong, but that nigga daddy deserved that shit. When you do wrong, that shit comes back on you twice as hard," I said.

"Nigga you sound like a ole man," JoJo said.

"Aight a ole man. We know what that boy AJ done been through. I hope he aight," I said.

"Me too," JoJo said

We both sat on the grey rocks in silence. I continued to smoke the blunt as I stared into the water, contemplating.

"Everybody ain't as lucky as you my boy," I said.

"What you talking my boy," JoJo quickly responded.

"You know having a daddy at home to chill with and talk too,"

JoJo laughed out loud as I passed him the blunt.

"Nigga what the fuck is you talking bout chilling. That nigga don't spend no time with me. You see my lip, that's all that nigga good for. Why you thank I'm out here hustling with my uncle. I gotta do something to help my momma feed us and pay them bills because that nigga won't work. I'm tired of seeing my momma struggling like she doing mane with a grown ass man in the house," JoJo continued pulling off the blunt as I stared at the water. "But this the life we was given so we got to deal with it my boy, the best way we can,"

"Now that's real," I said. "Yo, do you ever have dreams of making it out of here though,"

"Hell naw. Why the fuck would I even thank bout dreaming my boy, ain't nobody round here going to help me achieve them. So why fuck with it like that. Round here you got to lie, cheat, and steal to get what you need. As fucked up as it sounds my boy, it's true. We way too young for this shit. You see them kids cross them tracks, they don't go through the shit like we go through. The fights, the hurt, that shit adds up. Life shouldn't be this way my boy, but hey, what do I know. I am just another nigga,"

"You right though. We gone make it through though one day," I said. I knew JoJo may have been many things to many people, but one thing about JoJo was that he was trying the best he could with what he was born into, just like the rest of us from around the way. All of our wrong actions were unavoidable sort to speak, like it was meant for us to travel down the unfortunate road of despair. Making it out, to most, was a folk tale.

The two of us stood by the lake in silence as we finished up the last blunt of the set. It seemed as though talking about life always brought about a weird silence amongst children our age that lived around the way. Most of us smoked to escape the pain, instead of talking about it. The relaxation from the high eased the pain. We discovered early that talking about life problems would only deepen the wound that we already had on our hearts and minds, so we avoided it.

"Yo, my boy Imma get at you later aight. I got to run to the store for my momma before I go back to the crib," JoJo said as he gave me a fist pound.

"Oh you go make groceries too my boy. You like a mini house wife ain't it," I said with a smile.

"You got jokes I see," JoJo said smirking," You know I gotta be the man for my momma. Yo, I will have that package for you tomar, so be looking for me,"

"Aight," I said. "Yo, before you leave, let me use yo phone right quick,"

JoJo reached into his pocket and pulled out his cell phone that his uncle Bay had gotten him for making runs.

"Do not. I repeat, do not, call five-O on my phone," JoJo yelled.

"LIES," I jokingly replied.

"For real though," JoJo said with a semi serious tone.

"Nigga you know ain't nobody finna call the po-po like that,"

JoJo slowly handed me the phone. I started to dial out.

The phone rang about five times before Sea'Sea picked up.

"Hello," Sea'Sea answered.

"Sea'Sea," I said.

"Who this," Sea'Sea responded. It was a no-no to call Sea'Sea's phone without her permission.

"Oh you don't know who this is,"

"No I don't so tell me. You called me," Sea'Sea screamed.

"It's yo daddy,"

Sea'Sea hung up the phone in my face. I knew that her attitude with people other than me was off the charts and out of control. So I called back, hoping to God she would answer.

"Bitch, don't call here playing on my phone. Now, who this is," Sea'Sea answered with an attitude.

"Calm damn Sea'Sea damn, this Amel," I said.

"Oh what's up Boo," Sea'Sea asked.

"But I pose to be yo boy though and you can't even recognize my voice," I said.

"You know I didn't mean that. I'm gone make it up to you, ok Boo. Who phone you on," Sea'Sea said.

"JoJo," I said.

"I keep telling you stop fucking with that shasty ass nigga. That nigga fake as all out doors. I'm telling you Amel," Sea'Sea said.

"He cool," I said walking further away from JoJo so he wouldn't hear Sea'Sea talking about him.

"So what's up. You ok," Sea'Sea asked.

"Yeah I'm straight. The real question is what you doing later on tonight," I asked.

"Shit, waiting on you to come over and ...," Sea'Sea said with a slight laugh.

"And what Sea'Sea," I said with a smile.

"Nothing," Sea'Sea said.

"Naw, tell me," I insisted.

"I said nothing," Sea'Sea said.

"That's what I thought," I said.

"Whatever scary cat," Sea'Sea said with a chuckle. "How you gone get here,"

"That boy Mr. Lim usually come up that way just bout eleven every night. If he strike out tonight, Imma hop that ride with him," I said. "So if I strike out, Imma be over there. You cool with that little gul,"

"Is that even a question Boo," Sea'Sea said.

"Stop calling me that shit already," I said.

"Whatever Boo. See when you get here Boo. Bye Boo," Sea'Sea said.

I hung up the phone and shook my head with a smile.

"Mane that gul something else," I thought.

JoJo snatched the phone out of my hand.

"I forgot to tell you not to call hoes on my phone too," JoJo said.

"I told you bout talking bout her like that," I responded with irritation in my voice. People who knew me knew I didn't allow nobody to bad talk about Sea'Sea while I was around.

"Nigga you know she a hoe," JoJo said.

"I don't know shit nigga. Chill with the bullshit aight," I said getting upset.

"How you gone get mad over some pussy that you ain't never even smelt yet,"

"You better get on down before I put one in ya homeboy "

"Whatever lil nigga, with yo sensitive ass," JoJo said with a chuckle. "But Imma bout to strike out,"

"Aight. Fuck with me later on then my boy," I said as I watched JoJo walk away. "And don't be bullshitting bout getting this money cuz I need it. So handle me,"

"I got you lil nigga,"

Chapter 4

I hid in the woods a couple houses down from Baby Sister's House, waiting to hop a ride to Itta Bena from my 60 something year old neighbor, Mr. Lim, from down the road. I knew that every night around 11:15pm, Mr. Lim made his way to Itta Bena to buy drinks at the juke joint Blue Heaven and to buy pussy from the young girls and women who were selling.

I waited and waited until I seen Mr. Lim old red pickup truck pull out of his yard about 100 yards away. I stood in the road until he approached me. I asked him to give me a ride to Itta Bena. Mr. Lim agreed to take me and the two of us struck out up Highway 7.

"Fuck everything in sight," Mr. Lim said. "Knock down every piece of pussy that come yo way, you hear me boy. Fucking pussy is good for yo soul boy. Just look at me. I look 44 but I'm 64," he continued with a chuckle. Mr. Lim reiterated his "lots of pussy is good" argument over and over again with stories of the past and present as we descended into Itta Bena.

As Mr. Lim crazy ass kept on, I just laughed and kept quiet. He was the total opposite of the man Baby Sister wanted me to be.

Upon our arrival, I instructed Mr. Lim to drop me off on Kaine Street where Sea'Sea lived, just three streets over from Blue Heaven.

Sea'Andrea "Sea'Sea" Harris was my best friend ever since we both could remember. Even though she was a female, our friendship was unique, loyal, and pure in the sense that it never crossed over into being intimate. Me and Sea'Sea were one in the same sort to speak. We had grown up the exact way; poor, problematic, fatherless, and adventurous; which made us relate to each other in good and bad ways. We fought each other all the time but always made up shortly thereafter. Sea'Sea knew she was the only person that really understood me for who I was; the unpredictability, the complexity and all. She knew when to back off on my moody days and what to say to send me over the deep end when she felt like getting on my nerves. I trusted and cared for her and our friendship, even though I had a strange way of showing it. I valued how down to earth she was and her attitude towards life, she reminded me a lot of the old Melo before Melo got fucked up by the streets. Many people around the way thought Sea'Sea would turn out to be a food stamp baby, like most girls her age from around the way who grew up like we did: to have 4 babies before 23 years of age.

I made my way up the steps and knocked three times on the red front door of the old green trailer home. I already knew Sea'Sea mother, Jackie Harris, was at Blue Heaven doing God knows what with Gods knows who to chase another hit of crack. Jackie was never at home and had been battling her crack addiction before Sea'Sea was born. Sea'Sea's father was an unknown as most of the kid's daddies were from around the way. To most of us, including Sea'Sea, her father could have been any man walking the streets of any town within a 20 miles radius of Itta Bena.

Sea'Sea living situation had been fucked up since she was little, which explained her attitude and low tolerance for bullshit. I remember when Sea'Sea use to stay at home alone by herself every night when she was 8 years old. Nobody else knew that except for me. It was our little secret that we pinky swore over. Sea'Sea use to tell me how scared she felt when she was left at home alone at night. She was really fearful on days it stormed. Sea'Sea sometimes told me stories of how some of Jackie men friends snuck to her house from Blue Heaven and touched on her. To be honest, that's when I started to write. I started to write her short stories to help her cope with her fear of the men, darkness and storms. I hoped that my stories would make her happy.

"Who is it," Sea'Sea said walking towards the door.

"Amel," I said.

"Who," Sea'Sea said.

"Amel," I said louder.

"I don't know nobody named Amel," Sea'Sea said. "Is this my Boo,"

"Nah, this is Amel,"

"Ok, Mr. Amel, just stay outside then. You not coming in here until I know for sure that this is my Boo at the door,"

I paused for a second as I looked down to the ground with a grin. I knew I had to give in.

"Is this my Boo,"

"Yea this yo Boo now open up the door ole big head gul," I said with a smile.

Sea'Sea opened up the door and greeted me with a smile and a slight punch to the stomach as she usually did.

"That's what I thought," Sea'Sea said.

I walked passed her and said "Please don't do me Boo Boo," We both laughed. Our energy and chemistry together was different than any other relationship that I had in my life.

I made my way into the living room and dropped down on the old run down couch, with both hands on top of my head looking up at the ceiling. "Today definitely ain't my day," I whispered to myself.

"Do you really know what time it is Amel," Sea'Sea said as she threw a pillow at me.

"Do you really thank I care Sea'Sea," I said.

"Well for the record it's 11:43pm," Sea'Sea said.

"OooooooooK. Yo point," I asked.

"I don't have a point but I thought you should know that shit. I thought you was coming over earlier, not no eleven almost twelve o'clock. You act like you pay bills round here or something. Like this yo house,"

"Shit I do and it is, yeen know," I said.

"Whatever big head," Sea'Sea said. "So what up. Why you in my neck of the woods this time of night,"

"Just got into it with Baby Sister. Just got kicked out of the house. Nothing too unusual," I said being sarcastic.

"Damn. I see that black eye. What you do," Sea'Sea asked.

"Shid, I snapped," I said.

"Snap like how," Sea'Sea said with intrigue. "You didn't kill her did you,"

"Naw mane. Snapped like I grabbed her by her neck and choked the shit out of her,"

Sea'Sea burst into laughter. "LIES,"

"Aight LIES. I ain't bullshitting," I said with a grin.

"No bullshit," Sea'Sea asked.

"If I'm lying I'm flying my nigga. Straight up. I choked her. Just saying that is scaring the shit out of me right now because I know if she catch me anywhere in these streets, my life is over,"

"I KNOW. Baby Sister crazy as hell" Sea'Sea said. "But she ain't always use to be that way. Well at least I don't remember her being crazy growing up. But what made you choke her though,"

"She said some shit bout that pussy ass daddy of mine not loving me or something like that. I don't know. I really don't want to talk bout it right now," I said.

"So that's what we on now. We don't talk bout stuff no more,"

"Nah it ain't like that. I'll talk bout it later. Cool,"

"I mean that's cool. But you ok though right,"

"I am good little lady," I said with a smile.

"Cause, I'm just saying though. Baby Sister don't want nothing coming from this way. I will put these paws on her for messing with my Boo. You hear me shawty," Sea'Sea said laughing.

"I hear ya Shawty," I said with a grin. "Yo let me use yo phone right quick,"

"It's in there on the deep freezer," Sea'Sea said pointing to the kitchen.

I made my way into the kitchen and dialed a number I had memorized from Baby Sister's caller Id awhile back. The phone ranged about 5 times until someone answered.

"Hello," A voice said in a deep sleepy tone.

"Is Ben there," I asked.

"This is he. May I ask who is calling my house this time of night," Ben asked.

"Yo son, Amel," I said.

The phone got silent for a couple of seconds. I could hear the sound fade quickly from the background, knowing he had put me on mute and that he probably moved to another room to talk.

"Hello," Ben voice returned in a whisper. "Boy why are you calling my house this late at night,"

"You the man that made me ain't it,"

"Don't call my house with that nonsense this late at night. You are not my son, we been passed that point. You know that, we all know that. Did your momma put you up to this," Ben asked.

"Naw she ain't put me up to nothing, this me calling you. Baby Sister put me out and I ain't got nowhere to go so I hollered at you," I said.

The phone went silent. I was expecting this pussy ass motherfucker to have empathy towards my situation.

"That's your problem not mine," Ben responded.

"So that's how you do somebody you know is yo flesh and blood. That's how you do yo own child,"

"Look," Ben silently yelled. "You are not my son, how many times we got to go through this. And you know got damn well you not coming up in this house. You know that,"

"Why not though," I quickly responded.

"Get off my phone with this nonsense. Go find a job," Ben said sounding frustrated.

"Nigga I'm 15. Find a job where?"

"I don't know what to tell you, I guess good luck and have a nice life. That's the only advice I can give you. But don't call this house no more, I'm serious. I got a family to tend to. Now get off my phone before you get me in some trouble that I don't need,"

I heard the phone click, followed by the dial tone.

I stood there with the phone still to my ear. The conversation that I had with that pussy ass nigga reconfirmed what Baby Sister had said. My father wanted no part in my life. But I knew that if me and him stood side by side in public, that pussy ass nigga couldn't deny me and people would know for sure I was his seed.

For some reason I started to remember when I was younger, how every single day I use to look at the pictures of my father that Baby Sister kept in her chest. Baby Sister and my father looked so happy and normal together back then. I remembered rubbing those pictures and smiling at them. They gave me hope and a sense of family that I had longed for but never had.

I can't even front. That conversation with my father fucked me up a little bit. I even felt the tears forming in my eyes, but I quickly caught them. I dared not to cry for a motherfucker who made it his business not to acknowledge my very existence.

"Fuck them pictures," I said in my feelings.

"You ok," Sea'Sea said as she walked into the kitchen. She could feel something was wrong. She could read my demeanor and vibe like the back of her hand.

"Yeah I am good lil lady," I responded.

"No you not. What's wrong for real though," Sea'Sea insisted.

"Nothing just thanking bout some thangs," I said.

"Like what," Sea'Sea asked.

I paused. "I don't know. It's stupid, so just don't worry bout it,"

"See there you go. You do this shit all the time. Always running from yo feelings. Always shutting down. What's on yo mind Amel, for real for real," Sea'Sea insisted.

"Nothing man, just thanking bout what it would be like to have a real family round here. I'm talking bout a good momma, hardworking daddy, just normal stuff. You know like them TV shows on channel 6," I said.

Sea'Sea smacked her mouth and put her hand on my shoulder.

"That ain't never gone exist round here, you know that. I don't know why but that shit on TV ain't gone never compare to our lives. That is not our normal. Our normal is chaos and not having shit. But outside of this motherfucker though, maybe being fun, loving and outgoing is normal. I don't know cuz I never been outside of here before,"

"I know. I know. But do you ever have dreams of living a better life though. Just getting away from this place,"

"All the time but those are just dreams, nothing more. They don't mean shit to me though," Sea'Sea said. "Dreams are for dreamers, and I ain't no dreamer Amel. We live this shit not dreams,"

"Don't say that," I said.

"Name me one person that you know that done dreamed up some shit and that shit came true in real life. Name me one person,"

I twisted my mouth and looked to the sky as I went deep into thought. A few seconds turned into minutes. Sea'Sea stood there waiting on my response.

"Any thang," Sea'Sea asked.

"Nothing" I said. "But it ain't nothing wrong with me wanting a normal life, a normal family,"

"I'm normal and I'm yo family right," Sea'Sea said with a smile.

"You thank you my family," I said sarcastically as I glanced at her with a smile.

"I better be yo family," Sea'Sea responded snapping her neck, rolling her eyes, and twisting her mouth.

The both of us stood right in front of each other, looking into each other's eyes. The hurt and tiredness were evident. I could read the softness in her eyes and that shit spooked me a little.

"Come here," Sea'Sea said as she grabbed me and gave me a big hug, then kissed me on the forehead.

Sea'Sea looked me in the eyes "Promise me that until we die, what mine is yos and what yos is mine. That way we always be there for each other,"

I looked down. I hated commitments or somebody trying to slick me into some shit that would come back to bite me, but this was Sea'Sea. I knew that if I committed to anything, I wanted my word to be my bond, unlike what I had seen in my life where people broke bonds like it was nothing.

Sea'Sea looked down to get to my eye level. "Promise me,"

I didn't say nothing because I was scared.

"Fuck it then," Sea'Sea said as she tried to release from me.

I held on to her and squeezed her tighter.

"That's my word," I said. "I swear you be too serious some times,"

"I just wish you would stop playing so much when people trying to be serious with you," Sea'Sea said as she released from my tight grip.

"I'm sorry," I said. Sea'Sea didn't respond. "AIGHT,"

"I got you," Sea'Sea said with a smirk. "Now come on so I can feed you because I know yo lil self hungry," she continued as she walked into the kitchen. I followed behind her.

For some reason, in that moment, I started to notice how Sea'Sea appearance had changed over the years. She had gone from a slicked gel, tiny ponytail wearing, snotty nose little girl running around to a high yellow, bright red hair and micro braid wearing, big breasted, pudgy stomach, big hips and booty young lady. She was what people from around the way called "big bone-did". On the flip side, she would fight anybody anywhere. On any given day, you could find Sea'Sea dressed like a stripper going to school, and cursing out teachers and students. She stayed getting suspended from school for acting out. She was ghetto fabulous and I loved that.

"Boy look at that thang there," I thought as I watched Sea'Sea booty shake from side to side in her basketball shorts.

"You want some buttermilk and cornbread," Sea'Sea asked.

I didn't answer, my mind was on that booty.

"Amel,"

"Huh,"

"I said do you want to buttermilk and cornbread,"

"Yeah that's cool," I said. "Damn sounds like its finna storm," I continued as we both jumped when the loud thunder sounded. I could see the fear in Sea'Sea eyes. I knew every time it stormed, she would turn back into that little girl home alone again.

"You staying over tonight right," Sea'Sea asked.

"Yeah. Why though? You must be scared of the storms," I said jokingly.

Sea'Sea smacked her mouth, twisted her head and squinted her eyes at me all at the same time. She looked at me with a "I can't believe you" look for a couple of seconds. I knew I had fucked up.

"No the fuck you didn't," Sea'Sea said. I could see the tears beginning to form in her eyes.

"I was just joking Sea'Sea, damn. You act like you can't take a joke,"

Sea'Sea got up and tried to flee from the table, but I quickly grabbed her arm and held onto it tightly.

"Let me go Amel," Sea'Sea said screaming and crying in unison. "You act like you don't have feelings sometimes. Just cold hearted,"

"Sea'Sea you know I was just playing witcha," I said looking at her. She tried her best not to look at me.

"I said let me go motherfucker," Sea'Sea said wiping her face with her loose arm and huffing and puffing from anger. "Let me go. Let me go. Leeet meee goooooo," she continued being dramatic. She finally snatched away from me.

We both stood there looking at each other. Sea'Sea was still huffing and puffing trying to calm down. I stood there and observed her with a blank stare.

Before I could react to it, that crazy motherfucker spit in my face and ran off to her bedroom and slammed the door, locking it in unison.

"You motherfucker," I screamed as I stood there in shock. That wasn't the first time Sea'Sea had spit in my face. The last time she did it, I let her slide without whipping her ass. But I made it clear to her that if she ever did that again, she would not like the outcome. "I am going to beat yo motherfucking ass Sea'Sea,"

I stood there, still in shock trying my best to calm down but I couldn't. I slowly made my way to Sea'Sea bedroom.

I knocked hard on Sea'Sea bedroom door about five times.

"Open the door Sea'Sea," I demanded.

Sea'Sea didn't respond.

"Open the motherfucking door Sea'Sea. You know you done fucked up so let's go head and handle it and get it out the way,"

I knocked hard on the door a few more times but Sea'Sea still didn't answer.

"You know what, don't even worry bout it. Fuck you," I said as I stormed into the living room.

Sea'Sea quickly emerged from her bedroom. "I said I'm sorry, did you not hear me," she screamed.

I quickly turned around and ran towards the bedroom trying to catch the door before she closed it, but fell over the end table. Sea'Sea quickly slammed the door and locked it again.

Sea'Sea heard the loud thump and peaked out the door. She burst into laughter.

"You ain't said shit. Matter of fact, fuck yo apology. I better not see you at school. Imma try to kill yo motherfucking ass,"

"I said I'm sorry damn. You alright though," Sea'Sea said while laughing.

"Yeah you hehe-ing and haha-ing now, just watch," I said as I made my way back to the living room.

"You still staying right. You know how I get when it storm. You know that make me angry and scared," Sea'Sea yelled.

"I wish I would stay after you spit in my motherfucking face. And then you laughing when I fell. I coulda killed myself in this raggedy ass house," I said as I walked out the door.

"I am sorry, I was just playing witcha. Can't you take a joke," Sea'Sea screamed from her bedroom trying her best to make peace with me for the sake of me staying till morning.

Chapter 5

I slept in the broke down white '69 Mustang that was parked behind Sea'Sea's house. I loved that car since I laid eyes on it when I was a little boy and hoped one day I would get a chance to buy it from Jackie. The white outside plus the dark red inside made for a perfect vehicle to me.

I woke up before the sunrise to go find where Melo and Javion were staying. After being turned down by my father, I tried to call my two aunts, Constance and Rosie that lived in Itta Bena. Rosie lived in the Project on Sunflower Road and Constance lived in the Low End on MLK Street, but both declined to let me stay with them due to my so called disrespect and constant disobedience towards Baby Sister.

I didn't want to push my situation off on Sea'Sea because she didn't make the rules at her house even though she was there alone most of the time. When I slept in that car, I decided not to stay the night with Sea'Sea anymore, but go over to eat, wash clothes, and bath. I knew if I was around Sea'Sea too long, either she would kill me or I would kill her, and that was the bottom line. Family wise, I was all alone and I knew Melo, despite her shortcomings and living condition, was my only option to have a consistent roof over my head.

After asking around all day, I found myself standing on the doorstep of the house Melo and Javion was supposedly staying. It was a small wooden house that was located on a reclusive dirt road just outside of Itta Bena.

I knocked three times on the door.

"Damn I know she in there because I hear my Champ Javion crying," I thought with a smile. Even though it was a cry from Javion, it made me smile just to hear him.

"Who the fuck is it," a man said walking towards the door.

I was confused. I wondered why this dude was answering the door like that.

"It's Shake," I responded.

"Who," the man asked.

"Shake. Melo brother," I said.

The door cracked opened a little and a face emerged behind it.

"What you need lil nigga. Melo ain't here right now," the man said. I could smell the weed smoke through the door.

"Where she at," I replied.

"I don't know nigga. I don't baby sit her. What you need though," the man responded trying his best to be tough and rude at the same time.

Then it hit me. Javion was still crying and I knew that kind of cry. It was a cry that sounded like he was hurt.

"Since you can't tell me where Melo at, let me see my nephew," I anxiously said.

"He busy my nigga," the man said.

"What the fuck you mean he busy, he 3. What's yo name again homeboy," I said getting upset.

"Nigga don't be at my door step cussing and shit, like you tough or something,"

I heard Javion little footsteps as he made his way towards the door, still crying.

"Loc, you hurt my head," Javion cried.

"Get yo ass back in there. I don't give a fuck bout yo head nigga. Now stop all that crying little bitch ass nigga," Loc said to Javion.

I stood there in shock as I felt myself shoot to boiling hot. My heart started to hurt as I witnessed this motherfucker talk to my 3 year old nephew like he was a grown man. I couldn't believe that Melo dumb ass would let Javion be subjected to such hate and abuse, and not do anything about it. The one thing I tried to protect Javion from, he was now experiencing.

"What the fuck you just called him," I said with a confused look, still in disbelief. I was wondering how someone could treat a baby so mean with so much anger and ill spirit.

"I called him a bitch ass nigga, bitch ass nigga. Oh I guess you don't like that huh. If you don't like that then I know you ain't going to like this," Loc said as he opened the door wider, letting me see Javion.

I smiled at my little Champ standing there crying, looking passed the big knot on his head.

As soon as Javion recognized my face, he stopped crying and his face lit up like he had seen heaven. Javion started to run full speed towards me.

I opened my arms to embrace Javion, you know, because I missed him.

But In mid running stride, this dirty motherfucker Loc kicked my little Champ in the back so hard. He kicked him so hard that Javion little body flew out the door and passed me. Javion landed face first on the concrete, knocking one of his teeth out his mouth and putting a nasty scar on his jaw.

I can't front, my heart dropped for a second. Javion didn't move or say a word. His little body just laid there on the concrete, lifeless. I can't lie, it scared me. I thought Javion was dead.

I looked at Javion, then at Loc, then back at Javion, still in shock.

"Say something Champ. Cry for me or something," I whispered.

In mid thought, Javion let out a big loud cry. I figured the fall had knocked him out for a couple of seconds.

I sighed and smiled. Then I looked back at that no good motherfucker Loc.

I stared at Loc little bitty ass still standing in the door. He was a tall nigga, about 6-0 and 130 pounds soak and wet. I guess he was a supposedly quote-unquote dope boy/hard nigga from around the way.

"You and that little nigga need to get off my door step before I out both of yall," Loc said with a mean mug on his face. I can remember him holding his mouth in a way that his gold across the front and bottom teeth could show. And something about him holding his mouth like that pissed me off even more.

I popped my neck and looked around to see who was out and about around the way. One thing I did notice was that the house was hiding behind some big ass trees from the main road that went into town.

"Cool my nigga. No troubles," I said with both hands in the air, slowly walking from the door.

"Damn right, bitch ass nigga," Loc responded with a smirk. Being the dumb nigga he was, he felt that he had conquered yet another nigga around town to elevate his respect level.

Loc slammed the front door of the house.

"You aight Champ," I asked Javion as I kneeled down and checked on him.

Javion shook his little head to say no with a poked out lip like he was sad. I took off my coat to put it around Javion to keep him warm and took off my shirt and put it on his face to stop the bleeding from the scar. I instructed Javion to continue to spit the blood from his mouth due to his teeth being knocked out. I then noticed that Javion had bruises on his legs and arms. I knew Loc had something to do with that too.

"I can't believe yo momma let this motherfucker do you like this. What the fuck is wrong with Melo," I whispered to myself.

As I was wrapping my coat around him, Javion started to pout, wanting to cry. He poked out his little lip again.

"What's wrong Champ, yo mouth still hurting," I asked.

Javion nodded my head to say no. Then tears started to flow from his little eyes. He put his little head down in his chest, looking under eyed.

"Look at me Champ," I said, wanting to look into those innocence eyes of hope that I always admired.

Javion still held his head down.

I put one finger under his chin and lifted his head.

"What's wrong Champ," I asked again.

Javion tried to drop his head again but I caught it.

"Look at me Javion. What's wrong Champ? You can tell me, you know I'm not going to hurt you," I insisted.

Tears started to pour from Javion's eyes.

"Shake you left me. Loc and momma hurt me," Javion said in a sweet but sad voice.

I noticed that those eyes of his weren't as innocent as they once were. When looking at them this time, I found sadness in them. How Javion was looking and how his eyes read and what he said about Melo and Loc hurting him broke my heart into pieces.

"What you mean momma and Loc. Yo momma hit on you too," I said trying to get to the bottom of the problem.

"Yes. Momma be whooping me with that white tension cord," Javion said. I knew he wasn't lying. I knew that babies that age wouldn't have a reason to lie.

"With a fucking extension cord," I said with a grimace. My heart started to hurt even worse and my anger towards Melo started to grow by the second.

"And Loc be burning me sometimes with my cigderett on my arm," Javion said.

I just stood there looking at Javion as he described more terrible shit that both Melo and Loc had done to him. My heart grew heavy with every word. Guilt started to set in. I didn't know Melo was a dirty motherfucker too. Now I was starting to feel played by her motherfucking ass.

"I want to go with you Shake," Javion said whining.

I pulled Javion into my arms tightly and started to cry real tears. It hurt me to see my little bitty nephew go through what he was going through. But on the flip side, it made me feel good to know there was somebody in the world that wanted me around and that loved me.

"You going with me. I am right here now. I will never let you out of my sight again. You hear me. You my responsibility now. Ok," I said.

Javion nodded his little head to say ok.

"So yo coward ass going to sit here and let this motherfucker do this little baby like that. What is this some kind of turning the other cheek bullshit these church folk talk bout. So this nigga done kicked yo nephew down some steps and you sitting here crying and shit. You a fucking coward," the small voice inside my head said.

It fucked me up because that was the first time that voice came at me like that. On some other shit, you know, not on fucking a girl or something. But attacking me personally almost.

"I just want to squash all of this. I have my Champ now so I am good," I whispered.

"Squash what? Squash the fact that this motherfucker burn yo nephew with cigarettes and beat his ass for no reason. Look at yo motherfucking nephew nigga. Just look at him," that voice in my head demanded.

I reluctantly looked down at Javion and focused in on him.

"Look at those eyes again. Do they deserve what they have been given. Do yo Champ deserve that kind of treatment," that voice in my head said.

"Hell naw he don't," I responded in a whisper.

"Well go off this nigga then. Put this nigga out of his misery. What kind of nigga deserves to live who do stuff like that to lil bitty babies," That voice in my head screamed.

"Shake, I'm hungry," Javion said as I snapped out of my daze. I knew what I had to do. That nigga life was about to come to an end in a few minutes.

"Ok, just hold still for a minute," I said making my way back to the house.

"Don't leave me Shake," Javion said sounding like he was scared.

"I ain't leaving, I'm going back to the house for a minute. I be right back ok, just hold still. Matter of fact let's play a game. Let's see who can stand behind the tree the longest," I said walking back to Javion. I took Javion and placed him behind one of the big oak trees in the yard.

"Now if you stay behind this tree until I get back, I will go get you some ice cream. Ok," I said.

"Yay ice cream," Javion said with joy. I smiled at his happiness.

"So are you going to stay here like a big boy and get ice cream," I asked.

"Yes," Javion said.

"Alright Champ. Hold still right here. I will be right back," I said. As I was walking towards the house doorstep, I was thinking what I could use to off this motherfucker. I'm talking about offing this nigga badly.

"This might work," I said as I picked up a red brick from the flower bed beside the doorsteps.

I knocked on the door two or three times. I could hear Loc footsteps coming to the door.

"Hold on baby here I come," Loc said obviously expecting somebody else.

It angered me even more that Loc was ok with what he had just done and didn't feel any guilt whatsoever. I knew that Loc was ok with being a bad person and that didn't sit well with me. He was ok with abusing babies and women. Shit like that made him who he was.

As soon as the door swung open, I speared that motherfucker to the ground and started to beat him in the face with the red brick over and over again.

"You like beating little babies huh motherfucker," I said, hitting him harder and harder every time Javion sad eyes flashed in my mind.

With every hit of the brick, Loc body became less responsive. It didn't take long for me to beat him to the point where he couldn't move any more. He couldn't do nothing but moan for his life. I made it my business not to kill him though, I wanted him to slowly suffer for his bad-hearted ways.

"You don't deserve to live, bitch," I whispered to Loc as I spit in his bloody, disconfigured face.

I got up, washed my hands and chest off, and made my way to the shed on the side of the house. In the shed I found a jug of gas beside the lawn mower. I grabbed the gas jug and headed back into the house where Loc's punk ass body was.

Before I entered the house, I yelled "Javion are you still being a good boy,"

"Yes," Javion said.

"Alright," I said with a smile.

I went back into the house and made my way to the kitchen.

My mission: find a knife, a box of nails, and a hammer. Too bad for Loc, I found all three.

I went back to the front room with my redemption tool kit. Loc was still moaning for his life.

"This coulda turned out way different if you wasn't a bad hearted person. But you the one wanted to be tough. So you gone take this L and die slow bitch ass nigga. You remember that,"

I started to take off all the little bitty nigga clothes. I wanted Loc to suffer by all means. I wanted the pain to be pure, nothing to interfere with it.

When Loc was completely butt naked, I took the nails and the hammer and nailed 5 nails in each hand, and 5 nails in each foot. He screamed with every swing of the hammer. I smiled. It made me feel good to put this motherfucker through so much pain.

For each finger and toe, I busted them wide open with the hammer one by one. Again the bitch nigga screamed with pain. And again I smiled with joy.

Then I thought about it. Let me go get some rubbing alcohol from the bathroom. Everybody from around the way kept white rubbing alcohol in the bathroom.

I went to the bathroom and found some alcohol. "Gotta be my lucky day," I thought.

I headed back to the front room, untopping the alcohol slowly.

I started to dash Loc's body with the alcohol, again that bitch nigga screamed. I laughed out loud at this tough guy laying on the floor, helpless.

"Let me wrap this shit up right quick," I said. I knew I could do that all day and make the motherfucker suffer. But Javion was outside and we needed to be getting on our way.

I went into the kitchen and turned on all the eyes on the gas stove so the gas could circulate through the house.

I waited.

I poured half the jug of gas on Loc's body. I noticed a blunt on the end table in the living. I grabbed the blunt, lit it with the lighter beside the ashtray, took a pull, and threw it on Loc's body, causing it to burn like charcoals would burn on a barbeque grill.

He started to scream so loud. I could hear and smell the nigga flesh burn.

I threw the red brick on his body so there wouldn't be any finger prints.

I stood there for a few seconds and observed the body as it burned.

I smiled. It was like I was watching the birth of a child. Like I was a proud parent seeing the result of my discipline come to pass.

"I bet you won't hurt nobody else," I whispered as I placed the half-filled gas jug on his body.

I quickly ran out the house.

"You ready Champ," I yelled to Javion.

"I'm going with you," Javion asked with his eyes popped open with excitement.

"Yep you going with me," I responded.

"Yay," Javion said with joy as he tried to dance around in a circle.

I smiled.

"Now let's go get you that ice cream for being a good boy, ok Champ," I said.

I grabbed Javion and quickly ran behind the house and got on the back pathway to town.

This was the beginnings of our journey together into the unknown. I knew that Javion was all I had that cared for me no matter what, and I was all Javion had. We were a perfect match.

Halfway up the pathway, Loc's house exploded into flames.

I turned around with Javion in my arms.

"Say goodbye to yo old life Javion and say hello to yo new life," I said as we watched the flames tip the sky. I kissed Javion on the jaw.

"Bye old life. Hey new life," Javion said.

"That's my Champ,"

Chapter 6

It was a cold night out as I found myself searching for a place to stay for the night. In my right hand, I held a plastic bag filled with clothes while struggling to hold and support Javion, sound asleep on my shoulder, in my left hand. Javion was buddle up tightly in an old rugged blanket with a blue tractor skull hat on his head to keep warm. I had gotten Javion that old rugged blanket, 3 pants, 3 shirts, a pair of shoes, 3 pairs of socks, 2 pairs of long johns, 3 pairs of undies, 3 pairs of t-shirts, a backpack, paper, pencil, and that blue tractor skull hat from the local Salvation Army with the 34 dollars I had panhandled for at the corner of the Double Dip store in town. I had searched most of the town the entire day looking for a decent abandoned house that Javion could keep warm inside of. I knew that I would be ok but my main concern was the wellbeing of my Champ. Sea'Sea's house was out of the question. Out of all fucking days, Sea'Sea wanted to take her ass to Jackson and stay the night.

So I walked and walked, still without luck. The night was wearing thin and I knew I needed to find somewhere to lay for the night so me and Javion could get a good rest to prepare for the next day. I was going back to school for the first time in a week. I wanted to get there early to sign Javion up for the government funded daycare that my high school, Sammie Beans High, provided to students with children.

I walked another ten minutes until it don on me where I was. I can remember the dark vivid image that stood before me and how scared I got. It was an image that painted the perfect picture of violence, despair, anger, and ignorance. It was an image that represented, in essence, death. It was like standing face to face with a hungry and angry pit-bull on a vicious hunt for food.

What stood before me was the infamous small community known as Alley Whip aka Whip City aka The City. The City was a place like no other. It was located slap dead in the middle of Itta Bena. It was the slum within the slums of the already poverty stricken town. Some people said that The City got its name because people were known to get their asses whipped, killed, and robbed if they were caught in it without permission, whether it was day or night. Others said that it got its name to signify the struggle of the people and how life whipped everybody asses that stayed there.

The City ran about 4 miles long and 5 miles wide. Each shotgun house that it embodied seemed to be a replication of the old white shotgun house Baby Sister occupied. All of the shotgun houses were located on 13 narrow, pot-hole filled roads. The entire area of The City was surrounded by a ten feet bob wire fence due to its violent nature. It was something like a prison; one way in and one way out. Walking into The City was just as worst as walking into a wild jungle at night. They both consisted of the same things, wild animals that would hunt and kill at the drop of a dime if its prey showed its head. Most considered people who lived or hung out in The City as being animals. Most people around said it was the place where dreams and hope were no more. That it was a breeding ground for the next wave of criminals and murders; and a nursing home for old drunks and hoes. It was a place where Baby Sister had moved us from many years ago to escape The City life.

"The City? How in the hell did we end up here? Hold tight Champ," I whispered to the sleeping Javion as I slowly started to move forward through the front gates of The City.

Instantly upon entering The City gates, I was approached by several men and women looking to sell me pussy, drugs, stolen goods, and food stamps. I declined all offers for the sake of not waking Javion and not being set up for a potential robbery.

As I respectfully fought my way through the neighborhood sellers, I cautiously navigated my way to the guts of The City, looking for a place to lay for the night. Every single house seemed occupied with people.

"Damn there go one right there," I said as I noticed little small grey house with no lights or activity on the corner of 11th Alley Whip Lane. "Let me check it out,"

I made my way to the house, but stopped in my tracks. I could smell the shit, piss, crack smoke, and other foul odors from 50 feet away. I knew it was a whore house and crack house.

"That's it baby," I heard a fragile voice coming from the porch of the grey house.

Then I looked closer. I could see this 80 something old man barely standing getting sucked off by a woman on her knees.

"What the fuck," I thought.

"Boy get yo ass on somewhere now. Don't you see grown folks handling business," The old man said with irritation.

Then the woman looked around at me. "Oh, Hey Ms. Harris," I said as I spoke to Sea'Sea mother Jackie.

"Hey there Amel," Jackie said. "You don't want yo dick sucked do you? I don't charge nothing but 5 dollars,"

"No ma'am," I quickly responded respectfully. I was scared to death. Nobody had ever asked me that before, let alone a grown person.

"You got any on you," Jackie asked.

"Any what," I asked.

"Butter," Jackie said referring to crack.

"No ma'am, I don't mess with that stuff like that,"

"Ok then. Well you be careful out here ok. You go by there and see Sea'Sea cuz she always talking bout you. And if you want yo little dick sucked, let me know ok baby," Jackie said. Then she turned back around to the old man and started to suck him off again.

"Yes ma'am," I said walking off fast. To my surprise Javion was still sleep.

"Who the fuck you thank you talking to," A man said. He had a lady penned on a car with his arm around her neck.

"Nobody," the woman said to the man crying.

He punched her two times in the face. She screamed for help. He punched her again in the face.

"Shut the fuck up bitch. I wish somebody would come try to help you. I own you bitch,"

I quickly walked by the altercation trying not to make eye contact or be noticed. I succeeded. I didn't want any parts of that.

"Man what is going on," I thought. I was spooked by all of the crazy things that were happening in The City at one time. If it wasn't one bad thing, it was another. It was starting to feel as worst as being at home with Baby Sister.

As I continued to walk, I noticed a light blue shotgun house on the corner of 15th Whip Avenue Lane that stood out amongst the others in the darkness. It was something about the light blue shotgun house that intrigued me, like something was drawing me to it. I moved towards the light blue shotgun house with keen eyes. I could see a small red light coming from the porch in the pitch black dark that turned bright red every few seconds. Those bright red lights were followed by smoke.

"Damn who is this on this porch smoking? I hope they ain't got no gun," I thought scared out of my mind at this point.

As I moved closer to the house, I could hear a rocking chair consistently rocking back and forth.

"And a young man shall appear unto thee like a thief in the night and be delivered unto thee like a baby being delivered unto thou mother. Thou shall know it is him by what he possess in both hands. One hand will possess destruction while the other will possess hope. That's what he told me and I be got damn if it isn't true," A man's voice said coming from the old light blue shotgun house. It was a voice that sounded of conviction, disbelief, and a sense of shock wrapped all in one. "You know the old folks use to say that if you see something broken, you can either do three things: walk over it, pick it up and throw it away, or pick it up and try to fix it. I can feel your brokenness from here young man,"

I stopped in my tracks. For some reason, I could feel the power of the man's words within my soul, but what the man had said confused me.

"You got the wrong person sir. Ain't nothing broken about me," I said trying to keep focus and looking around to make sure I kept out of danger, but I couldn't keep my eyes off of the light blue shotgun house.

"What's a young boy like yourself doing out this time of night in this kind of city with a baby in your arm and a bag of goods in your hands,"

"Just minding our business and looking for a place to stay sir. We don't want any trouble," I responded respectfully. Baby Sister had always told me to respect my elders.

"That makes two of us young man. Do you need a place to stay for the night," the man said still submerged in the darkness on the porch.

The smell from the house reeked of piss and liquor. I knew the man had to be a drunk.

"Yeah but I wasn't expecting to burden nobody," I said.

The man emerged from the darkness of the porch into the dim street light. "You won't be a burden. He said that I had to do this for me and for you. I have a spare bedroom and mattress. You and the little one can stay here,"

I looked sideways at the man as he stood in the dim street light just 15 feet from where I was standing. The man looked like he was in his 70's. From the looks of it, he looked like he had a hard life and was missing a couple of screws upstairs.

"What's your name young man," the man asked me.

"Amel," I said. "And this little guy on my shoulder is Javion. And you,"

"The name is King Lee Greene but people around here call me King Lee. So you can call me the same," King Lee said.

"Do that explain the crown and the cape," I quickly asked.

King Lee stood in the dim street light with a gold crown with red padding on his head, something like a king would wear. His cape was red with white spotted fur trimming on it. It looked like he was dressed in his best Halloween custom. King Lee, the man, stood about 6'0 150 pounds with a head full of long straight silky hair with a dark brown face. From the looks of it, he looked like he was a mix of Indian and black.

King Lee face was old and his eyes told the story of his life, hard and unforgiving. I could tell that once upon a time he had an athletic build but the drinking and other things along his life journey had long taken over it. He was missing his two front teeth and his face was filled with hair. King Lee blue shirt and blue pants were all covered in dirt, like he hadn't bath in months. He had no shoes on and it was clear that he was a bit drunk. Although I noticed all of the bad exterior things about King Lee, what I noticed the most was how well he spoke for a dirty drunken man.

"Well," King Lee said. "I wear a crown and cap because I am the king of my world and not of this world. You understand,"

"I ain't got a clue what you talking bout to be real witcha Mr. King Lee,"

"Please, call me King Lee, I insist. Now come on in the house and let me explain myself a bit more so you will understand why I am the king of my world and not of this world," King Lee said. He noticed I was still a bit reluctant to come inside the house. "There is no harm here, haven't you seen by now that I am not of this world you see around you. Now come on in here and let me get you a piece of cornbread and a glass of water,"

I finally obliged and followed King Lee into the light blue shotgun house.

"Welcome to my kingdom," King Lee said stumbling into the house, almost falling. "This is where I rule the world,"

I continued to follow King Lee as I observed his kingdom. I noticed an old steel heater in the middle of the living room with a round table and a chair surrounding it. I also noticed all the glass that was on the floor and all the marks and stains on the wall. The living room was filled with large bookshelves that were all occupied by tons of books and old records.

"Here is the spare room that you will stay in. I know it ain't much but it will do,"

"Thank you," I said in a humble tone. I noticed the old mattress on the floor with a dirty white sheet on it.

"Ain't no way I am letting my Champ sleep on that," I thought.

"Now if you have to defecate or urinate, you will have to go in a bucket. Make sure that you place lye in the bucket when you are done to kill the smell. You can use the bathroom in the other spare room,"

"Ok,"

We made our way back into the living room where the heater and table was. King Lee grabbed a piece of cornbread from the old gas stove and poured me a glass a water from the kitchen faucet.

"Have a sit," King Lee insisted. "Here is the cornbread and water I promised you," he continued as he placed the water and cornbread on the table.

I sat down in the chair and laid Javion across my lap. I started to undress him because of the heat that was coming from the heater.

"Where do you take a bath at," I asked.

"When I do bath, I run water in the kitchen sink in there. You can bath with the soap I made from wood ashes or with the dish washing liquid in there," King Lee said.

"Ok, do you mind if I wash them sheets on that mattress in there,"

"Go ahead, I don't mind. There is a wash board in the kitchen under the sink. You can wash your clothes and the sheets in the kitchen sink,"

"Thank you," I said politely.

King Lee left the living room for a split second. He quickly emerged from the back with a fresh bottle of corn whiskey in hand. He cracked the bottle opened and gestured towards me to offer me some. I declined. The liquor smelled too much like rubbing alcohol.

"This is the source of my power Amel," King Lee said as he held up the bottle. "It is the root of my wisdom and understanding. It is my salvation and destruction, so they say,"

I observed King Lee as I rocked and rubbed Javion back to ensure he stayed comfortable as he slept. For some reason, King Lee was intriguing to me.

"You know the world that you see every day can be as cruel and wicked as anything you can imagine. But in my world, in this kingdom, everything is peaceful. Everything is good. There is no pain. There is no hurt. Just me and my queen. And I like that,"

I knew for sure I didn't see or hear anybody else in the house when King Lee showed me to my room. I knew that no woman could live in such conditions unless she was crazy or a cracked out of her mind.

"Where is the misses," I said looking around, trying to play it safe and not come off as rude or ungrateful. "Is she sleep,"

"There she is in that corner over there," King Lee said pointing over to the dark corner. He proceeded to get up, barely walking, to get his queen. "I make love to this old gal every single night. I like to hear her moan with pain and pleasure," he continued as he sat back down and admired his old guitar. King Lee began to stare at it in a daze and started to gently stroke it like it was an actual woman.

"Now let me explain why I am the king of my world and not this world," King Lee said. "Let me ask you something Amel. Are you free,"

I hunched my shoulders as to say I didn't know.

"That isn't an answer. In this house, we don't hunch shoulders nor do we say we don't know. We give answers to questions. Understand,"

I nodded my head as to say I understood.

"Again, are you free," King asked.

"I would thank that I am free," I said.

"Why would you think such a thing and I don't want to hear that you don't know," King Lee said.

"I just am," I said.

"Let me ask you this then, do you look at a man like me and feel sorry for me. A man that looks dirty and smells like me. Do you feel sorry for me Amel," King asked.

"A lil bit, I can't front," I said.

King Lee moved closer to me. "How can you feel sorry for me as a grown man, when I feel sorry for you and you are just a child? Do you know the difference between this drunken fool and you,"

I shook my head as to say no.

"I am free and you're not. These people out here ain't free Amel. They are broken, just……like…..you," King Lee said as he took another big gulp of the brown liquor. "That is why I am the king of my world and not this world. I am free and the world isn't. The only attachments I got in this world is this bottle and this gal of mine, you understand,"

I nodded my head.

"Just something to think about in your free time. Freedom of this world is the starting point to having self-peace. And self-peace is the starting point of fixing that brokenness inside of us all,"

Chapter 7

I was still in my feelings about Sea'Sea spitting in my damn face. But like we did so many times, we fought to make up. I had to forgive her this time not because I wanted to, but because I had to. I was having doubts about living with King Lee. I wanted to make sure I was straight with Sea'Sea just in case me and Javion needed her for something.

Earlier that day, I used the pay phone at the Double Dip store to make sure Sea'Sea would be at home before me and Javion went by. Around 6pm, me and Javion made our way from The City to Sea'Sea's house. Sea'Sea lived about a mile from The City.

I knocked three times on the red door of the light green trailer house. I knew Jackie wasn't home. I could smell the food Sea'Sea was cooking from outside of the house.

"Who is it," Sea'Sea said working fast towards the door.

"Amel," I yelled.

Sea'Sea quickly opened the door to let us in.

"Hey yall," Sea'Sea said.

"Hey Sea'Sea," Javion said.

"Hey my little Lightbread," Sea'Sea said as she journeyed into the living room. Sea'Sea started calling Javion "Lightbread" because every time we turned around, he was eating a piece of light bread. That's all he wanted to eat. She told him that if he continued to eat light bread so much, he would turn into a slice of light bread.

I quickly noticed that Sea'Sea was not her usual playful self. She didn't even welcome me inside the house with a smile and punch in the stomach that she did 99.9% of the time.

"You ok," I asked slightly concerned.

"Yeah I am good why,"

"Nothing," I said dismissing the subject. "Damn it smells good in here. What you got cooking in there,"

"It's a surprise," Sea'Sea said. "But I got a special treat that you can eat later on though," she continued with a smile as she repeatedly hiked up both eye brows.

"I'm telling you this now. If it smell like fish or swim under water, I ain't eating it," I said.

We both burst into laughter. "You too stupid," Sea'Sea replied.

Sea'Sea moved from the living room into the kitchen to check on the food. Me and Javion sat on the couch and started to get comfortable.

"Have you been watching the news," Sea'Sea asked me from the kitchen.

"Naw, you know I don't watch no news gul," I responded. "A better question is why in the hell we keep watching this wack ass Crosby Show. It's so depressing,"

Sea'Sea returned to the living room wiping her hands on her shirt. Javion ran and jumped into her arms.

"I don't know why we watching that, it was on that channel when I cut the TV on. Shit change it if you don't like it. But then again, you know that you don't have nothing but two other stations to choose from anyway so let it stay. But anyway, the news lady say that the police said they investigating that fire over there by Shadow Lane Road. You know where I am talking bout," Sea'Sea stated.

"Yeah I know where that at. You talking bout over there by the white folk's neighborhood," I asked.

"Yea over there by all them trees and stuff. But anyway, they say that yesterday evening that little wooden house over there exploded and killed everybody in there," Sea'Sea said.

"Oh for real," I nonchalantly responded.

Sea'Sea paused and squinted her eyes at me.

"Damn why you got to be so cold bout every fucking thing,"

"I mean what you want me to say Sea'Sea," I responded with my arms in the air.

Sea'Sea rolled her eyes.

"ANYWAYS. They say it was that boy Loc from around the way. You know skinny Loc, don't you," Sea'Sea asked.

"I know of him, but I never just been round him like that. They say Melo was fucking round with him, so, that's all I know bout him,"

Sea'Sea paused with intrigue. She looked like she was contemplating something.

"What's wrong with you, why you get all quiet and shit," I asked.

"Nothing," Sea'Sea said. "But Loc momma was on the news talking bout how good of a person he was and how he had a good heart. She said that he wouldn't hurt a fly and everybody around the way loved him.

She said he was the type that made people laugh. That he loved his family, especially his kids,"

"That's what she said huh. I heard otherwise bout the nigga," I said with a mean mug.

"What you heard," Sea'Sea asked.

"I heard the nigga beat women and lil children. I heard he molested lil babies too," I responded. I knew that last statement about molesting babies was a lie but I wanted to make Loc look like the animal he was.

"Who told you that," Sea'Sea asked.

"Don't worry bout who told me what. Just know that the nigga ain't what they say he is," I said.

"I don't know bout all that, but I just thank it's sad that somebody had to die like that," Sea'Sea said.

I don't know what she say that for. I raised up from the couch and looked up at Sea'Sea pissed to the max.

"What's so sad bout it Sea'Sea. Just tell me what's so fucking sad bout it," I screamed.

"Because somebody died. That's what's sad bout it Amel," Sea'Sea screamed back.

"What do you know bout this nigga to be all sad and shit. The motherfucker didn't deserve to live if you ask me. I know niggas who knew the nigga. They say he was fake and shasty. Didn't give a fuck bout nobody but himself. If you ask me, the world is better without that weak ass motherfucker,"

"I'm just saying it doesn't matter what somebody done did, they don't deserve to die. He was young. He could have changed, who knows," Sea'Sea responded being a little bit too sensitive about the situation.

"Got damn Sea'Sea you must was going with the nigga or something. Or fucking him one. Mane fuck that nigga," I yelled.

Sea'Sea quickly looked at me with that "I know you didn't" look. She knew that I was complex and difficult to read, but she could feel that something was not right with me. The way I was talking about the situation was different than how we talked about other situations that went on around the way.

"Damn, you didn't kill the nigga did it," Sea'Sea asked jokingly to see what kind of reaction she would get from me.

"Naw nigga I ain't kill nobody, where the fuck that come from," I asked.

"Never mind," Sea'Sea responded trying to change the subject. It was clear I was not in a joking mood.

"Naw, never mind my ass, where did that come from," I asked yelling at this point.

"Forget bout it Amel damn," Sea'Sea insisted.

"Naw, tell me what you talking bout," I asked.

"I ain't talking bout anythang. I'm just trying to make conversation with you," Sea'Sea said.

I grabbed her by the arm tightly and looked her in the eyes to see if she was lying or not. Sea'Sea stared back without saying a word. I know she noticed something different in my eyes that began to scare her a little.

"You done cooking," I said with irritation in my voice as I came to the conclusion that she was just trying to make conversation. I released her arm. "Because you losing yo motherfucking mind, for real,"

"Ain't nobody trying to piss you off Amel, I was just saying," Sea'Sea said.

"You ain't saying shit Sea'Sea. You ain't saying shit bout nothing. You just running yo mouth and feeling sorry for a motherfucker who didn't deserve to breathe air. You talk too fucking much," I said.

"Ok, you right," Sea'Sea said trying to quickly put an end to the conversation before it turned ugly.

"Ain't nobody trying to be right Sea'Sea, I am just saying. Stop it with the bullshit. Just quit," I insisted.

"I said Ok," Sea'Sea said as she rolled her eyes. She knew I always had to have the last word.

"Cool. Now, is the food done yet," I asked.

Sea'Sea looked at me and let out a little chuckle. "Mane you something else with yoself," she said as she walked off.

"So I already fixed yall plates. I want us to eat at the kitchen table instead of eating in the living room," Sea'Sea said with a glimpse of happiness and enthusiasm on her face. Me and Javion were like her little family and she treated us as such. She had made my favorite meal: homemade hamburgers with chopped onions in them, homemade french fries with season salt, and red Kool-Aid. "Come on Javion so I can wash them nasty hands of yos," she continued as she grabbed Javion from my arms and took him to the bathroom to wash his hands.

I made my way into the kitchen and sat at the table tickled a little bit.

"Man Sea'Sea talk too much and get on my nerves sometimes. But one thang for sho, she know how to treat a nigga for real though," I thought as I waited for Sea'Sea and Javion to come to the table.

Sea'Sea and Javion emerged from the bathroom as Sea'Sea sat Javion in a seat.

"This my plate," I asked while pointing to the plate in front of me and looking at Sea'Sea as she walked over to her chair to seat down.

"Don't it have ketchup on the side and not on the fries? Don't the burger have extra mayo on it and that's it," Sea'Sea said with slight irritation while rolling her eyes and smiling at the same time.

I rolled my eyes with a smile too. "You something else Sea'Sea. You something else girl," I said. Sea'Sea always knew what to say to bring a smile to my face when I wasn't feeling my best or was pissed off. She knew exactly how I liked all of my meals fixed down to the tee.

"Oh you can thank me later for cooking yo favorite meal too," Sea'Sea said.

"I ain't thanking you for something you pose to do," I responded.

"Nigga you ain't my man. My man just left before you came here. I don't pose to do shit for you, so don't play with it like that now," Sea'Sea in a semi-serious tone.

I fell silent and stared off towards the front door, jaw on the floor and feeling hurt like a motherfucker.

Sea'Sea started to apologize but left it alone. She wanted us to have a good meal and didn't want Javion to witness us fight.

I continued to stare off for another minute.

 Sea'Sea observed me.

"You ok Amel," Sea'Sea said softly trying to deflect her earlier actions.

"Yeah I'm good," I responded back in almost a whisper.

We all started to dig into the food until Sea'Sea halted everyone.

"Javion, what do you pose to say before you eat yo food. What did we go over the other day," Sea'Sea asked.

Javion hunched his shoulders as to say he didn't know.

"You do know big head. Say grace," Sea'Sea insisted.

Javion gave off a shy smile.

"Go ahead, say yo grace Lightbread," Sea'Sea egged him on.

Javion looked at me. I nodded to tell him to go on. Javion closed his little eyes, put both hands together around his mouth, and started to speak. "Thank you God for this food, A...man. Now everybody can eat,"

The table fell to a complete silence. Everybody sat in their chairs motionless waiting for somebody to move. I sat in my seat with my head down. Sea'Sea noticed what I was doing.

"You better not," Sea'Sea said with a smile.

I burst into laughter. "That's what you taught me. That's how you taught him to say grace. I thought it pose to be 'God is grace, God is good....' "

Sea'Sea burst into laughter.

"Chill. He did good," Sea'Sea said laughing even harder. Javion started to laugh too. Me and Cee started to laugh even harder.

"Why you laughing Javion. We laughing at you buddy," I said. "But you did a good job though Champ. That was really good," I continued as I wiped the tears from my eyes.

"Yeah that was a good job Javion," Sea'Sea said wiping her own eyes.

We began to dig into the food. As we were eating, I could feel Sea'Sea looking at me. Every time I would look up she would look down.

"Why you keep staring at me Sea'Sea. It must be something over here that you like," I said with a smile.

Sea'Sea paused.

"They say they found two charred bodies in that house," Sea'Sea said as she started to look down at her plate.

I sat up straight in my chair with intrigue. I scooted my chair closer to the table to make sure I heard Sea'Sea right.

"What you mean they said they found two bodies," I asked.

"I mean they saying that the police is saying that it is a potential double homicide," Sea'Sea said still looking down.

"Look at me Sea'Sea. You bullshitting ain't it," I said as my heart dropped. I hoped Sea'Sea was just playing. I knew for sure it was just one person in that house.

"No bullshit. I wouldn't play bout nothing like that," Sea'Sea said with a serious tone. "And they say that they looking for the other person little boy," she continued as she raised her eyes to me and then to Javion. "They say the other person was 7 months pregnant,"

I stared at her, squinting my eyes. Confusion was written all over my face.

"There is no fucking way," I thought. "No fucking way,"

I could feel myself going into panic mode. I felt like I was having a heart attack.

I suddenly jumped up and ran to the kitchen sink where I started to vomit nonstop. As I slumped over the sink, I started to bang my head against it.

"Amel," Sea'Sea said as she jumped up from the table. I continued to bang my head against the sink. "Amel you scaring us, stop......please," Sea'Sea ran full speed into me and knocked me to the floor.

"I didn't know. I didn't know. I didn't know. I didn't know," I whispered to myself over again.

"Well I be damn. You killed Melo. Yo fake ass killed Melo. Just look at you crying and shit. You knew she was in that house when you blew it up with yo lying ass," the small voice inside my head said.

"No I didn't," I screamed.

Sea'Sea looked like "Who the hell is he talking to". It looked like her worry instantly turned into fear.

"Why did you do it? Why did you do it Shake? Why did you blow up that house in the first place," The small voice inside my head said.

"Because you told me to do it motherfucker," I screamed as my voice started to crack. I could feel the tears forming in my eyes. I began to pound on the floor repeatedly until my knuckles started to bleed.

Sea'Sea kneeled down and tried to console me but I pushed her away. "Get off me," I screamed.

"Let me help you Amel," Sea'Sea insisted.

"I said get the fuck off of me," I said as I got up and ran to the bathroom and locked the door.

Sea'Sea ran behind me in hot pursuit as Javion followed her.

Sea'Sea pounded on the door. "Amel I understand, trust me. Just let me in," She continued to pound on the door constantly.

I stood motionless as I hovered over the bathroom sink with my head down as the tears flowed from my eyes. Images of Melo started to play over again in my head. Even though she was going through rough patches in her life, and I was feeling salty about what her and Loc did to Javion, at the end of the day she was still my sister. I still loved her. She was still my Melo.

I wanted to hurt her for what she did to Javion, but not kill her. Killing her wasn't even a choice for her but beating her ass real good was.

I raised my head to look at myself in the mirror. As soon as I caught my own eyes, I quickly lowered my head back down. I couldn't stand to see myself in the mirror, it was too much. It made me sick to my stomach.

"End it now. Just end it already. Who gives a fuck bout you anyway," That small voice inside my head said. "The razor is on the tub,"

"I ain't gone off myself. That's out the window," I whispered.

"Why not? Might as well. You ain't shit anyway," that small voice inside my head said.

"Mane get gone," I said.

"Get gone my ass. Stop bullshitting. Stop being a pussy all yo life. Just listen to me. Go head, it's on the tub," the small voice inside my head said.

"No," I screamed.

"Nigga you killed yo sister, so handle that. You ain't no better than that nigga Loc. Melo died just like he did. You knew she didn't deserve to live that's why you did it," the small voice inside my head said.

"No I didn't," I screamed.

"Yes you did. Handle that. It's on the tub. End this shit already," the small voice inside my head insisted.

For some reason Melo burned body kept playing in my head. I couldn't control it, the thoughts wouldn't stop even when I tried to close my eyes real tight and refocus my mind.

The more stressed I got, the stronger the thoughts got, the more real they got, the more vivid they got.

The tears started to flow from my eyes again as I started to pound on my head with my hands, wanting the thoughts to end.

"They won't stop," I cried out.

"They will when you be at peace my boy. Handle that. I promise you, death is the best thang that can happen to you. You can choose to suffer or choose to live without pain,"

The small voice inside my head finally made sense to me. Peace was what I needed in my life. Peace was what I was searching for. The small voice inside my head convinced me to move over to the tube and sit down. I didn't want to do it but I knew it may have very well been my destiny to off myself.

"Get the razor and gently go around yo wrist until you see blood. For once in yo life have some balls my boy. Go head," the small voice inside my head said.

I stretched out both arms to look at both of my wrists. I stared at them.

"You know what to do,"

I nodded to say I knew.

I grabbed the razor from the tube.

"I am sorry everybody," I whispered.

"Go ahead and free everybody from the burden you have put on them. Go ahead, free yoself. You will be free, trust me," the small voice inside my head said over and over again. "You will be free,"

I put the razor to my skin, just piecing it a little.

"Don't nobody care bout me anyway, I might as well do it," I whispered. "Don't nobody care bout me," I said, this time screaming out loud.

I could slightly hear Sea'Sea trying to break down the door. But that sound soon faded out. Now it was just me, the small voice inside my head, my thoughts, and the razor. Everything else was just a blur.

"You will be free," the small voice inside my head said.

"Free," I said with a chuckle. Freedom was what I was searching for my entire life.

"Free Amel," that voice in my head said.

I pieced my skin even more. The more I pressed down the razor, the more I could see blood coming from my left wrist.

"Go over a little, hit that vein," the small voice inside my head said.

It seemed like everything around me started to turn into slow motion. As I attempted to move the razor over to cut the vein in my left wrist, I looked up with a face filled with tears and seen Sea'Sea running at me in slow motion, like a movie. I could see her mouth moving, but I couldn't hear anything that she was saying. The only thing I saw was her running towards me with tears flowing from her eyes, reaching out her hands to me

I stared at Sea'Sea in a daze with a peaceful smirk. What was crazy is that, for some reason, I could see Sea'Sea soul through her crying eyes as she approached. I seen the fear, the love, the commitment.

I remember looking down at the razor and digging deeper into my skin with it, still smirking.

Then all went blank.

Chapter 8

Sammie Beans High School was the pride of Itta Bena. The school was a landmark around the Mississippi Delta because of its rich history, especially the history of how the school was founded. The old folks around Itta Bena and Bear Ridge us to say that Sammie Beans was a former slave turned business man that took it upon himself to open a school for young black children in the summer of 1932. They said it originally started out as a white wooden school with one room and had grown over the years into a small campus that consisted of an elementary school, junior high school, and high school.

The old folks use to say that each section of the school told a story of the past. The tree stomp that resided in front of the high school building, represented one of many trees that were used to hang black folks in the early 1930's. Baby Sister use to say that white people did that to prove a point to black folks that they were not allowed to have a decent education like the rest of decent folks around town. "They want to keep you dumb and ignorant," Baby Sister use to say all the time. Baby Sister may have been many of things, but Baby Sister made sure me and Melo knew where we came from and our history.

In the old City Hall building, when I was little, Baby Sister use to take me up there and look at articles from the 1930's that had photos of black folks hanging from the trees right in front of the white school that

Sammie Beans built. The parking lot of the junior high building was said to be a place where black folks were sold in slavery time, which is why Sammie Beans decided to build on the land. It was the very land that Sammie Beans was sold on. Behind the elementary building, spreads of cotton fields were as far as the eye can see. Most, if not all, of the children around Itta Bena, Bear Ridge, Morgan City, and Quito had kin that picked cotton in those fields.

Many teachers told different stories of Sammie Beans, the man, and what he meant to the community. They told why the school was built and the lives that were lost trying to uphold a certain dignity and standard at the school. But some older folks around town had a different to tell about ole Sammie Beans. A few older folks around the community said that they knew the truth about ole Sammie Beans and knew why the school was in the condition it was. They said it was cursed and rightfully so because of what ole Sammie Beans had done. "He was a snake," they said "That did any and every thang for them white folks"

Sammie Beans High School, as it stood then when I was in school, was a school like no other, far from the rich history it once knew. It was now a school that had a daycare for students with children, a reserved smoking place for students who had permission to smoke on campus from their parents, a perpetual use of subject books 20 years too old, and school buildings that had holes in the floors and ceilings. From guns, drugs, and students having sex in the bathroom, the school had become a direct contradiction of it's past.

Sammie Beans placed last in the state of Mississippi in every category possible from an education standpoint, but ranked almost first in every sport.

Chapter 9

Me, Sea'Sea, and Javion walked silently to school together. I could feel the stinging in my wrist from the fresh razor cuts that was covered by several bandages.

Once we made it to school, me and Javion parted ways with Sea'Sea. Sea'Sea made her way to the cafeteria to eat breakfast as I made my way to the daycare in the junior high building.

"May I help you," the daycare assistant said.

"I need to sign him up for the program," I said.

"Whats yo name," the daycare assistant said

"Amel...A-M-E-L...River....R-I-V-E-R," I said.

"Are you the father," the daycare assistant said

I looked at Javion and smiled.

"Yeah I'm his daddy," I said.

"You not my daddy," Javion said.

"Boy be quiet," I quickly snapped at Javion. "I'm his daddy,"

The assistant went to the back room for a few minutes and came back.

"Alrighty Mr. River. Here is his need sheet. He will need everything on there. Ok," The assistant said.

"Ok," I said.

"Can he stay with yall today," I asked. "Cuz I really need to get to class today,"

"He sure can," the assistant said.

I smiled.

I enjoyed how pleasant and nice the assistant was towards me, which made me feel comfortable with leaving Javion there.

"Come on little man," The assistant said as she grabbed Javion hand and walked him over to the other 20 or so kids his age.

"You be a good boy ok Champ," I said.

Javion was so busy with playing with the other kids that he didn't hear me.

"Javion," I said louder to get his attention.

Javion looked back at me.

"You be a good boy ok," I repeated.

"Ok," Javion responded.

I looked at the need sheet that the daycare assistant had given me.

"Got damn, why do these little kids need 1...2...4...6...13....19...19 items. Where am I going to get the money from to get all of this shit," I whispered.

I made my way to the cafeteria and posted up outside so I could see the line of buses coming in. I knew that JoJo's bus, 017, hadn't made it to school yet.

"I hope this nigga got something on him," I thought.

I noticed it looked like bad weather was coming into the horizon. The sky was beginning to get darker, an obvious indicator that bad weather was approaching quickly.

"When it rain, it pours," I thought.

I never carried books to school, only a towel around my neck and a backpack that contained my notepad. I was a SPED in school. I took special education classes, except for English and Art classes. It wasn't that I was unable to learn, I was in those special education classes to collect a monthly check to help Baby Sister pay bills. I knew I could compete with the "best students" at Sammie Beans, but school was boring and uninteresting to me. I knew I could not show my true potential or else I would be pulled from my special education classes and then stop getting those monthly checks Baby Sister needed.

JoJo spotted me posted up on the cafeteria wall before his bus stopped.

"What's up boy," JoJo said pounding hands with me.

"What's good my boy," I asked.

"Shit, chillin,"JoJo said. "Where you been at. I been looking for you for the past three days,"

"It's a long story my boy. Long story,"

"Yo, yo momma been looking for you too. It looked like she was worried bout you my boy,"

"Ain't fucking with Baby Sister like that, at least not now. She gots to calm down first,"

"I feel you my boy. Yo, I got them goods for you too,"

"It's bout time you came through,"

"What," JoJo said laughing. "You the one been missing in action. Come fuck with ya boy right quick,"

Me and JoJo cautiously made our way to the bathroom of the old science building. When we got to the building's bathroom, we both looked around to make sure that there were no teachers in sight before we went in. I stood behind the door, blocking the entrance, as JoJo got situated. JoJo opened his book bag as I looked inside, finding a half brick of weed, four 8 balls of coke and two guns enclosed in it. JoJo always carried loaded guns at school for some reason. I guess he was scared of getting robbed or something.

"You finna go to war with some niggas ain't it my boy," I said. "Mane, you get caught with those two burners, yo life is over with my nigga, for real for real,"

"And if you get caught with this dope yo life is over with too little nigga, for real for real," JoJo responded.

"True that," I responded with a smile.

"Why you bring coke though. I ain't fucking with my nose at all," I asked.

"I ain't asking you to fuck with yo nose, but some niggas out here need that white bitch in they life sometimes. Nigga you would be surprise who on that white gul like that. I don't fuck with, I just pass it along my nigga," JoJo said. "You ready to make this money though," JoJo said looking at me with a serious look.

"Hell yeah," I quickly responded. I knew I could buy all of the stuff off Javion need sheet with this little run at school. "Let's make this bread my boy,"

"Shit, we got like 15 minutes to make something happen though. Let's ride my boy," JoJo said.

We knew our homeroom teacher would not be in the room until 8am because she had to be on duty watching the students in the cafeteria. It was 7:40am and JoJo knew we had to move fast. We quickly exited the bathroom and made our way to our homeroom. JoJo had set up a couple of deals and wanted the opportunity to make a few dollars before the school day began.

JoJo rushed to his desk and started to get set up to make his first sale of the day.

"Amel pass me that brown bag that Pee Wee had his jungle juice in right quick," JoJo said to me. As JoJo opened his book bag, his face lit up with excitement. It was like an adrenaline rush to him to sell and smoke dope at school. I guess it was the thought of getting caught that made it so much fun to him.

I passed JoJo the brown bag, and JoJo began to break the weed up as he carefully sectioned it off while rolling it in pieces of the brown bag. The loud weed smell coming from JoJo book bag dominated the air.

"Who got that sconion? That's some fire dope there, believe that," A student standing outside of the classroom said, now peeping in the door trying to see who had the supply.

Before the first deal came in the room, JoJo gave me my share of dope rolled in school paper. It was about 3 ounces. I got extra because I was helping with the deals and because of my relationship with JoJo. JoJo was going to split the profit with me for everything that I help sell, so that was a good look for me too.

"Don't say I never did nothing for you little nigga," JoJo said. JoJo always called me little for some reason, even though we were the same age and the same height. I guess he felt that because of all of the responsibilities that he had to take on at home, he had manly years over me.

As the deals came in, I was responsible for getting the money and passing the customers the goods.

I was in the middle of making my third or fourth deal of the day when a teacher walked in the room. Boy! When I tell you my heart dropped to the floor so fast as I tried playing that shit off by pretending to read a book that I found on my home girl Kenisha Taylor desk.

"Kenisha, do you really thank that the president of Nigeria would do something like that," I said looking spooked. My hands were shaking uncontrollably.

"What the hell is you talking bout Shake," Kenisha asked looking up at me, making a confused face. She was in the middle of trying to do her homework and was being disturbed by me I guess.

I bucked my eyes to tell her to just go with the flow and stop asking questions. "Imma beat yo ass," I said slowly and silently to Kenisha.

"You seen JoJo, Shake," Mr. Petey Williams, the 8th grade Social Studies teacher asked. I had my back turned to him and played like I didn't hear him. I continued to act like I was trying to talk to Kenisha about the president of Nigeria.

"Shake, have you seen JoJo," Mr. Williams said again, this time louder with a slight irritation in his voice.

I turned around slowly and said "Yyyeah, he bbback there,"

I was so scared and nervous that my knees started to buckle. I was so scared that I had to hold on to Kenisha desk to keep from falling.

Mr. Williams made his way to the back of the room where JoJo desk was. I knew for sure that Mr. Williams could smell the weed in the air, like we all could, and hoped that he just let us ride this time.

"What's good Mr. Williams, what you need on this lovely Tuesday morning," I heard JoJo say joking.

Mr. Williams walked over to JoJo and began to whisper something in his ear. JoJo then shook his hand and exchanged an 8 ball of coke with him without anyone knowing. It was a perfect exchange between a student and teacher. Before I turned around, Mr. Williams secured the bag of goods in his pants tightly.

"Ain't this bout a bitch," I thought, still shaking like a leaf because of my nerves. "A teacher getting served by a student at school. Ain't this some shit? Nigga pose to be teaching us but the nigga too busy getting high. And my dumbass sitting up here scared out of my mind and this nigga bout to buy some dope from JoJo,"

Selling to teachers was nothing new to JoJo. Most teachers he sold to were from around the way and were accustomed to smoking and tooting with his uncle Bay and his cousins.

As the last deal of the morning walked out, the teacher, Mrs. Kay Appletree, walked into the classroom. She was a white teacher from Wisconsin in her mid-thirties with a petite body and big ass, so attention from boys and men came her way quite often. Mrs. Appletree was a good teacher to us students at Sammie Beans High. She always talked to us about this world of dreams that existed miles away and how much that world had to offer us, even if we were from the Mississippi Delta. I played like I never listened to her lectures, but deep down I listened to every word that she use to speak religiously.

"Oh my God, What is that smell you guys. Would someone please let up the window, good grief," Mrs. Appletree said in a sweet and innocent voice. All of us students laughed. We thought it was funny that she didn't know what weed smelled like and we did.

"Looks like bad weather coming this way huh Mrs. Appletree," I said to take her mind off of the smell.

"It sure does Shake. It's looking really bad out there," Mrs. Appletree said. It made me laugh at the fact that an innocent white lady from Wisconsin was calling me by a name that was created in a world so unknown to her.

Knowing what I know now, Mrs. Appletree perception to us students was that of a saint that knew nothing of the hood and streets in which we were from, but I later found out that the truth was, Mrs. Appletree actually came from a hard background herself. She knew the smell of weed and of meth, due to her meth addiction in her past life. In her students, Mrs. Appletree saw plenty of herself in us. We gave her a reason to live and she knew in her heart that most of us were good kids living without proper guidance. She made it her business to try to provide that to us. Mrs. Appletree overlooked most of the bad activity we did because she knew that most of us, if we got caught, were going to end up on the streets, becoming another statistic. She wanted more for us.

For some reason, Mrs. Appletree took a liking to me I guess because of my respectful and nice demeanor. I think it was something about me that was different to her, a coolness and charm that she liked. My positive energy made me stand out amongst my peers.

As we were gathering our things for the next class, the school siren started to sound through the intercom system. Bad weather had finally arrived and it was time for everyone to gather in the hall for the tornado drill.

All of us gathered in the hallway of the Junior High School building. The drill consisted of us laying on the floor with our butts tilted up and our hands covering their heads.

So we all got into position on the floor on both sides of the hall. Mrs. Appletree, Mr. Williams, and Mr. Edwards were assigned the duty of monitoring us students, making sure everyone was doing what they were told.

Seconds turned into minutes as we held our positions.

I laid there, chilling, until I felt something poking me in my side really hard.

"Nigga, get yo shit," AJ whispered to me as he pointed to the three blunts on the floor by my head. I hadn't noticed that AJ was beside me until then. I paused for a second looking at AJ, remembering what JoJo had told me the day before about him being accused of killing his father. Then my mind instantly came to me and realized what AJ had just told me.

"Oh shit," I whispered. As soon as I grabbed the three blunts off of the floor, and within a fraction of a second, I swear to God, Mrs. Appletree walked right passed me.

I kept my head down. My heart was beating faster than I don't know what. I was scared to look up, scared that I would find Mrs. Appletree looking down at me with that "I caught you look".

Seconds seemed like hours as Mrs. Appletree made her way back towards where I was laying, still monitoring the hall gracefully. To my surprise, she kept walking.

"There is no fucking way she didn't see those blunts on the floor. There is no fucking way," I whispered. Now I was sweating like a got damn pig in heat. My heart felt like it was about to jump out of my chest.

Mrs. Appletree walked passed me again, still monitoring the hall with grace, but she kept on walking and never looked my way.

"Thank you God....Thank you.... Thank you....Thank you," I prayed silently.

As the bad weather moved on, all the students got up from the floor and started to go back to our scheduled classes. As everyone was scattering, I looked over at AJ and said "I owe you my boy,"

AJ looked at me with a weird cold stare for a second, and then smiled.

"You good Shake. You straight," AJ said as he waved me off nonchalantly. "Just be careful next time"

"Bet that my boy," I responded. "Fuck with me later aight,"

"Aight," AJ responded walking off.

And I be damned if it wasn't one minute later that the police surrounded AJ with guns and told him to get on the ground and don't move. He had been on the run from police for the past couple of days and finally came to school to eat some food.

"What I do," I could hear AJ pleading, "I didn't do nothing mane. Somebody call my grandma," he continued as they rushed him away in handcuffs.

"Damn my boy," I thought.

Chapter 10

The last period bell rang to dismiss school for the day. My 7th period class was located in the Junior High School building, the same building in which Mrs. Appletree room was located. For the entire day, I made it my business to avoid coming into that building, trying not to be seen by Mrs. Appletree because I still didn't know if she had seen the weed I had dropped on the floor or not. Coming to my last class, I hid beside two big girls as I passed Mrs. Appletree room, avoiding her with ease.

Now that school was dismissed and without the two big girls to hide behind, I found myself in a dilemma as I walked down the hall of the Junior High building towards Mrs. Appletree room. As I approached Mrs. Appletree room, I noticed that she was not standing outside of her door as she did daily to monitor students walking the halls after school.

"Let me speed my ass up. I don't want her to see me," I thought as I started to speed walk.

As I sped passed her door, I made sure my head stayed focused on the blue exit door. I didn't want to turn my head and make eye contact with Mrs. Appletree by looking into her room as I passed it.

"Thank you God," I said as I hastily passed by the room, trying to get to the exit door as fast as I could.

"Amel," Mrs. Appletree yelled out to me just as I was exiting the door.

"Ma'am," I responded rolling my eyes and biting my lip. I knew something was up. Now what's the odds of her calling me out the same day I drop dope on the floor that she supposedly didn't see.

"You got a minute, I need to talk to you about something," Mrs. Appletree said.

"Motherfucker! How in the hell did she see me," I thought as I walked up the steps.

I slowly walked into the room, and noticed that there weren't any students in there.

Mrs. Appletree closed the door behind her and locked it as I entered.

I kept walking on into the room, afraid to turn around like a little bitch. I was too scared to face Mrs. Appletree under the perceived circumstances.

"Please God, please don't let her tell me that she saw that dope on the floor. Please," I thought as I tightly squeezed my eyes.

"Shake," Mrs. Appletree said with a soft tone.

"Yes, Mrs. Appletree," I said nervously with my back still turned to her.

"Why do you have your back turned to me? Turn around and let me ask you something," Mrs. Appletree said softly.

"Damn. Here comes the bullshit. I knew she seen that dope on the floor," I thought.

As I turned around to face Mrs. Appletree, I found her sitting on top of a desk with one leg on the floor and the other leg hiked on a desk. Mrs. Appletree always wore little professional skirts to school that fitted her body just right. That booty looked so good in anything she wore.

"Have you ever seen a white pussy before," Mrs. Appletree said as she started to unbutton her shirt and then her bra to let her breast hang. "Have you ever seen white titties like these before Amel," she continued as she squeezed both breast together, licking each nipple one by one.

Being a young boy I was scared and excited at the same time. I didn't know whether to run or get hard.

Mrs. Appletree stood up from the desk and took her skirt and shirt off, getting butt booty naked. When I tell you that body looked so good naked, that's what I mean. But I was young, I didn't know the first thing to do with a grown woman.

"I see how you look at my ass all the time and I think it's cute. You know, I see your little fine ass walking around here and it just gets my pussy wet every time I think about that walk of yours," Mrs. Appletree said as she sat back down on the desk.

"Ummmm," I said nervous than a motherfucker. I never saw a woman naked before in real life. I can't front, me, JoJo, Freddy Boy, and Slim had watched plenty of flixs, but that shit there was different. This what I was witnessing was on a whole nother level.

"Come here and let Mrs. Appletree teach you how to say your alphabets while you eat this pussy," Mrs. Appletree said, telling me to come here with her one finger.

And like a little puppy, I went.

Mrs. Appletree instructed me to kneel down in front of her. I kneeled on one knee in front of her. Then she grabbed my head and put my face like two inches from her pussy.

I can't even front, that pussy smelled a little bit like buttermilk and cornbread. It kind of fucked me up because Mrs. Appletree looked like her pussy would smell like strawberries, you know, smell like something sweet. It had to be that she was sweating or something.

Mrs. Appletree took her hands and spread her pussy lips apart. "You see that little pump right there, I want you to suck on that," Mrs. Appletree said as she started to rub on her clitoris.

It didn't matter how that pussy smelled at that point, all I knew was my dumbass was down there doing whatever she asked me to do. That was my first time making a woman scream like that. Mrs. Appletree body was shaking like she was a vibrator, that's how much she enjoyed it.

After Mrs. Appletree took all she could from me, she threw me a towel and told me to wash my mouth because I had pussy juice on it.

 "Oh yeah, now we are even. If you don't tell nobody about this, I won't tell nobody about the blunts I seen on the floor earlier," Mrs. Appletree said with a slight smirk on her face as she unlocked the door. "Have a good day Shake"

I couldn't do shit but smile as I walked out the door on my way to get Javion and then go to basketball practice for tryouts.

--

Before basketball tryouts started, I found myself sitting on the sidewalk in front of the gym with Javion, reflecting on what Mr. Lim had told me about having sex.

"Fuck'em. That's what men do. Pussy is too good to pass up boy," Mr. Lim use to say.

I knew in my heart what had happened between me and Mrs. Appletree wasn't right, but after thinking about what Mr. Lim had said, I figured it was just part of me becoming a man.

"Yo KO," I said to my boy Brace McKinely aka KO as he walked down the sidewalk.

Brace earned his nickname, KO, from streets fights, and knocking dudes out cold with those big hands he had. KO was new around the way, so you already know how that went. KO had every girl knocking at his door trying to have sex and every dude knocking him upside his head trying to fight. It was like a rite of passage sort to speak around the way. KO was high yellow with gray eyes, wavy good hair, and was 6'7 200 pounds or so. He was a basketball star from Julian High School in Nashville that transferred to Sammie Beans High due to his grandmother falling ill, forcing his family to move to take care of her. KO came from a decent family that had more than most. His father was an electrician, his mother a nurse, and his grandmother, Miss Arma McKinely, was a prominent figure in Itta Bena for years until she became ill. Although he came from a good life, KO had a little hood in him too.

"What's up my boy. What's up Champ," KO said. All of my partners called Javion Champ like I did.

"What's up KO," Javion replied.

"You seen Sea'Sea," I asked.

"I seen her earlier, but she looked like she was crying bout something though," KO said.

"Crying? Crying bout what," I asked with intrigue.

"I don't know. Ain't no telling with her though my boy. You out of all people know how crazy Sea'Sea is. But I did see her walking off campus like she do every day. You know she don't give a fuck," KO said.

"She ain't crazy my boy, she just got problems. She good peoples though," I insisted.

"There you go always taking up for her," KO said laughing. "But you ready for this tryout. I been trying to get yo ass on the team to run the point since forever, but you been bullshitting," KO said.

"Been busy my boy," I replied.

"Busy with what though," KO asked.

"Trying to stay out the way," I said.

"I feel ya on staying out the way. Ain't nothing out here but trouble," KO said as he picked up Javion. "Let's gone on in here before Coach start acting crazy and shit. You know he be lying like he served in the Gulf War and shit. They say the nigga was the lead drummer in the Army band and he be acting like he done been to war and shit. You know the drummer that be leading the men to war when they be walking," KO continued as we started to laugh.

"Mane, everybody know Coach be lying. That boy too crazy serving them lies like that," I said.

"Hell yeah," KO said.

Me, KO, and Javion made our way into the gym.

"Yo you seen that boy Money though. He pose be coming out too for tryouts," I said.

D'Money "Money," Wilson was my best friend and closest dude to me. Me and Money did everything together. We played sports together since we were small kids going to NYSP. Money lived a few blocks from the City over by the JW's Ranch.

"Money with that slow ass crossover," KO said with laughter.

"It sho is slow but he swear it be killing everybody on the court. That boy too funny," I said.

"On the line," Coach yelled.

Coach was a heavy set mid age man. He was known for being dramatic when it came to coaching. Throwing chairs, kicking benches, and pointing his finger at his players was all a part of his makeup. The students, his players, and people around the community loved how crazy that motherfucker was.

"But Coach we gotta change our clothes first," KO said. "I can't run in these," KO said pointing to his timbos.

"Yo ass shouldn't been late," Coach screamed pointing his finger. "Now all of yall get on that line. 20 suicides. Now Hit It,"

Money finally walked his slow ass in the gym already dressed for practice. Coach had given him another chance to come out to practice despite him quitting the team the year before. This was his last chance to impress Coach.

"There he go," KO yelled. "With that slow ass crossover,"

"I bet you can't stop it though my boy," Money yelled back.

"Bring yo last ass here," Coach screamed to Money. "I told yo ass if you bullshit me, Imma bullshit you. Now get yo ass on the line. You gone do 30,"

Money chuckled and got in line. "I got you Coach," he said.

"My boy walking up in here like he been lying between some legs," I said out loud.

"Oh what you thank I been doing, beating my meat," Money yelled.

"Who legs you been laying between," I said trying to challenge Money.

"Sea'Sea who else," Money said as he laughed and stuck out his tongue.

"I DON'T BELIEVE YOU," I said with laughter. The entire gym laughed out loud.

"Aight then, smell my finger and tell me if it don't smell like Sea'Sea pussy," Money said.

"Chill with all that," I said running in the opposite direction as Money.

"KO, smell my finger," Money said as he quickly put his finger under KO nose and ran off laughing.

"Imma beat yo a......," KO yelled as he was about to run after Money.

"GOT DAMMITTTTTTTTTTTTT," Coach screamed. "GET OUTTTTTTTTTTTTTTTTTTTTTTTTTTTTTTTTTTTT,"

The gym didn't move.

"GET THE FUCK OUTTTTTTTTTTTT. YALLLLLLLLLLLLLLLLLLLL AIN'T SERIOUS," Coach screamed.

Coach went to the bench to sit down and put his head in his hand, frustrated as shit with us. He started to pour bottled water on his hand, wiping his face with it, trying to cool off his anger. The gym still didn't move.

"Aight, since yall don't want to get out, yall gone run 40 suicides," Coach said. "AFTER running 45 minutes around the gym. Put that 45 minutes on that clock up there,"

The entire gym sighed and smacked their mouth.

"Shut up ug-e man," Money said to PeeJay.

Pete "PeeJay," Fellows Jr. was a normal around the way nigga that grew up in the City but had money since his father, Pete Fellows Sr. was a hustler. He thought he was a tough guy since his father was a "tough guy". PeeJay was the kid that when he got in trouble, his momma and daddy took up for him even though they were the ones teaching him all the bad shit. Everybody around the way hated PeeJay because he was spoiled and hard to deal with for no reason.

"I got yo ug-e man nigga," PeeJay said jumping in Money face.

Me and KO stepped around PJ.

"You got problems don't it my boy," KO said with my fist balled up.

"HIT IT," Coach yelled as the clock started to tick down from 45 minutes.

"You lucky nigga," KO said to PeeJay as we all started to run. "Imma bring that tough guy shit outta you. You gone have to live that tough shit, you feel me my boy,"

"RIVER. NO CUTTING THE COURT," Coach yelled to me. I started to run wider around the court.

"Damn, I wonder what's up with Sea'Sea though," I asked myself.

Chapter 11

After basketball tryouts, me and Javion made our way to Sea'Sea's house. When we arrived at her house, we found her on the front door steps crying with her knees bent and her head hidden in her arms.

"Javion go play in the house," I said as I maneuvered by Sea'Sea to let Javion in the front door.

Then I focused on Sea'Sea.

"Why you wasn't at school today," I asked in concern. "You ok Sea'Sea,"

Sea'Sea sat there with her head hidden in her arms without a response. It seemed like me being there made her cry even harder.

"What's wrong," I asked, waiting on a response from her. "Don't you hear me talking to you Sea'Sea,"

"Nothing," Sea'Sea screamed in a muffled sound.

"What it is? Who did it," I asked.

"I did it," Sea'Sea mumbled.

"Did what," I asked. "Look at me,"

Then my heart dropped. Maybe Sea'Sea was trying to figure out a way to break the same news to me that Melo had done just 2 years before. Maybe she had HIV and didn't know how to tell me.

"Look at me gul," I said raising my voice.

Sea'Sea slowly raised her head from the pits of her arms. I could see the snot running from her nose and how puffy her eyes were.

Sea'Sea sat there and cried for another minute, not saying a word, just glazing off into the sky.

"What did you do Sea'Sea," I asked anxiously.

Sea'Sea started to shake her head from side to side, wanting to say something but didn't.

"Fuck it then. Just sit yo ass up there and cry then. I don't care. I am not going to sit up here and beg to see what's wrong with you,"

"That's right, I know you don't care and I don't want yo ass to care either,"

"Yeah I know you don't care but I am still sitting my dumb ass up here trying to see what's wrong witcha and you act like you can't tell me," I said. "You ain't gotta cop no attitude. Ain't nobody trying to piss you off Sea'Sea,"

"Tell you what Amel, tell you that I thank I am pregnant. Tell you that," Sea'Sea said with attitude.

I was both relieved and taken back at the same time. I knew Sea'Sea was young and had her faults, as I did, but I always viewed her differently than other people around the way. Even though she was 15, like me, I held her to a higher standard.

"You what," I asked.

"I thank I am pregnant. You heard me. I haven't gotten my period in two months, been throwing up every day," Sea'Sea said.

I paused to gather my thoughts, trying to put two and two together. I was damn near certain that Sea'Sea was a born again virgin. She was pure in my eyes not including the shit that went on when she was a little girl.

"Maybe God wanted me to be Joseph and Sea'Sea to be Mary. They didn't have to smash to have a baby. It just happened," I thought. Since I was a little boy, Baby Sister always talked to me about the story of Jesus. She said Jesus was made without anybody having sex. I believed her and I still believed that could happen.

"Is it mine," I asked in a serious tone.

"Is it yo what Amel," Sea'Sea responded with attitude. Thinking back on it now, I bet she thought I was out of my got damn mind.

"Is it my baby," I repeated.

"How in the fuck... Nothing, never mind. See now you acting stupid,"

"How am I acting stupid? I ask you a real question. What, you scared to answer it,"

Sea'Sea rolled her eyes as she looked off with a slight chuckle, obviously irritated by me and my antics.

"Yeah it's yos. It's yo baby, if that's what you want to hear," Sea'Sea snapped.

"What the fuck do that pose to mean," I asked raising my voice.

"How in the hell can we have a baby when we ain't never fucked Amel," Sea'Sea yelled.

"Did Mary and Joseph have to smash to have Jesus? No. So what's so different between us. Maybe God wanted us to be like them,"

Sea'Sea gave me a "This nigga can't be serious," look and chuckled a little with disbelief.

"Is you a fool Amel. Is you a fucking fool? Our situation ain't nothing like no Joseph and Mary. I know you done lost yo mind now. You, out of all people, should know that God don't see people like us, so how is He going to give us a baby. Who says shit like that anyway," Sea'Sea said. "And plus, you act like you scared of pussy anyway, at least mine. Hell I am starting to thank you playing for the other team,"

"Just quit while you ahead now Sea'Sea. Now you being stupid," I said getting upset.

"What? It's true and you know it's true. That's why yo ass can't say nothing. How many times have you seen me butt ass naked and ain't never tried to touch me or make a move,"

"Sea'Sea I ain't trying to go there with you like that, can't you understand that,"

"Go there with what. It's just fucking Amel. Dick and pussy, that's it,"

I looked at Sea'Sea. "It's more than just dick and pussy to me. Do you thank I just view you as just a piece of pussy,"

Sea'Sea looked down.

"You might as well, these other niggas sho do. What makes you different from the rest of them niggas," Sea'Sea asked.

I stared at her and was shocked that she was coming at me like that. It was like she was trying to play me.

"You know what Sea'Sea, fuck you and that baby," I said, trying to hurt her like she was trying to hurt me.

"Naw nigga, fuck you and yo momma, bitch," Sea'Sea said pointing her finger towards me. "Like I said, you just like the rest of these niggas

Amel. Don't give a fuck bout nobody but yoself," she continued as she began to cry.

I observed Sea'Sea in silence. I figured that she was indeed pregnant because of how emotional she was. I remembered how emotional Melo was when she was pregnant too. Melo use to say things she didn't mean when she was pregnant so I figured Sea'Sea was doing the same. I decided to back off a little.

"Who baby is it if it ain't mine,"'

Sea'Sea looked at me with an "I can't believe you just ask me that," look.

"I don't know who baby it is," Sea'Sea said.

"You do know who baby it is," I said.

"What you want me to say Amel. That the baby daddy is one of them niggas they use to fuck me when I was 8. Yeah Amel, it's one of them niggas. Or maybe it's JoJo baby. Didn't you notice my number saved in his phone. Yeah me and JoJo been fucking, now what,"

I stepped back and put my hand under my chin. I did remember Sea'Sea number being saved in JoJo's phone. Then I thought about how JoJo always acted when I brought up Sea'Sea name in a conversation, how he use to try to talk bad about her, calling her a hoe, trying to deflect the relationship they had going.

"You did what now," I said, obviously caught off guard by what Sea'Sea said. "Sea'Sea, you did what with who. I didn't hear you,"

I moved slowly towards Sea'Sea, biting my lip, damn near in a rage of anger. Sea'Sea stared me in the eyes the entire time without blinking. She knew I was about to give her what she wanted. She knew I was about to show her some good love and affection the way she liked it, to remind her that I still cared.

I grabbed that motherfucker by her throat so hard and slapped her twice in the face with all of my might.

"So I guess you out here selling pussy too, being a fucking hoe like these niggas say you is. Just like yo momma," I said as I started to squeeze Sea'Sea's neck even tighter. Sea'Sea didn't try to fight me off. She just sat there. "You fucked JoJo," I asked.

Sea'Sea didn't respond.

"Did ….you… fuck… JoJo," I screamed. I was trying to see if she was lying or not. I squeezed her neck even tighter.

Sea'Sea still didn't respond. Her eyes started to roll into the back of her head from the grip I had on her neck.

"Kill this bitch Amel," the small voice inside my head said. "She doesn't deserve to live,"

I shook the small voice inside my head off, I didn't want to kill her. But I did want to prove a point that I was not about to be played like a motherfucking sucker. So I continued to stare into the eyes of Sea'Sea while I choked her ass. The more I thought about what she had just said, the angrier I got.

"Imma kill yo motherfucking ass if you don't answer me this time," I said. "Did you fuck JoJo, Sea'Sea,"

Sea'Sea slowly shook her head as to say yes.

I squeezed her neck as hard as I could for a second longer and threw her to the ground. Sea'Sea started to breathe heavily as she tried to catch her breath.

Minutes passed as I observed Sea'Sea gather herself. I wanted her to say that she and JoJo fucked.

"Say you fucked JoJo,"

Sea'Sea stared at me. I know she debated whether telling me what I wanted to hear would send me over the deep end and make me do something really crazy. But I guess she figured she didn't have nothing to lose. We would make up in a couple days like we usually did.

"Yeah I fucked him. Now what you gone do, kill me? Why you care so much? You ain't my man nigga. "

"I know I ain't yo motherfucking man, but why you got to go fuck one of my partners though? To prove a point to me or something? How low can you get Sea'Sea,"

"You know what Amel, fuck you. At least JoJo show me some kind of affection. At least he tells me he love me. At least he look at me and tell me I'm sexy and pretty. Shit nigga, when you look at me, you look right through me. You ain't never told me I was pretty or sexy,"

"For what Sea'Sea, so I can fuck like that nigga. Is that all you thank of yoself as being? I guess I should just fuck you, the next bitch, and the next one after that. Is that what you looking for me to do? You want a motherfucker to feed you that bullshit cuz you like bullshit,"

"I don't like bullshit Amel, I just like for people to make me feel good bout myself, unlike you. So what if I fucked JoJo or not. You ain't never tried to fuck me, go with me. You ain't never showed me what I showed you, motherfucker,"

"What the fuck you talking bout," I asked.

"What the fuck I said nigga, don't play motherfucker," Sea'Sea said. "I take care of you and that baby. I do that Amel, nobody else. I take care of yall like I would take care of my family because yall are my family. And this how you try to do me," she continued as she began to cry.

"Fuck you and them fake ass tears Sea'Sea," I said with disgust. "You just like the rest of these bitches and hoes around here. Got me out here looking like a fucking fool with this nigga,"

people houses to either: scope it out to steal something, come in the house to talk about it, or to bring mess into it.

After staying with King Lee for a few months, I took it upon myself to clean the old shotgun house every other day to show a little appreciation to King Lee for being so kind to let me and Javion stay there. I even started to buy food for the house, a little furniture here and there, and cloths for myself, Javion, and King Lee.

People around The City started to notice the way me and Javion had started dressing and how I was fixing up the old shotgun house. I know they figured I was either robbing or slanging, which was cool for a young nigga from around the way. King Lee noticed my improved dress attire too. He started to question me about where I got money from, but I always told him that I was just washing cars and mowing grass for money. King Lee took my word for it until he would see something else new in the house, then he would ask me the same questions over again. "All that bad money is going to catch up to you one day and you will pay the price for it. Just don't bring no trouble to my door step," King Lee would say.

King Lee was away picking up cans around the way to earn a little cash to buy for the house and to buy his moonshine.

Javion was at weekend daycare at Sammie Beans that lasted until noon on Saturdays. I knew that I could sneak JoJo in without any problems.

After waiting outside for about 30 minutes, JoJo finally pulled up driving somebody's black car.

"What's up," I said, avoiding not to call him my homeboy.

"What's up with it," JoJo asked.

"Chillin on it. Yo the shoes in the house though," I said.

We both walked in the house as I lead the way back to me and Javion room.

"These the shoes I was talking bout. You can get them for the low. They cold ain't it," I said as I walked into the closet and grabbed a pair of all white Reebok classics. When I turned around to walk out of the closet, I was met by JoJo at the closet door.

"Yeah they aight," JoJo said looking around in the closet and not the shoes. I had a closet filled with clothes and shoes, all named brand.

I noticed how disinterested JoJo appeared to be in the shoes and how hard he was looking at the clothes in the closet. Most of the clothes and shoes still had the tag on them due to me wanting to preserve a fresh outfit for a game or dance.

"Yo, a nigga running low on cash right now, but......But if you can let me slide today, I will drop you off this coming Friday when my momma get that fish plant check," JoJo said still looking at the clothes in the closet. He was now fully immersed in the closet looking through the clothes like he was in a clothing store.

"Why the FUCK you come over here knowing you ain't got no money. Don't try to play me my nigga. I ain't letting you slide with shit. I ain't fucking witcha like that my nigga," I said getting upset. JoJo had been running me down all yesterday about getting the shoes, already knowing that he didn't have money to buy anything.

"Chill my nigga, damn. I was just trying to cut a deal with ya so I can go head and stunt on these hoes with them on today. You feel what I'm saying though my nigga," JoJo said with a smirk on his face.

I started to feel some kind of way about JoJo and the energy he was giving off. I started to put the situation in perspective and came to the conclusion that JoJo was really trying to play me, on some slick shit.

"Mane, fuck what you talking bout. You sitting up here bullshitting wasting my time and yo time. Let's ride my nigga," I said with an attitude. "Take me over Sea'Sea house right quick since you ain't gone do no business. That's the least you can do,"

The two of us made our way outside. I noticed how slow JoJo was walking. It was like he didn't want to leave the house and had something on his mind.

"You know momma kicked me out the house two weeks ago right. I been out here fucked up. Yo boy doing bad out here," JoJo said with intent of gaining empathy from me. "She kicked me out but she still got that pussy ass nigga living there,"

I had noticed how different JoJo looked when he pulled up at the house and got out of the car. It had been a month since I had actually seen him. JoJo looked like he was 30 though he was just 15. He was still smoking weed, but I had heard some people say that he had started smoking crack. JoJo appearance was that of a crackhead that was strung out. His clothes were dirty and big and he had a twitch about him, something like Jackie had when she would be on the hunt for her next hit.

"You know like I know that yo momma just going through it with yo daddy," I said. "She just don't know how to show you that love right now. Can you blame her though? You been getting into so much shit for the past couple of years that she done bailed you out of over and over again. It's only so much yo momma can take my nigga. I thought you was the man of the house and helping her so much. What, all of a sudden she kicked you out for no reason? That shit ain't adding up. It's something you ain't saying,"

JoJo walked over to the black car he pulled up in and grabbed a beer and a cigarette. He lit the cigarette and started to sip off of his beer.

JoJo sighed as he blew a puff of smoke in the air as he leaned against the black car and stared into the sky.

"She chose that bitch ass nigga over me. After all that I seen that nigga put her through, she chose that pussy ass nigga over me for trying to take up for her," JoJo said with animated hands. "So this how the shit went down. That pussy nigga was beating her ass and shit right, for no reason at all, you feel me. So I jumped in and hit the nigga in the mouth.

Next thang I know, she yelling at me, like I did something wrong, you feel me. Then she tells me, and these her exact words, to get the fuck out because no child of mine is never going to disrespect their parents, not in my house," JoJo said taking another pull off of the cigarette. "That shit fucked me up so bad my nigga. So I left. Mane, I ain't never heard my momma cuss like that before, ever. All this shit happen because I tried to stop the nigga from beating her ass,"

"Shhiiidddd. Thangs gone get better for you, believe that. You just got to keep praying my nigga. Keep praying for a better day and the Man upstairs will send somebody or something yo way soon. It don't rain out here forever. For real though," I said.

I was giving advice to JoJo that I barely believed in myself because I had prayed many of times for a better day and was still waiting on that something or somebody to show up. The truth was, I had stolen those words from Ms. Maggy that lived two houses down from King Lee. She was trying to heal King Lee of his "drinking problem" and those were the words she was telling him as she wiped holy oil on his head.

"The Man upstairs don't answer prayers around here my nigga, you know that just like I know that. Just look around you my nigga. Hell look at me. Look at you. Look at this City. You thank if the Man upstairs cared bout anybody around this motherfucker He would let us live like this. Be born into this shit," JoJo said to me with a serious look in his face.

"Naw don't say that. A better day coming for you, for me, for yo momma, for my momma, and for everybody around here mane. We just got to believe my nigga," I responded in a serious tone.

"Fuck all that bullshit, because you finna start preaching and shit in a minute and I ain't trying to have you throw oil on me. But hell yeah, that shit fucked me up bad. So bad that I need another cigarette. You know that boy Kam selling these cigs for a quarter a pop. But shiddd, you got a quarter on you that I can borrow. I gotta go take a shit. You know I gotta have a cigarette while I drop a couple of loads," JoJo said with a smile. "Plus that would be yo payoff for me taking you to Sea'Sea house," I continued.

"I'll fuck witcha today," I said as I reached in my pocket and gave JoJo a quarter.

Me and JoJo made our way to the black car. But before I got in, I said. "Before I step a foot in this motherfucker, this car clean ain't it. You ain't got no shit on you do it,"

"Fuck no boy, you know better than that," JoJo responded.

"I ain't trying to fuck with them laws in no way, shape, or form. You sho you clean," I repeated.

"Yeeeeaaaaa nigga, just get in and stop acting so paranoid," JoJo said.

"Who car is this again," I asked.

"You ask to many questions my boy. It's up to me to know and for you to find out," JoJo said as we both got into the car and drove off.

Chapter 13

I stayed over Sea'Sea's house and watched "The Young and the Holy" soap opera rerun until it was time to pick Javion up from weekend daycare at Sammie Beans. I was surprised to see Jackie at home. To me, she looked different at home than she did in the streets. She seemed almost normal.

"Remember what I said," Jackie said to me as she swept the kitchen floor while winking her eye at me with a slight smile.

Sea'Sea looked at Jackie and then at me.

"What she say to you," Sea'Sea asked. She wanted to know what all the smiling and playfulness was about. She knew that I didn't interact with Jackie like that.

I didn't say a word, only continued to stare at the floor.

Sea'Sea looked at Jackie and said "Ma, what you say to Amel,"

Jackie continued to sweep the kitchen floor like she didn't hear her.

"Did you hear me Ma," Sea'Sea yelled.

"Yeah I heard you Sea'Sea damn. It ain't none of yo damn business what I said to him. That's between me and him," Jackie yelled back.

Sea'Sea turned back to me.

"What she say to you," Sea'Sea asked again.

I still didn't answer.

Sea'Sea punched me hard in the stomach with a frown on her face.

I laughed while holding my stomach.

"Chill mane. She didn't say nothing to me," I said.

"Do it look like I'm fucking smiling Amel? What the fuck she say to you," Sea'Sea screamed.

"Watch yo fucking mouth little bitch," Jackie screamed.

"Naw you watch yo mouth. What the fuck you say to Amel," Sea'Sea screamed.

"Say another word and watch don't I slap the piss out of yo ass," Jackie screamed, now pointing her finger at Sea'Sea.

"You ain't gone slap nobody bitch. Now get beat the fuck down if you want to," Sea'Sea responded.

I intervened. "Don't talk to yo momma like that Sea'Sea, what's wrong with you gul," I whispered with a frown. I knew Sea'Sea had a bad attitude but I didn't know she talked to Jackie like that.

"Fuck that crack head bitch. Don't be talking to her like that. That bitch nasty. Ole crack hoe," Sea'Sea yelled.

"Yeah I got yo crack hoe, bitch," Jackie said as she charged at Sea'Sea.

I stepped in between the both of them and grabbed Jackie.

"Let that bitch go. Let that bitch go," Sea'Sea said, squared up, ready to fight.

It was obvious that Sea'Sea and Jackie talked to each other like that often. It was just the way the two of them communicated and the way they fully understood one another. The streets had raised Jackie like they were currently raising Sea'Sea.

"Let's go Sea'Sea before you do something real stupid and be like me with nowhere to go. Now chill aight," I said as I grabbed her arm and dragged her out of the house. "I gotta go get Javion by 12pm anyway. It's 11:37am now,"

Sea'Sea snatched away from my hold, trying to get to Jackie.

"Sea'Sea, would you please stop it with the bullshit. PLEASE," I said. "Now come on, let's go,"

"You lucky bitch," Sea'Sea said as I dragged her out of the door.

Sea'Sea and I jumped in the old pickup truck Jackie drove all the time.

"Bitch, I didn't tell you to get in my truck and go nowhere," Jackie screamed from the front door.

Sea'Sea put the truck in reverse as she stuck her left hand out the window, pointing her middle finger up and started to wave her hand like a beauty queen at Jackie.

"Bye crackhead," Sea'Sea said with a smile.

"Ok bitch, you thank I'm playing. You thank I'm playing,"

Jackie jumped off out of the front door, got on her purple ten speed bike and started towards the truck in hot pursuit.

"Oh shit, here she come with that motherfucker in 5th gear, flying," I said laughing as I looked at Jackie in the rearview mirror. "Mane you need to speed yo ass up. Ain't no telling what yo momma got on her mind,"

Sea'Sea and I burst into laughter as Sea'Sea drove faster until Jackie was out of sight. We drove about a mile and stopped at a stop sign to catch our breath from laughing.

"For real though Sea'Sea, you gotta stop talking to yo momma like that," I said.

"And this coming from somebody who choked they momma. Nigga please," Sea'Sea said.

"I mean my situation was ..." I said as I was interrupted by a peck on the passenger window. Sea'Sea and I quickly looked to the window.

"You thought you lost me, didn't it bitch," Jackie said as she stood beside the truck on her purple ten speed bike.

"Oh shit," I said as I burst out into a huge laughter.

Sea'Sea sped off in the truck again, laughing trying to control the wheel. I was laughing so hard my stomach started hurt. I could barely breathe.

"I keep telling you that bitch crazy," Sea'Sea said laughing.

"Mane stop the car, please," I said with tears pouring down my face with laughter. "I thank I am gonna die. My stomach hurting so bad,"

Sea'Sea drove about two more miles and stopped the truck. I jumped out of the truck, still laughing, holding my stomach, trying to catch my breath and balance. I laid down in the middle of the street and replayed the stop sign incident over and over again, laughing harder and harder every time.

Sea'Sea watched from the truck as I cried my eyes out in laughter. We sat there and laughed together for about five minutes like it was no tomorrow.

"Get yo crazy ass back in this truck with all that damn laughing," Sea'Sea said still laughing "You just a fool boy,"

"Aight, give me one minute," I said wiping my face with my shirt, trying to compose myself. I got up from the ground and got back in the truck. "Damn, I needed that laugh,"

--

Sea'Sea and I arrived at Sammie Beans and picked up Javion 2 minutes before noon. Then we made our way to The City.

"Sea'Sea I got a surprise for yo big headed ass. I know Imma earn a couple of cool points," I said.

"What kind of surprise is it? I hope it's long, thick, black, and hard," Sea'Sea responded.

"You really thank I would surprise you with a billy club cuz that's the only thang you gots to be talking bout," I said.

"Hump," Sea'Sea said as she cut her eyes, looking me up and down. "I thought you was one of them gold pack, extra-large niggas,"

"Lies," I said smiling.

Sea'Sea looked over at me and smiled.

"For real. Every girl round school always talking bout how big Amel dick is. Hell, I know for sho I see that dick print every time you stand up and when you sit down. Dick just be swanging everywhere when you walking. You thank I don't see that dick print on yo left leg when you sit down," Sea'Sea said.

"What the fuck," I said with a smile. "How did we get on this subject again,"

"I don't know how we got on the subject. All I know is that I want to see it," Sea'Sea said.

"See what," I asked.

show. I sucked on each of her pussy lips one at a time to the tune of her moan. I started to make rings with my tongue around the opening of her pussy hole. I then stuck my tongue out as far as it could go and started to tongue fuck Sea'Sea.

Sea'Sea moaned even louder. "Oh shit," she said.

I moved with my tongue from the pussy hole to the clitoris. I flickered my tongue on it like a lizard. I could see that Sea'Sea was enjoying it by the way her body was jumping. I started to suck on the clitoris like I was sucking on one of her breast. Sea'Sea body started to jump uncontrollably as she moaned and screamed with passion.

"That's it, right there," she screamed repeatedly until she reached her orgasm.

I raised up and seen how exhausted Sea'Sea looked as her body continued to shake a little every other second.

"Shit I'm hot," Sea'Sea said as she started to fan herself. "Where you learn all that shit from,"

I humped my shoulders.

The two of us sat in silence for a couple of seconds. I was deep in thought about crossing me and Sea'Sea friendship boundary. Then it donned on me. I figured eating pussy didn't constitute as having sexual relations with somebody, only intercourse did.

"You still ain't showed me that dick. Oh, I ain't forgot bout that," Sea'Sea said with a smirk.

Sea'Sea reached over, unzipped my pants and struggled to take my dick out as it was fully erect.

"Damn, they wasn't lying. You got a fucking tree limb between yo legs boy," Sea'Sea said with a smirk as she held my dick in her hand. "I can lift weights with this big monster,"

Sea'Sea spit on her hand and started to jack me off slowly as she raised up my shirt and started to suck on my nipples like I had done hers.

"Taste that dick," I whispered to Sea'Sea as she sucked my left nipple then my right one repeatedly.

Right before Sea'Sea could put my dick in her mouth, a loud cry came from the front yard.

"Javion," I said as I snapped out of my pleasure daze. I quickly put my dick in my pants, zipped them up, and jumped out of the car to run to Javion's aid.

Sea'Sea rolled her eyes and let out a deep sigh, clearly irritated. She was ready for some serious jungle action with me. It seemed like every time she tried to fuck me, something always came up. It never failed.

Sea'Sea put back on her clothes too.

I approached Javion and seen that he had fallen from the steps and scratched his legs up.

"You ok Lightbread," Sea'Sea asked as she walked up behind me and put her arms around my waist.

"Yea, I ok," Javion said. Sea'Sea and I smiled.

"Can we finish what we started later," Sea'Sea whispered in my ear as she gently licked it.

"We will see. Let me show you that surprise I got for you though," I said. "Let's go get you a snack Champ,"

Chapter 14

I told Sea'Sea and Javion to wait in the front room. I had a surprise for not only Sea'Sea, but for Javion too.

I opened the door to my room only to find empty shoe boxes and clothes hangers on my bed. My heart dropped to my knees.

"What the fuck," I screamed.

Sea'Sea heard my outburst and quickly ran to the bedroom.

"Oh no," Sea'Sea said as she observed the mess. We both knew what it was. Somebody had broken into the house and stole my stuff.

"Are you fucking serious," I whispered to myself, almost in tears.

"You want me to call the police," Sea'Sea said.

"Them laws ain't coming to the City like that. Don't even worry bout it," I said.

Then I looked nervously under the bed where I was hiding Javion handheld video game, wrapped like a gift. The box was gone.

"Fuccccccckkkkkkkkkkkkkkkkkkk," I screamed with anger.

I looked in the closet to see if Sea'Sea gifts were still in there. They were gone. All the clothes I had bought Javion and myself were gone.

"Ain't no way somebody done stole all my shit like that. I just spent a grand on my clothes, Javion clothes and shoes, and Sea'Sea birthday gifts. Nigga just wiped me out for everything just like that," I thought as I made my way around the house to inspect. I found that a window had been broken in a back bedroom where we used the bathroom. Glass was everywhere.

I started to pace back and forth, wondering why this was happening to me. I wanted answers but couldn't understand why someone would steal everything from me like that.

"There go the four pair of shoes and four outfits I bought for you for yo birthday Sea'Sea," I said with anger. "There go the video game and clothes I bought you Champ," I continued as I held back the tears. I was hurt over Javion gifts being stolen because I knew that Javion deserved all that he was given since he was always being a good boy. Plus I had been promising him that game for a month.

As I continued to pace back and forth, asking myself "What could it be, who could it be," repeatedly.

Then a thought came to me that made me put my hand to my mouth, like a light bulb had gone off in my head.

Sea'Sea looked at me. "What,"

"Hell naw. Hell naw. No way. That motherfucker," I yelled. I thought about how JoJo was looking and acting when he was in my closet.

I stood there, thinking and thinking, trying to make sense of the situation. The more I thought about the situation and JoJo, the more upset I got.

"Let me use yo phone Sea'Sea," I asked.

Sea'Sea passed me her phone. I was so angry that I dialed the wrong number twice before getting it right.

When I dialed JoJo's number, the phone rang one time.

"What up," JoJo said

"Oh that's what you do to yo nigga, ole bitch ass nigga. Imma kill yo motherfucking ass when I see you, you hear me bitch. I pose to be yo boy and you played me like a motherfucking sucker," I yelled in a rage.

"Yeah this is JoJo," JoJo continued to say.

"Bitch I know who this is. Don't play with me nigga. When I see you, it's on, on site. You hear me bitch," I continued my rant.

"Oh snap, got you again, leave yo message at the peep," JoJo said.

I realized that I was talking to JoJo voice mail all along. I knew that JoJo was avoiding my call because the phone ranged one time and went straight to voice mail.

"Now this bitch still trying to play me like a sucker for real," I thought. I hung up the phone and stormed out of the door.

"Amel where you going," Sea'Sea asked.

"I'll be back. Yall don't go nowhere," I said walking without looking around. My mind was solely focused on JoJo and I knew exactly where he was.

Slaughter Park was located a couple of blocks over from The City. It was a place where most young kids hung out to play ball, shoot dice, and try to pick up girlfriends and boyfriends. It was right off the main road that ran through Itta Bena.

As I approached Slaughter Park, I spotted JoJo sitting on the monkey bars with the exact shoes on that he had said he could not afford just three hours earlier.

I started to yell his name, but I didn't want him to start running. I knew that a scared crackhead was a fast running crackhead.

"I'm bout to beat the living shit out this nigga. This nigga just broke in my house and got the nerve to be rocking my shit already. No fucking respect, trying to be tough and shit. Imma stomp a mut-hole in this motherfucker," I thought as I approached JoJo from behind.

I continued to creep towards JoJo. As I got about ten feet from him, I took off running full speed and dived and football tackled JoJo from behind. Because JoJo was acting so normal about the situation and didn't care if someone saw him with my clothes on, sent me into a deeper rage.

"What the fuck nigga," JoJo said as he laid face down on the ground.

I flipped JoJo over and pent him underneath my legs. I stared into his eyes for a second to find the guilt and guilt was written all in them.

"Get off me dog," JoJo screamed. "Get the fuck off me nigga,"

"Nigga, you steal from one of yo ace coon boom," I asked.

"Mane you already know what it is," JoJo responded.

"Naw nigga tell me. I don't know shit. I know one thang you finna get this heater put in yo mouth," I said knowing I didn't have a gun on me. I just wanted to scare JoJo.

"You seen me nigga. Even when I pulled up to yo house, I ain't even have no shoes on my nigga cuz I ain't got no shoes my nigga. You know that white bitch got me going out here my nigga,"

"What the fuck that got to do with me though," I screamed.

"Nigga you the one been stunning on niggas these past couple of months like you something. You ain't shit nigga, you ain't better than nobody. Nigga fuck you,"

"Oh, you thank I'm yo bitch huh. You thank you can just steal my shit and do me any kind of witcha way bitch nigga. You done lost yo motherfucking mind," I screamed as started to hit JoJo with open face shots.

JoJo tried to maneuver his way from my brace, but I was too strong.

"Make this nigga a believer," the small voice inside my head said.

"Oh he gone be a believer. He gone learn today. Matter of fact, this motherfucker gone die today," I continued, still punching JoJo harder and harder with every punch.

"You gonna kill him," JoJo girlfriend, Janet Seasy, screamed at me.

"Shut the fuck up bitch before I beat yo motherfucking ass," I said as I continued to hit JoJo with power I didn't know I had. JoJo face was bloody now and he was on the verge of going unconscious. It was turning into a replay of the Loc incident.

"Stop," King Lee said from a short distance.

"This motherfucker gone die today," I said, still punching JoJo. JoJo face was swelling like a balloon.

"Amel," King Lee said. This time he was louder and closer. "If he dies, you die. Is that what you want,"

King Lee always had a way with words. He said things a certain way that always grabbed my attention. It was like a gift he had.

I reluctantly stopped punching JoJo.

"From the looks of it, he has paid his debt to you," King Lee said.

"Fuck that. Off this nigga," the small voice inside my head said.

I looked at JoJo, then to King Lee, back to JoJo.

"What you waiting for, off him," the small voice inside my head said.

I continued to stare at JoJo, contemplating what to do.

"What did he do to deserve this," King Lee asked.

"The nigga a fake, a phony, and a crum snatcher," I screamed in JoJo face.

"Didn't I tell you all money ain't good money. He stole from you because you stole from others," King Lee said.

I smacked my mouth and rolled my eyes. I wasn't in the mood for that shit.

"Don't smack your mouth and roll your eyes at me, I didn't do it. Now tell me, what do you see different in him than what you see in yourself. What makes you two different," King Lee asked me. "It seems to me that you both are the same people fighting for the same thing,"

I looked up at King Lee.

"What," I asked with a frown. King Lee was beginning to piss me off.

"You know exactly what I am talking about. Yall both fighting for the same thing. And that is to repeat the same negative cycle of being a dumb, ignorant, and worthless man. You are not free Amel, remember. You are trapped both ways. You are a slave of your world and of this world," King Lee said. "Just remember that everything that you get in your world, you deserve it, both good and bad. Because you are the only one that can control your world, no one else," he continued to lecture me as he started to walk off.

"Man you talking out yo head," I said.

I jumped up, leaving JoJo on the ground bleeding. I started to dust myself off and wipe the blood from my knuckles onto my shirt.

A crowd started to gather around JoJo and the police and ambulance could be heard a few blocks away. King Lee nodded for me to walk with him, so I could avoid trouble.

"Walk with me," King Lee said.

As we started to walk down the street, I ran into a group of young boys I knew.

"Who this is Shake. That boy super ugly," Lil Dee, Toya Medley son from the City, said amongst his friends with laughter.

"Come here Dee," I said. Lil Dee obliged as I grabbed him by the ear. "It ain't nice to talk bout folks like that, aight. Now yall get on down and stay out the road, aight,"

King Lee smiled at my gesture as we continued to walk along the street.

"Somebody gotta teach these little knuckleheads something but they don't know no better sometimes. They just like I was when I was out here with a snotty nose and a nappy head. That's just what it is round here and how we grow up, you know that," I said with sincerity.

"I know," King Lee responded.

We continued to walk.

"What's the real reason behind you being so mad at that young man back there," King Lee asked.

"You mean JoJo? He stole the stuff I bought for me, Javion, and Sea'Sea out the house. I had him come over to look at some shoes and next thang I know, the nigga stealing from me," I said.

"You invited me over to my house when I specifically told you not too," King Lee said.

I dropped my head.

"Look at a man in his eyes when he is talking to you. Drunk or no drunk, I'm still a man, now look at me," King Lee insisted.

I raised my head slowly.

"Did you or did you not invite him over to my house when I specifically told you not to," King Lee repeated.

"I mean........ I was trying to do business and make some extra bread," I said.

"You see. You see now. Excuse my language but a hard head always make a soft ass. Now you see why I don't have company. Now you see," King Lee said.

"Yeah I see that now. That fool lucky I didn't kill me," I said.

"No I think you are lucky you didn't kill him. So tell me about this stuff. What kind of stuff were they," King Lee asked.

"Jordans, Polo, Hilfiger, all that. All the stuff you seen me come in the house with all the time. The stuff you was always questioning me bout, remember," I said.

"No, I don't remember questioning you about anything," King Lee replied.

"That's cuz you was drunk," I said.

"Watch your mouth when you talking to a man, drunk or no drunk, still have some respect, you understand," King Lee yelled.

I didn't say a word.

"Do you understand," King Lee demanded.

I shook my head to say yes.

"Now. This isn't about me being drunk, this isn't about me at all. It's about you understanding that you had a hand in having these things stolen from you," King Lee said. "So answer this for me Amel, why do you like wearing these things that have you so upset that you are wanting to kill somebody over,"

"I don't know," I said as I hunched my shoulders.

"That's not an answer. Let me ask you that again. So why do you like wearing these things that have you wanting to kill somebody," King Lee said with a more direct tone.

"This nigga outta his mind," I thought before answering the question.

"Because they make me feel good," I said, not knowing how to answer the question.

"I see. So, your heart lies within materialistic things huh, meaning that you are a materialistic person," King Lee said.

"How you figure I'm materialistic," I added.

"Because you couldn't give me an answer to my question and the answer you gave me was one that a materialistic person would say. A wise man once told me that where a man's heart lies, so lies his value. So I gather that your value is based on these dead things you wear. Is that true," King Lee said, now looking me in my eyes.

"Nope," I said looking away.

King Lee grabbed my face and turned it back around.

"So you were about to kill somebody for stealing these things from you. Aren't those things dead? Don't those materialistic things depreciate over time? So, who is really at fault here," King Lee said. "Do you know of the two things in this world that don't die and depreciate over time if you grow and feed them the right things," King Lee said before I could answer his last question.

I shook my head as to say no, looking at the ground.

"I told you to look at a man in my eyes when he is talking to you. I said do you know of the two things in this world that don't die and depreciate over time if you grow and feed them the right things," King Lee said raising his voice, lifting my head with his hand. "It's your mind Amel," King Lee said pointing to my forehead. Then he pointed to my chest. "It's your heart. But everything starts with your mind and the heart will follow,"

"You know why that boy stole from you," King Lee asked.

"Because the nigga is shasty and fake, that's why," I responded.

"No, that's not it. He stole from you because you both are one in the same and I think you know that. Wasn't he your friend," King Lee asked.

"He was pose to be my friend," I said.

"I see, but understand this Amel and hear me loud and clear. Your mindset attracts everything that happens to you in life. I call it 'the magnet rule,'. If you have troubled friends, trouble will find you. If you hang with thieves, you will be stolen from or begin stealing yourself. And so on, there is no way of getting around it. Now, on the other hand, if you hang around those who have businesses, you will learn from those people and make yourself more attractive to having a business. You never see pigeons flying with eagles Amel, never!!! Look around you. I haven't known you long, but I know that I know you more than you even know yourself. And that's a problem Amel, that's a real problem," King Lee said.

I stood there listening with reverence.

"The Creator Himself is telling you that your value doesn't lie within materialistic things, that is why He took that junk away from you. He has more in store for you and is trying to teach you a lesson that you probably will not understand now, but trust me, you will understand it when you get older. Understand that The Creator blesses us all to experience both good and bad situations. Those bad situations are put in place to test our faith and teach us lessons about life. Find your lesson Amel,"

I nodded my head to say ok.

"You are different Amel because I feel your spirit and it is good. But having a good spirit isn't good enough, not in this world or your world. You must become more of a magnet to success, to The Creator, to giving, and to all things that are positive in order to gravitate to positive things and to live a good life," King Lee added.

"I don't know King Lee," I said.

"You don't know what,"

"Sometimes I believe in some thangs, but most times I just don't believe in nothing. To be real King Lee, I can barely tie my shoes, and you talking bout being a magnet to something. I don't know how I pose to do that? Ain't nobody ever told me or taught me nothing, especially bout being a magnet to something. You must gonna tell me or teach me how to do this,"

"I can't tell you how to become a magnet to these things. That's up to you to figure out," King Lee said walking off.

"So you saying all this good stuff, but every time I see you, you got a bottle in your hand, dead drunk. You got a bottle in yo hand now,"

King looked at his bottle for a brief second and then looked back up at me. He then took three big gulps from the bottle and wiped the drips from his mouth with his forearm.

"Even a drunk man, such as myself, can teach you more about life than a rich man could. You know why," King Lee said.

"Why," I asked.

"Because that drunk man will tell you about the struggles of life while that rich man will tell you only about his successes. Life lessons comes from struggle. Growth comes from struggle. Faith comes from struggle. Everything good comes from struggle. But never judge a book by its cover because even though that cover might look ugly, the story that lies within it might be a beautiful one that could change your life forever. Remember I am a king of my world and not of this world. Know that every king has a flaw or two. My kingdom is ugly, but if you pay close attention, it indeed tells a beautiful story. Sometimes the ugliest things hold some of the most beautiful treasures. Pay attention Amel," King Lee said with a smile. "Now let's get on home before that sun catches us,"

Chapter 15

"Where do me and Javion pose to get some clothes from? I can't be out here doing all this bullshit like I been doing. But then again, a nigga too young to get a real job, so I'm fucked any way it goes. Can't do right for doing wrong seems like," I thought as I sat on my bed, observing Javion as he slept. I knew I could try jacking somebody but at the same time, I knew my luck would soon run out and all the bad shit I had done would catch up to me eventually. I wanted to do something different, try to do right for a change. I believed in right and wrong, but it always seemed like doing wrong was just so much easier to do, to manage.

"Shhhiiiidddd, Imma try hitting Baby Sister up to see what she talking bout. She might kick me down something, a nigga gotta do something for me and Champ," I said.

I got up slowly from my bed, went into the living room, grabbed the phone from the wall and hesitantly dialed Baby Sister's number. I hoped that Baby Sister would have some kind of guilt in her heart for what she had put me and Melo through most of our lives. I hoped that she would be willing to do anything to be on good terms with me, to have me back in her life again.

My heart began to beat fast as the phone began to ring. It was a mixture of fear and anxiousness all rolled up into one.

"Hello," Baby Sister said.

"Baby Sister," I said apprehensively.

"Who this is," Baby Sister responded.

I rolled my eyes. I knew then it was going to be a long talk.

"This Amel,"

"You got some kind of nerves calling my house after cutting a rug with me like you did. What you calling here for. Ain't nothing here for you. You done burnt this bridge baby, so…" Baby Sister said with an attitude mixed in with a little disgust. She never had a child put their hands on her before and I had crossed that line.

"But anyway, I need you to come through for me with something," I said looking passed all the other stuff Baby Sister was talking about.

"Come through for you with what, with yo smart ass," Baby Sister said.

"Me and Javion need some clothes," I said. The phone fell silent for a couple of seconds, so I continued to talk. "Somebody done sat up here and stole all of our stuff that I paid for. Now I don't have no clothes to wear to school and Javion don't either," I said with the intent that Baby Sister would find it in her heart to have sympathy for me and for Javion.

"I knew it wouldn't be long before life slapped yo ass dead in the face," Baby Sister said. "What? You thank I pose to sit up here and feel sorry for you or something," she continued.

"Nah, I ain't looking for nobody to feel sorry for me. I'm just saying. But it's all good though," I said in defeat. I knew Baby Sister was out of the equation. "What bout Javion though,"

"What bout him," Baby Sister quickly responded.

"Baby Sister, come on now. He just a little boy. I been out here taking care of this boy like he mine. Melo ain't nowhere to be found. What I pose to do. You should be the one taking care of me and taking care of him. We ain't grown,"

"I don't pose to do a motherfucking thang. You showed yo ass, now you got to live with it. And that baby ain't my baby. I'm too old to be running up behind babies. That problem is you and Melo problem, not mine,"

I looked at the wall and shook my head. It was a never ending tale of disappointment and heartache. Baby Sister was impossible to deal with. It seemed like her heart was as cold as ice.

"You know what," I asked.

"What? What you got to say now. I done told you, I ain't got no money," Baby sister yelled.

"Ain't nobody asking you for no motherfucking money," I screamed with anger. My temper was getting the best of me. "And how you ain't never got no motherfucking money anyway when you ain't taking care of nobody but yoself. You on that shit ain't it,"

"Who the fuck you talking to like that motherfucker," Baby Sister screamed.

"I'm talking to you, who else. You ain't even got it in yo heart to give yo own grandbaby some money for some clothes. Hell, I don't want no money you got from them white folks, cleaning they toilets and shit. You can have that,"

"Well you coulda fooled me how you up here begging for shit, you ungrateful motherfucker. Them white folks money you talking bout is good hard earned money. Money you ain't got, now do you,"

"I ain't bout to do this with you. This shit is for the birds my nigga. Have a good life mane," I said giving up on the conversation. "But you know what Baby Sister, I got something for you to listen to,"

"Listen to what. If it's some of this bullshit you talking, you can keep that shit to yoself,"

"Nah for real though. You ready,"

Baby Sister fell silent on the phone waiting for this thang I wanted her to listen to.

I hung up the phone as hard as I could. I wanted her to listen to the sound of the dial tone. "Stupid bitch," I yelled.

I sat there and stared at the phone, breathing and contemplating heavily.

"Talking to people and hanging up in their face like that isn't good for the soul Amel," King Lee said walking to the kitchen to get some water.

"Fuck that bitch mane. And ain't nobody worried bout no soul. We just need some clothes to wear, that's it. That's the least she can do for us since we not living with her. Bitch just crazy. It's the same ole shit with her over and over again," I said angrily. "And why do I got to always ask my own momma to be buy me stuff anyway? Every...single...time... I ask her for something, she ain't never got it? I'm just 15 King Lee, what I pose to do for me and that boy in there without getting in trouble. Don't she owe me that much," I continued as my voice started to crack with emotions. I made it my business not to let Baby Sister's actions defeat me or make me cry.

King Lee sat there and studied me for a few seconds. Despite the hurt I was going through, King Lee knew this was an important moment in my life. He knew moments like these taught lessons that couldn't be learned in school, for he knew that life itself was the greatest teacher of all.

"Let me tell you something that you are not going to like it. The truth is, your mother doesn't owe you nothing, I don't owe you nothing, the world doesn't owe you nothing. No one owes you one red cent, you hear me. For as long as you live, don't you ever tell anybody that they owe you something because they don't, you hear me Amel," King Lee said sternly. King Lee knew this wasn't the time to hold my hand and baby me up. This was a time to give a straight talk with no beating around the bush. King Lee didn't believe in excuses but believed in hard work even though his disposition didn't show it. "A man just don't sit around and wait on things to happen to him, a man go out there and make things happen for himself," King Lee continued.

I dropped my head and looked to the floor, trying my hardest not to cry.

"Look a man in his eyes when he is talking to you. Boys drop their head and hide their faces, hide their eyes. You see, your eyes tells the story, it tells your makings," King Lee said with authority as he hit the table as hard as he could with his fist.

I slowly raised my head and looked King Lee square in the eyes. I knew King Lee could see the hurt, the loneliness, the disappointment in them. He knew he had to look passed those elements in order to help me. He understood the journey in which I was currently traveling, for he had been on the same journey once upon a time. He understood the fork in the road that was standing before me.

King Lee proceeded to put a bottle of fine Mississippi brandy on the table. He then slowly placed it right in front of me.

"Go on," King Lee said as he egged me on to drink the brandy straight from the bottle.

I stared at the bottle. Then looked up at King Lee with a "You can't be serious," look.

"Go on I said," King Lee repeated.

I slowly grabbed the brandy bottle and untwisted the cap. I slowly put it to my nose to smell the aroma. The smell made me quickly turn my head due to its strong odor.

King Lee carefully observed my every move.

I looked up at King Lee again and back at the brandy bottle. I put the bottle at the tip of my lips.

Before I could gulp the brandy, King Lee quickly knocked the bottle out of my hand. The bottle went into pieces on the floor.

"So now you putting bottles to your mouth," King Lee screamed. "That's how you handle your problems now, drinking like me. Do you see me,"

King Lee stared me down as I timidly looked him in his eyes.

"What are you going to do when you have a family Amel, when you have kids, have bills, have real responsibility? What are you going to do then? Put a bottle to your mouth? You going to ask someone to help you feed your fucking family, help you feed your fucking kids? What the fuck are you gonna do? Better yet, what are you going to do when that little boy in there tell you that he is hungry. What are you going to do, panhandler for money on the corner, and beg like a fucking slave," King Lee yelled all while pounding on the table again with his fist.

The more King Lee talked, the angrier he got. I know now that he hated seeing young men complain and make excuses for what they didn't have rather than getting up and working for what they wanted to have. King Lee was thinking about his own family that he once had and how once upon a time he took pride in working and caring for them. King Lee didn't care what my age was, he knew I was learning how hard life could be.

I sat quietly at the table, still trying to hold back my tears as King Lee lectured me. I was determined not to let the situation make me cry, not this time. I was older and stronger now.

"Being a man is more than just saying you are a man Amel, being a man is about action and never about words. You are a man now, whether you like it or not. Things will be hard out here in both your world and this world. Believe me when I say that no one is going to give you nothing in this world, so don't expect them to. You will understand soon enough that people in this world will chew your ass up and spit you right back out and keep on moving and won't look back. It's time for you to be a man Amel, because you are a man even at your age. Those are just the cards life has dealt you, that it dealt me long ago. Don't ever depend on somebody to do anything for you, you owe it to yourself to get out there and do things for you and for your future family. Your momma means well by what she told you, even if you can't see it now. If she feed you too long, you will turn out to be no good, like the rest of these men around here. This is good for you, struggle always bring about good things if you let it," King Lee said looking me in the eyes.

I leaned back in the chair and put both hands behind my head as I stared into space.

"I ain't gone ask her for nothing, for real. I rather die first," I said. "Excuse me mane," I told King Lee as I put my head down in my lap.

"Everybody act like I'm a bad nigga or something, like I'm a burden on them. Don't nobody care bout me. Don't nobody love me like that," I thought in a muffle as I was on the verge of letting my tears flow.

It was obvious that I had too many inner question marks and not enough answers. I was confused, I was hurt. My soul was slowly dying as each day passed. I didn't understand why every time I asked somebody for something, they never had it. But they always found time to do things for themselves. Everyone had their own family, their own life that didn't include me. The only things I had, at this point in my life were Javion, unreachable dreams, and a notepad that I never used anymore. I wanted my own family to love, to show my family how it supposed to be done. I started to think about my friends and how worry free they were.

"I'm still a boy, I ain't no man," I said as I raised my head and looked at King Lee.

"What I do wrong to get treated like this. I'm a good nigga King Lee. I treat people nice and everything. The wrong I be doing, feed me and that boy in there. I can't even be a kid cuz people keep saying I got to be a man, got to be a daddy to that boy. I love that boy King Lee, I do, but I want to be a kid too, I want to be somebody baby too," I thought with tears on the tip of my eyes. "I don't know how to be anythang but myself. That's all I can be and I ain't even good at doing that. I ain't shit. Don't nobody even love me, so…,"

I started to shake my head trying to hold the tears. I didn't want to seem weak around another man. I wanted to show my strength.

King Lee stared at me for a second.

"It's ok to cry Amel," King Lee said. He could feel and see the brokenness written all over me. "Crying isn't the worst thing a man can do. Crying is the best thing a man can do, but we think it makes us soft, it makes us weak, it makes us unmanly. You see, crying cleanses your soul of hurt and sin,"

The reason I tried to hold my tears was because my whole life, everybody told me to suck my tears up and to keep my emotions to myself. "Men don't cry, sissies do. You a sissy," They told me. King Lee was the first person in my life that gave me permission to cry, to express my pain, without judgment.

I stared at King Lee as the tears began to pour from my eyes like a well.

"Ain't I still a kid," I repeated.

King Lee sat and observed me as I waited on him to respond to my question. King Lee didn't know how to respond to what was asked, matter of fact, it seemed like he was holding back tears too.

All King Lee knew was, as bad as the situation might have seemed, what I was experiencing was the first step to a new beginning that awaited me. It was something that King Lee anticipated since we had met.

I laid my head on the table and began to cry. The pain, resentment, and hurt that I was holding in was coming out.

As I sat at the table crying, I suddenly felt these little hands touch my leg as I had my head submerged in my arms. I tried to quickly compose myself and wipe my face, but I couldn't keep the tears from flowing.

"SHAKE, you crying," Javion asked as he put his two little hands on my cheeks. The concern in his little eyes made me smile. "You ok SHAKE. It's ok. You a good boy SHAKE. Don't cry, ok," Javion continued in the sweetest voice. I kissed him on the forehead and hugged him. He hugged me back tightly and held on to me as I began to cry again. It was Javion loving, innocent nature that made me feel warm inside. Everyone knew that I took care of Javion and loved him, but the truth was, in a sense, Javion emotionally cared for me with his love.

"You see," King Lee said. "Those little hands are your hope. Those little hands are touches from the Creator himself,"

Chapter 16

Two months passed and my resentment towards Baby Sister was at an all-time high, but I knew I had a balance to that situation in Sea'Sea.

I dropped Javion off at weekend daycare and made my way over Sea'Sea's house to check on her and to see if she needed anything. I wanted her to ride to the store with me so she could get out of the house for a change. Since being pregnant, her energy levels had dropped and she forfeited most school days to get in extra sleep that her body craved.

I knocked on the door three times as usual. I waited for two minutes, no answer. I knocked three more times, waited a minute, still no answer.

"Sea'Sea, open up," I yelled as I started to pound on the door. I knew Sea'Sea was at home at 8 in the morning.

Sea'Sea snatched the door open. "Stop beating on the fucking door like you crazy, damn. I am trying to sleep," Sea'Sea said. Her belly was starting to poke out a little. She was 3 or 4 months.

"Ok damn, Sea'Sea. You want me to go home then since I am bothering you so much," I said.

"You can," Sea'Sea responded.

"Well I ain't, now you and yo belly get out my way. I'm trying to go buy you something to eat and you sitting up here acting like that," I said. "Now you going or what big nose," I continued as I pinched her nose. Sea'Sea quickly slapped my hand away and rolled her eyes. She gave a slight smile.

"See I knew you be being mean to me on purpose. It ain't got shit to do with you being knocked up," I said. "I miss that smile though. Now you going to the store or what,"

"Naw I ain't going. I am bout to go back to sleep. You can go by yoself, can't it," Sea'Sea said as she switched back to being mean again. She left me at the door and walked over and laid down on the couch.

"Well fuck it then," I barked. I struggled to deal with her attitude.

"Fuck it then Amel. Don't come over here with that bullshit today. Today ain't the day for it, for real though," Sea'Sea said. "Just leave me alone, I ain't in the mood. You just don't know when to stop," she continued as she started to cry.

I knew that the best thing I could do at this point was to stay quiet. It was obvious that Sea'Sea was a hormonal and emotional wreck.

I loped down on the love seat and started to flip through the three TV channels with no avail.

"Sea'Sea," I said. Sea'Sea didn't respond. "Sea'Sea, I know you hear me,"

"Amel, seriously, you finna get on my last nerves. What do you want now," Sea'Sea snapped.

"Did you cook," I asked.

"Do you smell some food," Sea'Sea snapped.

"Nope," I said.

"Well then," Sea'Sea said.

I sat in silence for a few minutes with a stupid and sad look. Sea'Sea was my home girl and all, but since being pregnant, she was constantly snapping at me and hurting my feelings although I didn't show it.

"Ok, I ain't gone say nothing else to you. And you don't say nothing else to me. Ok Sea'Sea,"

"Thank you, now be quiet," Sea'Sea said.

I sat back on the love seat with my arms behind my head, bored, watching the "The Young and the Holy" trying to pass time. I looked around the room to find something that would keep my interest for a good bit. I then noticed a newspaper on the floor beside the couch Sea'Sea was laying on. I went over and picked it up and went back to sit down. As I unfolded the paper, I browsed the sports section first and made my way to the front page. It read "Man of the year," in big bold beautiful letters.

"What the fuck," I thought with my mouth open, still in shock.

I looked over to Sea'Sea with a smile. "Sea'Sea, you see this shit,"

"Whaaatttt Amel...If you gone keep waking me up, you can leave, for real," Sea'Sea snapped.

"Naw, I'm for real now. Look at this," I said walking over to Sea'Sea. I loped down on the couch where her feet were.

"Do you see this fake ass nigga on the front page smiling and shit," I said.

"Who Mark," Sea'Sea asked.

"Naw the nigga on the front page Sea'Sea," I said.

"Who Mark," Sea'Sea said raising up, squinting her eyes trying to see the front newspaper. "Yeah that's Mark with that big ass smile, looking like he got sugar in his tank,"

I looked at the paper and back at Sea'Sea, and then back at the paper. "Where in the fuck she get Mark from," I asked myself.

"This nigga name ain't no Mark, where you get that name from," I said. "Did you even read the article,"

The room instantly fell silent. Sea'Sea slowly sat up a little on the couch. I could see the tears begin to form in her eyes. I knew I had fucked up, as usual in these times. "What, you trying to be funny now. You trying to be funny Amel,"

"Naw, ain't nobody trying to be funny, I'm, just saying. I didn't mean it like that, on everything I love I didn't mean it like that," I said with my hands in the air trying to plead my case. I knew how sensitive Sea'Sea was about that subject, but I didn't think before I spoke. Me and Sea'Sea shared the same three special education classes. I took the classes because Baby Sister forced me to for the monthly check to help with bills, Sea'Sea took the classes because she had a mild learning disability and a severe case of dyslexia. She could say her alphabets, count, multiply, and all, but she struggled with reading. She read on a 2nd grade level.

"Then why you say it," Sea'Sea asked.

"I wasn't thanking. I swear to God I wasn't trying to be funny. Come on now. You know I don't make fun of nobody, at least not to hurt somebody feelings," I said as I moved to the center of the couch. I started to rub her hair to calm her down. Slowly but surely, I was starting to understand the makings of a young pregnant mother. "Sea'Sea, for real for real, how do you know this dude," I continued in a soothing voice as I stared at the newspaper.

"Amel. Don't you thank I would know my baby daddy when I see him. That is Mark. Mark Davis from over by the way. We been fucking around on and off for bout 2 years now," Sea'Sea said.

I didn't move and stood still for about a minute to compose my thoughts.

"Say what," I said as I sat up on the couch. Sea'Sea didn't answer me. "Say what Sea'Sea, who this is. You say, this yo who now,"

"That's my baby daddy, you heard me, damn. Sometimes you just act like you crazy," Sea'Sea said sounding more and more irritated with every word.

"This nigga here is yo baby daddy and you been fucking with this nigga since you was 13" I said, still in disbelief, holding the newspaper to Sea'Sea face and pointing to the picture. She buried her face in the pillow. "Look at the fucking picture Sea'Sea,"

"Look, you can get the fuck out with this bullshit you trying to run. I just told yo ass who that is. What the fuck is it to you anyway, didn't we go through this one time before. And you call yoself getting mad at me. So now, you know who my baby daddy is and it ain't yo ass. Feel better now,"

I sat there in silence, staring at the newspaper, biting my lip to keep the tears in, but I couldn't hold them. My right leg started to bounce up and down, like my nerves were beginning to unravel. The image of the man on the front page and Sea'Sea fucking started to play in my head over and over again.

I quickly got up and made my way to the bathroom and locked the door behind me. I didn't want Sea'Sea to know how emotional I was becoming.

I started to pace back and forth in the small bathroom, trying to avoid looking in the mirror, but I couldn't resist it. I had to look at it, I had to read myself, read my eyes.

So, there I stood once again in front of a mirror, searching, trying to find something positive.

I looked into the depths of my own eyes and wondered if my life was a curse, filled with sorrow and luck of a different kind. I started to breathe out heavily as I wiped my face clear of tears with my hand over and over again. Those tears represented betrayal and I didn't want any parts of them, especially if they were for Sea'Sea. I could feel my heart growing with resentment towards her.

"So what you gone do. Sit here and cry or go do something bout this problem, like a real man would," the small voice inside my head said. "Do she deserve to live Shake after doing this,"

I looked away from the mirror and tried to dismiss what the small voice inside my head had just said. "Chill, Chill, Chill, Chill," I repeated, trying to calm myself down.

"This bitch pregnant with yo motherfucking brother. After all you have done for her, this is how she do you. She played you with JoJo, now she fucking yo daddy behind yo back," The small voice inside my head said. "Off this bitch already," that voice inside my head said even louder.

"I can't fuck with it. That's Sea'Sea. I can't. She the only thang I got other than Javion,"

"Nigga this is yo fucking daddy she fucking behind yo back and you sitting yo dumb ass up here talking bout this Sea'Sea. Who gives a fuck? You don't thank her and that nigga laughing at you behind yo back while he fucking her and you spending time with her like a fool. She fucking a nigga that hate you and told you to yo face that he didn't want you. And you cool with that? You cool with her playing you like a motherfucking sucker,"

I looked down into the sink and visualized Sea'Sea and Ben laying up somewhere, making jokes about me and how I was a fool. I could feel myself getting boiling hot mad at the imagery.

"That's why they did it. To show you. To show that nobody in this world care bout you. That pose to be yo girl and she fucked you over, bad, just like everybody else. She ain't no different than those other bitches out there. Ben still fucking her, why you thank she been treating you like shit, because that nigga told her to treat you like that. He told her to treat you like he treat you,"

"Oh, now she doing me bad because of this nigga. You know what," I said as I looked out the window. "Fuck Sea'Sea and that pussy nigga baby,"

I stormed out the bathroom and into the kitchen. I looked for the biggest knife I could find. I wanted to send a message to everyone in the world that wanted to fuck with me. Sea'Sea was going to be the next example, and a good one at that. I found a midsize butcher knife, tested it's sharpness by cutting a small section of hair on my arm, headed back to living room with blood in my eyes.

I violently snatched Sea'Sea up by her shirt with force and raised her to my eye level. I placed the knife to her throat. Sea'Sea fate was upon her and she didn't even know it.

"Amel, what you doing," Sea'Sea screamed with fear. Then she looked into my eyes and seen death in them. She could feel the sharpness of the knife piecing her throat.

"Did you know," I screamed to her. The tears started to pour from my eyes. I couldn't hold back the hurt that I felt. Sea'Sea may have been and done many of things, but she had never betrayed me like this before. This was a death before dishonor principal that she had crossed carelessly.

"Know what Amel. Just breathe, ok," Sea'Sea said as she began to cry. She thought I was going through one of those crazy episodes I would every so often go through and just spaz out.

"Did you fucking know," I repeated, this time with more anger. The imagery of her and Ben laughing at me was replaying in my head again.

"I don't know what you talking bout,"

"Answer the question or Imma gut you like a fish, ok," I said calmly with a smile as the tears continued to pour from my eyes. I could feel my heart hurting. "Answer my question Sea'Sea. Did you know,"

Sea'Sea knew she had to guess on an answer because she had no earthly idea what I was talking about. She didn't know Mark was actually my sperm donor. We never talked about our fathers because none of them were around. She never met my father nor did I ever meet hers.

Sea'Sea could feel the knife pressing on her neck even harder. She could see in my eyes that I was going to kill her if she didn't give the right answer. She began to cry and proceeded to give an answer that would determine if she lived or if she died.

"No I didn't know," Sea'Sea screamed with agony. She knew that saying no to the question would be better than saying yes to it, for most situations. She waited on my verdict. She was scared to look me in the eyes. She didn't want to trigger an uncalled for reaction.

I looked her in the eyes to determine the verdict of her life. I stared at them with the knife still at her throat ready to slice on demand.

I concluded that she wasn't lying.

"After all we have been through, this how you do me," I whispered to Sea'Sea. I stared at her for a while, still in disbelief.

I said my final goodbyes to her with a kiss on her cheek, threw her down on the couch violently, walked out the door, and never looked back.

Chapter 17

I arrived at Sammie Beans the next morning with a head filled with bad thoughts. As I thought more about the Sea'Sea situation, the angrier I got.

As I was walking to class after the morning bell had rung, I spotted Sea'Sea walking towards me with a smile she always welcomed me with.

"What's up Amel," Sea'Sea said in good spirits. Today was one of her good days. "Listen, don't worry bout what happened yesterday. You good now? You know I can't do this by myself. I been feeling so bad lately. This baby kicking my ass, for real though,"

Usually I would stop, laugh, and talk with her. This day, I continued walking like I didn't see her ass.

"I should punch her dead in her fucking jaw. Embarrassing me like that. Gone fuck this nigga without telling me. Now she looking stupid. Didn't even speak to her ass. I don't fuck witcha," I thought walking passed her without even looking at her. My face was filled with anger.

Sea'Sea grabbed my arm as I walked passed her.

I snatched my arm away from her grip real hard. I then stopped and stared at her for a few seconds, biting my lip as I continued walking.

Sea'Sea was taken back at how hard I snatched away from her. I knew she still seen the anger in my eyes. I think she thought that I would be over what happened the night before, that we would be good, like always.

"Well fuck you too. You the one that pulled a knife on me nigga and you trying to act like that with me. Fuck you," Sea'Sea yelled at me.

I kept walking like I didn't hear her.

"I got you though. You better not say a word to me, you hear me. And I mean that," Sea'Sea screamed.

--

"You feeling better," Sea'Sea said to me with a smile as I entered homeroom. She beat me to the room first to sit in my seat like she usually did.

I looked at her and found an empty seat on the other side of the room.

"You need to check ya boy before I put his ass on blast in here," I overhead Sea'Sea say to Money.

"Shake, I know you hear Sea'Sea up here talking bad bout you," Money said to me.

I nodded my head as to say I heard her.

"Oh now you can't talk to me. Naw, I know what it is. The little pussy is on his period this week," Sea'Sea said to me rolling her eyes and smiling. "Pass that stupid motherfucker this homework that I know he didn't do," she continued as she passed the paper to Money to pass to me.

"Watch your mouth Sea'Sea," Mrs. White said.

"Sorry Mrs. White," Sea'Sea responded.

I waved my hand at Money to indicate I didn't want the homework. Money passed Sea'Sea back the paper.

"Oh, ok. You going to look REAL stupid when you get a zero on this homework just for being stupid," Sea'Sea said raising her voice.

I stared at her with the darkest eyes, but I never said a word to her. I had vowed the night before I wouldn't even look at her, let alone say a word to her.

"Why you still talking to me? I ain't got shit for you. I don't fuck with you," I thought.

As I stared down Sea'Sea, I heard the door to the classroom open.

"Hey Kris. You look so pretty today," Mrs. White said.

"Hey Mrs. White. How are you? Mr. Willis told me to bring you these papers by here," Kris said.

"Thank you Kris," Mrs. White said.

"You're so welcome Mrs. White. Have a good day," Kris said.

"Hey Amel," Kris said to me smiling as she was making her exit out of the classroom.

I nodded my head to say what's up to her. Then I gave off a little smile.

"Oh you can talk to that bitch but can't say a word to me," Sea'Sea screamed.

"Get out," Mrs. White screamed at Sea'Sea.

"Sorry Mrs. White. You know my hormones acting up,"

"One more time and you are out of here,"

"Ok,"

Sea'Sea focused her attention back at me.

"Oh I see what it is now. Oh I guess that's yo little girlfriend now," Sea'Sea said to me, rolling her eyes. I didn't respond again. She hated when I went into silence mode with her.

"Wouldn't you want to know," I thought, still staring at her, smirking, not saying a word.

"Just keep on smiling and watch me slap that smile right off yo face. You got the right one you playing with nigga. Watch me beat that little girl down and we gone see how you gone be laughing then,"

I still didn't respond.

"I know you hear me. See I hate niggas that act more girly than I do. Ain't that right Amel," Sea'Sea said in a playful tone and rolling her eyes at me.

As the bell rung to go to 2nd period, I jumped up first and made my way out the door.

"Amel," Sea'Sea yelled walking out the door, grimacing a little as she held her stomach.

When she made it to the building hallway, she spotted me walking out the exit of the building, clearly trying to avoid her. She walked hastily to the exit and burst through the door.

"Amel, bring yo ass back here," Sea'Sea said, sounding worried why I was acting like that with her.

We fought almost weekly but made up the next day or a few days afterwards. She had a knife put to her throat a few times in several fights besides the one with me. She had even caught a brick to the forehead in a fight that almost killed her. Fighting was what we did. Cussing violently at each other was what we did. Making up with each other was what we did. I know she knew that my actions had carried on from the night before, and knew I was still hurt and acting distant.

For some reason, something in me told me to stop walking and turn to face her.

"For real though, the question you ask last night, I don't know what you talking bout. Hell I don't even know what happened, or what I did? You just put a knife to my motherfucking throat for no reason. What's going on? What did I do to you? I hate it when you act like this with me. I don't want you to be mad," Sea'Sea said in a serious but sincere voice. She was acting really concerned.

I didn't show any emotion but gave her a poker face. I know my eyes were blood shot red and told the verdict of our relationship at that moment. I sat there and listened, trying my best not to break down into tears.

"I know you not tripping over a newspaper. Come on now. Really? You really acting like a baby over a fucking newspaper," Sea'Sea said, trying to find the problem in the situation.

I continued to stare at her, standing there like I was about to swing on her. Then I walked off. Sea'Sea hated when I did that. She couldn't stand it.

"Well fuck you then. You don't treat nobody like that over no damn newspaper or that other shit you thanking bout. And I pose to be yo girl," Sea'Sea screamed. "Fuck you nigga. I thought we was pose to be niggas,"

I know she was trying to act hard, but deep down my actions bothered her and she was left not knowing why I was acting that way towards her.

`"I thought we pose to be niggas too Sea'Sea," I silently said.

I knew that the chapter to my friendship with Sea'Sea was rapidly coming to a close.

Chapter 18

I was in my fifth period class as I dreadfully awaited my turn to stand before the class and recite my newly composed poem. The English teacher, Mr. James Jackson, had given a creative writing assignment with two parts: The students were to compose a poem on any subject matter and each student was to analyze one another's poems through a paragraph to capture the symbolism it contained. Ironically, I was listed on the white sheet of paper on Mr. Jackson's door to follow Sea'Sea, who was now standing before the class reciting her poem about pregnancy and loneliness. I wrote "FUCK THAT LYING NASTY MOTHER....FUCKER," for my paragraph relating to Sea'Sea's poem. I was willing to take a zero to express my ever growing resentment towards her.

As Sea'Sea finished her poem and wiped her face of tears due to her emotions, I could feel her still standing before the class, staring at me. It was like Sea'Sea and I was the only ones in the room and the spotlight was on me to look up.

I slowly looked at her with a deep under eye to somewhat hide my eyes and not make full eye contact with her. With a quick glimpse, I could see in her eyes that she awaited my reaction to her poem. I knew that her poem was a plea to me in a sense to let me know that I was the only thing she had in her life that made her feel like somebody, that made her feel wanted, and that gave her a reason to get up and live another day. I felt the poem sincerity but I chose to play it off like I wasn't listening to it when I really was.

"You can sit down now," Mr. Jackson told Sea'Sea. As she walked back to her seat, I could feel her still eyeing me, but I refused to look at her. I was determined to stick to my guns and vow to never give her the time of day again.

"Amel River," Mr. Jackson said.

I slowly got up from my seat. I could feel my knees begin to get weak due to my nervousness. As I stood before the class, trying not to look out into the audience because of my shyness, I let out a big sigh. I could feel everyone looking at me and could hear small giggles here and there throughout the room. Mostly everyone in school thought I was continually getting a bit strange as I got older, far from the cool kid they all once knew. It seemed like I was the only person in the entire school that liked painting, drawing, and writing, that also took special education courses. But I knew most of the giggles came from my appearance and some to make fun of my so called learning disability that they thought I had. Since the day JoJo stole my clothes, I wore mostly clothes that I found on the street or old clothes that people had given me in the City. Since that day, I no longer could hide behind the clothes anymore, I was back to being the old me. The me that had nothing, no money, no clothes, and no self-esteem.

Mr. Jackson gave me the node to begin.

I spoke:

She

She asks: What is a young girl to do when she has the heart and resolve of a queen but lives amidst the harsh realities and circumstances equal to that of a slave?

Young by age, trying to keep a beaten head above water, starving with an obligation to a younger brother and a baby, looking to do just about anything to get paid.

She says: What happens to a beautiful life that is destroyed by prayers that went unheard

Searching for a chance to be better, to get out, to change, to escape the death nest, like a fleeing baby bird

She screams: He just sits up there all high and Mighty, looking, observing, carefully choosing who should live and breathe good

But she, like us, are only step children to Him, as always, bamboozled into thinking that being poor is ok, it's just entirely misunderstood

She pleads: Ain't we yo children too? Ain't we got good hearts and souls? Ain't we good enough to be issued a fair shake?

But each day that passes, good things slowly starts to happen, until she realizes that, life is indeed just a humiliating waste.

She knows: When babies in heaven, like she, are asked by angels "Do you want to be born to her," she replied "hell no, not her please"

But then she, like her, prematurely brings a baby into this world, looks into his eyes and thinks, I wonder what you said to the angels when they asked you that same question they asked me.

I ask: Is she good enough to be born? Good enough to live? Good enough to die and finally be free?

I think so. Because, she, like her, has the same DNA as me.

-Shake

--

The room fell silent and everything seemed like it stood still.

I just stood there and stared at the floor, apprehensive to look up. I was waiting on Mr. Jackson to give me my que to sit down.

"Amel just stand up there for a few minutes and let me show the class something that I think is important for them to hear. And I want all of you to listen good because this is important," Mr. Jackson said. "You see this young man standing before you, this young man represents all that you….. should not strive to be in life. This young man is the prime example of what some of you will look like in 20 years. He is well on his way to being a drunk, crack addict or a drug dealer. Do you want this for yoselves,"

The entire class stared at me. They were taking what Mr. Jackson was saying to heart. They silently sat in their seats as quiet as they could be, contemplating their future that they hoped didn't include turning out to be the loser that stood before them. They all continued to listen attentively to what Mr. Jackson had to say. They obsessed over every word, like a child would its father. And since most, if not all, were fatherless, Mr. Jackson gained their trust easily and knew he could feed off that and strategically manipulate them. Mr. Jackson was funny and animated, something the children naturally gravitated too.

I stared at the floor, embarrassed to look up. I could feel everyone looking at me, I could feel their thoughts, I could feel their judgments. I knew Mr. Jackson didn't like me and he made it his business to let it be known that he didn't like me every chance he got. Mr. Jackson was one of those so called classy types: uppity, clean cut and self-absorbed. If any student didn't meet his level of "smartness" of what he thought they should have, which he could disingenuously take interest in for future trust and investment, he didn't want any dealings with them. It was clear that I fell into the "dumb" category on Mr. Jackson growing list of students that wouldn't pan out to be anything in life.

"That's the worst piece of shit I have ever heard before in my whole entire life. Mr. Amel, you should be completely ashamed of yoself. And yo art teacher told me you would be a good fit for my class due to yo artistic nature. I have seen yo drawings and paintings and wasn't too impressed with those either. I think I am going to talk to Mr. Conely about this. I can't take yo lack of effort anymore. I am going to recommend that you take strictly special education courses from here on out. Maybe, just maybe, you could get yo GED and clean up somebody Buster Burgers,"

The room burst into laughter. It was always a good joke to make fun of someone's learning ability by calling them SPED or saying that they took special education classes. Being a SPED student meant that you were at the bottom of the pit. It didn't matter how poor someone was, how hungry they were, in their minds, they had one thing going, they weren't a special education student.

I stood there and twirled my pen in my hands, still staring at the floor. My anger was beginning to grow. Mr. Jackson was starting to piss me off. That poem was near and dear to my heart. It was about Melo. Plus, he was making fun of cleaning up places, something that Baby Sister had done her entire life. With each word that came out of Mr. Jackson's mouth, I wanted to put a gun in that motherfucker's mouth and proudly pull the trigger.

I looked at Mr. Jackson with a cold stare as I bit my lip to contain myself. Sea'Sea eased out of her seat and quietly made her way to the front of the class. She knew what could potentially happen next.

"What, I guess you want to fight me. I see now that you can't take it when someone is telling you the truth, now can you Amel. If it quacks like a duck, you best to believe that it's a got damn duck. Now get yo smelly ass out my room, smelling like feet," Mr. Jackson said as he started to laugh.

The students laughed out loud again. To them, Mr. Jackson was getting the best of me from a joking perspective. To me, Mr. Jackson was trying to maliciously tear every ounce of me down, with words, just like Baby Sister use to do to me and Melo.

I started to move towards Mr. Jackson, but Sea'Sea grabbed my arm.

I looked back and saw that it was Sea'Sea that had my arm. I squinted my eyes and stared at her for a couple of seconds.

"Let it go Amel, just let it go," Sea'Sea whispered. She knew firsthand what I was capable of doing.

"No, let him go, since he is so big and bad," Mr. Jackson said with a chuckle. He was a tall and heavy set man, standing almost 6'2 280 pounds.

"Amel you going straight to jail. It's too many people in here, you know that. So fall back," Sea'Sea pleaded with me in a whisper.

I looked at Mr. Jackson for a second. I saw that grin on his face that reminded me of Sea'Sea and my father laughing at me for being a fool for Sea'Sea.

"Come on tough guy and watch me knock yo ass straight out. Don't get this shirt and tie misconstrued," Mr. Jackson said. "Damn that's the new word of the week class: misconstrued. Write that down class and I want to see it being used correctly in yo next report,"

I started to reach for my hunting knife at my side. Sea'Sea grabbed my hand.

"Amel for real though, you don't want to do this. Just let it alone. You gotta learn to walk away from some thangs and this is one of them thangs,"

I looked at Mr. Jackson, back at Sea'Sea, and then back at Mr. Jackson. He was still grinning. Now waving his hand to tell me to come on.

"Imma see you my nigga, don't worry bout it. Imma see how tough yo ass be in these streets ole fat bitch. I know where yo eat at motherfucker," I thought. I stood there shaking my head and biting my lip as Sea'Sea held my arm.

The class still was in an uproar with laughter.

"Cuz mad ain't it," One boy yelled in the class, tickled to death over how I was looking.

I snatched away from Sea'Sea and said "Let me the fuck go," and stormed out of the door.

Sea'Sea stood there holding her belly, wishing that I would go back to being the old me. The little boy who use to write her stories when she was alone and afraid, was now lost, alone, and afraid himself. The caring me, the loving me, the friendly me, is what she missed the most.

I burst out of the exit door of the high school building.

"Amel River," a police in uniform said as he was meeting me at the exit door with his hand on his gun. It was about ten police cars in front of the high school building.

"What up," I responded, looking a bit confused.

"Get on the ground, now," the policemen screamed as they charged me. They had their weapons out like they were making a drug bust that I had seen countless times before. I knew the procedure of not moving or else I could risk being shot for no reason. I easily laid on the ground.

"You got the wrong man officer," I said as they put the handcuffs on me and threw me in the police car.

A crowd started to gather outside of the high school. Through the crowd I could see Sea'Sea standing there, holding her hands to her mouth, crying relentlessly. I could hear Mr. Jackson saying to someone "Didn't I tell yeah. See I just told my class that that boy was going to turn out like that. I just said it,"

I looked away from everybody, embarrassed to look up again.

"Damn, I got this knife on me too. I'm fucked both ways," I thought.

The police car drove off.

Chapter 19

The police tried their best to corner me with "I know you killed Loc" bullshit. I knew how to play the silent game, I had watched too many detective shows on TV. Word on the street was Melo was still alive and been telling everybody and their momma that I killed Loc.

--

As I made my way to the City from the police station, my teacher Mr. Jackson car passed me driving straight towards the City.

"Now what's the chances of me running into this nigga after all the shit he was talking in class? Trying to front on me and shit," I thought.

I started to jog towards entrance of the City. I made sure I had my hunting knife on my side.

Mr. Jackson car slowly pulled up to Rico Chill's house. Rico was known in the neighborhood as being a rainbow or a gay man. For more reason than one, people in the City loved Rico because he wasn't afraid to be who he was and he was one of their own. Even those who went to church and self-proclaimed Bible thumpers from the City, secretly loved and fooled around with Rico too. Word was that Rico had always been that way before he even took his first step. The old folks in the City said he was just placed in the wrong body. Outside of the City, Rico had to be careful of the Bible thumpers and ignorant folks that prejudged him before getting to know him. They said that he was a sinner with much shame that needed healing and sometimes to them, healing meant death.

I hid behind a tree to see what was going on and why Mr. Jackson was at Rico Chill's house.

"This nigga thank he all that, trying to be tough and shit. Mane, this nigga gay as a whistle," I whispered.

As Rico opened the car door, the inside light of the car came on. I witnessed Mr. Jackson lean over and kiss Rico, like a man would kiss a woman.

I laughed. 'Ooooooooooh shit. Ain't no way this shit happening right now,"

I sat there and paid close attention to how Rico and Mr. Jackson interacted. I noticed how they were laughing and joking with one another, like they were husband and wife, or in this case husband and husband. They seemed really happy to be around one another.

"No wonder this nigga all out in the open like this, its 2:30 in the morning. Fake ass," I whispered. "Mr. Lim said real happiness only exist in the wee hours of the morning. Creeping and shit,"

Rico closed the car door and waved goodbye to Mr. Jackson as he drove off.

I dashed onto the street. I wanted Mr. Jackson to look me in the face as he passed me.

As Mr. Jackson passed me, I smiled and waved. I knew Mr. Jackson was paranoid and was checking everybody in his path, trying to duck and dodge without being seen.

The car instantly hit on breaks and quickly reversed back to where I was proudly standing.

Mr. Jackson rolled the passenger side window down.

"What's up Mr. Tough Guy," I said with a smile. "Didn't know you fucked with dudes. Ain't you got a wife and some kids,"

Mr. Jackson quietly sat in his car, scared to death that someone other than me, Rico, and God knew his little secret.

"Get in the car," Mr. Jackson said.

"I don't fuck with dudes, sorry my nigga," I responded with a chuckle.

"Just get in the fucking car, NOW,"

"See, that tough guy shit don't work out here in these streets. Either you bout it or you ain't," I said as I saw Mr. Jackson about to get out of the car. "Now if you get out that car, it's on you. I owe you anyway,"

Mr. Jackson got out of the car anyway. I placed my hand on my hunting knife.

I knew I was in a bad predicament. I knew I couldn't hit Mr. Jackson with the hunting knife in the middle of the City without somebody seeing me. But I knew if it came down to it, I had to defend myself, especially against a gay, big, black man weighing almost 300 pounds.

"I shoulda beat yo motherfucker ass. I never liked yo ass any way," Mr. Jackson said. "Now, either we can keep this between us or I can try to kill you with my bear hands,"

"You talking to the wrong nigga Action Jackson. You ain't killing shit this way," I said in a serious tone. "You just don't want nobody to know bout yo boyfriend. Rico Chill cool peoples though. I know yo wife and kids would love to meet him. Ole shit, don't you coach football too. I know Coach Hines and them football players gone love to hear bout yo boyfriend too,"

"Fuck you and that faggot Rico. I was just giving him a ride home. It ain't even like that. That's just my homeboy,"

"A ride home? Nigga you can't be serious. I saw you with my own eyes kiss the nigga,"

I heard a voice coming from behind that sounded like Rico. "Who you calling a faggot Jackson," Rico was on his front porch listening the entire time.

I laughed. "Uh Oh, somebody in trouble now. You done fucked with the wrong nigga Action Jackson," I sarcastically said. I called him Action Jackson because he always acted like he was about action and business. I knew that once the news about Mr. Jackson gayness got out, the death of his manhood would lead to a life far worse than death. A life of shame, regret, and embarrassment for an alpha male turned gay dude.

"I said……Who you calling a faggot Jackson," Rico screamed as he popped his mouth. Rico was one those flamboyant gay men that talked, danced, walked, and dressed like a woman. "Oh, hey Shake,"

"What's up Chill," I said as I stepped back to let the two do their thing.

Mr. Jackson motioned to Rico to keep his voice down.

"Don't tell me to hush up. You don't run me, hell," Rico screamed as he rolled his eyes harder than any hood girl.

"Chill, did you know Action Jackson was married with children," I said.

"Married," Rico yelled with his mouth open. "See, I told you when we first started fucking that I don't play no games. And you tried it,"

"Shut the fuck up Amel," Mr. Jackson screamed about to charge me.

"Just leave Shake out this, ok. Don't try to jump the subject mister. Is you married," Rico asked popping his mouth. Mr. Jackson didn't answer, he just looked away. "Is you married," Rico repeated.

"I'm separated," Mr. Jackson said.

"That nigga ain't separated, I just seen him with his wife two days ago at the game," I interjected.

Mr. Jackson looked at me with a death stare. I smiled at him.

"You know what," Rico said as he started to cry. "I knew you was some bullshit. You just was too good to be true,"

By this time, a crowd had slowly gathered around the three of us without us knowing.

"Don't that nigga work at the school," a bystander said.

"Yea that's one of the football coaches," somebody else said.

We were stunned at how many people had gathered around us so quickly.

"Yall, this my husband. This the nigga I been fucking, sho is. Now nigga if you fuck with me, Imma fuck with you. Yo wife will hear bout this to....mor...row. I can be messy too boo boo,"

Mr. Jackson looked around at everyone standing, watching him. The look on his face was complete disbelief. He couldn't believe something like this was happening to him.

"Oh it's real Action Jackson," I said with a smile. I already knew what Mr. Jackson was contemplating.

Mr. Jackson quickly jumped in his car. I knocked on his window and gave him a huge smile, a wink of the eye, and a thumbs up as he drove off into the night.

"Yall quit it," Ms. Betty Joe said. "Embarrassing that man like that,"

"That's him out here lying Ms. Betty Joe," Rico said. "Got me out here looking stupid and cute,"

"Now I know you know you better Rico," Ms. Betty Joe said.

"No I don't either Ms. Betty Joe. He gone get what he deserve with his gay ass," Rico said out loud. "I mean his gay self. I'm sorry Ms. Betty Joe, you know my mouth gets nasty sometimes. I mean like cursing and stuff, not what you thinking Ms. Betty Joe,"

Ms. Betty Joe laughed. "You a mess Rico, you hear me. You a mess child,"

"I know, that's why you love me don't it," Rico said.

"That's right," Ms. Betty Joe said.

I left the crowd and made my way to the old light blue shotgun house. I met King Lee sitting on the porch lightly playing his queen.

"What is all that fuss down there," King Lee asked.

"Ole nothing. Just somebody that try to treat somebody dirty, got treated dirty himself. That's all,"

"If you throw dirt, you will soon get dirty too," King Lee said.

"That's exactly what I be screaming to these dude out here King Lee, but they act like they don't understand nothing though,"

Chapter 20

The room was mildly lit as I laid in bed with my eyes glued to the ceiling pondering my future. Then I felt Javion little hands touch my arm.

I gestured to get up, but I couldn't. I gestured to move my mouth to talk, but I couldn't. My entire body was paralyzed, the only thing I could move were my eyes.

"Come on Javion, DAMN," Melo screamed. "He don't care bout you. You see he ain't moving,"

I tried hard to get up again but couldn't.

Melo snatched Javion by the arm. "Didn't I tell yo ass to come on," Melo said but Javion snatched away from her and clinged back to my arm again.

"I want Shake," Javion screamed. "You hurt me,"

I was trying all my might to move but I couldn't.

"Gone go with yo momma boy," I heard Baby Sister say from the corner of the room. She was submerged in darkness but I could see her shadow. "Cause I can't keep ya. I had mine and I ain't raising no more,"

I watched as Melo took Javion into the darkness. I knew I couldn't move. I knew I was helpless. I knew I couldn't save him.

I felt the tears running down the side of my face.

I knew I couldn't give up on Javion, so I tried with all my might and finally broke free.

--

"Imma kill them motherfuckers," I said as I awoke from my sleep. To me, the dream symbolized Melo and Baby sister betrayal towards me and what they were secretly contemplating behind my back.

Infuriated with anger from the constant playback of Melo shasty ass, from the conversation I had with Baby Sister a few nights before, and my dream, I decided to sneak out while Javion and King Lee was sound asleep. In my heart, I knew what I had to do not just for my sake, but for Javion sake too. There was no way they were taking him from me.

I stood outside of the ole light blue shotgun house as the cool breeze wiped across my face. I loved how quiet the City when all was just about sleep, except for the dope heads. I waited and waited, I knew eventually someone would show and they finally did.

"Can I get that ride to Baby Sister house," I asked Caralyn Dent, who was leaving her boyfriend house in the City going to Bear Ridge. Caralyn was from Bear Ridge, she had gone to school with my oldest cousin, Jaqueline Simon.

She said I could catch a ride.

Me and Caralyn rode in complete silence without saying a word. People around the City use to talk about how quiet Caralyn was but how she was sleeping with everybody around the way. "You got to watch them quiet ones," the old women use to say in the City.

People said Caralyn went both ways, because one night she would be with a man, the other night with a woman, and the next night with both at the same time. They said she was one of those nymphs' type women.

I never heard of her smashing young dudes, only grown dudes, so I knew she didn't have her ass on me.

Caralyn dropped me off on the highway. I walked down the side road until I made it to Baby Sister's house. I cautiously looked around twice, making sure Baby Sister was nowhere in sight and that no cars were coming as I opened the window to Melo's old room. My heart began to race with adrenaline. I was on a mission, as I had been before, to rid the world of bad hearted people. Just so happen, tonight I had my mind focused on Baby Sister, nothing else.

As I eased my way through the Melo's window, I tried my best not to make a sound.

I stood still. I wanted to make sure I didn't hear Baby Sister near the room.

I didn't hear anything so I relaxed a bit.

The smell alone of the old wooden house brought back many memories, both good and bad. I started to remember how me and Melo use to laugh and play together.

For some reason, I started to get a tingling sensation all over my body. The feeling was strange.

I quickly shook the emotions off. It wasn't the time and place for it. I looked around the room and noticed that the room still looked identical to how Melo had left it when she left that day with Javion. Javion toys were still in the floor and Melo's bed was still messy just as I remembered. It was like Baby Sister was preserving the room to keep her memory of Melo close.

Then I snapped out of my trance of reminiscing. I started to get back focus on my mission. I pulled my hunting knife out from its holder, looked at it, cut a small patch of hair from my arm to make sure the knife was sharp enough, and braced myself to finish a deed that I thought should have been done a long time ago.

I cautiously opened the door and crept into the living room on my toes, trying not to make any noise on the old wooden floors. As I stood in the middle of the living room, knife in hand, I could vaguely see Baby Sister and JoJo's mother, Mae, talking at the kitchen table through the old china cabinet glass in the kitchen. I could smell Mae smoking a cigarette and I knew they both were drinking like fish.

"Dump that motherfucker like a bad habit," Baby Sister told Mae. "Don't take that shit off no man, you hear me, nan motherfucker,"

"I know Baby Sister," Mae responded. "But you don't understand, I been with this man 30 years, where do I pose to go,"

"Go to the river and dump that motherfucker body in it after you kill him. It couldn't be Mae, it couldn't be me, I'm telling you gul. I woulda dropped that bitch as soon as he put his hands on me," Baby Sister said. "That's why I don't have a man now cuz if one put they hands on me or even try to do something to my kids, that's gonna be a dead motherfucker, you hear me,"

"Baby Sister, you stone crazy, you know that. And that reminds me gul, I knew I had to tell you something and it just fell on my mind. Do you know what Joseph had the nerve to do to me," Mae said.

"What gul," Baby Sister responded.

"He had the nerve to try to beat me in front of JoJo," Mae said.

"Beat you in front of JoJo," Baby Sister responded.

"Beat me in front of JoJo, you hear me Baby Sister," Mae responded.

I started to remember how Baby Sister use to talk about how pretty Mae use to be when they were young girls growing up in the cotton fields of Bear Ridge. She said Mae was the talk of the town. She was voted most likely to succeed, most beautiful, most outgoing, wittiest, all by her high school class. She was even the Valedictorian of her class.

"She was a pretty something nother back in the day, let me tell you. She was something else. You talking bout pretty. She looked like something you woulda seen in a movie, you hear me. Every man wanted her," Baby Sister use to say about Mae. "Too bad she let that no good bitch bring her down. It's a crying shame too cuz she coulda been something special to somebody. She could have made it out of them fields. Shit, she still living in them same fields as sho as my name is Baby Sister,"

I knew Baby Sister loved Mae, probably more than she did me and Melo. Baby Sister loved Mae's spirit and good heart, even though she was a weak woman mentally, the total opposite of her. Once upon a time, Baby Sister use to find inspiration from Mae's ambition, drive, beauty and character. But as of now, character, drive, beauty and ambition were things of the past for Mae. She now dressed in rags and looked 20 years her senior. She never held a job because her husband, Joseph, barred her from doing so. Mae's skin was now black and dirty, far from the caramel brown skin Baby Sister use to tell me about.

To me, Mae never seemed happy, only depressed and sad. Her eyes told a million sad stories about her past, present, and future. Sometimes, I would catch her just staring off into space, talking to herself.

The reason for all of her trouble was because Joseph beat the living shit out of her. One time, they say Joseph slammed Mae's head in a closet door just because she asked him to pick up his shoes that were lying in the floor. Joseph was known to beat Mae ass often just because he said that she was worthless and no good, and beat JoJo too because he said JoJo looked just like her.

"Everyone round town told you good not to mess with that no good ass nigga. The nigga musta got a gold tip on his dick cuz it makes no sense why you let that bitch do you like that," Baby Sister yelled.

"It's just love Baby Sister. Love can make people do some crazy thangs," Mae added.

"Fuck love. If love gotta get my ass beat and get treated like that, just so I can say that I am in love, then I don't want it. No sir re bob. You can have that shit Mae. You can have it, you hear me. Hell, the motherfucker already tryna beat you in front of yo son. And guess how yo son gone turn out," Baby Sister said, making direct eye contact with Mae, being a little bit more serious.

"How he gone turn out Baby Sister," Mae responded, looking concerned. She didn't want to tell Baby Sister that she had put JoJo out of the house for fighting Joseph for beating on her a few months back.

"Just like that no good motherfucker you got living in yo house right now. The nigga eat yo food, shit when he want to, sleep when he want to, beat yo ass when he want to, and here's the kicker, the bitch won't even work. Hell yo son is in a lose-lose situation. See, Amel didn't grow up with no man in my house. He didn't have a daddy to teach him how to be no good, hell I rather for him not to have a daddy than to have a daddy in his life that ain't teaching him shit but how not to work and beat women. JoJo deserve more than that. You can raise him by yoself Mae. Hell you can come stay with me and I bet you that nigga won't show up at my door step. You don't need that nigga," Baby Sister said.

"But didn't you put Amel out Baby Sister," Mae asked.

"See that's different. That little motherfucker put his hands on me. He was gonna die that day if he didn't run, you hear me. Son or no son," Baby Sister said.

"Awwww Baby Sister, don't say that," Mae said.

"Thank I'm lying if you want to, gul please. But we not talking bout me and mine right now, that's a whole nother talk. We talking bout you and JoJo," Baby Sister insisted.

Baby Sister could see that she had struck a nerve with Mae talking about JoJo by the way Mae was in a daze.

We all knew Mae loved JoJo but deep down we knew she cursed the day she married Joseph. JoJo was her life. Her only reason for living was to show him a better life and not have him to turn out to be like his father.

Mae started to realize that she had chosen a no good man over her own son. She started to notice the way JoJo was starting to react to situations like Joseph and take up his violent ways. Regardless of his struggles, JoJo was the only thing in the world that kept Mae sane and living.

"I don't know what it is Mae. And I guess I will never understand it. Matter of fact, I will never understand why women lessen themselves just to be with a man. It's like you settling for anythang, like you feel as though you don't deserve better. That nigga done took you for all you have, even yo spirit and soul. He own you Mae and he knows he do. And you just sitting yo foolish ass round here and being a slave to him and you don't even know it. You let that nigga take yo life and spirit from you and that ain't right. That ain't right at all Mae," Baby Sister said.

"I know Baby Sister, I know," Mae said in a sad tone.

Baby Sister abruptly jumped up from the kitchen table.

My heart dropped to my knees as I stood still in the living room, in the same spot, trying not to move. I thought that crazy motherfucker was coming straight to the living but luckily for me, Baby Sister was headed to her room.

"What's that you got Baby Sister," Mae said still confused as to why Baby Sister jumped up from the table so quickly. "Gul you scared me getting up from this table like that. Damn near scared the life out me,"

"Why you worried bout what I got. It's none of yo business what I got. You don't be asking that nigga what he got, now do you," Baby Sister said.

"Don't you take no picture of me Baby Sister, I'm serious now. You know I don't take good pictures," Mae insisted as she realized that Baby Sister had a picture camera.

Baby Sister took Mae's picture against her will, catching a good shot of Mae's face.

"Gul didn't I tell you good not to take no picture of me. See you start playing and don't know when to stop," Mae said getting upset.

"Oh shut up Mae. You acting like I'm beating yo ass or something. Hell if you don't get mad at that nigga over at yo house that beat yo ass, then don't cope no attitude with me, Ok," Baby Sister said as she paused for a second. "Wait a minute. I'll be right back,"

Baby Sister went back to her bedroom and returned.

"See she ain't got no respect for nobody. Now the woman done told her good not to take her picture and she still done it," I whispered with irritation.

Baby Sister paced back and forth in front of the table with the picture she had taken of Mae in her hand, wavering it to make the picture come faster.

She then sat down at the table.

Baby Sister started to finger through the photo album she had gotten from her room, searching for a particular picture she remembered. She finally found the one she was looking for. She then placed the two pictures on the table side by side.

Mae nonchalantly glazed at the pictures on the table, still trying to make sense of what was going on.

"Now why you went and got my high school picture," Mae said with a smile. "Now, who is this you got beside my picture," Mae asked.

"That's the picture I just took of you Mae," Baby Sister said in a low tone. I could tell the way Mae reacted to the picture affected Baby Sister.

Both of Mae hands landed at her mouth in shock. She didn't recognize herself in the photo Baby Sister had just taken of her.

Mae started to cry.

"Who is that Baby Sister? That can't be me. Please tell me that ain't me Baby Sister," Mae screamed.

Baby Sister got up from the table, grabbed Mae and hugged her.

"It's ok Mae, it's ok. You can't run from happiness all yo life. Trust me Mae, I know. That's you Mae. That's you," Baby Sister said with a tear rolling down her face. She wanted Mae to start searching for happiness like she had started to do in her own life. Baby Sister stood there and tried her best to be strong for her friend. "You have paid yo dues to life, you hear me Mae. You have paid yo dues, now it's time for you to live again. Ain't no experience in life like bought experience,"

The two of them embraced each other and cried together until Mae became stable.

"This is the Mae that I know and want to see again," Baby Sister said, pointing to Mae's high school senior portrait.

"That's the Mae that I want to know and see again too Baby Sister," Mae said with tears rolling down her face again. It had been a long time since she had seen pictures of herself when she was young. Joseph had burned all of her pictures and photo albums years back to make a point to her that she wasn't shit.

"That Mae died many years ago Baby Sister, many many years ago," Mae said as she lit a cigarette and grabbed another beer out of the refrigerator. What depressed Mae so much was she once had dreams of becoming a lawyer, but she felt that she had turned out to be a failure.

"I wasted my life Baby Sister. I know God is punishing me for a reason. Maybe I deserve this life," Mae said.

Baby Sister let out a small sigh and dropped her head.

"This is long overdue Mae and I shoulda told you this a long time ago." Baby Sister said looking up. "You can't let nobody tear you down like that. Man, woman or child. When you get with somebody, they should help you build a life, not help you destroy yo life. Yo man should bring something to yo life, not take away from it, you hear me. So I am telling you this, don't you let no dick or a no good nigga be yo down fall. Don't you die like this Mae, you better than what I see before me. You still young and pretty. Hell if I was a man, I would try to colt ya. You need a man in yo life child, not a shell of a man,"

Baby Sister wanted to be sure Mae understood her sincerity.

"Today, you can either choose to let that younger Mae die or you can choose to let that younger Mae live again. Do you want to live again Mae? If you don't do it for yoself, do it for JoJo. He deserves better, you hear me Mae, he deserves better than what you given him. Choose now to change yo life and get that Mae back for you and yo son," Baby Sister said.

"I want that Mae back, but I just don't know how to get her back Baby Sister," Mae said staring at the floor, wiping her eyes from the tears that continued to flow from them.

"I know how. Look to Jesus Mae. Look to the Lord. He can help you forgive yoself and help you move on to the next chapter in yo life. Now, by no means am I a Bible thumping woman but I am a praying woman now Mae. I learned that I have to pray to keep going. I want you to learn to pray to keep going too. Let's pray Mae, let's pray together," Baby Sister said. For the past three weeks, Baby Sister had been reading her Bible more and was getting better with her relationship with God.

Baby Sister grabbed both of Mae's hands from across the table and they began to pray:

Dear Heavenly Father,

We come to You today with a humble heart and open mind.

First, we like to thank you for all that You are and all that You provide for us.

We thank ya Father.

Have mercy on us.

Father, bless Mae so that her life become full and vibrant again.

Bless her to understand her past in order for her to understand her future.

Bless her Father with knowledge, wisdom, and courage.

Bless her to forgive that bitch of a husband of hers and allow her to be a good momma to her son.

--

Mae laughed out loud and slapped Baby Sister's hand. Baby Sister smiled. "You a mess Baby Sister,"

"Hell I'm serious gul, you playing,"

"Keep it clean. It's a prayer Baby Sister for crying out loud. Now keep going," Mae said.

--

Now I was rudely interrupted Lord, so forgive Mae for that

But Bless Mae heart to be lifted from all of her past burdens and help bring light to the rest of her days.

Help her find her way in this dark world.

Bless us both to seek You in the midst of adversity and good times.

Bless us both to put You first and to be good Christian people with good hearts.

We thank ya Father.

We ask these and other blessings in ya Son Jesus name we pray.

Amen.

--

"Find that Mae again. Live for God and find motivation to live for yo son," Baby Sister added as her and Mae released hands and started to look at one another.

"You ready to live Mae," Baby Sister asked.

"I am ready Baby Sister," Mae said.

"Alright then. Now I am not going to hold you over here too long, but know that I'm here for you Mae," Baby Sister said.

As Mae got up from the table, a tear rolled down her face.

"I am ready Baby Sister. I am ready to live again. Thank you Baby Sister for those words. You know words can come to life sometimes and show you thangs that can break you or make you. You made your words come to life in a good way tonight Baby Sister and I thank you for that. You know you always been a good person and everyone round town knows that. God gonna bless you Baby Sister, He gonna bless you one day," Mae said as she hugged Baby Sister. "Now I want you to do one thang for me,"

"What's that Mae," Baby Sister asked.

"I want you to make thangs right with yo babies too. I'm talking bout Amel and Melo," Mae said.

Baby Sister fell silent.

"I know you love them chilren Baby Sister, you just had a tough life just like the rest of us. Make thangs right with them, can you do that for me," Mae asked.

Baby Sister sat there still in silence. She wasn't ready to face her own problems. She thought the conversation was going to be strictly about Mae. She knew it was easier to tell other people about their problems and how to solve them, but it was so hard to talk about and solve her own.

"Baby Sister, will you do that for me," Mae asked again.

"I will try," Baby Sister said nonchalantly as she dazed at the table, deep in thought.

Mae grabbed Baby Sister's hand.

"Don't try, do," Mae said.

Baby Sister looked up at Mae.

"I will do it for you Mae. I will do it for you," Baby Sister said with a smile.

"Don't do it for me Baby Sister, do it for yoself. Yo chilren need you too just like you say JoJo need me. Maybe both of our happiness will be found when we just start over," Mae said. "Well let me get on back over here to this house before he start trying to come look for me. I'll holla at you later, ok Baby Sister,"

I was caught in a flux. I knew the conversation between Baby Sister and Mae was over, but I didn't want to run and make noise to bring attention to myself. I knew Baby Sister was just a skip and a hop away from her gun that resided in her dresser.

I tiptoed quickly back to Melo's room. As soon as I gently closed the door to Melo's room, I heard footsteps coming towards the living room as Baby Sister was walking Mae to the door.

"Now how is she good to everybody else except for me and Melo," I whispered in a confused state.

But something dawned on me. "What about the goodness she showed though" I thought.

I knew Baby Sister still had goodness in her heart to have a conversation like that with Mae.

In that moment, I was no longer angry with Baby Sister. I no longer wanted to kill her. Now I wanted a chance to just sit down and really talk to her.

Seconds turned into minutes as I listened for Baby Sister in the front room. At first I heard Baby Sister and Mae talking, but that soon turned into silence.

"What they doing," I thought.

Then Baby Sister opened the door to Melo's room, closed the door and sat on the bed in complete silence and darkness.

I could feel Baby Sister rocking back and forth on the bed.

"I can feel my babies," Baby Sister yelled. "I can feel them hurting"

Baby Sister rocked back and forth.

"I did care bout my babies, you don't know nothing bout me. It ain't my fault. They chose to leave. It ain't my fault, hell," Baby Sister yelled again. "They turned they back on me. I loved them chilren but they didn't love me back. See you always talking that bullshit and don't know what the hell you talking bout,"

Baby Sister rocked harder.

"I know motherfucker, you thank I don't know that," Baby Sister screamed.

"Nope, them my babies. Them my babies. I ain't gone kill my babies. So you can get on with that mess. I ain't doing it. I ain't doing it. I ain't doing it, so quit. This ain't the old Baby Sister that you could talk that shit to and I do. I am done with all that. Lord please bless me," Baby Sister pleaded.

"I know," Baby Sister cried out. "I know I am. I know nobody don't. That ain't nothing new. I know nobody don't love me. I know I ain't shit just like you motherfucker. You can't run that shit on me now, I got God on my side now. So you can get on Satan,"

Baby Sister stopped rocking.

"Now what you gots to say now," Baby Sister said with a chuckle. "That's what I thought, not a damn thang. See you can't outsmart me no mo,"

Baby Sister got up and left the room. I could hear her mumbling in the other room.

"Damn, she hear that motherfucker too," I whispered.

I quickly got up from under the bed, opened the window, and vanished into the night.

Chapter 21

I entered the City in a complexed state of mind in the wee hours of the night. I hitched a ride from Bear Ridge with a truck driver by the name of Jerry. He was an older white man that wore a cowboy hat and thick bifocals. It was something strange about Jerry. I didn't fear him and he didn't fear me even though we were strangers. For some reason, he kept repeating "She knows everything". I didn't know if he was talking to me or to himself so I left it alone and sat quietly until he dropped me off.

--

As I slowly approached the light blue shotgun house in the darkness of the night, I could hear King Lee playing his queen and humming at the same time from the front porch. It was something beautiful and painful about the music that he played.

"Who goes there," King Lee asked as he suddenly stopped playing his queen. He could instinctively feel someone approaching the house.

"It's me, King Lee," I said.

"Come sit with this old man young fella," King Lee insisted.

"You not old. You still a young buck," I said with a smile.

King Lee laughed out loud. "Is that right,"

I walked to the steps and sat just below where King Lee was playing. I looked into the sky and noticed how pretty the sky and stars were.

"She knows everything," I thought with confusion.

King Lee started to play a light tune on his queen. Minutes turned into hours as we sat there on the porch in the heat of the night, fanning mosquitoes and all. We sat there and didn't say a word. We were silently thinking. I was thinking about Jerry and what he meant by what he said to me. King Lee was thinking about the life that he once had. Reflecting on his past life always ended in King Lee playing tunes of pain, then killing that pain through some good ole whiskey or brandy.

"Pass me that brown bag special over there," King Lee demanded as he abruptly stopped playing, breaking the silence between us. "It's time for me to taste a piece of heaven," he continued.

I passed King Lee the bottle of home brew. I could smell the alcohol through the sealed top of the old bottle. King Lee took the bag, looked at the bottle, untopped it, ran the bottle back and forth beneath his nose a few times to smell it's sweetness, then took a big gulp from it.

"Ain't no wonder you ain't laid out here dead how strong this stuff is," I said.

"Oh hell fella, these people around here will kill me faster than this will," King Lee said.

King Lee looked at me for a second and then took another gulp from the bottom.

"Some people do other things to escape this world's pain. You know like robbing, stealing and killing. Drinking is what I choose. It keeps me living honest. But you listen to me and listen to me good. Don't you do what I do, you be a better man than the man you see before you, alright," King Lee said.

I shook my head to say ok.

"What," I asked.

"He was just as nice as he wanted to be. He was a yellow black man that was half white. They called him Pugh City Red, but his real name was Aaron Davis,"

"Pugh City Red," I said with a laughed. "Now that's a name,"

"Yessuh and he was a man to be left alone. And he didn't say too much either. See the quiet ones be the most dangerous," King Lee said.

"That what everybody say," I said.

"You know ole Candy Man down the road that walk with that limp," King Lee said.

"Yeah," I said.

"Ole Red beat him with a hammer and shot him six times. That's why Candy Man walks with that limp. But those were the good ole days. People would look out for you then. People cared for one another. But ole Red dead and gone now, but he was a good man that would kill,"

"Guy'lee. He was a bad man huh," I said with excitement.

"Sure was," King Lee said.

"Pugh City Red," I said silently with a grind.

King Lee and I sat there for a few minutes in silence, listening to the sound of the darkness. I was playing with little rocks on the ground as King Lee stared into space. I loved when King Lee told me about his friends and stories of the past.

"And then the situation with Sea'Sea is all messed up too," I said out of the blue.

"How is Sea'Sea doing? I don't see her around here that much anymore. At one point in time, you couldn't keep that lil gal from being over here, smiling all in your face. You can tell she got the hots for you. And I bet you haven't tried not one time to colt her, have you," King Lee said.

"She good and naw, she was my friend," I said.

"What do you mean she was your friend? That's past tense," King Lee said.

"I know it is. We was friends. I done found out that she been sleeping around behind my back with a dog nigga that I know. I ain't kicked it with her in like over a month but it seems like three years," I said.

"Is she your girlfriend," King Lee asked.

"Naw, I just told you we was just friends. She was my home girl, you know. Somebody to kick it with or what not," I said.

"Something like a do-girl," King Lee said.

"Naw, something like a home girl, like I said. That what home girls do for their homeboys, kick it and stuff. You know what I'm talking bout throwback," I said.

"I never heard nobody just 'kicking it' as you say and nobody got feelings for one another. So since she isn't your girlfriend why do you care so much about her sleeping with this person that you know," King Lee said.

"You know what's funny, she asked me the same exact question but I couldn't answer it," I said rubbing my chin. "But check this out though King Lee. I'm sitting my dumb self-up there taking care of Sea'Sea while she letting the man knock her down. It's all bout loyalty for me. I pose to be yo homeboy and stuff, and you can't tell me that you knocking this nigga off. Somebody that I know, mane I can't do that. I can't fool with her like that no more,"

"How do you know she did it," King Lee asked.

214

"Because she told me, that's how. I been knew she knocked the nigga off though, to be real with it," I said clearly lying through my teeth. "But I'm at her house right. Chilling, trying to make sure she good, you know. So I gets to reading the newspaper and saw the fake nigga she knocking off. So, I held up the newspaper and asked her did she know him, but this was before I knew she had knocked him off. She said she knew him. I told her to chill with the lies. She said that she knew her baby daddy when she seen him and that he was the baby daddy. No if, ands, or buts bout it. What gets me is I'm the one looking like a fool, nobody else," I said getting upset. "And I ain't even told the really messed up part bout the whole thing,"

"What's that," King Lee asked.

"She pregnant by the nigga. She is showing and everything. I was the one buying her stuff. I was the one spending time with her, making sure she was good. That was all me," I said.

"Just calm down now, don't get all bent out of shape for no reason. You sure that she knew that the person was somebody you knew," King Lee asked.

"Yeah I'm sure but she tried to deny it," I said.

"Why can't you just take her word for it and leave it alone," King Lee said.

I looked up at King Lee with a confused look like "what are you talking about".

"Because I can't. And even if I did, I still can't mess off with her like that. I just can't," I said.

"Well that's a question mark in your life that will always be there," King Lee said.

"So be it. I'm good with that. She nasty and I don't want no parts of that," I said. "But you know what I been thanking bout though King Lee,"

"What's that," King Lee asked.

I stared off into the night sky.

"I want a chance, King Lee," I said.

"A chance at what," King Lee asked.

"A chance to live," I said.

"You are living," King Lee said.

I looked at King Lee. "I mean a chance to live a good life. That's not too much to ask is it,"

"No it's not too much to ask," King Lee said with a smirk on his face. "You know what's the first step is, don't you,"

I stared at King Lee for a second, trying to read him.

"I don't," I said.

King Lee slowly raised from his seat and sat beside me on the steps. He reeked of alcohol but it was like his body was so immune to the alcohol that he couldn't get drunk anymore.

"Its start here," King Lee said, pointing to my head. "And here," he continued pointing at my heart.

I shook my head to say I understood.

"You must fix what has been broken. You must change how you view this world and your world," King Lee said.

"How though. It ain't just like talking bout it," I said.

216

said forgive, but you never forget. This is not a fool's journey, it's a journey of truth and revelation of self," King Lee explained.

"Is surrounding myself with positive thangs apart of self-discovery too," I asked.

"It is," King Lee said. "You must surround yourself with positive people in order to become a positive person. The same principle applies to anything else you are trying to become a magnet too. Always remember that you are what you attract, same as I have told you before,"

"So you telling that if I forgive my past, I will have a better future," I asked.

"You hit the nail on the head. Here is where my theory comes into play," King Lee said. "Are you ready to hear it,"

"I'm ready," I said.

King Lee spoke:

Theory: If one discover who they are and what they stand for early, for the sake of self-growth and prosperity, one will have a greater chance at avoiding illiteracy, prison, relationship woes, immature parenting, and so on. The real kicker is that self-discovery helps one to be at ease with oneself, finding ones strength and building on it, finding ones weakness and improving on it. The goal of self-discovery is to have one to become self-sufficient and confident in one's own skin with the result of creating goals, morals, and values based on one's own outlook on life. This way, when one is faced with adversity of any kind, one has their own standards on handling any situation the right and appropriate way, not having to look elsewhere for answers. It takes time to understand and develop into the person one is destined to become. It takes courage to endure hard times. It takes hope to dream of things unseen. It takes patience to await blessings that are longed for. It takes life experiences and circumstance to be able to give and share life with others. Self-discovery also brings about hard work, simply because self-discovery within itself is a life journey. One has to be able to work hard not only for things of this world, but for things within oneself as well. Hard work is a vital component of self-discovery that poses the following points: if a journeyman never worked hard for anything in life, how can he encourage another to work hard; if a journeyman never made good grades in school, how can he encourage others to make good grades in school, especially his own children. Most importantly, if a journeyman never dared to dream and defy the odds, how could he encourage others to dream and defy the odds? The point is, experience life and approach each life situation with doing the best you can. If you don't, you will be a hypocrite in telling someone else to do the same. Advice is only given through experience of the advisor, don't be afraid to experience things and endure hardships in hopes of helping another get through the same experience. Lastly, remember that every journey has its purpose, and every life has its meaning. Discover life and discover true riches beyond this world.

--

"Now, understand that this theory is just the advice of this ole man. I am just a man that lived a lifetime of experiences and is able to live and share my stories with young people like you. Once upon a time, I had dreams Amel, real dreams just like you have. I wanted a real chance at living too, but look at me. I am the decision that you don't want to make. One decision can make you me one day," King Lee said with a serious tone. "I look around now and see that my dreams as a child were mere dreams, just a fantasy. But your dreams are real and possible. Remember that in life, there is nothing definite and everything has its place and opinion. Take my theory and make it your own, the right way," King Lee added

"You make it sounds so simple though," I said.

"It is. Everyday people tend to overcomplicate simplest things for some reason or another. It's those simple things that adds up to be bigger things," King Lee said.

I glazed off into the night sky as King Lee continued to talk.

"Imma go back to my momma house tomar and try to talk to her. Probably catch out first thang in the morning," I thought.

Chapter 22

I sat on the porch of the old light blue shotgun house and watched as Javion played in the yard. As usual, King Lee was out picking up cans to buy food and liquor. It was moments like those that convinced me that I was doing the right thing by Javion. I could see the same innocence and joy in his eyes as I seen when he was a little baby. It was those moments that brought a smile of joy to my face.

As I sat on the porch, still observing Javion, I noticed a brand new Yukon with 26 inch rims pull up in front of the old light blue shotgun house.

"I'm bout to head down by yo momma way. Come fuck with me," Tough Cat said. Mike Peoples, aka Tough Cat, was a 29 years old guy that lived in the City and had a girlfriend, Jessica Daniels, who lived three houses down from Baby Sister. I didn't take well to Tough Cat. He was one of those shasty niggas that liked to brag and boast about what he had, even though he lived in the City just like the rest of the poor folks. Tough Cat dressed well, drove an expensive truck, but had the personality of a tree.

I eased off the porch and headed towards the truck to see who it really was. I figured it was Tough Cat but I wanted to make sure.

"Cuz, on them sixes. You doing it ain't it my boy," I said with a smile as I dapped Tough Cat up, all along ponding what Tough Cat wanted and why he was so anxious to give me a ride to Baby Sister's house.

"You already know what it is my boy," Tough Cat responded with a smile. "Shiddd, hop in and fuck with ya boy though,"

"Imma fuck with ya fosho my boy. Let me get me and my lil Champ ready right quick. Give me a minute," I said to Tough Cat.

"That's Melo boy ain't it," Tough Cat said.

"Yep," I responded.

"Javion, come on so I can grab us a bag," I said to Javion.

Javion obliged and quickly ran inside of the house.

I ran inside of the house right behind Javion, put me and Javion a few pieces of clothing in my book bag, just in case we had to stay in Bear Ridge for some reason. I washed Javion's face, changed both of our clothes, put my knife on my side, locked the house up, and headed to the truck.

I placed Javion in the backseat, fastened his seat belt, and jumped in the front seat.

"This a good look my boy. I preciate it, for real though," I said to Tough Cat.

Tough Cat nodded his head upward to say it was cool.

"Before we leave my nigga, I gotta get right real quick, you feel me," Tough Cat said as he pulled out a small bag of cocaine from his pocket, placed a dab on his pinky, and took a bump. He took three more bumps, in different nostrils. "Hell yeah, Imma put this shit on that pussy tonight and have that bitch cumming everywhere," he continued to whisper to himself. Tough Cat placed the cocaine back in his pocket, checked his nose for residue, checked his gold teeth for shininess, checked his hair for placement, gave me dap again, and drove off.

From the time Tough Cat drove off, it was a nonstop talk fest. If he wasn't talking about how much dope he sold, he was talking about how many bitches and hoes he had or how much money he had. I wondered if it was the coke that had him going on and on about nothing.

"These bitches out here be all on a nigga dick, you feel me Shake. I'm talking bout, bitches be digging a nigga, for real though mane. Be sucking a nigga up, swallowing all that shit my nigga," Tough Cat said. He was holding his mouth so that his top and bottom gold teeth could show.

"Oh for real though," I said looking off with a "what the fuck this nigga talking bout" look. I knew Tough Cat was about to hit me with about twenty more lies back to back.

"Hell yeah, no bullshit. I bet you ain't never had a threesome before, have you my nigga," Tough Cat asked.

"What," I asked with a confused look. I then looked back at Javion and saw that he was fast asleep.

"See what I mean, nigga don't even know what that shit is. I be having three bitches at one time, you hear me my nigga," Tough Cat said.

"So you be having three bitches at one time in a threesome," I said with a slight chuckle. It was obvious that Tough Cat didn't know how many people it took to even have a threesome.

"Hell yeaaa my nigga, shit crazy ain't it. Niggas out here be hating on a nigga but you already know what it is," Tough Cat said.

I stared out the window, rolling my eyes, wishing for the ride to be over with already.

"But shiidddd, what up with yo girl Sea'Sea though my boy," Tough Cat asked.

"Ain't shit up with her. Why," I asked.

"I'm trying to knock that down my nigga, what you mean why. Niggas say she a straight freak though, that's why," Tough Cat said.

"Who the fuck told you that," I responded with an attitude. "She ain't no freak my nigga. She good, aight,"

"Damn you talking like thats yo ole lady or something," Tough Cat said.

"Naw she ain't my ole lady, but ain't no nigga finna sit up here and talk bad bout her like that. Like I said, she good,"

Tough Cat smacked his mouth and said "Aight then,"

The truck fell silent for a few minutes. I was thinking about how fake Tough Cat was. I knew Tough Cat was pondering how he was going to bring up the real reason why he asked me to ride with him in the first place.

"Shiiiiidd, what you know bout getting this money though little nigga," Tough Cat said as he pulled out a wad of money from his front pocket. It was about ten thousand dollars rolled up and wrapped with a thick brown rubber band.

I stared at the money. Never in my life had I seen that much money at one time. I knew it was flossing season for Tough Cat since he was riding in a new car on rims that were about as tall as me.

"Niggas wish they had that kind of money. Where you get that kind of money from," I asked.

"You already know my nigga. Hustling and shit, pimping and shit, you already know what it is," Tough Cat said.

Then Tough Cat casually reached into his pants waist and placed a 9mm on his lap.

I looked at the gun and knew something was up. Then it hit me out of the blue why Tough Cat just voluntarily offered me a ride to Bear Ridge for no reason. I knew that Tough Cat never really fucked with nobody unless it was about business, either dope or killing.

I nervously looked back at Javion and then back at Tough Cat as he drove. I didn't want Javion in the middle of any bullshit. I especially didn't want him to get hurt or killed over nonsense or over something I did wrong.

"What you know bout handling a nigga that fucked over one of yo partners, you know what I mean Shake. You feel me," Tough Cat said with conviction, licking his lips, and bouncing like he was itching to kill somebody. I knew if I died, Javion would die too. I knew Tough Cat was a geek monster that didn't have no conscious when it came to business.

I could feel the mood changing.

"I feel you my nigga," I said staring at Tough Cat.

"I'm finna stop the bullshit and be 100 witcha my nigga. Niggas round the way been saying that you the nigga that handled my brother Loc over some bullshit. They say, 'yeah you know Melo little brother did that shit to Loc'. I done heard that from bout 5 niggas in the hood, so what up nigga," Tough Cat yelled.

"Mane I don't know WHERE you get that shit from. I ain't got shit to do with what you talking bout right now. I didn't even know that nigga Loc like that. You know that and you know me my nigga. You know I'm a good nigga so why you trying to play me like this," I said trying to make peace.

"Then answer me this, how you get Melo little boy then," Tough Cat asked. "Nigga yo own sister told me you killed Loc, so what up,"

I smacked my mouth and said "Nigga you thank Imma believe that. Melo been dead,"

"How Melo dead and I just seen her over Dice house just this morning. I gave her 20 dollars and she dropped the dime on yo ass," Tough Cat said.

"Melo ain't seen me do shit my nigga. It's clear she cracked out her motherfucking mind and that's real," I said, still looking back and forth at Tough Cat and the gun that was laying on his lap.

"See now you trying to play me. This ain't no game Shake. I'm dead motherfucking serious right now," Tough Cat said as he placed his hand on the gun. I was witnessing his demeanor change from violent to kill zone.

"I'm serious too. You know me my nigga. Do it look like I would do something like that? Imma scary nigga not no killer," I said animated, trying to prove my case. I knew I was one wrong move or one wrong word away from me and Javion being across a field somewhere in the back woods with 20 bullet filled holes in us both from Tough Cat's gun.

Tough Cat looked at me, biting his lip like he had blood on his mind, with his right hand on his gun. I knew that Tough Cat was going to try to blow my head off at any given moment. I slowly placed my right hand on my hunting knife.

"I know you killed my bro......," Tough Cat was suddenly interrupted by me as I quickly placed my hand on the gun, ambushing Tough Cat with my hunting knife. I hit him four times in the neck. Then six times in the chest. Then three more times in the head. I wanted to make sure he didn't survive.

I grabbed the gun from Tough Cat lap, who was gasping for air, trying to stop the blood from gushing out of his neck. I placed the gun on the floor.

As the car swerved in the road, I took control of the wheel, trying to make the car come to a complete stop and it finally did. I looked back and saw that Javion was still asleep on the back seat.

Tough Cat started to breathe slower and slower until I heard him take his last breath.

I observed him. I could still see the gold teeth still shining in his mouth.

"I should take them motherfuckers out yo mouth and go pawn them," I said laughing.

I then looked back at Javion.

"This guy can sleep through anythang," I whispered with a smile.

I got out of the car and made my way to the driver side where I pushed Tough Cat over to the passenger side. I put the ten thousand dollars that fell on the floor in my pocket. Luckily, the money only had a few spots of blood on it.

"Damn, I'm glad I listened to my first mind and grabbed some clothes," I whispered. "You know what, Lake Amel would love to have this nigga,"

Lake Amel was the lake that me and JoJo always went to under the bridge. I named it that because the lake knew me better than anyone. It was there, I talked about my life and secrets. It was there I felt the safest.

I drove off and finally made my way to the lake. I jumped out of the car and observed the surroundings. First, I made sure that no one was around. Next, I observed a path where I could drive the truck into the lake. I noticed it was a clear path down to the lake right by the bridge.

"How in the hell am I going to get this big ass truck in there. Do I drive it, then jump out? Do I put it in neutral and just let it drive itself in there," I pondered. If I was going to do anything, I knew I had to do it fast. I decided to drive it and jump out like I had seen on a show on channel six.

It was just about dark and I knew that by the time the sun rose the next day, the truck would be totally submerged under the water.

"If I angle it this way, the truck would be under the bridge and nobody will see it go down," I said. But I knew that I had to drive it into the water to make sure that it was at the right spot under the bridge.

I woke Javion up and placed him at the top of the drop and told him not to move. I made sure I got our bag out of the car that had our clothes in it. I knew I needed to clean myself up before I went to Baby Sister's house.

I jumped into the driver seat, put the truck in drive, and drove the truck down at the speed of 40 miles per hour at an angle down into the lake.

As I hit the water, the air bag came out due to the impact. I sat there dazed for a few minutes until I realized that the truck was slowly moving towards the center of the lake. I quickly jumped out into the waist high water.

I instantly started to cleanse myself and my hunting knife of blood in the lake. "Forgive me," I thought as I tried to wash away my sins with the lake water.

"Javion," I called out.

"Yes," Javion said at the top of the drop.

"Nothing, just making sure you there," I said.

I made my way out of the lake and to the top of the drop where Javion was. I grabbed the bag from Javion.

"Javion, turn yo head," I said.

I started to undress and put on my changing clothes.

"You ready to go see yo Grandma Champ," I asked.

"Yes," Javion responded.

"Then what we waiting on then," I said as we started our journey towards Baby Sister House, which was about a half mile away.

--

I knocked three times on Baby Sister front door and waited for a few seconds. I started to look around the porch and reminisce on how me and Javion use to look out and watch the trees against the sky.

Seconds turned to minutes of us standing at the door without a response from Baby Sister. So I knocked three more times. She still didn't answer.

I obliged.

Baby Sister sat at the table, placed her gun in front of her, and spoke:

What you seen out there with that bitch motherfucker, Imma put it like this. I can easily sit up here and tell you not to put yo hands on a woman, but I ain't gone do that. There is one thang bout a woman, if she know you a weak man, she will run over yo ass like a dump truck. You will be the doormat that she walk on every....single.....day. And the same can be said with a weak woman, like Mae. It's easy for anybody to tell you to leave a woman if she gives you a reason to put yo hands on her, but if you have kids with that woman and want to make it work, that can be tough. Now don't get me wrong, I ain't telling you to go out there beat a bitch ass for no reason, just because she is breathing. But if a woman ever challenge yo manhood and want to step to you like a man, she need to be treated like a man. If she don't want to be treated like a man, she ought not to be acting like one. You see, bitches get away with this victim shit too much, like they ain't never in the wrong. If a bitch spit in yo face, how many people you know gone walk away from that. Respect is everything, you hear me Amel. It is everything. If nobody respect you in yo own house, then how can you expect somebody outside of yo house to respect you? See that nigga who I just put them bullets in thought I was a weak woman, but look at that motherfucker now. That bitch gonna die a slow death. But you be a good man Amel, you hear me, not no weak man. Remember that respect is earned. Give yo family a reason to respect you.

--

"I hear ya," I said.

"Don't hear me. Listen," Baby Sister said pointing to her ear.

"Ok," I said.

We stood there for a moment as I watched Baby Sister staring at her gun.

"Why not end it now," Baby Sister said. "Just end the pain, end the struggle,"

I turned my attention to her.

"Because it's not yo time yet," I said.

"Says who," Baby Sister asked.

"Says God Baby Sister," I pleaded.

Baby Sister leg started to shake. She was getting anxious.

Then her leg stopped shaking. She looked at me and smiled.

"The devil stay business don't it," Baby Sister said.

I gave off a weird smile.

"Says God Baby Sister," Baby Sister mocked me grinning.

We both burst out into laughter.

"Amel, do me one favor," Baby Sister asked.

"What's that," I asked.

Baby Sister placed her hand on mine.

"Don't ever forget me, you hear me," Baby Sister said.

"I won't," I said.

"Naw promise me that," Baby Sister insisted.

I took some time to think about it.

"I promise," I said still looking down at the table. "Well me and Champ bout to hit this road. I gotta get him ready for school,"

I walked in Baby Sister's bedroom, reached into my pocket and pulled out the wad of money I had gotten from Tough Cat. I counted out 2 thousand dollars and put it in Baby Sister's purse on the bed.

"You ready Champ," I asked Javion.

"Yes," Javion said.

"Let's ride then," I said.

Chapter 23

After catching a ride from Mr. Lim from Bear Ridge that night, the next morning Javion and I found ourselves on Sea'Sea's door step. I knocked three times on the front door of the light green trailer house with Javion attached to my side. I was hoping that Sea'Sea wasn't at home. I didn't want no dealing with that motherfucker.

"Who is it," I heard a voice coming to the door.

"Fuck," I thought. I knew it was Sea'Sea.

Sea'Sea opened the door and stared at me for a few seconds with a disgusted look on her face. It was obvious that her once likings for me had grown into hate. Her belly had grown even more since the last time I had seen her. Although I had a grudge against her, deep within my heart I missed her being a part of my life and apart of Javion's life too.

"Hey Lightbread," Sea'Sea said to Javion. "How you been,"

"Good," Javion said with a smile as he shyly hid behind my leg.

Sea'Sea took her eyes off of Javion and placed them back on me. Instantly her smile turned right back into a "fuck you, have a nice day" look.

"Ma, somebody at the door for you cuz he can't be here for me," Sea'Sea said to Jackie in the back room.

"Who it is," Jackie said.

"Come and see," Sea'Sea yelled.

"Who it is got dammit, I'm trying to mop, shit," Jackie yelled back.

"It's Amel," Sea'Sea yelled.

"What he want," Jackie yelled.

"I don't know. He won't say," Sea'Sea yelled.

I stood at the front door looking down at the ground. Sea'Sea dared not to invite me into her home after how I did her.

"Amel, what you need baby," Jackie asked as she looked at me with a face full of confusion. It was clear that she was higher than a giraffe's pussy.

"I want to buy that Mustang out there," I said.

"That old Mustang ain't no mo good. The only thang good bout it is the inside and hell, you can't drive that," Jackie said.

"I know but I still want to buy it though. How much you want for it," I asked.

Jackie placed her hand on her chin and looked down as she started to think about a price.

"20,000 dollars, cash money," Jackie said as she quickly looked up and snapped her fingers with her best price.

"Ain't no way I'm giving you 20,000 dollars for a car that's been sitting up for ten years. I ain't even giving you 1,000 dollars for it. I'll give you 750, cash money right now," I offered.

"Mane you must be out yo got damn mind talking bout some 750 dollars. The damn hood of the car worth that damn much," Jackie responded.

"Sold," Sea'Sea said as she tried to snatch the money out of my hand but I quickly moved my hand out of the way.

I looked at Sea'Sea with a hard stare. Sea'Sea raised her middle finger two inches away from my nose. I then looked back at Jackie.

"Oh no. I ain't given that car away for no 750 dollars. Child please," Jackie said.

"But I got cash money, right here right now. This party money here. I know, like you know, that you like to party," I said.

Jackie paused and stared into space, clearly stoned out of her mind.

"You sho ain't lying. Ok, give me 850 and we can call it a deal," Jackie said.

"Deal," I said.

I turned my back to Sea'Sea and Jackie, looked around to make sure no one was watching me, and counted out 900 dollars. I knew Jackie was going to be sold on having a party with the money. That could be a couple weeks' worth of crack.

"What you turning yo back for like somebody want yo damn money. You ain't got shit nigga that nobody want," Sea'Sea yelled with an attitude.

I glanced at Sea'Sea over my shoulder while I was recounting my money.

"Sea'Sea quit it got dammit. The boy got money so shut yo damn mouth," Jackie yelled.

"Ain't nobody stunning bout that nigga money or that stupid ass car," Sea'Sea snapped.

"Hush yo damn mouth right now Sea'Sea. Just hush," Jackie demanded. Jackie didn't want to lose the money.

"Here is 850 and another 50 just because," I said.

"Well thank you Amel. That's sho nuff nice of you," Jackie said as her face lit up like a kid in a candy store.

"No problem. But look Imma come by damar and get the car, aight. So be looking for me," I said.

I looked at Sea'Sea as she just stared at me with curious eyes. I knew exactly what she was thinking and the questions that had to be running through her mind. I knew she was thinking that something wasn't quite right and was questioning where I got that kind of money from. She knew I had my hand in something wrong, she just needed time to figure it out.

"Damn Sea'Sea," I thought. Sea'Sea's pregnancy was doing a number on her. Her face was three times the size it had been and acne was taking over every inch of it. I noticed that Sea'Sea's clothes looked dirty, her skin looked nasty, her hair looked thin and was packed with dandruff, and I could smell her body odor from where I was standing. I also noticed the unlabeled Clorox jugs that I assumed were filled to the top with pump water.

"If I give her some money she gone thank we cool and we ain't cool," I thought. As I looked at Sea'Sea, she instantly snapped out of her dazed and slammed the door violently in my face. I could hear her say "I can't stand that motherfucker"

I stood at the front door and started to think. I knew that Sea'Sea's judgment of me was fair and my handling of her was fair too, since she was pregnant by my father. I was caught in a flux between wanting to help her and not wanting to help her. I thought it would make me look like a sucker for helping her but on the other hand, not helping her would make me feel like a bad hearted person.

"Go play in the yard," I said to Javion. Javion ran and started playing with an old bike in the front yard. "Don't hurt yoself on that bike aight,"

Javion nodded to say ok.

I walked off of the front porch and went to the hose that resided on the side of the trailer. I tried turning the water on but no water flowed out. "I knew how she smelled that their water was off," I thought.

I made my way back to the front porch. I turned my back to the door, looked around to make sure no one was watching me, and counted out 3,000 dollars.

I knocked three times on the door.

"Who is it," Sea'Sea said.

"Amel," I yelled.

"Ma, Amel want you again," Sea'Sea said.

Jackie opened the door with white residue on her nose.

"You must want to give me some mo of that money," Jackie said with a chuckle.

"Tell Sea'Sea to come to the door," I said.

"Sea'Sea come to the door, Amel want you," Jackie yelled.

"What he want," Sea'Sea yelled.

"I don't know shit. Hell I'm trying to get high and yall fucking it up. Bring yo ass to the door," Jackie said.

Sea'Sea slowly made her way to the front door. She looked at me and rolled her eyes.

"What," Sea'Sea asked smacking her mouth and looking at me sideways.

"Here," I said as I handed her 3000 dollars. "Count that,"

"Why I need to count it for," Sea'Sea asked.

"See if it's enough to get yall water cut back on," I said.

"This ain't no motherfucking pitty party. Don't you dare try to come up here and pull this shit, acting like we cool or something. Nigga we ain't cool," Sea'Sea yelled.

"Count the fucking money," I said looking her in the eyes without cracking a smile. She knew I was about business.

Sea'Sea reluctantly started to count the money. She looked up at me after counting every other 100 dollar.

"What I need all this for," Sea'Sea asked.

"Buy you some shit I guess," I said.

"I can't cuz I know this blood money, I can see it in yo eyes," Sea'Sea said.

"Its green money and it spend the same. Is that enough though," I asked.

"See, now I'm confused. You bring yo ass in here and drop me off 3 stacks like it ain't nothing. What you want from me, Amel. I ain't getting into no bullshit," Sea'Sea said.

"I don't want shit from you, guuyyyyyyyy damn. You see what I'm talking bout. See that's why I don't fuck witcha no mo. You too fucking stupid. I should....," I said.

"You should what nigga. You should what Amel," Sea'Sea immediately said pointing her finger in my face. "What you gone do. Stick a knife to my throat and finish what you started last time. Or you gone kill me like you did that nigga you got that money from cuz I know you ain't just stumble up on that kind of money,"

I stood there with a cold stare. I knew it wasn't in me to kill her. But I knew that if it was anybody else, I would have been buried this motherfucker.

"Something done got into you and you just ain't the same no mo. You ain't the same. You act like you crazy, like you done lost yo mine or something," Sea'Sea said.

"I ain't got to be the same to give yo ass some motherfucking money," I said getting angry. "If you don't want the money just throw the shit away, I don't give a fuck. I don't want it. So take it or throw it away my nigga," I said as I started to walk off the porch.

"Come on," I said waving my hand to Javion.

Sea'Sea stared at me as I walked almost to the end of the street.

"Well…. I guess…… Thank you," Sea'Sea yelled from her front porch. She waited for me to turn around and acknowledge her but I never did. "Ole crazy ass," she whispered as she closed the door with her face dominated by a slight smile. She knew deep down that I still cared for her despite our differences. She could see a small glimpse of light in me that gave her hope to think that one day we would reunite and be just regular ole Sea'Sea and Amel again.

Chapter 24

"LETS GO............GO..............GO.............GO, FIGHT, WIN," the Sammie Beans High basketball cheerleaders cheered.

It was the first game of the season and the gym, the Den, smelled of popcorn and floor wax. The Den was like it always had been: hot, smelly, and packed with people. Although the high school basketball team averaged at most 2 to 3 wins a year, the people around Itta Bena loved and took pride in their Groundhogs. I had earned the starting point guard spot on the team alongside K.O., who was the star shooting guard.

"You ready Shake," Tresee Williams and James "Jumbo" Smith asked me as I entered the Den with Javion attached to my hip. They were at the concession stand getting Jumbo food as usual. I had known both boys since we met at LS Rogers Elementary in the fourth grade.

"I thank so," I said. I always had butterflies before the game, the reason why my nails were chewed off so much and the reason why I had to take a shit before each game.

"Nigga you still sorry," Tresee said. "You know you ain't better than me. You remember how I use to drop you off behind my house. Don't trip,"

"You need to wake up my boy cuz you still dreaming. I always dropped you off, always," I said making my way passed the concession stand.

In full walking stride, I stopped dead in my tracks and looked to my left and observed what was inside of the concession stand.

"Damn look at those big ol pretty eyes on that thang there. " I said of the girl in the concession stand, who happened to be the girl that had spoken to me in Mrs. White's classroom that day me and Sea'Sea were in to it. For some reason, I couldn't remember her name for shit.

I had seen her around school a few times but never really paid attention to her like that.

Before I could look away, she caught me staring at her in a daze and was now staring back at me.

"Can I help you sir," the girl in the concession stand yelled across the lobby with a smile on her face.

"Is she talking to me," I thought as I nervously shook off the daze and started to walk off. My shyness was dominant when it came to people like her, well-kept and put together.

"Can I help you sir," the girl in the concession stand yelled again across the lobby still smiling. I kept walking like I didn't hear her.

As I walked in the gym, I spotted Money sitting in the midsection of the bleachers with his father, Boomer Wilson.

"My boy," I said to Money walking up. "What's up with it,"

"My boy, my boy. Not a thang but a chicken wang on a strang," Money said.

I chuckled. "You out of control,"

Money would always watch those old 70's movies and repeat the funny phrases from them.

"What's shaken Boomer," I said. Rain, sleet or snow, Boomer was going to be there to support Money. Mostly everybody around the way admired their relationship, especially me.

"What's up Shake, you ready for tonight," Boomer asked.

I gave Boomer a pound. "Yeah, I thank I am ready,"

"Aw you ain't gone do shit. You need to start shooting the ball more Shake," Boomer said jokingly.

"Leave my boy alone. " Money said. "Say Shake, you heard bout yo girl Sea'Sea being preggo by ole boy,"

I looked over at Money with an intriguing look. I wanted to know what Money knew.

"Who is ole boy," I said.

"I ain't gone to tell you cuz I know you gone get mad like you always do when somebody try to tell you something bout Sea'Sea," Money said.

"Ain't nobody gone get mad. Who is ole dude for real though? Chill with all the playing my boy," I said.

"See what I'm saying. You already getting mad," Money said.

"Don't bring it up if you gone beat round the bush with it. What you talking bout though," I asked.

"They say she smashing AJ," Money said.

"AJ," I said.

"AJ, AJ. That boy AJ from the City. Daddy, my boy over here acting like he senile," Money said. AJ was the one that saved me from getting caught with those three blunts that dropped on the floor that day of the tornado drill a while back and the one accused of killing his father in broad daylight.

"She told me she was preggo by another dude," I said with a fake smile. I now was staring at my shoes ruminating how hoe-ish Sea'Sea was.

"Naw my boy, that's AJ baby fasho. AJ say he be over there just bout every night knocking that down," Money said.

"Somebody gots to be lying somewhere. This is what she told me my boy. This came from her mouth not mines," I said getting upset. "Yall playing games and I ain't good at playing games,"

"See daddy, I told you my boy be getting mad over anythang. The boy got issues," Money said.

"Naw, I'm good my boy. Ain't nobody mad bout nothing. All yall will be aight," I said getting up to go to the bathroom. Although I had already been through this with Sea'Sea, every time someone brought these types of things to me, it still hurt me for some reason.

"Yeah right my boy. Stop acting like don't care bout Sea'Sea," Money said.

"I don't," I said as I started making my way to the bathroom.

"I hope you got yo game face on tonight my boy," K.O. said as he passed me to sit down.

"I'm dropping off 20 dimes tonight. You just be ready to dunk on somebody my boy," I responded.

"You already know," K.O. said. "Where that boy Javion at,"

"He over there with Money," I said walking off.

I arrived at the bathroom and started to use the urinal. My mind was on Sea'Sea and how much of a hoe she was. I started to count all the niggas that Sea'Sea had been with. I figured that she had fucked just about all of my homeboys and maybe their homeboys too. I came to the conclusion that I had been avoiding on purpose, that Sea'Sea was a straight up hoe.

"Yo Amel," Tresee said with his head halfway in the bathroom.

"Nigga can't you see that I'm trying to piss," I said sounding irritated.

"Kris said come here right quick," Tresee said.

"Who," I yelled.

I flushed the urinal, passed by the sink without washing my hands, and made my way out of the bathroom to meet Tresee at the door.

"Who the fuck is Kris" I asked. "I know one thang she better not be one of those chicken heads you stay talking to," I said.

"LIES....You know Kris. Kris Wilson. She stay down the street from me. You know her. The girl that get all them awards at the awards program all the time. That Kris," Tresee said.

"Still don't know her," I said.

"Nigga just come and see what she want," Tresee said as he walked me over to the concession stand.

"May I help you sir," Kris said to me while I was standing second in line.

"Amel this is Kris. Kris, this is Amel. Yall be safe," Tresee said walking off.

"That's her name, Kris. Kris is so fucking bad. Look at that booty. Look at them eyes. She badder than Sea'Sea hands down. But I wonder what she want with me though," I thought. "I don't know what Imma say to her,"

Just by observing Kris in the concession stand, I could feel her spirit. She seemed happy and worry free. It reminded me of Javion when he was little. It was like she was a little baby living in a world filled with wolves. It was obvious that Kris wasn't poor like me and my friends. Kris had something to smile about every day and a family to look forward to.

"May I help you sir," Kris said with a smile as I moved first in line. Word was that Kris had been watching me for a couple of months and started to form a thing for me. She enjoyed watching me play basketball.

"Can you talk sir," Kris said to me, still smiling.

"Yeah. Yeah. I can talk," I shyly said, looking down at the counter.

"I know Sea'Sea gone hate me for talking to this motherfucker. But you know what, fuck Sea'Sea," I thought as I looked up at Kris.

"Yo Shake, it's time to go into the locker room, it's halftime of the girls game," Money said, coming into the lobby to find me.

"My name is Amel River. What's yo name," I said to Kris before leaving.

"Nigga would you bring yo lame ass on here. Ain't like you gone lay in between no legs anyway. Oh virgin ass nigga," Money said smiling and walking towards the locker room.

I looked out of the corner of my eyes at Money with a smirk.

"Don't worry about him," Kris said waving off Money. "But that's real cute trying to act like you don't know my name. That's real cute. I know you know me and I know you so stop acting up," Kris said to me smiling.

"Damn she act like them girls on TV. She talk like she white. She smile like she white. She act like she white. This motherfucker is straight out a movie. Straight Crobsy show," I thought cracking a smile walking off.

"Imma holla at you later aight miss lady," I said walking off.

"The name is Kris mister," Kris said with a chuckle. "Bye Amel,"

"Tresee come here," Kris pointed to Tresee to come over as she waited for me to disappear into the locker room.

"Call me, Shundra, and your boy Amel on three way tonight," Kris said. "I know you are going to hook us up, right. You better not mess this up for me,"

"You sure," Tresee said. "Cause Shake is a different kind of nigga. But that's you though,"

"What's that suppose to mean," Kris asked.

"I mean you better know what you getting into," Tresee said.

"I do. He seems nice and shy. I like that," Kris said smiling.

"Aight. Just know I warned you. I mean Shake a good dude but he got issues. Real issues Kris," Tresee insisted.

"That's fine. Now are you going to hook us up or what," Kris asked.

Tresee looked at Kris and smiled. Truth was, Tresee wanted Kris for himself but she had long put him in the friend category.

"I will make that happen if you give me those pack of skittles on the free. You know a nigga running low on cash. If you give me those skittles right there, I promise Imma have Shake on the phone tonight. Swear to God," Tresee said as Kris reached for the pack of skittles to sneak to him.

"You better not play me Tresee. I'm so serious right now," Kris said.

"I got you girl, damn. Ole buttermilk biscuit head ass girl," Tresee said.

--

I finished my bath, put Javion to bed, and started to relax in my bed, tired from the long game. I started to think about Kris from the concession stand. I couldn't stop thinking about how her eyes resembled Javion eyes so much. The innocence, the pureness, the untaintedness.

Then I felt my newly purchased cell phone vibrate on my leg.

"Yo, Who this," I answered the phone.

"Hello, this is Mrs. Appletree, I am calling looking for Mrs. River. Is she there sir," Tresee said with his voice disguised as Mrs. Appletree.

I knew it was Tresee on the phone playing, he forgot to block his phone number from showing on the caller id.

"Yes, hold on please," I said as I dropped the phone from my ear. "Baby Sister, Mrs. Appletree on the phone for you," I screamed, acting like Baby Sister was in the other room.

"Shake, nigga stop playing. You know yo momma crazy nigga," Tresee said in a low voice, now being serious.

"Hello," I said smiling.

"See nigga you play too much. You play entirely too much. Ole sandwich meat face ass boy," Tresee said.

"Oh I thought you wanted to speak to Baby Sister," I said laughing.

The phone fell silent.

"Say hey girl. Don't act like you shy now. You done begged me to get this man on this phone. Now you acting brand new," Tresee said to Kris in a joking voice.

"Hey Amel," Kris said.

My mouth flew open in shock. I didn't expect to hear that voice. I thought Jumbo was on the phone like he usual was when Tresee called. I found it ironic that I was just thinking about Kris.

"I'm going to kill you my boy," I said to Tresee.

"Don't hurt Tresee, Amel. I made him call you," Kris said. Kris had been looking forward to this since the game earlier. She had gone home, bath, did her homework, and cleaned the kitchen so she had no worries while on the phone with me.

"Soooooo.....What's up," I asked Kris in a sarcastic tone.

"Nigga what's up. Is yall gone hook up. That's what's up. I told you this nigga was lame Kris," Tresee said.

"What you mean hook up. Like a boyfriend or something," I asked.

"Naw nigga, like hooking up a PlayStation. What you thank we talking bout crazy boy," Tresee said jokingly.

"I mean, we can be cool. I don't want no girlfriend right now. Let's just be cool first then we will see what it is," I said "I ain't trying to be mean or nothing but,"

"LIES!!! Enough of the bullshit. Shake, you gone call her or what. Yall need to get off my damn phone. I got bitches to call," Tresee said.

"Hey Tresee, you know that bridge over there by yo house," I said.

"Yeah, what bout it," Tresee said.

"Drive to it. Stop, get out of the car. And jump off into that motherfucker and kill yo self my boy. You know you ain't got no bitches," I said laughing.

"You guys sure know how to curse. Jeez louweez," Kris said with concern.

"What the fuck," Me and Tresee said in unison. We both started to laugh.

"I don't see nothing funny. I mean you guys do curse quite a bit to be in our age group," Kris said with confusion. "Why is that so funny, I don't understand,"

"Oh my God, who is this we talking to," I said crying laughing. "This motherfucker sound like a robot. Talking bout, 'you guys'. It's ' yall' got dammit, not no 'you guys' "

Then Tresee and I heard the dial tone. Kris had hung up the phone.

"My boy, she serious ain't it," I said. I didn't know we could offend Kris by joking about something so minor to us.

"Mane you know Kris come from that life where she ain't like us. She don't speak like us and shit. On some upper class shit," Tresee said.

"She really like them people on TV huh. Like different and shit," I said.

"Yep. Just like them," Tresee said. "She a good girl though. Squeaky clean my nigga if you know what I mean. She squeaky clean my nigga, for real. You gotta call her,"

I paused for a second. I was scared to call her. She was a different kind of girl, way different than girls like Sea'Sea.

"Imma fuck with her," I said.

"Don't bullshit me my nigga cuz she ran me down trying to call yo ugly ass," Tresee said.

"Nigga I told you Imma fuck with her," I said.

"Well get off my phone then ole square ass nigga," Tresee said.

"Hey Tresee, last word," I said as I hung up the phone. "Last word," was a game we played amongst one another to see who would remember to get off the phone first to say those words.

I hung up the phone and apprehensively called Kris, scared to death to joke or play with her. I was scared to even talk to her like I would my other homeboys.

I dialed her number and the phone started to ring. It seemed like after every ring, my heart started to race even faster.

"Hello," Kris answered.

"May I speak to Kris," I said.

"This is she," Kris said.

"This Amel," I said.

Kris laughed at how I introduced myself.

"This is who again," Kris asked.

"This me, Amel," I repeated, not knowing she was making fun of my ass.

"You are too cute. Hey Amel," Kris said.

Kris and I conversation lasted almost an hour until it was time for me to hit the sack to prepare for the next day. I told her about Javion and she thought it was cute that I took care of my nephew the way I did. I told her a little about how I grew up and she felt compassion for me. She told me that it was something good about me that she couldn't put her finger on. I knew then that I was right about Kris, she was as innocent as a baby in a world filled with wolves. She knew nothing of my world and I found that to be comforting and awkward at the same time. I found kindness in her voice and notice how pure her spirit was towards life and others. She was the total opposite of me and I liked that. I knew that she could bring balance to my life in the mist of my struggles. I vowed to never tell her about my entire past unless I absolutely had too.

Chapter 25

"What's the key to long life," I reluctantly asked King Lee as we sat on the back porch of the old light blue shotgun house, cleaning a turtle. I thought it was a stupid question.

"Well, let's see. One, you have to put your trust in the Good Lord above. Two, you have to treat people right. Three, you have to eat your corn bread to absorb all that grease from these foods now a days. And you have to have a little bit of luck too along the way too," King Lee said.

"It can't be like talking bout it though," I said.

"It is harder than it sounds for sure. We both know firsthand that life can be hard on us, but those are just the three principals of life that I live by. Understood," King Lee said.

I nodded to say I understood.

"Hey King Lee, tell me that story bout yo daddy again. I know you done told me that story bout a hundred times but I just can't get enough of it," I asked. From my time living with him, King Lee told me stories about the past, his past. I loved his stories.

"Which story you want to hear," King Lee said. "You know I have many stories,"

"The one bout him getting caught in them white folks house," I responded getting excited.

"Oh, that story," King Lee said with a chuckle. "See, my daddy was a crazy ole high yellow man. Short, rough little something nother. And you talking about somebody that can beat some tale, boy let me tell you something. We were scared to even move around him,"

"I thought he was Indian," I said. King Lee turned and looked at me.

"He was an Indian, a Cherokee Indian. But if your skin wasn't pure white in those days, you were just a nigga still. Didn't matter what you were. An Indian, Mexican, them Arabs, you were still a nigga, the lowest of the low," King Lee said as he started to throw the turtle to the ground trying to crack its shell.

"Hot damn, that damn thing cut my finger," King Lee said in reaction to the cracked turtle shell cutting his finger as he picked it up to slam it to the ground again.

"Anyhow, my daddy practiced something he called The Third Degree, a strange form of black magic that can be used to read a person energy and vibe; and used to control a person thoughts, dreams, healings, among other things. Some said that it's the key to a long life and some say it's the key to insanity. But you know, my daddy use to say when we were little that he could see our dreams and sometimes told us exactly what we had dreamed about. He knew what we were feeling. And we never, not one time, went to the doctor. As a matter of fact I never been to the doctor," King Lee said.

"How could he tell though? You know, what yall was dreaming bout and thanking bout and stuff," I said with deep interest.

"It's here," King Lee said, pointing to my left eye. "There is where yo thoughts and dreams are developed. There is where the mind gets what it needs to think and to make a decision,"

I sat there like a kid listening to the greatest story on earth. These kinds of talks gave me chills and eagerness to want to know more about The Third Degree every time I heard the story.

"If you can trick and manipulate the mind into believing in something, then you can control the mind, its thoughts and dreams just like magic, only this magic can sometime be a matter between living and dying. We all have the power to control people souls, their destinies, if we learn to believe in the principals of The Third Degree," King Lee said. "What you choose to see and believe, will determine whether you have complete control over your own dreams, destiny and thoughts,"

King Lee started to gut the turtle with his pocket knife. The two of us started to watch the sun set from the back porch.

"Do you ever practice The Third Degree," I asked.

"I do, but I don't abuse it's powers. Few know of it so it's a sacred type of thing, passed down from generations to generations," King Lee said.

"Can you show me if it's real or not," I asked.

King Lee looked at me.

"So, you don't believe that it's real or that my word is good," King Lee asked.

"I mean...," I said with doubt.

Out of nowhere, King Lee sliced my arm with his pocket knife. Blood started to spew everywhere.

"Got damn King Lee. What the fuck mane," I yelled.

"Just trying to show you that it's real, that's all. Now pay close attention," King Lee said.

King Lee stepped down from the porch, went into the house and grabbed a bag of red clay dirt from the hills, and blew softly on the dirt while saying words I didn't understand. He then walked over to me and blew the dirt on my wound, like he was blowing a kiss.

I looked at my arm and looked back at King Lee.

"Just let it be. Let The Third Degree do its work," King Lee said as he observed my arm. He started back gutting the turtle. "But let me tell you some more about my story,"

I watched my arm carefully as King Lee began to talk. I could see the dirt circulating, like magic, in my wound although it was still bleeding.

"You listening," King Lee asked.

"Yeah I'm listening, go head," I said.

"My daddy abused the power of The Third Degree and used it to steal money from white folks. He was smart now and knew how to play it. But one day all that stealing caught up with him, like I knew it would. Because when you abuse The Third Degree, something bad will almost certainly follow your actions. It was meant to be used with good intent," King Lee said while I was looking at him like I was watching a movie.

"So, one day my daddy decided he wanted all those white folks money, not just some, but all of it. He wanted to make his move while they ate supper. Don't you know the day before this little slick devil boiled a black cat all day long until a wishbone floated to the top of the water. You know those wishbones have power too, but that's that evil stuff. He performed a ritual on that wishbone and every time he put that wishbone in his mouth, my daddy disappeared," King Lee said with animation.

"No way," I said, still intrigued by the story even though I heard it a thousand times before. It was something about the past that made me use my imagination in a unique way. I could visualize every moment.

"I'm telling you now, that's what happened," King Lee said, trying to convince me that he had no reason to lie.

"Those white folks that my daddy was working for were good white folks too. They treated him good, gave him work and a place to live. You know back in those days, it was rare in these parts that you would find white folks that would treat you like something. Hell most of those white folks treated the dirt on the ground better than they treated us coloreds," King Lee said.

"But anyhow, one day this slick devil got buck naked and slid that wishbone in his mouth and disappeared when he was at work for those white folks. Don't you know he walked in the house, sat at those white folks table, and started to eat dinner with them," King Lee said laughing. "Those white folks thought it was a ghost, they were scared to death. "

"Then my daddy got up and started throwing chairs and stuff. Getting violent you know. Acting a fool trying his best to make them leave that house, but for some reason they never did," King Lee said getting a bit serious.

"And you not going to believe what happened. You not going to believe me, you going to think I'm lying," King Lee said shaking his head.

"What happened," I asked with excitement.

"Before I tell you, put this turtle in the bucket over there and don't drop it, that blood attract too much dirt. " King Lee said as he handed me the turtle. I jumped back with a look of disgust. King Lee had gutted the turtle and skinned it. He was handing me a piece of skinless meat.

"Lord have mercy boy. A little blood ain't gone hurt you," King Lee said. "Now here,"

I grabbed the turtle and threw it in the bucket, almost missing it.

"Now if that turtle would have hit that ground, we would have had some problems out here, you understand," King Lee said looking at me.

I nodded to say I understood.

"What happened to your daddy after all that stuff happened in the house," I said.

"Oh yeah, you not going to believe this Amel. I'm telling you this is the God honest truth," King Lee said.

"What happened King Lee," I asked as the suspense was building.

"That damn wishbone fell out of his mouth," King Lee said with a grin.

"Oh no," I said with my hands on my head.

"Now you got a little colored man, butt naked in a white man house in front of his wife and children, with nowhere to go. You want to know what else kind of colored man was in there," King Lee said with a smile.

"What kind," I asked smiling.

"A dead colored man because those white folks beat the shit out of that ole devil and almost killed him. My daddy said he had to set in a tub of buzzer grease to numb his body because of all the pain. They damn near killed my daddy that night and you know what, he never did that no more," King Lee said laughing.

"I bet he didn't," I said laughing too.

"See I told you, when you abuse the power of The Third Degree, something bad always follows. My daddy was too smart for his own good, he let the bad take over his life completely until there were no more good," King Lee said.

"So how yall end up getting down here from the hills in West Point? Didn't you say yall daddy had to change his name from Johnson to Leflore because he killed two white men in them hills," I said, hoping that King Lee would tell the story the same as before so I would know that it was still true.

"Sure did. My daddy killed those white men for trying to beat him out of his money for work he had done. See these weren't the white folks I was just talking about, these were some more white folks. Those dirty white folks that would treat you like dirt. We had to move because if we didn't, they would have killed all of us. See, back in the 30's things were much different than they are now. It was a time where white folks would kill you for just looking at them wrong," King Lee said.

"Just by looking at them wrong," I said with a look of concern. I knew I had done wrong but I never hurt nobody just for looking at me wrong. "They musta was some bad, cold hearted people huh,"

"Bad and cold hearted don't come close to describing what kind of folks they were. Now not all of them were like that, but most was," King Lee said. "For you to understand the importance of where you are now and where you are going, you must know and understand the struggles and hardships of the past," King Lee continued.

Before we got up King Lee stopped me and grabbed my wounded arm to observe it.

"Dust that dirt from your arm," King Lee insisted.

I looked at my arm and dusted all of the dirt from it.

"My arm is like you didn't even cut it," I said with my mouth open wide.

King Lee chuckled.

"How did you do that," I asked.

"The Third Degree," King Lee responded. "Do you believe now,"

"You dog gone right I do," I said looking up at King Lee in amazement. "I want you to teach it to me,"

"You are not ready yet. I will teach it to you when it is time," King Lee said.

"When will that be," I asked.

"You will have to determine that. Now let's go boil this turtle and eat it," King Lee said.

Chapter 26

With the white '69 Mustang running with a rebuilt motor and transmission that I paid $5,000 to Fish Tail, the best mechanic in the City, I shot out down Highway 7 headed to Bear Ridge to pay Baby Sister a visit again.

"What's up Baby Sister," I said as Baby Sister opened the door to let me in after my third knock. I had caught her unwinding from a long day's work of cleaning houses.

"Hey Mane. What you up to no good," Baby Sister said with a welcoming tone.

"Ole nothing. Just wanted to talk to you bout some thangs," I nervously said.

"Lord have mercy. If it ain't one thang it's another with you and yo sister," Baby Sister said with a slight chuckle.

"I want to wait til you get settle first. I know you fresh off work," I said.

"You hungry," Baby Sister asked. "I done put some gravy and onions to a coon and fixed some rice,"

"Coon," I asked. "Where you get a coon from,"

"From Bune Holloway down there on 4 mile lake. I guess he went hunting and killed a few coons and brought me one," Baby Sister said.

"I ain't eating no coon," I said in disgust.

"I told you bout acting like you sissified. I ain't raise no sissy, you hear me. Sitting up there acting like you don't eat coon. You ate it all the time when you was little. Now quit all that nonsense," Baby Sister said.

Baby Sister went to the back to take her a hot bath. I knew she would stay in the tub for at least an hour, just soaking in the damn near scorching hot bath water. I remembered how I use to bath in Baby Sister's water when I was a little boy when she was finished bathing, trying to save on the water bill.

"What you want to talk bout," Baby Sister said entering the living room with a beer in her hand.

"Just trying to see something," I said.

"Something like what. It better not be nothing crazy, I tell you that," Baby Sister said.

"It ain't," I said with a smile. "Just wanted to know how you and Ben met, that's all,"

Baby Sister paused and looked at me sideways with a sly smirk on her face.

"How me and Ben met? Where this coming from Amel," Baby Sister said as she giggled like a schoolgirl talking about a boy for the first time. "You ain't never asked me nothing bout him before like that. Why you ask now,"

I hunched up my shoulders to say I didn't know why.

"Well. Let's see," Baby Sister said with a smile trying to find a place to start telling her and Ben story. "Let me see if I can remember back that far,"

I stood on the edge of the couch and paid close attention to Baby Sister's words.

"I was 25," Baby Sister looked into the air trying to remember. "And he was, I thank 45 or 46, one of the two. But Ben was a fine man. He had the strongest arms and hands that any woman would love, you hear me. He was something Amel, he was something. You mind me of a younger him every time I see you,"

I studied Baby Sister as she spoke.

"Me and momma worked for him and his first wife. Come to thank bout it, she was a good lady too. Treated us like we was something,"

"If she was so nice then why........." I responded.

"Shut yo got damn mouth right motherfucking now before I slap you dead in it, you hear me. Now if you gone let me tell the motherfucking story, then let me tell the motherfucking story, shit. Ain't nobody asked you nothing, you asked me, hell. If that's the case, you tell the damn story then," Baby Sister yelled,

I sighed loudly and rolled my eyes.

"Ain't no need to be huffing and buffing and shit. You asked me to tell the story, ain't nobody asked you nothing. Now if somebody hada asked you something, you wouldn't know a got damn thang, be over there quiet and shit, like a cat got yo tongue,"

"Go head and tell the story, guy'lee," I insisted.

"Anyhow," Baby Sister said as she rolled her eyes. She smiled at the flash of memories that sparked in her head. "His wife was a good woman to us but I guess she wasn't treating him right cuz he came flying to me. Flying, you hear me,"

"This motherfucker crazier than a bat," I thought.

"We had a good time together. The sneaking around, the meet up spots, all THAT was a turn on for me. I guess it was the fact that he was older, and he wanted me, that got my juices flow,"

"Now I don't need to know nothing bout no juices flowing," I said with a chuckle.

"Hush yo mouth boy," Baby Sister said smiling as she slapped me on the arm. "But Ben, when we was having fun, he was the best thang that happened to me. But when we started to have problems, he was the worst thang that happened to me. You know when you first meet somebody, it be fresh to you. They treat you nice, you treat them nice, it's new, you know. But when you start getting use to each other, that's when all hell breaks loose then. That's what happened to me and Ben,"

"You thank Ben ever loved me," I asked Baby Sister.

"I can't answer that. That's something you got to ask him," Baby Sister responded.

"You thank he ashamed of me," I asked.

"I don't know," Baby Sister responded.

"Sometimes I wonder is it me or was it something I did, you know. Let me ask you this Baby Sister. Why you thank Ben act like he don't know me," I asked as I looked on in anticipation. Baby Sister could sense that I was trying to get at something. She didn't know how much I knew about how her and Ben relationship ended.

Baby Sister looked over her shoulder and out the opened back screen door.

"I done some bad thangs in my life Amel, thangs that I ain't proud of. Thangs that I keep to myself, that bother me sometimes," Baby Sister said.

"Me too Baby Sister," I said.

"But some thangs just meant to happen the way they do and people get hurt. I'm talking bout good and innocent people get hurt too. It ain't right but...," Baby Sister said staring at the table. "My heart hurt for some of the thangs I done. My heart is heavy, too heavy sometimes,"

I stood there shaking my head to say I understood. I knew Baby Sister had deep secrets, I just didn't know how deep. I knew that the conversation about Ben was over. I could feel Baby Sister's mood change to sadness and sensed she didn't want to talk about it no more. I didn't want to tell her that I was going to pay Ben a visit soon so I jumped conversations.

"What bout yo momma though," I asked.

"What bout her," Baby Sister asked.

"I been wanting to ask you what really happened to her too. You never talk bout her, so I wanted to ask you bout it," I said.

"Pass me a beer outta there," Baby Sister said pointing to the refrigerator. "And pass me my bacca off that bed in there too. And my spit bottle off the floor by the bed,"

I got up and did what she asked.

Baby Sister paused as she bit off a chunk of tobacco and took a big gulp from her beer. I knew she never explained the story of her mother, Bunny Sue, to anyone, nor did she disclose the details about her journey that followed her mother's death.

"I mean...damn Amel," Baby Sister said with a smirk on her face "You asking some tough questions, ain't cha,"

I awaited the story with a serious stare.

"Well," Baby Sister said as her eyes glazed the floor. She paused again. It was like she was visually seeing her thoughts.

"I mean you don't have to talk bout it if you don't want to. I understand," I said. I could tell she was becoming a little uneasy. I knew when not to push her too far.

"Naw, you need to hear this. I need to get this out my system. It's bout time for me to lift this burden off me," Baby Sister said.

"My momma was a good woman, you hear me. You best believe everybody knew Ms. Bunny Sue, let me tell you honey. A jack of all trades she was," Baby Sister said with a chuckle. "She cooked, cleaned, and cared for her children the best she could. I watched her help people in them cotton fields when we didn't have a dime to our name, you hear me. I watched her beat the shit out people in them cotton fields who had the nerve to want to try her too. She didn't take no shit from nobody, NOBODY, you hear me. But her heart was good as gold. Good as gold, you hear me," Baby Sister said looking at me in the eyes.

"You see, momma came from good stock, good decent folk that was well off," Baby Sister said.

"She came from money," I asked with a confused look.

"Sho did, momma came from a family with money, real money. Not that bullshit you see niggas round here talking bout," Baby Sister said.

"Then why in the hell we living like we been living then," I thought, wanting to believe Baby Sister but at the same time was confused about where all this so called money was.

"She was a show stopper now. Let...me...tell...you. Babbbyyy, momma had five mink coats, five silk dresses, ten pairs of fine shoes, and get this, had the purses to match. She was sharp as a tack. She had these thangs even when we was living out there across them cotton fields.

But I know you wondering how did she end up across those cotton field ain't cha," Baby Sister said.

"Yep," I said with a look of pure interest.

"Momma first ole man, Dank, did her like a dog. He was a no good motherfucker, something like that Joseph over there with Mae," Baby Sister said.

"How old was he," I asked.

"They say he was bout 40 something and momma was 14 or 15," Baby Sister said.

"Guuuyyyy'lee. She was just a lil girl," I said.

"Oh boy people was marrying at 13 back then. But they say Dank did momma real bad you hear me. They say Dank use to beat momma from here to there and then had the nerve to give her a baby when she was 15. But when folks in them days was 15, they had full families so that wasn't nothing new. But she had Dankie to that man. They say that Dank took her to Chicago, pregnant and all, and left her up there with no money or nothing. See in them days, you couldn't just call back home and ask somebody to come get you when you was in trouble. Being that she came from money, they say momma had a nervous breakdown. They say she lost her mind and was never the same since," Baby Sister said.

"What you mean lost her mind," I asked.

"You know, talking to herself, pacing all the time. Just out of wack with life," Baby Sister said. "Momma had issues that she never talked bout. We knew when to leave her alone most times," Baby Sister said.

"Or what," I asked.

"What you mean or what," Baby Sister asked.

"What happened if you messed with her on most days," I asked again.

"You get yo ass beat, that's what," Baby Sister said with her eyes bucked. "A good ass whooping is what you got,"

I shook my head to say I understood.

"But how her and yo daddy meet though," I asked.

Baby Sister smacked her mouth with an ounce of anger.

"Somehow she made her way back down this way. Dankie was sent off to live with his daddy folks in California, and momma caught a ride from Chicago to Bear Ridge to live with her sister Annie. They say daddy started colting her and she fell for him," Baby Sister said.

Baby Sister paused and stared at the table.

"I remember when people use to laugh at momma cuz of the old clothes and bright red lipstick she use to wear out, you know, when her mind had left her. She wouldn't touch them nice clothes cuz I guess they reminded her of where she came from and she didn't want to mess those memories up. But sometimes momma would just sit up in different places, just rock back and forth, making conversation with herself, you know. And she moved a lot, her hands you know, cuz of her nerves," Baby Sister said as her eyes glazed at the ground. She was trying to keep those memories in her heart because they were the only ones she had of Bunny Sue. "But she would give the shirt off her back if you needed it more than she did,"

"But momma taught us all she could, she did her best with us. She taught us how to clean, to cook, to comb our hair, to iron, to wash, and everything else by the time we was six years old," Baby Sister continued.

"She did everything around the house and worked in the cotton field while that motherfucker was out chasing and spending all his money on a piece of pussy," Baby Sister said, getting upset.

I knew that Baby Sister resented her father, but I didn't know how deep it was until now. I just sat there and listened.

"He chose to take care of everybody else except for his own family. When them folks in them streets came calling, he ran. But when momma asked the motherfucker for a loaf of light bread, he never had no money. I remember times when momma walked fifteen miles to Belzoni to get us two sets of clothes and a pair of shoes from Old Man Billy consignment shop to wear to school. She had to walk cuz the motherfucker wouldn't take her. She fought him day and night to give to his family at home, not his family in them streets. All she wanted was him to be a man to her and he couldn't do that. He didn't teach us shit as a daddy. "Baby Sister said visibly upset now. "She wanted better thangs for us but the motherfucker wanted to stay in them cotton fields. He didn't want shit. Didn't want a motherfucking thang out of life but to chase pussy and get drunk,"

"I bet that nigga so fucking weak," I thought. I wanted to meet him so I could punch him in the face.

"How she end up dying though," I sadly asked.

Baby Sister paused yet again. This time I could see the tears forming in her glazing eyes as they were stuck looking at the floor. I never saw Baby Sister cry before.

"She disappeared without a trace," Baby Sister said.

"She disappeared," I asked.

Baby Sister looked at me and seen that I wanted to know the truth from her. It was a dark truth that she had long wanted to get off of her chest. She felt that today was the day.

"Let me stop lying. I ain't got a reason to lie to you. I know you ain't gone judge me Amel," Baby Sister said.

"Then what happened," I asked.

Baby Sister glazed back at the floor. The tears started to stream vastly down her face.

"I.........," Baby Sister said as she broke down even more.

"You what," I quickly asked. "You what Baby Sister,"

"I did it," Baby Sister yelled slamming her hand on the table.

"You did what," I asked.

"Killed her," Baby Sister screamed.

Baby Sister cried and cried. I observed her, her pain, her release.

"You killed yo own momma," I asked with a look of disbelief.

Baby Sister shook her head to say she did while she wiped tears that continued to stream down her face.

"Stabbed her in the heart," Baby Sister said in a crying mumble. "Killed the one thang that had hurt her the most,"

"Why Baby Sister? Yall couldn't have gotten her some help," I asked.

"I had too. You don't know how she was. You didn't see her like that, I did. There wasn't no helping for what she went through," Baby Sister said.

I backed off and let Baby Sister calm down some more for a few minutes.

"So did you go to jail," I asked.

Baby Sister shook her head to say no.

"I dumped her body in that river back there. Nobody was home when I did it so I cleaned up the blood before anybody came home," Baby Sister said pointing towards the river that resided behind the house. "I couldn't stand to see momma live like that, I just wouldn't stand for it. I couldn't take another minute of it, you hear me,"

"What did yo daddy do. How he take it," I asked.

"He thought she left. He didn't know how to function without momma. He cried every minute of the day for years. I bet till this day, he still hurting for her. You know they say you don't miss something good till it's gone," Baby Sister said with conviction. "But she buried in that river back there with some of them bitches he was doing her wrong with. I couldn't get them all, but I got enough. I never wanted that motherfucker to find love cuz he never showed momma any,"

"She didn't try to fight you off her or nothing. She just let you just stab her like that," I asked.

"She knew I was gonna do it like I knew what you was gonna do. It's a momma instinct I guess. It was the day she waited on her whole life. It was a day where she wasn't gone feel no more pain or heartaches," Baby Sister said. "And I told momma that her riches wasn't of this world but in the next. She had to leave this life to live the life I wanted her to have, the one I knew she deserved, you understand. She wanted to be free so I let her go on home,"

"Why not kill yo daddy instead of yo momma though," I asked.

"The only reason I ain't killed that motherfucker is because she made me make her a promise to her that I would take care of him no matter how I felt bout me. I told her I would. That was my momma, I couldn't tell her naw. But the thang is, even in her last breath, she still loved the motherfucker. That's why I ain't killed him but Lord knows it took every bone in my body not to,"

"You ain't the only one that got blood on they hands Baby Sister, I know people who done worst thangs. At least you had a reason for what you did," I intervened.

"But that was my momma Amel, you hear, MY momma. She was just as hard on me as I am on you and Melo asses. That hurt me and when I let her go on, a big piece of me went on with her," Baby Sister said as the tears again started to slowly roll down her face. She tried her best to be strong and hold them back. "I chose to kill her rather than let that motherfucker worry her to death. That's why I don't respect the motherfucker. That's my daddy true enough and God forgive me if I'm wrong, but I don't got no love for the motherfucker,"

Baby Sister held her head down and started to cry a little.

I slowly got up from my seat and tried to console her but she pushed me away.

"I don't want no pity from nobody, you hear me. I ain't no pity party," Baby Sister said as she held her hands out to keep me from trying to come near her. "I lost my momma before I was even born, you hear me. She was always hunted by her past, every single day of her life,"

"It's alright though Baby Sister," I said sincerely.

"My momma left this earth when I was 15. She was 41, hair was as white as snow from all that stress the motherfucker put her through. When she passed on, we ain't have nobody to look after us, to guide us. I ain't have no momma to ever tell me that she loved me. I ain't have no momma to ever hug me and tell me what was right and wrong. Hell I ain't have no daddy to do that either. I been struggling to love and to live my entire natural life. Misery been my company since the day she left me. You understand," Baby Sister said.

"That's why I am so hard on you and Melo. I don't want you to turn out like that motherfucker. I want you to be a good man, you hear me. I want you to take care of yo family, be there for yo family. I don't want you to let no pussy in the street fuck yo life up cuz all pussies on these bitches out here look the same, ain't nothing different bout them. Don't you be no fool for no bitch, you hear me," Baby Sister said as she wiped her eyes. "I know I ain't been the best momma to yall, but I tried

278

to give yall all that I got, the best way I know how. That was my prayer every single day, that yall turn out alright and decent. Just to be decent folk and I thank yall have,"

"Baby Sister, answer me this. Have you ever just sat down and talked to yo daddy bout his past so you could find out why he was the way he was," I said.

"What good would that do," Baby Sister asked. "Momma dead and gone now,"

"I thank it would do a lot of good, just like it's doing me a lot of good by me talking to you now. I didn't know you went through what you told me so I didn't understand you, but now I understand you a little more. You need to do it for you," I said. "Somebody told me that forgiveness is hard but forgiveness is necessary. I thank yo momma would want you to do that. A wise man told me that in order for you to understand yo life better, you must understand yo daddy life before it's too late. In order for me and Melo to forgive you for what we thank you done to us, I thank you should forgive yo daddy for what you thank he done to you," I said, moving closer to Baby Sister while I looked at her in her eyes.

"Oh, don't give me that forgiveness shit. I ain't got shit for the motherfucker," Baby Sister insisted.

"Baby Sister, you need to do this for you, not for him. Know his story like you know yo momma story. Give him a chance to speak his peace and explain his story, his life," I said. "Just talking to you have opened my eyes up to a few thangs I didn't know bout you, to tell you the truth. But now I understand you more as a person,"

Baby Sister stared at the floor.

"It ain't no overnight process, but it gots to start somewhere," I said.

"You right," Baby Sister said reluctantly.

I got up from the table and went into Baby Sister's room and returned to the kitchen table.

"I want to meet this Baby Sister cuz I never had a chance to," I said as I handed her the picture of my father and her that I always looked at as a boy. The picture captured a moment in her life when she was truly happy and feeling loved.

Baby Sister chuckled and patted my leg.

"You turned out to be alright, good hearted you know," Baby Sister said.

I smiled.

"I'm trying Baby Sister, but it's hard," I said. "But when you live in chaos for a long time it becomes you. Living happy is just like living bad. It don't seem normal,"

"See, I knew you turned out decent. I knew the day would come where you would teach me something," Baby Sister said with a chuckle. "Now, ain't that something,"

"That is something, ain't it," I said with a chuckle too.

"I will try to find the motherfucker and talk to him," Baby Sister said.

"Baby Sister," I said laughing.

"What, he still a motherfucker," Baby Sister responded with a grin.

"So, you don't know where he live at," I asked.

"Naw. I ain't seen him in over 20 or so years," Baby Sister said.

"It's bout time you find him," I said.

"I thank so too," Baby Sister said. "Let's find the motherfucker,"

We laughed out loud.

I exited Baby Sister's house with a smile and with a delighted heart. I jumped into the white '69 Mustang and grabbed my notepad and pen from my book bag.

I wrote:

Momma True Riches

I see momma hold back her tears every second of the hour that she lives

Her motives is understanding why God seems to care more for others than He does for her

Maybe life wasn't meant for everyone to live in blissful harmony everyday

Hell, the people living good seems to be the worst kind

Preachers with corrupted souls living like kings, hell I'm not judging nobody

Good hearted folk living like dogs in the bottom of the slums to fend themselves after every bill is due

Is this how life supposed to be?

Why poor folks get poorer and rich people get richer

Momma say that all riches and blessings don't come from God

Momma say being poor makes your faith stronger and gets you closer to God

Hell, no wonder momma don't mind crying

Her tears cleanses her soul of sin

She understands the meaning of living in hell on earth and what true riches are.

For she knows the true riches aren't here on earth, it is in the next life she will live.

-Shake

Chapter 27

I stepped out of the old light blue shotgun house to take the trash down the street to the field where everybody dumped their trash, to get it burned two days a week in a garbage can.

"Let me go Billy," Jasmine Wilson, Money half-sister, screamed to her husband Billy Mosely, who had her in a choke hold outside of their house in the City.

I quickly glanced their way but kept walking. I knew Billy from around the way and Billy was always good to me. I knew Jasmine from hanging tough with Money all the time.

"Help me," Jasmine said towards my way trying to catch her breath.

I continued to walk like I didn't hear her.

"Help me Shake," Jasmine repeated as Billy tightened his grip on her throat.

I looked around and seen that Jasmine eyes looked weak, like she was about to pass out.

"Yo Bill chill man," I yelled. "You choking her out,"

"Gone bout yo business Shake. This grown folks business here," Billy said.

"She can't breathe though. You can see it in her face she can't breathe," I yelled.

"She gone learn," Billy yelled.

"What she gone learn from you doing that though," I asked.

"Learn not to fuck with me," Billy said as his grip got tighter. "See you gone learn one day that being nice to these bitches, especially the one you call yo woman, ain't bout shit,"

"Naw…" I said but was interrupted.

"Get on to the house," I heard a whisper in my ear. "This isn't your business here,"

I knew it was King Lee from the peach brandy I smelled on his breathe. I obliged to King Lee's command.

I looked back. "But he gone kill her though,"

"That isn't your business, now keep walking," King Lee insisted.

The two of us walked in silence all the way to the old light blue shotgun house.

"What bout Jasmine," I asked.

"What about her," King Lee asked. "Leave that alone before you get yourself hurt. I'm going to show you the lie that you are looking for in a few minutes when it die down that way,"

"Aight,"

--

An hour passed.

"Come on, let me show you that lie you were looking for," King Lee said as he took me outside and down the road to where Billy and Jasmine were fighting earlier.

"You see that dark colored car over there," King Lee said without pointing.

"You mean that car" I said pointing towards the car. King Lee quickly hit my hand down.

"Look, don't point boy" King Lee insisted. "That's Jasmine over there with another man,"

"For real," I said.

"What? You thought Jasmine was an angel because she is nice and polite," King Lee said.

"I mean, she just don't look like the type that would be doing something like that in broad daylight," I said.

"Billy isn't a perfect man, don't get me wrong but he is a decent man, a good man. He treat her good and take care of her the way a man should," King Lee said.

"How should a man treat a woman," I asked.

"Feed her, clothe her, provide a roof over her head. That's how a man show that he loves his woman, by doing for her," King Lee said.

"So a man love comes from what he provide," I asked.

"A working man that treat a woman decent, not perfect, is a good man. There is no such thing as a perfect man. No matter how perfect you try to be to a woman, she will always find something that you are not doing. It's their nature, to want more. Men are not like that," King Lee said.

"Then why he fight her so much," I asked.

"Because he work 24/7 and don't spend enough time with her. He works hard for every penny, always has since he was a little boy," King Lee said. "Look over there in that car. That man she with gives her all the time in the world but he doesn't work. She would rather have a man that stays at home, stay under her, instead of a man that goes out and make a better life for them both. Billy is trying to get her from here but she will not let him,"

"Damn," I thought.

"How else do you want him to handle the situation," King Lee asked. "You want him to leave a woman he loves, a woman he think he can change,"

"Why not," I asked.

"Because when you love somebody it's not that easy to walk away," King Lee said. "Instead of leaving, he would rather beat the change in her, like beating a child to make them discipline,"

I looked at King Lee strangely.

"What else can he do? How else do you expect him to handle the situation? Billy never had a father to tell him better. That's his only solution, right or wrong. Who can blame him for trying to make her do right," King Lee said.

"So you saying what he did is right," I asked.

"No I'm saying look at the truth of the situation and then put yourself in Billy shoes," King Lee said. "Don't let people fool you like it's so easy to leave. That's a lie,"

I nodded my head and listened more.

"Now if that man had of killed you, she would still be in that car over there with another man, doing the same thing that got her beat in the first place," King Lee said. "And now you dead trying to defend somebody you don't even know, somebody who is going to do them regardless if you are dead or alive. "

I continued to listen.

"See that's why it's not your business. Don't die in vain Amel. Because Billy is still going to do what he wants to do and Jasmine is going to still do what she wants to do. And you are dead to the world, never more. You can't save the world from its trouble, so stop trying,"

"Ain't nothing wrong with helping people, is it," I asked.

"Just always be aware of situations. I'm not telling you not to help people. What I am saying is pick and choose carefully who you help because all people don't want help and all people don't mean you good," King Lee said.

"See it like those food stamp people," King Lee said getting angry. "Why would somebody like that change,"

"I think they would change to be better if they could," I said.

"You would think, but when somebody give you everything you need, without working for it, why would you change. There is no reason to change," King Lee said.

"As old as I am, an old man like me can't get 5 dollars in food stamps but a 20 year old with a healthy body can get $600. I paid my dues to this life. I worked for 25 years without complaint," King Lee said.

"You want to hear something strange but true Amel," King Lee asked.

"Bout what," I asked.

"About poor folks," King Lee said.

"Yeah," I said. "What theory is this,"

"The Poor Folks Theory," King Lee said.

King Lee spoke:

No matter what the circumstances are, what help you give, people will always find anyway to be poor. If you tell them you got a job for them, they will say they don't have clothes. If you say you have clothes, they will say I don't have a ride. If you say I will provide the ride for you, they will say I don't have nobody to keep my kids. You tell them that their children can go to daycare for free, they will tell you oh ok then, looking for a way out but everything they had an excuse for is given to them, for free. You say, I will be here tomorrow at 6:00am sharp, they will roll their eyes because they only wake up at 10am to watch their stories. They ask about the pay, you say it doesn't matter, it's hard earned money. They say no not really, for what that job is paying I can just stay at home. You ask, do you have an education. They say, I have my GED. You say, how much do you think you can make on a GED alone. They say, more than minimum wage, why would I give up a free phone, a light bill check, a water bill check, food stamps, without working. You think to yourself, that's interesting. They say, my momma was on food stamps, my momma momma was on food stamps, her momma was on food stamps, so why you think I'm not going to be on food stamps. Why would I work? You say, good point.

You will pitch your best ideas to convince them that working for a living is good and being lazy is bad. They will say, oh ok then.

You will say that you will, again, be there at 6am sharp, to take their children to daycare for them, to take them to work, to give them work clothes. You basically are holding success in your hands, everything they need to make a positive change in their lives is there, right in your hands.

Then the next day comes. You pull up at 5:57am, on time, excited and ready to change somebody's life, to give somebody a reason to live and take care of their children themselves. You walk up to the door proudly, with the wind to your back, and knock graciously three times on the door.

No answer.

You think to yourself, ok, they may be getting ready in the back and can't hear my knock. So you knock again, this time harder and louder, and put your ear closer to the door. You hear a TV playing in the distance and you hear movement in the house. You hear a baby crying and the sound of somebody putting their hand over the child's mouth.

Again, No answer. Then you start to feel played. You start to think, how could someone deny everything that is given to them to help them achieve a positive change in their lives. You think to yourself, it's free, why do they not want it. You think to yourself, if this was you, if you didn't have a job, you would do all you can to get a job and would welcome anybody trying to help you. But there you are, at this door, knowing that you don't make that much money either but you still get up every day, strap on your shoes, put on your clothes, and go to work like most people do.

Anger sets in your heart. Your one reason for going up to the door in the first place is now blinded by what is growing in your heart.

Despite your growing feelings, you are a reasonable person, you knock again, this time harder and louder than before.

In your heart, you know that this lazy piece of shit, pardon my language Amel, won't answer the door, but you want them too, to take advantage of all that you hold in your hands.

Then you move to the closest window, just curious of what is inside, and look through the blinds. You see them, with their children, on the couch, flipping through the channels, intentionally ignoring your knocks. Content with the future before them and content with the repeated future for their children.

Now you are at odds with yourself. A part of you is saying fuck'em, pardon my language again. The other part of you is saying, just knock one more time for hope sake. Maybe a miracle will happen.

You knock three more times, this time mildly, knowing it's a 99.3% percent chance that they won't open the door.

Then hope shows it's face. A dead situation manifested itself into a miracle.

You hear footsteps walking towards the door, not with the intentions of getting what you have in your hands, but irritated that you keep knocking at their door so early in the morning.

You can feel the irritation in their breathing, it's clear you are bothering them and their current work life of nothingness.

Then the door opens. You can see the invisible fork in the road before them. You know they can take the right path or the wrong path, but in your heart you know exactly what path they will take, like most of their kind take.

You say with a somewhat angry smile, I have all the things you need to be successful in my hands, your future is bright, it's free to you, no worries, I just need you to get up, put on these clothes, get the kids ready, and Let's start this journey together.

They say, I don't want help anymore.

You say why.

They say because I don't. I don't need help so leave.

You ask what happened between yesterday and today.

They say it doesn't make sense to work. As you anticipated they would say.

You ask, what do you mean.

They say they have everything that they need to survive without ever having to work.

You ask, what about your future and what about the example you are setting for your kids.

They say, what about it.

Now your understanding deepens, the anger in your heart deepens. The fact that you knew it was a losing battle before you even pulled up to their house, gives you less hope for the future. Because this house, like the hundreds of thousands of houses you pulled up to before, gave you the same exact answer, acted the same exact way, had the same outlook on their children future and wellbeing.

Then the hatred grows slowly but everlasting in your heart because you know that you left your wife and children in bed at 4am in the morning, with hope of changing some lazy person life who refuses to work. You know that food is barely in your refrigerator, you are barely making ends meet, even though you and your wife work a 9 to 5, but hope and fear motivates you to drive to their houses. The fear is that you know that their children will one day have to interact with your children. The hope is that you know that if you somehow change their lives, then you will change an entire generation life going forward.

Then your understanding deepens even more. The fact that deep down in your heart you know it doesn't matter who they are, the more you give unsolicited tools to people, the more they will turn away from it. The more free stuff you give people, the more content they will be without having a future and without having dreams to chase after.

--

"You understand that," King Lee asked.

"That's deep King Lee," I said.

"But you know how they can solve that problem. " King Lee said.

"How," I asked.

"Make them work like those inmates work. Pick up paper on the side of the road, work on the farms, work for the government, for free," King Lee said. "That's all it will take and their lazy butts will get a paying job then,"

"I know they will," I said.

"Always work for what you want and never wait on nobody to give you anything, you hear me," King Lee said.

"I hear you," I said.

"Life is an everlasting door Amel, there are no guarantees. Work hard for what you want in this life. Die trying to take care of your family the right way. Die trying to protect your family from falling into these traps of life. Most importantly, die trying to instill good values in your family. Change somebody world just by you being the change you think the world needs," King Lee said as he patted me on the shoulder. "You will be just fine, it's in you,"

Chapter 28

"Mr. Dandress, my man," I said as I shook hands with Mr. Dandress and entered Itta Bena's new rotary club, located across the railroad tracks, by the town's library, on the white folks side of town.

"Is it this way," I asked.

The two of us had struck a deal that would allow me to sneak into the rotary club, unpronounced to anyone except for me and Mr. Dandress. Even though the event was opened to the "public", me and Mr. Dandress both knew what "public" meant in the scope of things, "no poor folks allowed". In order to solidify our deal, I had to cook Mr. Dandress three filets of catfish, spaghetti, hot water cornbread, and make some grape kool aid to flush the food down.

I knew Mr. Bo Dandress from the City. He was an older fellow, in his late 70s that always kept a clean cut with a freshly creased white dress shirt, flawlessly creased black slacks, a black top hat, and the cleanest white church shoes ever worn. Mr. Dandress had known me ever since I moved in with King Lee. I helped him out around his yard and brought him food that I cooked from time to time. People around the way said Mr. Dandress use to be a motherfucker with the ladies back in the day and it showed.

"Just round that corner. And young blood," Mr. Dandress said.

"Sir," I replied with respect.

"Just don't bring too much attention to yoself. I don't want you getting into no trouble, you hear. These white folks ain't gone have no mercy on you so don't start nothing," Mr. Dandress said.

"Yes sir. Preciate it Mr. Dandress," I said as I made my way to the auditorium.

Before I entered the auditorium I stopped, took a deep breath, and looked inside. I had never been around so many important people before in my life. Everything reminded me of movies I had seen on television.

I was dressed to the tee with a fresh red t-shirt tucked neatly in my black jeans with my old white and black gangsta Nikes on. My hair was crisply cut into a high top fade with a duck tail at the back.

I stood nervously on the side wall of the auditorium, mid crowd, so everyone could see me, including the honoree. I could feel the awkwardness and silent chatter in the room. It seemed like all eyes were glazing my way with the intent to pass judgment.

"Evening everyone," Jessie Dodd said with a smile as he started to speak to the crowd of about 90 people. "I would like to say that it is indeed a pleasure to stand before you today on such a glorious occasion. We all know why we are here. The man that we are celebrating tonight is the epitome of what it means to be a great family man, to be a great father, to be a great integral part of this community. I have never seen anyone care for others like this man does for family or just people in general. He is indeed one of a kind. Hence, this is why he is our man of the year. Without any further a due, ladies and gentlemen, I present to you, our man of the year, my friend, our friend, Ben Fisher,"

The audience stood to a roaring standing ovation. All were dressed in their best formal attire, far from what I had on. All were considered the high class amongst the poor folks, the ones that stuck their noses up at people from the City and people from other less fortunate places around town.

Ben approached the podium with a smile 7 miles wide. He carefully observed the room. First Ben nodded to his wife, Mary Fisher, son Jacob Fisher, and daughter Belle Fisher. He surveyed the room to make sure all the powerful political players were in the audience and they were.

As he continued to survey the room, looking briefly into the eyes of everyone, he caught eyes with me.

Ben smile turned to worry as I could see him began to sweat like a pig in heat. It was like he could see the death of his potential career in my eyes. Ben opened his bottled water and gulped it down hard two times.

Ben finally snapped out of his nervous trance after a few seconds, took a deep breath and calmed down.

"The meaning of what it means to be a great man," Ben said into the microphone.

I laughed out loud as I shook my head. Everyone in the room sighed loudly, including Ben who was shocked by my outburst like everyone else was. I could feel all eyes on me and I could hear the chatter again, but I didn't care. I wanted to make my presence be felt.

Mr. Jake Johnson from the City, who was ushering the event, walked over to me and whispered "Don't start no bullshit you hear. These white folks will hang yo little black ass from them rafters and you know that. Now quit. Now this my last warning,"

 Mr. Johnson looked around and gave a fake smile to the audience as to say he had the situation under control.

I nodded in agreement. "Sorry bout that Mr. Johnson. He just fake, that's all," I whispered.

"Son, I don't give a damn bout that. You need to quit or leave. I'm just looking out for yo own good now. You understand," Mr. Johnson responded in a whisper.

I nodded in agreement.

The room took about five minutes to settle down. Ben waited on everyone to come to a complete silence before he continued on with his speech. He was so uncomfortable standing up there that he had to loosen his tie a bit and unbutton the top button of his dress shirt.

"The meaning of what it means to be a great man," Ben said cutting his eyes at me. Everyone looked at me to gauge my reaction. I didn't say anything. I smiled and shook my head in amazement.

"If only these motherfuckers knew. But they gone find out today though," I thought.

Ben delivered his speech not like he intended. The usually profound and powerful speaker sounded timid and nervous. I noticed that every time he looked up at the audience from reading his speech, his eyes would connect with mine.

An hour passed of Ben talking bullshit about the importance of being a man, the importance of family, his belief in the Good Lord above, and his mission forward.

Ben finished his speech to the tune of a roaring ovation. The speech reassured all in the audience that Ben was the apple of their eyes. Ben knew he couldn't do any wrong in their eyes, he was their golden child, their next big political player.

Three weeks prior, Ben had made national news with his "brave," efforts of fighting against teenage pregnancy, obesity, and poverty, three things that plague the Mississippi Delta the most. With his efforts, Ben had gotten the attention of Washington most powerful Republicans, the party which he was affiliated with.

But the one thing that could hurt Ben's political dreams the most, he wanted to keep a secret. However, his secret was standing right dead in the middle of the room.

Ben started to make his rounds around the room as usual, to shake everyone hands especially Senator Conrad Smith, who flew in from Washington just for the event.

"This motherfucker dodging the shit out of me," I thought from afar as I noticed Ben avoiding me on purpose because every time I would walk in Ben's direction, Ben would walk the other way.

"Let me get a picture with you, the wife and children," I overheard the photographer say to Ben and his family from about 20 feet away. The camera man from the local news was also there to get footage of the grand night.

I hastily approached the family and proceeded to get into the picture like I was the missing piece to the family's puzzle.

"Excuse me," Ben said. "Do I know you,"

I chuckled as Ben wife and kids all gave curious looks.

"I thought the camera man said the wife and children," I responded, ready to make my presence felt once again. I wanted to kill Ben, but with a different approach.

Ben grabbed me by the arm and took me to the side, not trying to make a scene. For he knew his future political career hung in the balance.

"What are you doing," Ben asked. "Who paid you to do this,"

"Nobody put me up to this. I wanted to watch you get yo award," I said with a sinister smirk.

"Now you have seen me get it, now leave. PLEASE," Ben insisted.

Ben hurried back to his family.

I politely walked back over to the family and posed to take the photograph again.

"Ben seriously, who is this," Mary said getting frustrated.

Ben charged at me and pushed me down to the ground. I didn't try to fight back, I wanted everyone to see their golden boy in action.

"Ben what are you doing," Mary asked.

"I TOLD YOU TO LEAVE. NOW LEAVE GOT DAMMIT," Ben yelled.

I got up and smiled.

"Ok," I said. "If you want me to leave and not take a picture with my brother and sister, then I will,"

"Brother and sister," Mary yelled. "What a minute Ben. What is this boy talking about,"

"I don't know what this boy is talking about and who he is. He must be crazy," Ben said with frustration.

"Ain't nobody crazy. Don't I look just like him," I asked pointing to Ben.

"Is this true Ben," Senator Smith said as the crowd started to gather around.

"This is my family," Ben yelled pointing to his wife and two children. "I don't know this boy,"

Ben stood silently. It was like he was reflecting hard on what was going on. He could not believe that this was going on, especially in front of Senator Conrad.

"How old are you young man," Mary asked with curiosity.

"15," I responded.

"I see. So Ben," Mary said as she folded her arms and looked at Ben with a "you better not lie," look. In her mind, she was doing the math. They had been happily married for 22 years but they both were in their mid 60's. "Is this black boy your son,"

Ben cut his eyes at me and then charged at me like a bull. Senator Conrad grabbed him. "Ben, let it go. It's not worth it,"

"You gone have some respect for her and everybody in here, you hear me boy," Ben yelled.

"Yeah like you had respect for my momma. You don't want these problems over this way man of the year,"

Mary eased behind Ben with fear.

Ben and I continued to exchange words until we were separated by Mr. Johnson.

"Didn't I tell yo ass not to start no trouble," Mr. Dandress said as he approached me while Mr. Johnson held me. "What you thank you doing. You trying to get yoself in jail or killed, huh,"

"He fake Mr. Dandress," I said holding back my tears. "He know he my daddy but he don't want nothing to do with me. All I want is for him to tell people I'm his son, that's it,"

Mr. Dandress looked into my eyes and seen the hurt in them. He knew I was a boy searching for answers, the same as he probably did when he was a boy.

"Ok. Alright," Mr. Dandress said as he patted me on the shoulder. "Jake let him go. He need to get this off his chest,"

Mr. Johnson slowly let me go.

"Ben, is this your son or what," Mary asked in a high pitch, increasingly feeling more and more embarrassed as a bigger crowd started to gather.

"NO IT IS NOT MARY. This is just somebody who wants to get us for some money. I don't know this boy, I'm telling you the Gods honest truth," Ben pleaded with my wife. I could see in her eyes that she was starting to believe him over me. "BOY, GET YOUR NIGGA ASS OUT OF HERE AND LEAVE I SAID,"

Ben charged through his retainers and grabbed me by the shirt but I snatched away violently. I too was growing frustrated of the situation.

"I got yo motherfucking nigga. And you wasn't calling my momma no nigga when you was fucking her, now was ya. Having a baby by the motherfucker that cleaned yo nasty ass toilets. You ain't shit nigga. Out here acting like you all that," I yelled.

Ben grabbed me by the neck violently and threw me to the ground. He started to punch me over and over again. It was like he wanted to kill me for good. I sat there wanting to kill Ben but I gathered strength to control myself. I wanted to stick to my original plan.

"Ben are you crazy. Are you trying to destroy your chances to get on the Hill," Senator Smith said as he grabbed Ben. "You do know that is a child you are fighting,"

"I don't care. I'm just sick of this," Ben screamed.

"Naw, let him kill me. He don't care bout me no way. This is yo man of the year though. Now give him a standing ovation now," I screamed as I stood up. I had tears in my eyes and blood running from my mouth. This was the most attention I had ever gotten from my father, whether it was good or bad, and somewhere deep down, that made me feel ok, it gave a small connection to him. Just the touch from Ben meant something, whether it was punches or hugs, it didn't matter. "You right though, that is yo family. It's always been yo family and I always been the mistake. You ain't never loved me. You ain't never been there for me. I ain't never been good enough for you to call me yo son,"

The crowd started to chatter amongst themselves. They all knew I was speaking with a sense of familiar truth, they could feel the sincerity and hurt in my voice.

"Come on son," Senator Smith said. "Let's go outside,"

"I ain't going nowhere," I yelled. "Tell yo wife how you use to call my momma all the time and lie like you was coming to spend time with me. TELL HER,"

Ben stood there with his head down, clearly embarrassed and knowing that his political career had taken a turn for the worst. Having a child out of wedlock in the Bible Belt meant instant political suicide.

"Who is your momma young man," Mary calmly asked.

"Why do it matter anyway," I asked. "Yall acting like yall don't believe me, so what's the point,"

"We do believe you, that's why I am asking," Mary said. She avoided eye contact with Ben and focused all her attention on me. "Go ahead and tell me who your folks are,"

I thought about it and decided to tell her.

"Baby Sister," I said.

"I'm sorry," Mary said.

"My momma name is Baby Sister," I repeated.

"Baby Sister? Baby Sister River? Augusta River you mean," Mary asked.

"Yeah, Bunny Sue daughter," I said.

Mary quickly looked at Ben with anger in her eyes.

"You had a baby by Bunny Sue daughter? The maid Bunny Sue," Mary yelled, trying to stay classy and keep her composure.

Ben stared at the ground and sucked his teeth, speechless.

I wasn't finished talking though. I wanted to air out all of Ben's dirty laundry. I wanted to destroy his life like he had destroyed mine by not being there and disowning me.

"Ask Ben about Sea'Sea," I said as I hit Senator Conrad on the shoulder.

"I DON'T KNOW NO SEA'SEA," Ben screamed.

"Yes you do and guess what," I said with pride. "She 15 and pregnant by Ben. You know he got a thang for young black guls,"

The crowd sighed loudly and began to chatter once again.

Ben quickly raised his head and tried to charge at me again but people from the crowd stopped him and held him back. Mary looked at him with her mouth so open that a dump truck could have driven through it.

All eyes were now on Ben and this disgusting rumor that I had just released in the air. I was the center of attention but this time for all the wrong reasons.

"15," Mary screamed. "Now, Bunny Sue daughter was a grown woman I know, but 15 isn't acceptable Ben. Absolutely unacceptable,"

"That's the same thing I said. And Imma tell you where she stay at too Mrs. Ben, if you thank I'm lying. She live in that light green trailer over by Blue Heaven. Ask for Sea'Sea when you knock," I said. "The truth hurt don't it Ben? Welcome to my world Mr. Family Man,"

Mary started to form tears in her eyes as she mentally wrote down everything I was saying. A majestic night had slowly turned into her worst nightmare. It wasn't the different revelations I had revealed about Ben that had her upset, her issue was much deeper than that.

Her once dream of one day living in the governor's mansion in Jackson had faded right before eyes. She always wanted that spot light, the parties, the life that came along with being a politician's wife.

"Would somebody get this lying boy out this place before I kill him," Ben screamed.

"He just a child Ben," Somebody in the crowd said.

"Child my ass. This is a heddon. A lying heddon. He is trying to destroy me, my family, and my life," Ben screamed as he pointed his finger at me. "Just get out of here and do us all a favor and go rob a bank or steal something, like most of you people do,"

Then I remembered the term "circumstance" that Baby Sister always used in reference to Ben. I guessed Ben circumstance was wishing I was never born. To know Baby Sister even conceived a child with such a low down dog, made me sick to my stomach. Truth be told, the lack of love for me from my father still stung my heart deep down.

I started to put two and two together. Ben was white with a little power, with a little money and was known as an up and coming power player. I started to understand that Ben had shame on his heart. He had shame for his family, for his parents, for his community. Ben knew that having a baby with a person of color coming from his background was the lowest of the low.

"Thanks Pops," I said sarcastically as I walked off.

Ben stared at me with fire in his eyes. I knew he wanted to wipe me off the face of the earth.

"Wait a minute," Ben yelled to me. "You know what, since everybody itching to know the truth, well here it is,"

I turned around and stood there waiting on Ben to tell his bullshit story.

Ben pulled his shirt out of his pants, unbuttoned his shirt, and showed his chest.

"This is what happens when you make mistakes in life," Ben said as he showed about 26 stabbed wounds. "You end up with wounds that you will feel and face for the rest of your life,"

Ben started to point his finger at me to make his point as he continued to lecture the crowd.

"You may say you look like me. Hell, your momma can say whatever she want. But I am not your daddy boy and never will be. You will never, ever be a son of mine. Some mistakes in life you can't fix, but some you can. You are somebody elses mistake, but not mine. And I will take that to my grave,"

I turned my back and walked out the door with my emotions still raw and feelings a little hurt. I knew my work had been achieved. Ben was exposed for who he really was and that had nothing to do with being a so called man of the year. My father was a bad person. I knew he deserved every single thing that was coming to him.

--

I hid behind Prospect Baptist Church in Quito, waiting on Ben and his family to arrive home. It was the church where they say the blues great Robert Johnson soul was buried. Old folks in the City talked about how that church was the center piece of the quarters they use to live in back in the 30's, how the entire area of Quito use to be a profitable slave plantation once upon a time that belonged to Matthew Quito and his folks.

The white folks had long turned the church into a nice brick church that resided right off of Highway 7, going towards Sidon. All of the quarter houses had been torn down and were replaced by cotton and soy bean fields.

I had gotten directions to where Ben lived from Mr. Dandress, "Take Highway 7 south and Ben house should be on the left, right in front of that brick church, You can't miss it,", Mr. Dandress said. "Don't go down there acting no fool at that man house. It don't matter what he done did to you, he still a man with a family, you understand,"

As I waited, I realized that I was sitting on a tombstone embedded in the ground. I stood up, and dust the tombstone off. The tombstone had a small hand print on it.

The tombstone read:

Milia Fisher

Sunrise: June 2, 1985 Sunset: June 2, 1987

"A wonderful joy to the world,"

"Sorry for sitting on yo grave Milia. Don't hunt me for that," I whispered, did the cross sign across my body, asked God for forgiveness, and moved to another spot.

Ten minutes passed. Ben and his family finally pulled up to their red bricked country house.

"Let me check the mail. You need anythang," I overheard Ben say to Mary. It seemed like he was trying to be extra nice with the intent of earning cool points to avoid the bad verbal lashing that awaited him later.

"Stop asking me stupid questions Ben. We both know that you are in deep shit, so shut up. Don't come near me, don't touch me. That couch is your bed now," Mary yelled.

I chuckled as I watched Mary and their children go into the house. I waited on Ben to walk down the 20 feet drive way to the mailbox, get his mail, and turn back to go home to make my move. I wanted to creep up on him, to scare him a bit.

To my surprise, Ben kept walking passed the mailbox. It seemed like he was walking directly towards me.

I quietly crept over and hide behind the silver gas tank that was submerged in the darkness.

"I seen him today and you wouldn't believe what he tried to pull on your ole man tonight," Ben said into the night with a chuckle. "Yep, you guessed it. He comes in the place dressed God awful and ready to make trouble. I had to defend me and you. And the thangs coming out of his mouth Milia, you shoulda heard them. I know you wouldn't have acted like that in a million years. See, that there is pure evil walking and he get it honestly,"

"Who in the hell is Ben talking too. Sounds like he talking bout me though," I thought.

"Like I have told you a thousand times Milia, he will never replace you, you hear me, never. But please don't give your granddad and grandma no trouble up there, ok little lady. Daddy loves you and always will," Ben said as he wiped a tear from his eye, turned around, and started walking back home.

"Man of the year huh," I said walking towards Ben.

"What the hell are you doing here," Ben said sniffling.

"I come to see you and see who you be talking to over here by this church. You some kind of witch doctor or something," I asked.

"I said what I had to say to you and it ain't none of your business who I talk to. Now, leave before I call the police," Ben insisted.

I followed Ben across the highway onto his property. I knew I couldn't say what was on my mind on church grounds. The old folks from the City said it was disrespectful to God to curse on His holy grounds because bad things would happen to anyone who dared to do so.

304

"Call the police Ben, ain't nobody scared of no police. You know I got a real problem dealing with bad hearted people," I said.

"Well you must got a problem with dealing with yourself. I don't see what's so good about you. Now get out of here before I have to hurt you, and then call the police," Ben said.

"Hurt me," I said with a chuckle. "So now you a tough guy Ben. You too old for that ain't it,"

I pulled out my hunting knife from my side and carefully shaved a patch of hair from my arm to test the knife's sharpness.

"Hold on now. Let's talk about this before you do something you will regret later," Ben said trying to reason with me. His hands were gesturing like he was nervous.

"Naw. Ain't nothing to talk bout really. You said what you had to say so now I gotta do what I gotta do," I said.

"You know those wounds I showed you," Ben said.

"Ain't nobody trying to hear that shit Ben. You just saying that cuz yo ass scared. We been passed that," I said moving closer to Ben to make my move. Ben started to move backwards with his hands in the air trying not to make any sudden moves that would make me do something crazy. "You knew this was coming to you so chill Ben. Bad thangs follow bad people, we both know that,"

"You know like I know your momma put them wounds on me. She stabbed me 24 times. Then she..." Ben said getting emotional.

"Then she what Ben," I yelled. Ben was close to pissing me off. "Then she what? I'm sick of you crying like a bitch,"

I felt as though Ben was trying to make me turn against Baby Sister in some way. It was like he was trying to give a sorry plea so I wouldn't hurt him.

"She killed my baby and tried to kill me all because I wouldn't leave my family for her, thinking I was playing games with her," Ben said.

I stopped and looked at Ben. I knew Baby Sister had dirt on her, I just didn't know how much.

"What the fuck you talking bout Ben," I asked.

Ben started to cry.

"I loved your momma, I swear I did, but I was trying to make thangs work with my wife," Ben said. "Your momma was too crazy to deal with. I told her over and over again that she needed help, but she wouldn't listen. She constantly accused me of playing games and playing with her feelings, but I wasn't. I really loved your momma, it was the circumstances I was faced with,"

"See, now you lying. Ain't nobody tried to kill you or yo baby," I screamed. "Don't lie on Baby Sister Ben, on everything I love. Don't fucking lie on her to make yoself look good,"

"I had to tell my wife that me and my baby was attacked by robbers that tried to kill me but killed her instead. I couldn't tell my wife that it was your momma and have her double blame me for our daughter murder. I'm the one walking around here with that on my chest, ME not you or your momma," Ben said as tears continued to flow down his face.

"Milia and me came over to see your momma because she said she wanted to see Milia before I took her to get ice cream for her birthday, to bait me over to her house. That's when your momma showed me the positive pregnancy test. Like a fool, I blew it off, knowing that it would send her over the edge and it did. She went stone crazy. Out of the blue she started stabbing me and the next thing I know, she started stabbing Milia in a rage. She killed her and I can't never get that day back,"

I thought about the grave I had stepped on at the church. The name read Milia. I realized that I was standing on my dead sister grave.

"What about me though. You ain't never loved me," I yelled.

"I won't betray Milia like that, I gave her my promise that you will never replace her. And my word is my bond to her forever," Ben said. "I will not love you over my baby, that will never happen. Your momma took a life from me that day and I gave her back a life in return. If I could reverse it, I would have my Milia back instead of you without blinking an eye. That's just how I feel and I will never stop feeling that way,"

I realized that Ben didn't care for me because of something that I did, it was because of something Baby Sister had done.

"Why Baby Sister ain't never told me bout this," I asked.

"Because she never had too. Baby Sister comes from a troubled past that hunts her," Ben said. "Her past drove her crazy,"

"If you knew she was crazy, why you messed with her then," I asked.

"Some men just are attracted to crazy women. That's just how life is. You will understand one day what I am talking about,"

"I ain't gone understand nothing. Don't preach to me Ben cuz I ain't for all that shit tonight," I said as I pointed my hunting knife at Ben.

Ben took a couple of steps back with his hands in the air.

"Ok," Ben said calmly.

"Kill this lying motherfucker, Amel," the small voice inside my head said. "You know out of all people, this nigga don't deserve to live,"

I shook my head to agree, bit my lip, griped my hunting knife tighter and moved towards Ben with question marks still in my heart. Something in me wanted more answers.

"What about Sea'Sea though. You ain't said a word bout her, like it's a secret or something. Nigga I been knew bout yall. Been knew," I yelled.

"Been knew about what? And about Who," Ben asked with confusion.

"Sea'Sea, don't play. You know exactly who I'm talking bout. She the motherfucker you got pregnant," I yelled.

"Oh wait, just calm down. Let me explain that. First of all, I know her by Sea'Andrea, not by Sea'Sea as you call her. Secondly, she told me she was 23. You seen her body, she looks like she is 30. I didn't know she was 15. Trust me,"

"Trust you," I yelled. "Nigga you gots to be on dope or dog food, talking bout trust you,"

"I didn't know that was your friend, ALRIGHT," Ben yelled getting upset. It was late and I knew he probably just wanted to end the night.

Before I knew it, I had sliced Ben twice in the face, one time under his left eye and one time on his lower jaw.

Ben put both hands to his face with his mouth open, shocked and scared for his life. He knew I meant business.

"Who the fuck you hollering at," I screamed as I grabbed Ben and put the knife to his throat, waiting on him to say one more thing or to move a muscle. "Who the fuck you hollering at Ben,"

The night fell silent between us two. The only thing that could be heard were the frogs and crickets in the woods. I stood there with my hunting knife to Ben's throat, observing him, trying to study his eyes. Ben didn't say a word but stared back.

A tear begin to roll down Ben's face as he tried to look off.

"Look at me," I said softly.

Ben looked back at me.

"Fuck yo tears. You just a boy Ben, you ain't no man. You just like me," I said with a chuckle.

"I got a family to take care of, can't you see that. You don't know me and what I been through," Ben pleaded.

"Fuck you and yo family Ben. You ain't never gave a fuck bout me and I'm yo blood . Baby Sister said them kids ain't even yo kids and you care for them more than you even care for me,"

Ben just stared at me with a blank look on his face.

"Now if you lie to me one more time, it won't end well for ya Ben I swear fo God," I whispered. I was beginning to get emotional myself. Life as I knew it was filled with lies and confusion. "If you lie to my motherfucking face one more time, I'm finna kill you and go in there and kill yo whole family,"

"How would I know that was your friend? Think about it," Ben said.

"Ain't nobody talking bout no friend now. I'm talking bout me," I said. "You fucked over and hurt too many people Ben. I don't thank you deserve to live,"

"What, you think you God now," Ben asked.

"Naw. But I know I got yo soul in my hands. I can choose if you live or die tonight. That's my choosing, you know bout that don't you Ben," I said with a smile.

"What do you want from me," Ben asked in a defeated tone.

"The truth bout you," I said.

Ben laughed out loud.

"So you want to know the truth about me," Ben said sarcastically. "It's all the hateful thangs your momma has told you about me,"

"She ain't never told me nothing hateful bout you," I said.

"Come on now," Ben said in disbelief. "I know your momma told you how I was to her. I did use to drink a lot and do some thangs I shouldn't have to her but I loved her,"

I listened.

"I'm not that guy anymore, I have changed," Ben said.

"I told you she ain't never said nothing bad bout you," I said.

"You know what," Ben yelled. "Fuck that and fuck you,"

"What," I asked.

"You heard me. If you gone kill me, then kill me. That's the only truth I have," Ben said. "Now you know the truth,"

I gripped my knife tighter and bit my lip harder. I was ready to hit Ben with a kill shot straight to the throat.

"What bout yo family in there. You say you care bout them so much," I said.

"I don't care anymore. They are probably better off without me. Truth is, when Milia died I died. I will never be happy again. That's why I built that house across from the church so I can be close to her always,"

I continued to stare at Ben, pondering whether I should kill him or not.

"I'm no different than any other man. I got faults and you will too," Ben said

"What you waiting on," the small voice inside my head said. "Straight to the throat, end it now. Stop bullshitting,"

I looked Ben in the eyes with his face covered in blood from the two knife wounds.

"Do it," the small voice inside my head said. "Don't bitch out now,"

"Lets go," I said as I escorted Ben across the highway to the back of the church.

"Where we going," Ben said as he stared down at Milia grave.

"Tell Milia the truth bout who I am," I said with a serious tone.

Ben looked at me with a 'you can't be serious' look.

"Over my dead body," Ben said.

I hit Ben with the hunting knife in the arm. It wasn't a big wound but a wound that sent a message.

Ben jumped and yelled with pain.

"Tell her Ben and I will let you go back home to yo family," I yelled

"Fuck you," Ben screamed.

I hit Ben again in the opposite arm the exact same way I did the other one. Ben dropped to his knees in defeat.

"Me and Milia could of played together, but you fucked that up Ben," I said bending down. "Now the next slice is going from one ear to the other if you don't say it,"

"I would rather die," Ben said with conviction.

I hit Ben two time in the chest, three times in the stomach.

"Ben," I heard the voice of Mary coming towards the church. "Ben are you out here,"

"Mary, help me please," Ben said as I continued to stab him eleven more times. "He is trying to kill me. Please help me,"

I quickly put my hunting knife on my side, picked Ben bloody body up off the ground, looked into his defeated eyes for a second to feel his hurt, kissed him on the forehead, and ran off into the night.

"Hold on Ben. Don't die on me," I could hear Mary scream from a distance as I continued to run full speed ten miles north towards the City.

Then I heard a long and painful scream from Mary.

I knew Ben probably had passed on to be with Milia, which explained why he never once tried to fight back or run. He knew what his fate was and he accepted it.

Chapter 29

A month had passed as I kept tabs on Ben through the local news. To my surprise, Ben had survived the stabbing although they said he had several strokes shortly after. He was now unable to walk or eat on his own.

To be honest, I was patiently awaiting a visit from the police but they never came. I figured that Ben accepted his karma.

In my personal life, me and Kris relationship started to blossom. We talked on the phone every day. Kris presence in my life made me think twice about doing bad things. No more robbing, no more killing, no more anything is what I promised myself. I had released my anger towards Ben and started the journey to making my relationship with Baby Sister better. The sun was slowly trying to show through the dark clouds in my life without Sea'Sea being a part of it.

--

I laid in bed deep into the night thinking about Kris and Sea'Sea, wondering how I can one day fit them both in my life.

Then my phone rang. I instantly thought it was Kris calling me back to vent.

"Hello," I answered.

"Amel," a lady yelled.

"Who this," I yelled back. I didn't recognize the voice right off.

The lady didn't say a word. I could hear men in the background talking loud.

"Do you want to see me again," the lady asked.

"What the fuck," I whispered as I dropped the phone from my ear and stared at it with a confused look. My heart started to race. That voice on the phone sounded familiar but I couldn't put my finger on who it was. But I knew whoever it was sounded like they were in real trouble.

"Hello," I could hear the lady on the phone scream, breathing hard, and crying. I quickly put the phone back to my ear.

"Who this," I yelled again.

"If you want to see this bitch alive again, see me at 11:30pm at the Blue Heaven nigga. If you don't show, you gone find this bitch head in a field somewhere," a man said.

Before I could respond, I heard the dial tone.

"Who in the fuck is this and how they get my number," I said with confusion. Then it hit me. "Melo,"

I looked at the clock on my phone and saw that it was 11:09pm. I knew the Blue Heaven was five minutes away if I drove, but I knew if I drove I would wake up Javion due to the loudness of the new dual pipes I just put on the white '69 Mustang. By foot, it would take me about 15 to 20 minutes.

I quickly put on some clothes, grabbed my hunting knife, made sure Javion was situated and fully sleep, and bounced out of the door full speed towards the Blue Heaven.

As I approached the Blue Heaven, I looked at my watch and saw that it was 11:23pm. I noticed the parking lot was filled with old heads trying to get into the club to party. The lady didn't give me any description of a car or anything. "Just be there or somebody is going to die" kept playing over in my head. Even though me and Melo had bad blood and our differences, she was still my sister that I loved. If anybody had the right to kill Melo, it was me, her own flesh and blood, nobody else.

I combed the parking lot carefully for about 5 minutes trying to find the potential caller. As I walked passed an old beat up van with its lights on bright, I heard "Yea, what's up now nigga,"

I put my hands up trying to see through the brightness of the lights of the old van.

"What up," I responded. I already knew what it was. Then I matched that voice to the voice of the caller.

"You fucked over me last time my nigga. I owe you and these niggas in these streets owe you too and you know exactly what I'm talking bout. They paid me and Melo to off yo ass,"

"Nigga fuck you and Melo. You ain't built tough enough to kill nobody JoJo, with yo scary ass," I said. Then I heard the gun cock back. I knew I didn't have nothing on me but my hunting knife.

Still blinded by the old van bright lights, I took off across the parking lot to the tune of five gunshots.

To me, I was running away fast, but to those who witnessed what happened, I was moving in slow motion.

I ran as hard as I could until I fell to the ground.

As I laid there in a puddle of blood, my body started to feel numb. My mind started to race back when me and Melo were little children playing in the front yard of the old white shotgun house. I started to think about Javion, King Lee, and Baby Sister.

"We taking Javion too. Melo at homeboy house now, getting him," JoJo said.

I stared at JoJo as he put the gun in my mouth. I grimaced with pain. The heat from the gun barrel burnt my mouth.

Click. Click. Click.

"You lucky motherfucker," JoJo said with a chuckle. "I guess I will see when I see you if yo punk ass don't leave this motherfucker first," JoJo said as he spit in my face.

Then all went blank.

Chapter 30

Peep….Peep…Peep.

I slowly opened my eyes to the sound of the machine that was monitoring my heart. My vision was blurred and my mouth was dry.

I tried to move, but was stopped by a pain that shot all over my body as tears started to pour down my face.

"Just be still, don't try to move too fast," Baby Sister insisted.

"Baby Sister," I barely mumbled.

"You just be still, you hear me," Baby Sister said as she grabbed my hand.

I could feel Baby Sister's hurt without even looking at her. I could tell through her voice that she was concerned for me. Mr. Lim, who was in the parking lot of Blue Heaven, had hurried to Bear Ridge to tell Baby Sister about the news. They say Baby Sister dropped to her knees, prayed, got up, put on her clothes, and headed out the door on her way to the hospital in Greenwood.

"You gone be alright. Just rest, you hear. Just rest," Baby Sister said as she rubbed my head with tears in her eyes. She stood over me for a few minutes just staring at me and appreciating my being. She had heard an old lady say that sometimes bad things bring the good out of some people and this situation, was bringing the good out of her.

I looked in Baby Sister's eyes with a tight glance. I could see the concern, I could see the fear, I could see the love. For the first time, I seen my mother not Baby Sister, the one buried deep beneath all of life's mess. I slowly closed my eyes and drifted back to sleep with a small smirk. I could faintly hear Baby Sister say "Oh, they gone pay, oh they gone pay. You can bet yo ass on that,"

--

"Don't move," I heard a voice say as I slowly opened my eyes from a long medical induced sleep.

King Lee had my hospital grown open, sprinkling red clay dirt on my open wounds. I started to scream but King Lee quickly put his hand over my mouth.

"Just let The Third Degree work. Don't say a word. Let it work," King Lee said.

Upon hearing the news of me being shot, King Lee drove the white '69 Mustang to the hospital.

I let out a muffled scream as King Lee still held his hand over my mouth. My eyes filled with tears due to the pain.

"Don't move. Everything will work itself out. Just let it work," King Lee said almost moved to tears by seeing me laying in a hospital bed.

I slowly looked out the window, not wanting to show weakness, not wanting sympathy from a soul.

"Why this happen to me, out all people," I mumbled through the pain.

"When you do wrong, wrong always follow you. Isn't that what I tell you all the time," King Lee whispered. "It's what and who you attract here that makes the difference. Change this and you will change your world," King Lee continued as he pointed to my forehead.

"I tried that King Lee. Now look at me," I said still looking out of the window.

"I know you did," King Lee responded as he patted my leg. "But keep trying, keep going. Stay true to your self-discovery journey,"

I nodded my head as to say ok.

"Do you feel The Third Degree at work," King Lee asked.

I nodded my head as to say I could feel it.

"Let me ask you a question King Lee," I said.

"You need to rest," King Lee responded.

"But its important King Lee," I insisted.

King Lee observed me with a curious look on his face.

"Go ahead," King Lee said.

"Do you believe in dreams," I asked.

King Lee chuckled.

"That's quite a strange question coming from a young man lying in a hospital bed, don't you think," King Lee responded.

"I kind of figured that it was a dumb question, but I thought I would ask it anyway," I said.

King Lee looked at me with irritation in his eyes.

"You look at me. You always remember this until the day you die. No question is a dumb question, you hear me. The only dumb thing about asking a question is not asking one at all. If you want to know something, you got to ask somebody," King Lee yelled pointing his finger at me, lecturing me. "If you don't feel like asking a person, go find it in a book. That's how you learn and grow as a person. No matter how dumb you may think your question is, ask it. I guarantee you someone else is thinking about asking the same question. You understand," King Lee continued still in lecturing mode.

"I was just saying," I said.

"Then stop just saying. It makes you look foolish," King Lee snapped.

My eyes moved from side to side with a look of confusion. I was trying to figure out why King Lee was so on edge over the simplest thing. I smelled alcohol on him but I knew he wasn't pissy drunk because the alcohol smell wasn't overwhelming, and he wasn't wobbling to catch his balance.

King Lee put his head down and quickly raised it back up. I took a deep breath.

"I believe in dreams Amel. Dreams, to me, are real and majestic like The Third Degree. I think they are the gateway in which the Creator speaks to our souls. It is His way of painting a story for us to interpret and gain a valuable lesson from," King Lee said. "You know Amel, I had a special dream when I was a young boy like you. It was a dream that told the story of a good hearted young boy with great imperfections walking through a world of evil souls, with nowhere to run or hide. And in that dream, the young boy had no choice but to face and fight the evil of this world to stay good himself, to stay true to what he believed in and what he stood for. To me, dreams are apart of self-discovery because in order for you to achieve anything, you must dream it first," King Lee said.

I looked up at King Lee with a familiar look in my eyes.

"I have all kinds of crazy dreams. Them dreams felt real to me too. In them dreams, I was always a slave that stayed running away from my master," I said.

"Sounds like to me they were dreams that signified you always trying to escape your past with hopes of obtaining a better future for yourself. The slave master was the person who was always trying to catch you and put you back where you were trying to escape from. I think that was the Creator telling you to avoid those who are trying to keep you from growing and reaching your full potential as a person," King Lee said.

I nodded.

"You must understand that people will always try to pull you back to the places that you are trying to escape from, both mentally and physically. That's why I always say that you must surround yourself with people with good intent, people that can teach you something. You know, not all people you think mean well by you have your best interest at heart, if that makes sense. You see, sometimes your own family can be the main ones to bring you down. Spoiling you and not making you be responsible, trying to live their lives through you, and not allowing you to live your own life. Things like that can hurt you more than it can help you. Although your father is missing from your life Amel, never try to over compensate his absence with over spoiling your own kids. Always remember that," King Lee said.

I nodded again.

The room fell quiet. I looked out the window deep in thought. I started to think about why I was laying a hospital bed. I wanted to kill JoJo and Melo.

"What bout Javion, King Lee. I pose to just let them get away with that. My own sister trying to kill me," I asked.

"Just let it alone. Life will take care of it," King Lee said.

"I can't let it alone," I insisted.

"You just get better first before you start trying to get into some trouble. That little fella will find his way back to you, soon enough," King Lee said.

"I hope so. I miss my boy already," I said getting emotional.

"I know you do and I do too," King Lee said.

I wanted my strength back to go find Melo and JoJo because I knew they couldn't have traveled far. I knew they didn't have any money.

"What you thinking about," King Lee asked.

"Nothing," I responded.

"Oh you thinking about something and I bet it ain't good," King Lee said "I told you to let that alone,"

"I thank I want to go to college King Lee and really try to be something out here," I said.

"Oh really," King Lee replied.

"I'm just scared, I can't even lie," I said.

"Scared of what," King Lee asked.

"I really don't know. I guess scared to try to be something. Where we from, we are born being nothing. That's all we know. It's hard to change that," I said.

Then King Lee paused and then asked "Do you know what's one of the worst things that you can do in this life,"

"What's that," I asked.

"To ask the Creator for a blessing that you are not prepared for. Most people ask the Creator to bless them with a better job, knowing that they are not qualified to work a better job. Why ask for something when you know you really don't deserve it and haven't prepared yourself for it. If you do not have the proper education, why ask the Creator to bless you to be a doctor. It makes no sense. You have to prepare yourself for college both mentally and physically. The question is, how are you going to handle it? Are you going to persevere or are you going to fold," King Lee said.

"I don't know. I just don't thank I'm smart enough to even be in somebody college King Lee. I'm in special ed right now. Who gone give me a chance to go to college," I said.

King Lee hit the bed rail with force.

"See now he acting a fool. Now if he break this damn bed, he know he ain't got no money to pay for it," I thought.

"Let me to tell you something right now. Don't you ever use that word," King Lee said.

"What word," I asked. "You aight,"

"Don't you ever use the word 'smart' ever again. I want have it, you hear me," King Lee yelled.

"It's just a word King Lee," I responded.

"That word is dangerous and can hurt many people more than it can help them. We love to call kids smart. The truth is, that word is used to categorize people. Either you are dumb or smart, that's how people look at it. Don't you see that all people have the same ability to learn, it just take some longer to catch on than others. I don't think I am 'smarter' than anybody, I do think that I out work some people. To make a long story short, hard work defines your success, not smartness. The most successful people have worked relentless hours to learn their craft. It isn't a matter of being smart, it's a matter of working harder than anybody else. All knowledge is gained through hard work and life experiences. Work hard and study hard. That is the way to success and becoming a magnet to positive things and opportunities. I once heard a wise man say that when the mentee is ready, the mentor will appear out of the clear blue. That's why I stand before you today. You are ready for any opportunity. You understand," King Lee said looking me in the eyes. "So don't ever use that word again," he continued.

I nodded to say ok.

"What you are about to do from here on forward is write your own history and accept the calling that the Creator has in place for you, even if you don't know what that may be. I know you may be scared now, but trust me we all have that fear of stepping out and going against the odds. Change is scary but change is an essential part of life. This kind of change means that you are taking a chance on yourself and on your future. And soon you will be experiencing something that I call the "Power of Influence".

"What's that," I asked.

King Lee spoke:

Theory: *The power of influence is the understanding of the power you possess as it pertains to how you affect other people around you. It doesn't matter who you are or where you come from, you possess the power to influence someone directly or indirectly. Many people underestimate the value that they have on society, let alone on other people directly associated with them. With influence comes responsibility Amel. Responsibility in the sense that you can either influence someone to do good or do bad. Let's take the example of that junk music that I hear on that radio, just yelling and screaming, words not making sense. Most people don't know that words have power and that you can speak things into existence. You heard me right Amel, words have the power of creation and can influence people to do bad things. People should be responsible and accountable for every word that comes out of their mouths, but they're not. For example, if a song exist out there and one hundred people are murdered because the words to that song influenced the murderers to commit the crime, who is more responsible, the song or the murderers? Sure one will argue that the murderers were absolutely responsible, but the song planted the seed for them to do wrong Amel. So who is responsible? Understand that not just words can influence others, but your actions can too. If a journeyman is caught fighting in the street by a kid that looks up to him, then that kid is going to think it is ok to fight too. If a journeyman makes it his* *business to sleep with women outside of his marriage, then his son that studies his every move will think that it is ok to do that too. Influence is so powerful and people abuse it and manipulate it every single day. Just look at television, newspapers, politicians, and so on. That kind of influence is called deceit. Deceit is making you think something is real or genuine, when it is really not. My point to you Amel is to understand the influence that you have on people. Don't try to be perfect for nobody, but be a good person that means well and influences others to mean well too. Never be the one to deceive, always know your truth and speak it, good or bad. If you can influence more people to do good than bad, then that is a life worth living. You hear me Amel.....that is a life worth living.*

--

King Lee stopped for a second and looked out the hospital window. It was like he wanted to cry.

"Never lose sight of who you are and where you come from. When you get to wherever you're going in this life, always remember to listen before you speak. That's why you were blessed with two ears and one mouth so you can listen twice as much as can talk. Always be a man of few words and one that observe and study his surroundings. Wherever you go, make sure you represent your family and your community well. Show people that there are some people in the Mississippi Delta that have dreams, big dreams Amel that span beyond those cotton fields. You learn all you can from hard working folks, you hear me. Study how they work, how they conduct themselves, even how they learn. Everything has a strategy, so learn how the best go about doing things so you can come back home and teach others what you have learned. Remember that you are one step from making it out, and one step from being back across those cotton fields. You hear me," King Lee said.

"I hear you," I said.

I started to think about my father and the influence that he had on me. My father never had a positive impact on my life, which is the reason why I sliced his ass from top to bottom without blinking.

"King Lee," I said.

"What's that Amel," King Lee responded.

"Do you thank children need their daddy's around to make it out," I asked.

King Lee looked at me. He knew that I was trying to understand the impact and influence that a father can have on a child.

"I think children need fathers to survive and help them to understand the essence of what it means to live. Again, the power of influence and self-discovery are well represented in having a good and active father around, with emphasis on good and active. This falls into something I call the 'theory of a father'. Do you want me to explain more," King Lee said.

I nodded. I never had a man to sit down and talk to me about what a father was, nevertheless what being a father stood for. It meant so much to me since I had been trying to come to grips about my relationship with my own father and understanding his journey better. Before I met King Lee, I use to look in the mirror all the time and tell myself I would be a great father one day, even though I knew nothing about what being a great father meant. The truth was that my entire approach to wanting to get out of the Delta was to better myself not just for a better job, but to better myself to be there for my future kids and Javion, something I longed for from my own father.

"King Lee, answer me this," I asked.

"What's that," King Lee said.

"Do you have children," I asked, hoping that King Lee didn't get offended.

King Lee paused and took a deep breath.

"Before we get into the theory of a father, let's first understand the sacrifice of a man. You see, sometimes the Creator gives us a calling that takes us away from our families, not because we don't love them, but because of our love for them. There are men out there that aren't perfect by no means but they mean well. Many men have this undying fire to change the world in their own special way. Their calling takes them away from their families and their wives try their best to make their sons understand that. As the men sons get older, a calling may take them away from their family as well. Although a man wants to spend time with his family, his first duty is to take care of his family and make sure that they are stable and safe, even at his own expense. Sacrifice takes will and understanding on the part of a man's family, for they are the source of his sacrifice. To answer your question Amel, I had a wife and four daughters that I didn't know how to love when I had them. I just hope one day they all understand my calling and sacrifice as I understood the calling and sacrifice of my own father," King Lee said.

King Lee stared off into the distance, deep in thought. He started to think about his family, his mistakes, his own life's journey. I knew then that King Lee biggest regret was not being there for his family more and losing his wife in the mist of his sacrifice.

"King Lee," I said.

King Lee didn't respond.

"King Lee," I said louder.

King Lee snapped out of his daze.

"You ok," I asked "You going to tell me about the father theory,"

"Oh yea. Let's get to it,"

King Lee spoke:

Theory: *The word father has plenty of meaning to it and is quite powerful. It is a word that can change the course of an entire generation. A father is the key piece to any family structure. You have two kinds of fathers: present and non-present. A present father is directly around the child while a non-present father isn't. A present father can be broken down into two types: active and non-active. A present non active father doesn't do anything to promote and grow his family. However a present active father* *guides his family and teaches them about life and all that it brings. He uses his authority to teach discipline and responsibility. He teaches his son how to be a man and teaches his daughter how to love a man. Just like a mother teachers her daughter how to be a woman and teachers her son how to love a woman. In most cases, young girls with present active fathers compare their spouse to him and the same goes for boys comparing their spouse with their mothers. It tickles me to death to see so many women that think they know how to love a man, especially if they grew up without a present active father. How can they know how to love a man when they never experience the love of their fathers? They never connected with their father's spirit, energy, or embrace. The boy, on the other end, if he had a present active mother, most likely he will treat his spouse good. But he may lack the key qualities that a man possesses such as responsibility, reason, diligence, perseverance, and so on. That too is due to not having that connection with a present active father. In addition to that, a father doesn't think with his emotion, but he thinks with reason. He never gets too high or too low, and he always helps his family to understand the "why" behind every situation. Again, present active fathers represent understanding, reason, wisdom, security, diligence, and so on. That is why present active fathers are such a pivotal part of the family and that is why the world is the way it is. Present active fathers are the missing link and the solution. The guidance, the love, and the embrace are missing. I tell you one thing Amel, always remember the pain that you felt when you longed for your father as a young boy. Forgive it, but never forget it. Here is why. If you remember that hurt that you felt as a fatherless little boy, you will understand how that would affect your own child if you are not present. If you are a good man, how your child view you will mean the world to you. But most fatherless men and women today forget all too well how it felt when their own fathers broke promises, told lies, and never showed up. Now they are doing it to their own children, creating this negative cycle, making their own kids at risk of repeating the same cycle. A present active father number one fear in life is failing to be a good father to his kids. That's what he fears the most, you hear me Amel. I say that to say this, someone can either break the cycle of their past or they can relive it, which one will you choose Amel? Will you be just like your father or will you be better than he was to you. It is your choice.*

--

I stared out the window, deep in thought about how I wanted to be when it became my turn to father a child. I knew I wanted nothing more than to provide my own children with the best life I could possibly provide them, like I was trying to do with Javion. I wanted to be a present active father, the one that engaged my children and family. I knew I had plenty of growing to do, but one thing I knew for sure, no one would ever be afforded the opportunity to call me a bad father.

Chapter 31

Six weeks passed and I was back to full strength. The Third Degree had healed my wounds within a few weeks of being shot. The doctors said they couldn't believe how fast my body had healed, pointing out my youth as the reason why my wounds healed so fast, not knowing that King Lee blessed my body.

--

"King Lee ain't never around when you need him," I thought walking down the street passed the park store looking for King Lee.

A car slowly approached me as I stood in the road trying to figure out my next move. I noticed Sea'Sea was driving the car. Her eyes met mine as she passed by slow in an old white Ford Pinto.

"Watch her crazy ass keep going," I thought.

The car hit on breaks and proceeded to back up.

"Damn she musta read my mind," I whispered.

As the car approached me, Sea'Sea rolled her eyes as she let down the passenger side window.

"You need a ride Amel River," Sea'Sea asked looking forward. She refused to look at me.

"So when you start calling me by my whole name," I said with a mean mug.

"The day you put a knife to my fucking throat for no reason. But anyway, you need a ride somewhere," Sea'Sea asked. "Something told me to keep going, but I thought that I wouldn't be no better than him if I didn't stop and ask if you needed a ride,"

"Yeah I need one. You can take me back to the City," I said.

"Where Javion at," Sea'Sea asked.

"Melo took him and I ain't seen him since. She just took him away from me just like that," I said. "You know Melo the one who set me up to get shot,"

"Are you serious," Sea'Sea asked.

"Dead serious. But you know I got her when I see her. It ain't over by a long shot. Imma find her and get my Champ back. Believe that," I said.

"I know right. I miss my lil Lightbread too. With his lil self," Sea'Sea said. "But anyway how yo momma doing,"

"She good. She doing better, taking it one day at a time," I said.

"That's good. Yall back straight," Sea'Sea asked.

"Yeah we cool," I said. "You gone let me in the car or what,"

"Yeah, may bad. I'm bout to talk yo head off already," Sea'Sea said as a smile cracked across her face. She unlocked the door.

I jumped in the car.

"You sure this car ain't gone breakdown before we make it to the City. I'm telling you this now, Imma charge yo ass 50 dollars every hour I gotta push this motherfucker," I said with a chuckle.

"Oh, you got jokes now huh," Sea'Sea said as she cut her eyes at me. She still wouldn't fully look at me.

"I want to tell you something before we pull off and I'm for real," Sea'Sea said.

I looked out the window, scared that she was going to bring up old news that I didn't want to talk about.

"Look at me Amel, damn," Sea'Sea yelled. "Stop acting like a lil kid so much,"

I continued to look out the window.

Sea'Sea snatched my face around with her hand.

"I just want to thank you for that money you gave me and momma. That meant plenty to us and to me. Just know I appreciate you for that," Sea'Sea said.

"You ain't got to thank me for nothing. I did what I felt was right. Like I always do with you," I said.

"Just know it meant a lot aight," Sea'Sea said.

"Cool," I said.

Sea'Sea let go of my face.

"You ain't got to grab my face like that either," I said as I grabbed my jaw due to the slight pain from her grip. "That shit hurt,"

"Stop being a baby," Sea'Sea said. "So Amel, word around the way is that you quit the basketball team,"

"I did. You must got a problem with that or something," I responded.

"Naw, I ain't got a problem with it, but I just know how much you loved to play ball. You loved it so much that you stop writing to do it. So, I know how much it means to you," Sea'Sea said.

"Well, some thangs change over time. I ain't that Amel no more. I got to try to make something shake for me and Javion. You know how hard it is out here. You out of all people should know that," I said.

"Oh I know, you know I know. But I also know how hard it musta been for you give it up because I remember when you use to sleep with yo little basketball every single night. You remember that? I still know yo little ass, even if you don't fuck with me no more. So why you give it up," Sea'Sea said.

"Yeah I remember that, I loved that little basketball too. I'm shocked you still remembered that. But anyway, you know like I know that I can't depend on robbing or other people my whole life. I'm trying to change for the better so my life can get better. You seen me do my dirt, look where that took me. Straight to a hospital bed with gunshot wounds everywhere," I said.

"I know right. That makes both of us trying to do right," Sea'Sea said. "But that hurt me to my heart to see you in that hospital bed like that. I could barely look at you. I had to turn away a couple of times so I wouldn't lose it all the way,"

I smacked my mouth "When you came to see me in the hospital,"

"I was there before Baby Sister was there. I was the one in the ambulance. I was the first one at the hospital," Sea'Sea said getting offended. "What you thank I'm lying. Ask Baby Sister then,"

"I didn't know you was there though. I preciate that though," I said.

"You was out like a light. I thought you was dead in that parking lot. I was the one that called 911," Sea'Sea said.

332

"No bullshit," I asked.

"For real though. I saw when JoJo shot you and everything. I couldn't do nothing cuz he woulda shot me," Sea'Sea said.

"Naw, you did right," I said.

"I'm just glad you feeling better and doing better," Sea'Sea said.

"Me too, but anyway," I said trying to deflect and change the subject.

The car fell silent.

"You ain't even notice what's different bout me. Out of all people I thought you woulda caught it right off," Sea'Sea said.

I observed her but I couldn't find what she was talking about.

"You still yellow," I said.

Sea'Sea pointed to her flat stomach.

"You had the fucking baby without telling me," I yelled.

Sea'Sea chuckled. But then all of a sudden she got sad.

"I don't want to talk bout it," Sea'Sea said.

"What happened," I asked.

"I don't want to talk bout it I said," Sea'Sea insisted.

"Aight fuck it then," I yelled.

"My baby daddy beat my ass and I lost the baby," Sea'Sea said.

I looked at Sea'Sea to make sure she wasn't bullshitting. It was situations like those that brought the worse out of me.

"He what now," I asked.

"That nigga beat........my..........ass. You heard me," Sea'Sea said. "If you noticed, I missed like two weeks from school when it happened. I was in the hospital for a week,"

"Damn," I said. "That motherfucker in that newspaper did you like that,"

"Yep," Sea'Sea said.

"Bet," I said taking a mental note. There was no way I was going to let Ben get away with that. Now I regretted not slashing his throat from ear to ear when I had a chance.

"It was a blessing and curse. I know I couldn't afford no baby so I guess it was meant to be," Sea'Sea said.

"Don't say that. That nigga ain't had no reason to put his hands on you like that," I responded.

Sea'Sea looked at me with a "this nigga can't be serious face".

"Nigga ain't you the same nigga that put a sharp ass knife to my throat while I was pregnant," Sea'Sea said.

I sat quietly. Sea'Sea could see that the conversation was going for the worst, so she quickly changed subjects.

"But anyway, you know Mr. Jackson entire class was talking bad bout you. Talking about how you smell like feet sometimes, how you play ball in gangsta Nikes, and how you quit the team. I mean they was really going in on you hard," Sea'Sea said.

"Fuck Mr. Jackson gay ass and his whole class," I said with rage.

"They said he was gay for real though. He got that gay look bout him," Sea'Sea said.

"Yeah that fat bitch gay. And fuck all them motherfuckers in that class too. They gone get it too one day," I yelled.

"Damn don't get mad at me. You must didn't hear the part when I said I took up for you," Sea'Sea said.

"Yeah I heard you. But the real word on the street is that you hate me. I just can't see how you be friends with somebody one day and hate them the next," I said jokingly.

Sea'Sea quickly cut her eyes at me.

"You know what," Sea'Sea said with a slight pause. "You got some motherfucking nerves to say that to me. After how you did me, I should kick yo motherfucking ass out of my car right now. Don't fucking play with me bout that. I still got a bad taste in my mouth for yo trifling ass. My feelings still fucked up over that so don't play, aight," She continued.

"Damn, I was just joking," I said. "Still acting so damn crazy all the time I see,"

"Whatever nigga, don't play. Keep that crazy shit to yoself aight cuz we both know who crazy," Sea'Sea said.

"Ok. Whatever crazy lady," I said.

Sea'Sea cut her eyes at me. I didn't look back at her.

The car was in an awkward silence all the way to the City. Sea'Sea approached the old blue shotgun house and parked on the side of the road. We both continued to sit in silence until I tried to open the door.

"Why this door won't open," I asked.

"Because the handle is broke. I gotta let you out," Sea'Sea said.

"Just let the window down and I will let myself out," I said.

"Nope," Sea'Sea said.

"What you mean nope? Gul if you don't let this got damn window down, you better," I said.

"Not before you tell me why you did me like you did," Sea'Sea said.

"What you talking about now Sea'Sea," I asked.

"What the fuck you thank I'm talking bout Amel. This not the time to play stupid, ok. You just stop fucking with me all of a sudden without even telling me why. You just fucked over me like that. I thought I was yo girl," Sea'Sea said.

"I mean, I don't know what to say," I said, getting nervous because I didn't know how to get out of the conversation or the car. I was trapped.

"Say why you did it. I thought thangs was different between me and you," Sea'Sea said.

"Shiiiidddd, me too," I said.

"We went through a lot together and for you to do me like that. I don't know," Sea'Sea said.

"You don't know what Sea'Sea," I asked.

"I don't know where we stand Amel," Sea'Sea said.

"What the fuck do that pose to mean. Don't you got a boyfriend that you is happily in-love with," I said.

"Yeah but I'm talking bout our relationship now. This relationship is more important to me," Sea'Sea said.

"The hell you say. See now you just saying shit to make somebody feel good. You know I ain't shit to you," I said.

"You are Amel," Sea'Sea said as a tear fell down her cheek. "I miss our friendship. I miss you, Amel,"

I paused. Sea'Sea was actually crying.

"You know thangs between me and that girl Kris is getting serious. I just told her that I loved her," I said, not wanting to bring down the conversation, but wanted to be honest with her.

The car dropped to a dead silence. Sea'Sea had a look of disbelief on her face.

"You love who? So you love this bitch Kris," Sea'Sea said looking at me confused. "Look at me motherfucker. You love Kris. Kris? Are you serious,"

"Yeah. I love her. Me and you always been just friends Sea'Sea, nothing more than that. What do you want me to say," I added.

"I want you to say what happened Amel. What happened to us, I am not talking bout that bitch right now. What bout us? What bout how you left me hanging like I wasn't shit to you. What bout that Amel. Now you saying that you love this bitch. You told me that you would never use that word any way. I guess she is getting the best of you while I dealt with the worst of you. I am the one getting fucked over. Tell me something Amel. Don't I at least deserve to be told why you did me like you did," Sea'Sea said as her face flowed with tears.

"I don't have nothing to say," I said. I hated seeing her like that. I could feel that she was hurt. I never knew I had that kind of impact on her.

Sea'Sea stopped to gather herself. She felt that she was showing me a little too much emotion. She didn't want to tell me that she was in-love with me way before Kris even knew my name. She loved me ever since she could remember. She couldn't tell me that mainly because she didn't know how.

"Congrats on yo little fucking love story. I am happy for you and that bitch. You stopped fucking with me and all of a sudden, you love this bitch. What the fuck is that? Well halleluiah, God bless and thank you God that you happy. I wish you and that bitch the best. I guess you had to sacrifice my happiness and our relationship for a bitch you barely even know. I thought we was better than that," Sea'Sea said.

"Yeah I thought we was better than that too. Now let me out this motherfucking car," I said.

"What the fuck do that pose to mean. What did I do to you? You can't even answer the fucking question. I took care of you and Javion like yall my family and this how you do me nigga," Sea'Sea said yelling and swinging her hand to slap me.

I blocked her hand.

"What the fuck is wrong with you, ole crazy ass gul," I yelled.

"You what's wrong with me motherfucker," Sea'Sea said. "You ain't never cared bout me, did you," Sea'Sea said crying and yelling.

"That's what you going to hit me with when you have a boyfriend," I said. "Let me out this motherfucking car cuz I refuse to disrespect you," I continued, trying to open the door with no success.

"Disrespect me? I am the one sacrificing my body for you. Putting my body in danger for you. I'm the one sitting in the hospital with yo ass until Baby Sister came. That bitch ain't come to see you nan time. And this how you do me, yo girl Sea'Sea," Sea'Sea yelled.

"Put yo body in danger for me? What the fuck you talking bout Sea'Sea. It's always something with yo ass," I yelled.

Sea'Sea sat quietly trying to contain her emotions as the tears continued to flow from her face.

"What the fuck you crying for," I yelled.

"Abortion," Sea'Sea said.

"What you mean abortion," I asked.

"I had an abortion Amel. What you thank I mean," Sea'Sea yelled.

"I thought you said the nigga beat yo ass and made you lose the baby," I said.

"I LIED. SURPRISE," Sea'Sea said with a sarcastic but serious smile as the tears continued to flow from her eyes. "Ain't nobody beat my ass. Ain't nobody did nothing,"

"So why you lie then," I asked.

"Cause I didn't won't nobody knowing my business so I said the nigga fought me and I lost the baby," Sea'Sea said.

I sat quietly on the passenger side of the car. I was deep in thought. I didn't know how to feel about the situation.

"Why you had to get a abortion though. That baby deserved better than that," I said.

"Did you not hear me, I did it for you. I thought you was mad at me for being pregnant so I used some of that money you gave me and momma, and got one. That night I saw you laying in that hospital bed, it made me rethank everything in my life. I almost lost you," Sea'Sea said.

"I know but that still ain't right Sea'Sea," I said.

"I had to do what I had to do to get you back talking to me and get you back in my life," Sea'Sea said.

"Mane, fuck that," I yelled.

"See what I'm saying. I pour my heart out to you and that's all you gots to say is 'fuck that' like you proving something. Sometimes I thank yo heart is made of stone," Sea'Sea yelled.

"What you pouring yo heart out to me for Sea'Sea? I ain't......," I said about to say I didn't have shit for her anymore.

"You ain't what," Sea'Sea asked.

"Nothing," I said.

"Naw, say it," Sea'Sea insisted.

"I ain't got time for this shit. Now, you happy Sea'Sea. You get on my damn nerves sometimes," I said.

"And you get on my nerves too. That's what make us who we are. You piss me off and I piss you off. That's what we do," Sea'Sea yelled.

I didn't give a respond, just looked out the window.

"Look at us Amel. Once upon a time we was best friends. Laughing and playing with each other. Just look at us now, fighting like we enemies and distant strangers. I'm bout to move to Georgia with my momma in a couple of days. This ain't how I want to remember you. This ain't how I want to remember us. I don't know what else to say," Sea'Sea said, as her voice got low and sad.

"Didn't know you was leaving," I said, shocked to hear that Sea'Sea was moving to another state. I tried to hide my disappointment.

"I didn't know either until last month," Sea'Sea said.

"Sorry to hear you leaving. Can I skate now," I said in a calm tone as I looked out the window.

Sea'Sea stopped and looked at me like she was giving up on the situation, giving up on what she herself had dreamed of her entire life, to be with me, to love me. Sea'Sea rolled down the window so I could let myself out.

When I opened the door and was about to get out, Sea'Sea grabbed my arm and said "Tell me that you don't care bout me and I will leave you alone forever. I will erase our friendship. You will just be a part of my past, just a memory,"

I stopped and looked at her.

"What do you want from me Sea'Sea? You hurt me just as bad as I have hurt you. I don't know how to fix this," I thought.

I stared at her until she released my arm.

"I take that as being a no. Have a good life ok. Give Kris my fucking best, I mean that," Sea'Sea said as I got out of the car and walked onto the porch of the old light blue shotgun house.

I felt her still looking at me. I turned around and our eyes caught.

We stared at one another. Sea'Sea had this look of disbelief on her face as she shook her head.

Sea'Sea tried to turn her car on so she could leave but it wouldn't turn on. She turned it on again but it quit again.

"You need help with that," I asked.

"Fuck you," Sea'Sea said as the car finally cranked and she dug off in a furry of anger.

Chapter 32

Me and King Lee sat quietly on the front porch. I sipped slowly on a can of green tea as I looked out onto the day sky. King Lee gulped relentlessly on a bottle of homegrown brandy that he had gotten from Ms. Betty Joe down the road.

"He is going to be alright. Just believe it," King Lee said. "Everything will work itself out for the better. Just keep believing it will,"

"I don't know King Lee. Melo and that boy JoJo on some more stuff. They both on dope," I said.

King Lee didn't respond. He just kept drinking his brandy. One of King Lee greatest asset was his ability to listen first and give warranted advice at the right time.

"Deep down in my heart, I can feel him and it don't feel right King Lee. I know Melo ain't in no kind of shape to take care of my Champ. Especially how she let that other nigga do him. It just bothers me King Lee. I just know he is crying for me right now. Crying for me to come get him like I did before," I said. I wiped my eyes before the tears started to pour from them. "Melo know better. And then she got my Champ around JoJo like that. He may be just like that nigga Loc,"

"He will be just fine," King Lee insisted.

"No he ain't. Every time I just thank bout it I just wanna..." I said as I hit my fist against the wood step.

The porch fell silent and the only thing that could be heard was the wind sweeping across the City.

"The old folks use to say that when a wind is sweeping through like that, something is about to happen," King Lee said as he gulped down another shot of the brandy.

"I'm thanking bout joining the Navy King Lee. Ain't nothing else out here for me seem like," I said as my eyes dazed into the bright sky "I gotta do something for me and Champ,"

King Lee sat in his rocking chair nodding to say he understood. He knew that my mind was set through and through on finding Javion, to care for him, to love him again.

King Lee took another gulp of brandy.

"Why the Navy," King Lee asked.

"I don't know. Just something I saw on TV last night. When I saw the commercial, it just felt right," I said.

"Why not the Army or Air Force or the Marines," King Lee asked.

"That commercial said that the Navy Seals is what everybody would want to be. So I want to be a Navy Seal," I said.

"Oh I see. You want to be highly trained and skilled for combat. The best of the best is what they call a Navy Seal," King Lee said.

"That's exactly what they said on the commercial," I said. "The commercial said that the Navy pay for college and everything. I just got to sign up. That's a win win for me. I can go find Javion, take him with me and leave here for good. You know, just live a better life,"

"I understand. That's what it's all about. Trying to make something out yourself," King Lee said coughing repeatedly.

"You aight," I said with concern. I had been noticing that King Lee cough was getting worse as each day passed by.

"You know, I ain't been feeling so well as of late," King Lee said holding his stomach. "I just been short of breath and coughing like a horse,"

"I told you, you gotta stop all that drinking," I yelled.

"This ain't got nothing to do with no whiskey. It's just a little pain that's all. Pain comes and goes with old age," King Lee said.

King Lee screamed with pain as he grabbed his stomach.

I jumped up "Come on, let's go to the hospital,"

"I'm ok," King Lee said.

I grabbed his arm but King Lee snatched away.

"I'm ok, I said," King Lee yelled.

"You ain't gotta try and get no attitude. I'm just trying to help yo out King Lee," I said. "And why can't you just use The Third Degree to make yo body better like you did mine. It's clear you paining real bad,"

"The Third Degree has it's time and place. It ain't for everything and every situation. Sometimes you got to not use it to get the result you are looking for," King Lee said. "But go on and tell me more about the Navy,"

I looked at King Lee strangely for a second. I knew King Lee wasn't telling me something and knew he was avoiding talking about what was aliening him. I shrugged it off and started to look off into the distance again.

"They say boot camp is tough though. That's the only part I'm worried bout. Can you imagine me at a boot camp King Lee, trying to do all that running and stuff," I said.

King Lee didn't respond.

"You hear me King Lee," I said.

Then I heard a thump behind me. I quickly looked around and found King Lee lying flat on the ground, lifeless almost.

I jumped up and shook him. "King Lee. King Lee," I repeated. King Lee didn't move. His body was none responsive.

I nervously struggled for a few minutes to get King Lee off the ground and put him on my shoulder. King Lee wasn't a big man but he wasn't light in weight.

"Don't die on me," I whispered as I quickly carried King Lee to the white '69 Mustang, threw him in the back seat, and shot out to the hospital like a bat out of hell.

--

Peep. Peep. Peep. The heart monitor beeped to the rhythm of King Lee's heart.

I looked on at King Lee as he slept. It was the first time that King Lee looked clean, looked sober, looked at peace to me. I figured the nurses had taken him a bath in Clorox or something to get all the dirt off of him.

I got up and observed King Lee more, this time by his bed side.

"Look at you. You look like a king," I whispered. Seeing King Lee in that bed brought back memories of me in the hospital. "You look like a got damn king,"

"Watch your mouth, I ain't dead yet," King Lee said as he barely opened his eyes with a slight smile.

"Oh I know, I hear that heart machine still peeping. You look good though all clean and stuff," I said.

"Boy get on away from here with that, talking about how somebody looking," King Lee said.

"For real King Lee," I said with a chuckle.

King Lee sat up with slight pain.

"Take your time. Don't hurt yoself now," I insisted.

"Oh I'm alright," King Lee said.

King Lee looked off into the distance of the room. I could see the tears forming in my eyes.

"What's wrong King Lee," I said. "You gone be aight,"

"The time has come," King Lee said with a tear falling down his cheek.

"What you talking bout old man? Time for what," I said, knowing what King Lee meant but I chose to play stupid for hope sake. I sensed fear in King Lee for the first time ever. It kind of threw me for a loop to see a man that stood for bravery to me seem fearful all of a sudden.

"My time is upon me. I have lived a long life Amel. I have dotted all my I's and crossed all my T's in this life despite the wrong I have done. Time has finally caught up with this old fella," King Lee said.

"You gone be AIGHT King Lee so stop talking like that," I said.

The room stood still in an awkward silence.

"Remember when I said I was the king of my world and not of this world. This world has given me so much pain that I couldn't bare it. I couldn't live in it. I couldn't face what my life had become," King Lee said.

"We all do that in different ways, so you ain't no different than nobody else," I said.

"Look at me Amel," King Lee said as he looked at me with a cold stare.

I hesitantly obliged.

"You see this man," King Lee pointed to himself.

I nodded my head to say I did.

"This ain't life here. This is pain, you hear me. This is real pain," King Lee said as he teared up again. King Lee didn't want me to follow the same life path as he did. "You not going to end up like this. A lonely old man, dying a lonely and miserable life. This ain't life,"

I looked away as I whipped a tear from my own eye. I couldn't stand seeing King Lee that way.

"You aight King Lee. You aight," I whispered. "Just take it easy,"

King Lee stared out the window deep in thought as tears continued to flow from his eyes. I stood there trying to study his mood and what he was contemplating.

"What you thanking bout. You gotta stop all that thanking, everything gone be aight. Just believe. Ain't that what you told me," I said.

"Life has a beginning and an end, just like a normal day. Can't nobody change that," King Lee said.

"I kno. You talking like you scared of death. You told me you ain't scared to die," I said.

"Well, I lied. We all are brave until what we are brave about is upon us. But I will find strength in the Creator. He will give me courage," King Lee said.

The room fell silent again.

"Amel," King Lee said.

"What's that," I asked.

"When you find your truth, just let it be just that, the truth," King Lee said.

"Ok," I said looking confused.

"All I ask is forgiveness," King Lee said.

"For what," I asked.

"For not being the man I should have been. Now regrets are all I have to die with. You don't have to be that way," King Lee said.

"You more man than anybody I know. And don't feel like you the only one who got regrets, we all do. My biggest regret is not finding you sooner," I said.

"You know I knew you were coming to see me one day, but I didn't know when. I prayed to the Creator to let you come to me to make things right before I died. To give me a light of happiness before I left here. And you did and I am grateful for that," King Lee said.

"Preciate that," I said.

The room fell silent.

"Why you never taught me The Third Degree," I asked.

"It's nothing that you teach. It's something that you learn as you get older," King Lee said.

I looked away with confusion.

"I mean, how do you heal people and stuff with dirt," I asked.

"First thing you must know is that The Third Degree isn't anything magical that I once told you. The stories I told you were real, the healing was real, but The Third Degree isn't magic," King Lee said.

"How you do all that stuff then," I asked.

"You must understand the power of believing and persuasion," King Lee said as he grunted with pain. "The Third Degree persuades you into believing in the unseen and in the impossible, that you really can move a mountain from a muster seed. The mind is a powerful thing that can heal or kill,"

"How so," I asked.

"When it's all said and done, you can create or destroy reality in your mind. You are the king of your world and of this world, you see. That's how all of this is connected. You can persuade yourself into believing in anything," King Lee said.

"So the Third Degree is all about believing and persuading," I said.

"That's it, nothing more," King Lee said.

"Damn," whispered to myself with my right hand under my chin. "You sure,"

"What more do you want me to say. That's what it is," King Lee said. "Now if I persuade you into believing that the sky is red, then the sky will be red to you if you choose to believe. It's a choice that you have to make in a split second,"

"Interesting," I said still ruminating.

"Most people in this world are in search of something, to gain something, to achieve something. They will do or believe in just about anything to get what they are searching for," King Lee said. "At the point of choosing between real truth and fake truth, is where you know who you are dealing with,"

I listened.

"Once you have a person mind, you have everything, including their soul," King Lee said. "The Creator gives us all power to choose between right and wrong, fake and real, and lies and truth,"

"Learn to use your mind to receive truth. Remember that, in any situation, the truth is always right there in front of your nose, always," King Lee said. "But that's the Third Degree. That's all to it, now leave it alone,"

"Aight," I said.

I got the TV remote and started to flip through the channels. I had something on my heart that I wanted to tell King Lee.

"I want to thank you for not changing on me King Lee. You the only person that always kept it the same," I said.

"Oh I didn't do anything that I would hope a normal person would do when they see a young man with potential that needs to be reeled in," King Lee said. "Don't thank me, thank your mother. She is the one that prepared you for this marathon we call life, I am just a bystander that you came across while running that gave you water to help you keep going,"

I looked down to the ground.

"I wrote you a lil something King Lee," I said with embarrassment. "You want to hear it,"

King Lee nodded his head proudly to say he wanted to hear it.

It felt as though I was standing in front of thousands of people. King Lee was special to me, what I was about to say was special to me. I started to understand how certain situations that means the most to people produced feelings of having great fear to disappoint and to fail. That was the feeling I was having.

"It's alright. Go on and say what you have to say," King Lee said giving me reassurance that things would be ok regardless of how the speech read.

I spoke:

King

Sometimes the easiest thangs are the hardest thangs to do
And the hardest thangs seems like they are nothing to conquer or the easiest to go
through

Is it because the hardness of life is the only life I have ever known
Broken, until I found a king along this lonely and bumpy road

A King, to me, is a man that knows his worth and flaws all at the same time
Even though his own journey has been uneven, and walked about near sighted,
scattered, reaching for thangs like he was blind.

Blinded by deceit and distractions that any broken man would fall for.
But despite his ignorance, he holds his head, and fight, trying to catch life's ever closing
door

Is it me, or is the world filled with fake kings pretending to be real
Flashing their materialistic jewels, sharing their ill-advised knowledge, like selling their
souls wasn't a part of the deal

A King to me, is a man that, with integrity, accepts the harsh reality of his preconceived
destiny
Knowing that failure is the only future that he has, but still shows courage in the face of
defeat, screaming to the world, let me live and, if I choose too, let me mingle in my own
foolery

Who knows what this life has in store for you, for me, and for us all
Constantly falling on life's hard times, fearful to stand again, scared to succeed like
slaves that we were born to be; or will we get up, like a king, every time we stumble and
fall

I know one thing for sure that I want to share with the world and that I want all to see
If I ever become an ounce of what this man is that lay in front of me, I will surly become
Kingly

Just.....Like....Him...

-Shake

--

The room feel quiet. It was clear that emotions owned the room at the moment.

"Well done Amel," King Lee said proudly as he wiped a tear from his brow. "Well done,"

Chapter 33

"U up," a text came to my phone around 10:21pm as I laid in the bed, reflecting on Javion and King Lee, wishing everything would get back to where it was.

I checked my phone and noticed it was Sea'Sea. I sighed out loudly and put my phone back down. "I ain't got time for that bullshit today. Got too much on my mind,"

I laid there for another five minutes.

"I kno u up," Sea'Sea sent another text.

I looked at my phone again and rolled my eyes. "Why the fuck she keep texting me,"

"HELLO," another text came in.

"h,"

"e,"

"l,"

"l,"

"o,"

"a,"

"m,"

"Wat mane," I quickly texted. I knew she wouldn't stop. Besides I was reaching my text limit.

"Y u got to act like that with me :) " Sea'Sea texted.

"Wat CC. I'm sleep," I texted.

"I want to c u bfore I leave 2ma," Sea'Sea texted.

"I thought u dnt fuk wit me no mo," I texted.

About two minutes went by as I anticipated Sea'Sea's next text. "What the fuck she doing," I whispered, eagerly anticipating her response.

"Well fuk it then," I reluctantly texted.

"I just want to c u tonite," Sea'Sea texted.

"Tonite? Y tho CC," I texted.

"Yea. We leavin n da mornin. I want to c u to say gdbye," Sea'Sea texted.

I rubbed my face while shaking my head. I was wondering what Sea'Sea was up to.

"Aight. U betta nt b on no bullshit either," I sent my last text.

"I'm not I promise :)," Sea'Sea texted.

I got up slowly and put on my basketball shorts, flip flops with black socks, and my hoodie with "BASTARD CHILD" written on the front.

"Man I hope Sea'Sea ain't on that bullshit tonight," I thought as I exited the City on my way to Sea'Sea house.

As I walked, I constantly looked around to make sure I wasn't being followed or being set up again. I knew that at the same time I was walking to Sea'Sea's house, an auction was going on to see who would charge a lesser fee to take my life. I heard the whispers, the streets were talking.

I passed the Blue Heaven, jumped the ditch, and walked up the steps of Sea'Sea's house. I knocked my usual three times.

Sea'Sea opened the door with a smile wider than a 400 pound man.

I looked at her as she looked at me. I noticed how different she looked with her hair normal, cut in a bob, with no color. I noticed how smooth and clean her skin looked without all the ratchet makeup. She damn near looked like a college girl.

We stood there staring at each other. I gave off a blank stare as Sea'Sea turned her head to the side with a smile on her face. She knew I wanted to see her just as bad as she wanted to see me. I was trying to play hard to get.

"You gone come in or what. Or just sit out there looking crazy," Sea'Sea said.

I slowly walked into the house, still looking around.

I started to check behind each door, check each room, making sure the coast was clear.

"What you doing," Sea'Sea asked.

I didn't respond.

"Ain't nobody here but me. Stop acting brand new with me Amel. You know I'm the only one here so chill," Sea'Sea said.

I stood in the middle of the living room just staring at Sea'Sea. I noticed that the house looked better. The furniture and appliances were new, the carpet was new, and the house smelled like it had just been cleaned. I figured that they were really leaving and fixed up the trailer trying to sell it.

"You can sit down, damn," Sea'Sea said getting irritated.

"Why I'm here Sea'Sea," I asked rolling my eyes.

"Just sit down and I will tell you why you here," Sea'Sea quickly responded with a smile. I noticed she smelled of melons, like she had taken a real good bath.

I sighed as I obliged and sat on the couch.

Sea'Sea went into the kitchen and returned with a bottle of 4 dollar Zinfandel wine with two Black Burger 20oz cups.

"What you doing Sea'Sea," I asked as I observed her.

"What it look like I'm doing. I'm fixing us a drink. You always said that you want a normal life. This is me giving it to you," Sea'Sea said.

"You already know what it is with me and Kris," I said.

Sea'Sea put the cups and the wine on the table and gave me a devious stare.

"Don't speak that BITCH name in my presence," Sea'Sea yelled with authority as she pointed her finger at me.

"It is what it is," I said.

"It is what it is my ass," Sea'Sea said. "Just sit back and relax. And have a drink with me. This me na,"

I gave a slight chuckle.

"See. Just chill my boy. This ain't no stranger you dealing with," Sea'Sea said.

Sea'Sea poured a half cup of wine in both cups and handed me a cup.

"To our friendship. To us," Sea'Sea said as she raised her cup and waited on me to toast.

I reluctantly raised my cup and met Sea'Sea's cup.

"To us," I said with a smile. I couldn't front, it felt good to be around Sea'Sea.

--

"Amel why we ain't never fucked," Sea'Sea said with low eyes, clearly tipsy. "That's been on my heart to ask you for a minute now,"

I sat there tipsy too. I didn't respond.

Sea'Sea threw a pillow at me to wake me out of my daze.

"I don't know Sea'Sea. I mean I ate yo pussy before and sucked yo titties. Don't that count," I asked.

"No that's eating pussy and sucking titties. I'm talking about sticking that leg between yo legs right here," Sea'Sea said as she opened her legs wide in her mini skirt, pantyless.

I looked down and instantly got wood.

"You want to know the truth though," I responded still looking at Sea'Sea's pussy.

"About what," Sea'Sea asked.

"Bout why we ain't never fucked," I asked now looking at her in the eyes.

"Yea tell me," Sea'Sea said jokingly.

"To be real. I heard you fucked JoJo, that boy Mike, both ETs, Skinny Minny, Killa Voo, BaBa, that boy PeeWee, Jamison and his brother M, Thapo, Drill and Fred, Shocker House, CoCo, Gilmo, and yeah and the boy KO. You want me to keep going cuz I can,"

Sea'Sea closed her legs and just looked at me.

I looked back at her. "I mean you asked and there it is. Ain't no need to front like you ain't fucked them niggas,"

Sea'Sea grabbed the wine bottom from the table and threw it at me.

"GET THE FUCK OUT," Sea'Sea demanded as she pointed to the door.

"I thought we was drinking and playing the truth game," I said with a smirk.

"Get out," Sea'Sea screamed.

"I ain't going nowhere. Tell me why you fucked so many niggas and want me to act like everything cool. Fuck you Sea'Sea,"

"If you hada," Sea'Sea yelled.

"If I hada what Sea'Sea," I yelled.

"Nothing, get out," Sea'Sea yelled.

"I ain't going nowhere until you give me an answer to my question Sea'Sea," I said.

"OK then," Sea'Sea said as she went into the kitchen and grabbed a knife.

"Now if you don't get yo ass out my house, Imma put this motherfucker to yo throat like you did me," Sea'Sea said. "Now I'm asking you politely to get the fuck out my house,"

I stepped to Sea'Sea nose to nose.

"Who the fuck you thank you scaring Sea'Sea," I asked. "You know I ain't never been a bitch,"

Sea'Sea put the knife to my throat.

"Do ya thang Sea'Sea," I said.

We stood there and looked into each other eyes.

"Do it," I whispered. "Do what's on yo heart. You in control not me,"

Then a lightbulb went off in Sea'Sea head.

"Don't move or Imma cut yo damn throat," Sea'Sea said. "Now, you do what I tell you to do, you hear me motherfucker,"

I stared at her.

"Go sit down on the couch," Sea'Sea demanded with the knife still to my throat.

I didn't move.

"You thank I'm playing," Sea'Sea said as she pierced my skin with the knife.

I could feel the blood flowing down my neck. I took a deep breath and blew it out slowly.

Sea'Sea looked down and seen my dick jumping against my pants.

"I said go sit on the fucking couch," Sea'Sea said as she slowly ran her tongue up my left face cheek.

I took a deep breath again and blew it out slowly. Then I cautiously obliged to Sea'Sea's demand.

"Now take off them pants and boxers," Sea'Sea said sitting beside me with the knife at my throat.

I obliged. I struggled to them off due to my aroused dick.

"Don't move," Sea'Sea whispered as she tasted me and then saddled me.

Sea'Sea spit on her hand and rubbed it on my dick. Sea'Sea then slowly slid my penis in her vagina.

"Damn that dick big," Sea'Sea said as she leaned over to face with me with the knife still at my throat. "Don't move," she demanded.

I obliged.

Sea'Sea started to move back and forth and up and down on me, moaning louder with each movement.

"Choke me,"

I obliged. I put my hands around her neck and choked her slightly.

"Harder nigga,"

I squeezed her neck tighter.

"That's it," Sea'Sea moaned. She leaned back and started to ride me harder and harder, moaning louder and louder.

I could feel something coming to the tip of my dick as my moans increased. I didn't want Sea'Sea to stop.

I started to shake as I started to erupt like a volcano.

"Ooohhhhhh shhhhhhiiiiiittttttt," I screamed shaking like a leaf. It was clear my body was experiencing something I had never felt.

I jerked with tenderness. When I tell you all my energy was gone, you best believe it.

Sea'Sea leaned over and laid on me, both of us out of breath and sweaty. I knew she could feel my warm seed inside of her. Sea'Sea felt whole, she felt complete, she felt a piece of me in her.

Chapter 34

"Somebody just got they cherry popped tonight didn't it," Sea'Sea said with a smile as she slapped me on the arm.

I shook my head with a chuckle.

"How you figure you popped my cherry," I said. "My cherry been popped three years ago,"

Sea'Sea's mood changed.

"By who," Sea'Sea snapped.

"None of yo business," I said nonchalantly.

"It is my fucking business," Sea'Sea said twisting her neck and bucking her eyes. She was feeling some kind of way about what I had said. Sea'Sea felt a sense of pride about being my first.

"Says who," I asked.

"Says me nigga," Sea'Sea said as she punched me in the chest.

"See how you be playing. Now if I buss yo ass in the mouth, then I'm wrong," I said.

"Ain't nobody playing with you," Sea'Sea said. "I don't care who you fucked so whatever,"

"Why you all in yo feelings then," I asked.

"Ain't nobody in their feelings. Yo dick ain't that good nigga for me to be acting like that," Sea'Sea said.

"Whatever I'm bout to skate out anyway," I said.

"Leave then. I got what I wanted. Bye," Sea'Sea said as she rolled her eyes. I know deep down she wanted me to stay.

"The hell you say, talking bout you got what you wanted," I said as I took out my phone. "I knew I shouldn't have come over here. I shoulda listen to my first mind,"

"But you came though. Nigga stop fronting," Sea'Sea said with a laugh.

I called Money beeper and dialed in the number 1244. That was me and Money special code to come get me.

"And who you calling," Sea'Sea said. "I guess you calling yo bitch. You know, yo bitch Kris,"

"Chill with that bitch shit Sea'Sea, I keep telling you that. She ain't no bitch," I yelled.

"Where my phone at. I wonder what little Kris gone say if she knew you was over here with me, letting me do thangs to ya," Sea'Sea said as she took out her phone and started to dial a number.

"Would you chill with that bullshit," I yelled.

"Hello," Sea'Sea said.

I quickly jumped and ran towards Sea'Sea but Sea'Sea had a head start to the bathroom and I knew that.

"May I speak to Kris," Sea'Sea said as she ran into the bathroom and quickly locked the door.

"Sea'Sea chill out with all that mane," I said beating on the door. "See what I'm saying. That's why I didn't even want to come over here,"

Sea'Sea ignored me.

"Tell her this Sea'Sea," Sea'Sea said. "I am doing fine. Oh that's just my brother in the background making up noise,"

I felt my phone vibrate.

"What up," I answered.

"Shake, where you at my boy," Money said over the phone.

"Over here fucking with Sea'Sea bout to beat her ass," I yelled.

"Beat her ass? I hope you talking bout beating that red pussy up. Yall need to stop all that bullshit, every time you turn around, yall fighting bout something," Money said.

"You know how that motherfucker is," I yelled.

"I got yo motherfucker nigga," Sea'Sea screamed through the door.

"Come and scoop me though my boy," I said to Money.

"Why you trying to leave Amel," Sea'Sea said but I ignored her.

"Aight, I'll be through there in a minute," Money said. "Aye, what Sea'Sea cook,"

"Shit," I said as I walked back to the living room.

"Aight, with her lazy ass. I'll be through there to scoop you in a minute my boy," Money said.

"Where you going," Sea'Sea said as she opened the door to the bathroom.

"Fuck you Sea'Sea," I said not looking at her.

"I was just playing with you Amel, damn. You know I ain't even got that bitch number so how Imma call her," Sea'Sea said. "So get a grip on life,"

"You get a fucking grip on life and stop playing so much. You act like you 5 years old. Don't make no damn sense how much you be playing," I yelled.

"It was a joke Amel, hehe haha," Sea'Sea said with a chuckle.

"But you the only one over there sniggling and giggling though like the shit funny. Ain't nothing funny Sea'Sea, with yo crazy ass," I said.

"I wasn't crazy just a few minutes ago when I was riding that dick like a soldier," Sea'Sea said demonstrating how a cowgirl rode a horse.

I heard the horn blow outside and knew it was Money from the thump coming from the trunk.

"See, now you looking stupid," I said as I walked outside.

"Fuck you Amel," Sea'Sea yelled.

"You just did that so what's new on yo mind Sea'Sea. You got what you wanted right," I said.

Money rolled down his window and screamed "What's up Sea'Sea," with a smile.

"Fuck you too Money," Sea'Sea yelled.

I jumped into the car and we both stuck up our middle fingers at Sea'Sea and drove off laughing.

--

Me and Money blocked the City as we usually did when it was nothing else to do. Everybody in the City loved Money because he was a fun and outgoing dude that would make anybody laugh if they were in his presence. He was his father, Boomer, in a younger body, that's how much he acted like him.

"So Shake, what's up with you and yo girl Sea'Sea," Money asked.

"Shit. We just do what we do. Why you ask though," I said.

"Nothing. Yall just always fighting and making up like old married people," Money said.

"LIES," I said with a laughter.

"For real though my boy," Money said. "Do that girl Kris know you over Sea'Sea house this late at night,"

"Hell naw my boy, is you crazy," I said.

"Then why you doing it," Money asked.

"Who you pose to be, Matlock," I said. "You sound like a preacher my boy,"

"You know Kris is a good girl, right," Money said.

"I know that Money, guyyyy dammmnnnn mane. You keep telling me that. I'm starting to thank you fucking her," I said.

"I ain't fucking her cuz you know like I know, she would be chasing me out here and not yo lil ass. I'm just saying, it's fucked up that you fucking over her like that knowing she a good girl my boy," Money said.

"Get out yo feelings my boy," I said.

"I damn sho ain't in my feelings just letting you know cuz I know you got something good going with Kris," Money said. "I mean I fucks with Sea'Sea too but Sea'Sea and Kris apples and oranges my boy,"

"That's real," I said. I knew Money was telling me right, like he always tried to do. "I ain't trying to fuck over nan one of them though. I'm just doing me,"

"Doing you gone get you hurt out here my boy. I keep telling you," Money said.

"Mane catch out with all that bullshit my boy," I said with a chuckle. "You sound like King Lee,"

"Don't say ain't nobody ever tell you that when you out here fucked up," Money said, turned up the music, and left the conversation alone. I knew it was therapy time. Therapy time for us consisted of riding and blocking not saying a word, just thinking, trying to understand life as it was.

We blocked the City for about 15 minutes in pure silence until Money turned down the music. I looked at him with a strange look because it was unusual for him to do such a thing, especially when we were blocking.

"Let me ask you something my boy," Money said.

"What's that," I asked.

Money hesitated.

"What's that my boy. Sounds like you got something on yo mind," I said.

"Do you believe angels live in this world with us my boy," Money asked.

I hesitated, obviously caught off guard by what Money said.

"I don't know what to believe my boy," I said.

"Now tell me this, how you explain how miracles happen on earth then," Money asked.

"Mane, I can't tell ya my boy," I said looking out the window rubbing my chin.

"Cuz angels on earth have the touch of the Creator in them. They everywhere my boy and you don't even know it," Money said.

"The Creator," I asked.

"The Creator of the universe," Money said.

Money chuckled as he turned another block.

"Have you ever seen somebody heal a man with a touch," Money said with conviction. "Have you ever seen that my boy,"

"I seen King Lee do it a couple times. It blew my mind,"

"Exactly," Money said with confidence. "Now tell me this Shake, how do you explain miracles that happens on earth then. What you seen that boy King Lee do, got to be miracles, right,"

"I guess," I said. "Wait a minute. What you trying to say King Lee is a angel,"

"You said it not me my boy," Money said.

I smacked my mouth "Hell naw,"

"Tell me how you explain it then. You still ain't told me nothing," Money yelled.

"I can't explain it my boy. I seen it so I know it's real," I said. "The boy King Lee said it was a mind thing. Persuasion and belief he said it was. He called it The Third Degree,"

Money laughed out loud. "That's exactly what it is. The Third Degree and it's not just a mind thing, it's real my boy. King Lee told you that to throw you off. They got books and everything on The Third Degree,"

"Hell naw. You for real my boy," I asked.

"If I'm lying I'm flying my boy. What you thank I be doing when I be late for practice or late for school. I be reading my boy," Money said.

"Damn my boy," I said. "So how long you been on The Third Degree like that,"

"For bout a year now," Money said. "So let me ask you this then. Have you ever prayed for something and what you prayed for never happened,"

"Evvvvverrryyyy DAY," I said with a chuckle.

We both laughed.

"What if I told you that the Creator answered everything I asked Him for," Money said.

"I would tell you that it's impossible," I responded.

"With the Creator, anythang possible my boy. He makes no mistakes. He is pure. He is truth. And He found me," Money said with pride.

"Straight like that huh," I asked.

"Straight like that my boy," Money said.

My heart started to race a bit. The conversation was getting a little strange. I knew I believed in the God Baby Sister taught me about, but I was kind of uncomfortable getting so deep into this Creator talk.

"You scared to die my boy," I asked as I looked out the window.

"Nope," Money responded.

"Get the fuck out of here. So you not scared to die my boy," I asked in disbelief.

"Nope because I found the truth. The Creator is the truth, He is my truth. That's all I need my boy. I found that peace that make dying something to look forward too,"

"Damn," I said.

"We gone talk bout it later though. Until then, do some research on The Third Degree and the Creator," Money said in a serious manner.

"Aight," I said.

Money turned the radio up and immediately turned it back down.

"I knew I had to ask you something. Yo you going swimming with us this Satday down there on Robuck Lake," Money said.

"When," I asked.

"I just said Satday nigga. You got too much wax in yo ears," Money said.

I laughed.

"Oh hell yeah I'm going my boy. Bout what time yall skating out," I said with excitement.

"Early, bout 10am that morning," Money said.

"Bet. You already know we gone act a fool," I said.

"Damn straight," Money said as me and him gave each other dap.

Money pulled up to the old light blue shotgun house in the City.

I got out of the car and walked up to the door.

"I'm telling you this because I love you my boy and I want you to have that peace too," Money yelled with a smile.

"I kno…I love you too my boy," I yelled back with a smile. "I will get with you damar so be looking for me,"

"Aight bet,"

Chapter 35

It was 8 in the morning when I heard my cell phone ring in the other room of the old light blue shotgun house. I slowly rushed to get my phone because I wanted to let my bologna I was cooking burn around the edges until it was nice and crisp, completing my world famous triple decker fried bologna sandwich.

"Hello," I answered.

"Yo granddaddy say he wants to see you," A lady said.

I stepped back and looked at my phone.

"Hello, who this," I asked.

"This Baby Sister boy. Stop acting a fool here," Baby Sister yelled.

"Oh, my fault. What you say now, I couldn't hear you at first," I said.

"I said yo granddaddy said he wants to see you," Baby Sister repeated.

"My granddaddy," I asked.

"Ain't that what I said," Baby Sister yelled.

"Where bout you found him at," I asked.

"They called me from the hospital and told me to come get him cuz he only had two weeks to live. He bout gone cuz he starting to get real weak by the day. If you want to see him, you need to come on," Baby Sister said.

"I'm on my way. Yall just stay put," I said. "Fuck," I continued as I thought about going to Robuck Lake with Money.

It took me about 30 minutes to make it to Baby Sister's house in Bear Ridge. I wanted to meet my grandfather and find out more about him before it was too late.

I met Baby Sister sitting on the porch.

"He real weak in there but he said he wanted to see you," Baby Sister said.

I sat down beside Baby Sister. She spit out tobacco juice into her spit cup.

"So how they know to call you from the hospital," I asked. "How did they know you was his daughter,"

Baby Sister hunched her shoulders. "I guess he told them we was some kin,"

I nodded my head to say ok.

Me and Baby Sister sat on the porch for another minute or so, taking in the cool breeze.

"Did you talk to him," I asked, breaking the silence. "Did you ask him bout his past,"

"I did," Baby Sister responded looking down at her nails.

"Did you tell him bout yo momma and what happened to her," I asked.

"I did," Baby Sister said.

"What he say," I asked with intrigued.

"He cried," Baby Sister said still looking at her nails. "He cried like a baby. Then he asked me why and I told him why,"

"Then what he say," I asked.

"He said he understood. He told me every thang too. I told him all that what was on my heart. He told me he was sorry for everything," Baby Sister said.

"How you feel after that. I mean, like did you feel good behind saying all that stuff to him like that," I asked.

"I felt good. I felt a lil bit lighter round my heart, you know," Baby Sister said. "What I had inside me had me in a prison, like a prison of anger, you know that I been running from. But after I talked to him, I feel happy, I feel peace, you know. I ain't never felt like this in my life, at least not that I remember,"

"Well good Baby Sister," I responded. "Did he say any thang bout how he grew up,"

"He told me his side of the story," Baby Sister said.

"Do you believe him," I asked.

"I do," Baby Sister said as she sighed aloud. "I didn't want to believe him but what he said made sense,"

"What he say," I asked.

"Just how low down his daddy was to him and how his momma died when he was young. How he and momma met. How he loved momma and why he did some of the thangs he did," Baby Sister said. "Now just thanking bout it, just looking back at it, it make sense. Me and him the same. I did yall like I thought he was doing me. Ain't that something? Repeating every single thang he did,"

"As long as you in a good place now is all that matter Baby Sister," I said.

"You know I was so focused on not being like him that I turned out to be just like him. Ain't that something," Baby Sister said.

"It is," I said. "I thank the most important thang is, is did you forgive him,"

"I did, I sho did," Baby Sister said as she patted me on the leg. "It was hard to let go that anger, my past you know, but I did. You know you gave me strength to do that boy,"

"Well good Baby Sister. I'm glad that you feel better," I said. "He in there, right,"

"Yeah he in Melo room. Go head and go see him, he in there," Baby Sister insisted.

I got up and walked to the door. Then I looked back. "You coming too ain't it,"

"What you scared of. He ain't gone bite," Baby Sister said with a chuckle.

"I just want you to come with me. Imma lil nervous to meet him," I said.

Baby Sister slowly got up and slapped me on the back. "Boy I swear you act like you crazy sometimes,"

Baby Sister escorted me to the door.

"You ready," Baby Sister asked.

"Yeah I'm ready," I said.

Baby Sister slowly opened the door and there I found my grandfather in a hospital bed, hooked up to oxygen, sound asleep.

I stood in the door. I started to shake a little, put my hands to my mouth, and started to cry.

I turned and hugged Baby Sister.

"You acting like you know him or something. You ain't never even seen him before," Baby Sister said as she slowly patted me on the back trying to calm me down.

I didn't say a word but embraced Baby Sister harder.

It took another minute for me to even look at my grandfather laying in that bed.

When I finally calmed down, I walked over to my grandfather and touched his hand. They felt so cold to me.

"I heard you was looking for me ole man," I whispered with a smile as tears still rolled from my eyes. I wiped my face and sniffed loudly, awakening him.

My grandfather slowly reached up and touched my face with a shaken hand. A tear rolled down his face. He had finally met his long lost grandson his daughter had been telling him about the past two weeks.

I put my hand on my grandfather's hand.

"Why you didn't tell me," I asked.

"Tell you what," Baby Sister responded.

I looked at Baby Sister and then quickly looked back at my grandfather without responding to her.

My grandfather looked off into the light of the window, breathing heavy from anxiety.

"Do you know him," Baby Sister asked.

I didn't respond.

"Do you know him I said," Baby Sister screamed. She quickly walked over to me and snatched my face towards hers.

Baby Sister tried to look me in the eyes but I dropped my head. She then looked at her father lying in bed and saw how emotional he was too.

"Answer me Amel," Baby Sister snapped.

I nodded. Then I buried my head in Baby Sister's shoulder and began to cry again.

"What the hell is going on," Baby Sister screamed, clearly still confused.

I pushed away from her and focused my attention back on my grandfather.

"Why didn't you tell me," I asked again.

"You were the link to my salvation," My grandfather whispered in a weak voice. "The link to making a mends with my past and getting forgiveness from the one thing I lost, my family,"

I sat down on the stool beside the bed. I looked at Baby Sister and then looked to the floor.

"I told you that drinking was going to catch up with you," I said. "Didn't I, didn't I King Lee,"

King Lee just stared at me. He slowly pointed to the bottle of home brew on the dresser.

"I'm not giving you that, is you crazy," I quickly said.

"I'm dying Amel. A lil drink isn't going to hurt anything," King Lee said.

"I'm not giving it to you," I snapped.

Baby Sister snatched the bottle off the dresser and handed it to King Lee.

"What is you doing," I stood up and screamed.

"I'm giving him what he want," Baby Sister said.

I grabbed the bottle and threw it against the wall. "He don't need that shit. Can't you see he dying,"

"Didn't I tell yo ass bout yo mouth. Now cuss again if you all big and bad," Baby Sister yelled.

King Lee grunted, trying to raise up, "Yall stop,"

"See you gone upset the man, guy'lee," I said as I sat back down on the stool. "See what I been going through King Lee, now you see,"

--

Baby Sister was on the porch cleaning a catfish to eat. I was still by King Lee's bedside, watching him as he went in and out of sleeping.

"So that means that Javion is yo great-grandboy," I said.

King Lee nodded. He instructed me to get out of the way of the mirror that I was sitting in front of.

"What you need," I asked.

"Move," King Lee responded. "I want to see my death picture,"

I looked at King Lee with a defeated look as I moved out of the way of the mirror. I observed as King Lee studied his reflection in the mirror.

"It's my time my boy," King Lee said with a slight chuckle.

I gave off an uncomfortable smirk.

"Yall just bury me in a nice suit. I don't want no funeral. I just want to be put in the ground, a simple burial for a simple man. You gave me my flowers while I was here Amel and I thank you for that. Now I can die with a peaceful heart," King Lee said. "Do me a favor Amel,"

"Any thang you need King Lee," I said.

"Put that poem in my casket that you wrote me," King Lee said.

I nodded, "Ok".

"You know it's some kind of feeling when you know that you won't live to see the sunrise," King Lee said.

"Stop talking like that. You here now," I snapped.

King Lee started to scream with pain as he released fluid through his rectum like a pregnant woman would when her water broke.

King Lee reached out and grabbed my hand and squeezed it tightly.

"Where is his medicine," I screamed.

"He ain't got none," Baby Sister said bursting through Melo room door.

King Lee breathing went from heavy to light. His eyes began to glaze over as he stared without blinking into the ceiling, still holding on to my hand.

A tear rolled down King Lee's face as he displayed a slight smirk. I knew he was right where he wanted to be. Dying with his family and not alone.

"I....Love......You...," King Lee whispered, barely moving his mouth.

"I love you too King Lee," I responded.

King Lee took a deep breath and released his soul into the next life.

I stood beside King Lee, still holding his hand, crying for the one true king I have ever known.

Then I looked upon King Lee in the bed. He looked at peace. He looked free.

"You in a better place now," I said.

I grabbed King Lee's hand and took the brown rubber band from his wrist. King Lee always wore rubber bands on his wrists, he said they brought him luck.

I left out of the room and made my way onto the porch. There I found Baby Sister wiping tears from her eyes.

"He gone ain't it," Baby Sister said trying to hold her emotions as tight as she could.

I sighed loudly and shook my head to say he was gone.

"You ok," I said to Baby Sister as I sat beside her. I then placed my arm around her.

"Imma be alright," Baby Sister said as she patted my leg.

The two of us sat there in silence and cried together, remembering King Lee for what he was to the both of us.

"You know, ever since you talked to me bout him, thangs got so much better with our relationship. We stayed up a few nights, sharing stories and him explaining to me situations that I hated him for. I never knew that I could learn so much bout a person in so little time. These past couple of days taught me that it only takes a few moments to understand and love a person for a lifetime. You helped me turn my hate into love for my own daddy Amel, you helped me forgive him. I thank you for helping me make peace with him before he left this earth. Now, I don't have no regrets bout any thang," Baby Sister said.

I smiled.

"Everybody need somebody to help them look at the bigger picture, instead of looking at the small thangs so much. Now don't get me wrong Baby Sister, the smaller thangs in life count but we must put those thangs in perspective and not live within those small thangs in life but live within the bigger picture of life. Anybody can hold grudges against people for the smallest of thangs and forget how short life is. Forgiveness, courage, and peace are important thangs of life that most people take for granted," I said. "That king in that bed in there taught me that,"

Baby Sister laughed out loud and put her hands to her face with excitement. "Look at my boy talk. Keep on,"

"What's so funny bout how thangs turn out Baby Sister, is that you sat here and put yoself to the side to take yo daddy in even after having all that hate against him. It showed me what kind of person you was deep down that you didn't let him step a foot in a death home. He died where he wanted to be and that's in his family care. And that means something to me Baby Sister, it really do," I said wiping a tear from my eye.

"Oh that's all right," Baby Sister said as she wiped a tear from my eye. I felt like she was being a mother to me, I could feel her love, her compassion.

"God gone bless those who do the right thang and that have good hearts. Yeah, I had problems with my daddy but I couldn't let him die in no death home or by himself. He called and I came, just like I promised Momma before she died. I know God going to bless me, He going to bless us all. God knows his heart, mine and yos too. He knows we are good folk that mean well and I thank that stand for something," Baby Sister said.

"I thank it do too Baby Sister," I said.

"You know I never been so happy and at peace with myself in all my life," Baby Sister said. "And I want it to last forever,"

"It will. Like they say, trouble don't last always. Yo trouble over Baby Sister," I said.

"And I believe that Amel, I really do," Baby Sister said with a chuckle. "Well the death lady gone be here in a minute to carry him off so be looking for her,"

"Ok," I responded.

Baby Sister returned into the house. I stayed on the porch, closed my eyes, and appreciated the light breeze wiping across my face as me and King Lee always did on the porch of the light blue shotgun house.

"I can feel you King Lee," I said. "I know you still here with me out here somewhere,"

Chapter 36

King Lee died Wednesday and was being buried Saturday. Baby Sister abided by King Lee wishes to be buried without a funeral but Baby Sister and I both wanted to give King Lee a short graveside service. We wanted him to be sent off with a little grace and respect.

"You ready," Baby Sister asked me as King Lee's body made its way to the grave yard amidst the handful of people there. "Here he come,"

I started to cry. Just the sight of the hearse made me reflect on my memories with King Lee.

Ms. Betty Joe came over and hugged me and gave her condolences, as did Rico Love, Mr. Dandress and Mr. Ben.

Baby Sister put her arms around me and said, "It's gone be alright,"

"Look, there go yo friend," Baby Sister said as she pointed to Money pulling up, trying to cheer me up a little bit.

Money walked over to me. He didn't say a word but took me to the side and hugged me. "Its aight my boy," Money whispered to me as I cried on his shoulder.

Before the funeral home people started to roll King Lee casket in the ground, I stopped them.

"Can I put this in there," I asked as I took out a piece of paper from my pocket with the poem I had written for King Lee on it.

The funeral home moderator grabbed the poem, opened up the casket slightly and placed the poem inside of King Lee's casket.

The funeral home grave diggers started to roll King Lee's casket down into the eight feet hole. I stared at it, crying, still in disbelief that King Lee was gone.

"It's going to be aight my boy," Money said with his arm still around me. "You know he in a better place, right,"

I wiped my eyes and nodded.

"Aight then, so don't worry too much bout it," Money said.

I finally gathered myself enough to be functional.

"You ready to hit Robuck Lake right quick. Ah, I got something that gone make you feel better fosho," Money said.

I gave off a slight smile, still looking down, trying to finish gathering my emotions.

"What's that my boy," I asked wiping my nose with a tissue.

"They say Kris momma gone let her come," Money said.

I snatched my head up with excitement. "LIES,"

"Yep, see I knew that would bring yo lil butt up. That's what home girl Finny Bug told me yesterday," Money said.

"Kris bout hate me right bout now. I ain't hollered at her in soooooo long my boy. I mean when she call, I press ignore. Just been too much going on with your boy," I said.

"LIES. You know Kris ain't going nowhere, like I know she ain't going nowhere," Money said.

I chuckled.

"What we pose to be doing over at the lake anyway," I asked.

"Chill and watch ho...girls, what else my boy," Money responded.

"Hunting season," Money and I said at the same time as we started laughing out loud and dapping each other.

"Yo I gotta run by Baby Sister's house right quick. Come by and scoop me in like ten minutes. That's a bet," I said.

"That's a bet my boy," Money said.

--

Money pulled up to Baby Sister's house with a pickled pig feet and sunflower seeds in hand. He walked to the porch where he met Baby Sister sitting on one of the white plastic chairs, chewing tobacco and drinking a cold beer.

"Get yo stanky cock out my yard," Baby Sister screamed as she got up from her seat in a hurry.

Money looked around and pointed to himself.

"I'm sick of that got damn dog. Imma blow that motherfucker head off, just watch and see. I told him good to stay his nasty ass out my damn lilies," Baby Sister snapped.

"Amel here," Money asked respectfully.

"Yeah he in there," Baby Sister said calmly as she took her seat. "Amel," Baby Sister screamed.

"How yo momma doing baby," Baby Sister asked as she sipped on her beer.

"Oh she doing ok," Money said.

"Well tell her Baby Sister from Bear Ridge asked bout her when you see her," Baby Sister said.

"Yes ma'am," Money responded.

I burst out of the front door, eating a pork chop. "My boy," I said with a smile.

"I hope you ain't touched nothing while you acting a fool, bursting out my door like that," Baby Sister yelled.

"I ain't touch nothing. Just ready to hit this road right quick," I said licking my fingers. "Them pork chops on point though,"

"You ready my boy," Money asked.

"You already know," I said.

"Yall don't need to go down to that lake. Ain't nothing but trouble down there," Baby Sister said. "Yall just need to sit ya asses down somewhere,"

"Who said we was going to the lake," I said looking at Money with "do you hear this shit" look.

"I know where yall going and ain't nothing good gone come from it, you hear me," Baby Sister said.

"Ok Baby Sister," I said as me and Money walked to the car. "We gone protect ourselves,"

"It ain't gone be good, I'm telling you now. Ain't nobody gone survive it," Baby Sister yelled.

I looked around carefully to see if anybody was in sight while Baby Sister went on her rant.

"Yo momma got that divinity in her my boy," Money whispered. "I can feel it. She got it in her I'm telling you,"

"She bugging out, that's all I feel," I said feeling a bit embarrassed.

"Don't say I didn't tell you when shit she be saying go down," Money said.

--

Money and I headed up Highway 7, not saying a word just listening to music, until we got to Robuck Lake. When we arrived, Money and I knew it was going to be a good day because everybody and their momma was at the lake chilling.

"We just posting up right. I ain't getting in no water," I said just to make sure me and Money was on the same page.

"Nigga I ain't getting in no water either, you can't swim, and I can't swim. It's over with," Money said with a chuckle. "Ah, I just thought bout it. When you going to the Navy my boy,"

"Shid, I gotta go take that test first before I do anythang," I said.

Money rolled his eyes and shook his head, obviously irritated.

"Why you still bullshitting with that test though," Money snapped.

"Imma take that test. Man, I swear sometimes you act like you my daddy," I said.

"I just want you to do the right thang and stop bullshitting and get serious bout this shit," Money said. "You need to get yo ass outta here,"

"Why I need to get outta here. Why you don't need to get outta here," I asked.

"I'm straight. Ain't nothing out here for me my boy, just this shit you see and chasing hoes. It ain't bout me though, you just stick to what you need to do to get outta here," Money said. "Local jokers like me is meant to be round here my boy. That ain't you though, you feel me,"

"I feel you my boy. Imma take that test though next week," I said appreciating Money concern.

"Bet," Money said with a smile.

"Ah, look at that boy KO over there with Finny Bug and Pussy Cat, thanking he macking," I said.

We both laughed.

"He be on them hoes heavy though," Money said still laughing.

I rolled down my window.

"KO, my boy," I screamed.

KO threw both hands in the air with excitement like "all damn there go my boys".

"Ole weak ass," Money shouted to KO with laughter.

KO pimp walked over to the car with Finny Bug and Pussy Cat.

Desiree "Finny Bug" Jones and DaQuesha "Pussy Cat" Cross were two girls from the City attached to the hip like Money and me. They were good girls that got their lesson, but would fight anybody trying to get out of line with them at a drop of a dime. Finny Bug and Pussy Cat purposely hung out with boys more than they did girls. They said that girls were too messy and petty for them and boys were so much easier to get alone with. People around the way tried to say they were diking, but as in any hood, people told lies about anyone they didn't like, especially girls.

"Look at how this fool walking," I said. Money and I looked at each other, hesitated, and laughed out loud. "THIS NIGGA CRAZY,"

"What's so got damn funny? Yall know yall tickled," KO said walking up.

"Laughing at yo wack ass," Money said.

KO bent down and propped himself on the passenger side window.

"What yall wack ass boys doing for it on this fine evening," KO asked.

"Shit, just posting up my boy," Money said. "I see you got yo hands full don't it,"

"Mane you know, just doing a lil something, something. I'm just trying to stay out the way and stay in those legs. You feel me my boy," KO said with a chuckle. "I know fosho yall boys rolling today,"

"I ain't fucking with it today my boy," Money instantly said. "Too many laws out this way,"

"Shid, I'll blow one witcha my boy. Roll one," I said.

"Shid, fuck with me then Shake," KO said giving me a pound.

"Ah Finny Bug, I thought Kris pose to be here. " I said looking through the window trying to spot her. "I don't see her,"

"She said she was coming," Finny Bug said. "But you know how her momma is, she might have changed her mind bout letting her come. You know they don't too much fuck with local jokers like us,"

"Hell naw they don't," I responded.

"Shid, I'm surprise her momma let yo lil ass talk to her," Finny Bug said.

"I don't thank her momma know I'm from the City though," I responded.

"Now that make sense," Finny Bug said, finally getting an answer to a question she had been wondering since she heard me and Kris were talking on the phone.

I nudged Money on the shoulder. "Didn't I tell you she not coming. But naw, here you go, she coming trust me. See I can't take yo word for shit my boy cuz you don't know what you even be talking bout half the time,"

Money looked at me with a smile.

"You need to be getting on to Finny Bug, not me. She the one lying to me like Kris was coming," Money said.

"Aight then. Finny Bug, why you lie," I asked. "You got my boy Money out here lying and shit cuz you lying,"

Finny Bug snapped her neck with attitude.

"I didn't lie, that what Kris told me," Finny Bug yelled.

"I told you what," Kris said walking up.

"Speak of the devil and he will show his head," Money said. "I told you didn't it my boy,"

"You ain't told me shit," I responded with a smile.

"Hey Amel," Kris said as she kept walking passed Money's car.

"What's up," I said staring at her, but Kris didn't pay me no mind.

"Where the fuck she going," I whispered.

Money pointed to Pearlie Winston waiting in the distance for Kris. "Kris going right there my boy,"

Pearlie Winston was a smooth talking, nice dressing bastard from the white folks neighborhood just like Kris was. His parents were medical doctors, but wanted him to live and appreciate a humble life, that's why they sent him to Sammie Beans High and not a private school. I couldn't stand Pearlie ole spoil ass.

Kris hugged and kissed Pearlie on the cheek.

"Ain't this a bitch," I yelled in shock.

Money started to laugh.

"What's so got damn funny my boy," I asked.

"She walked straight passed yo ass and into the arms of another nigga. A good nigga too," Money said. "See I told yo ass good when you out here doing you and get fucked up, you gone be looking stupid like you looking now,"

I smacked my mouth and jerked back in the seat real hard.

"Got damn nigga don't break my seat," Money yelled with a smile.

"Mane fuck that bitch. They don't need to be out here anyway. They don't know bout this life. We from the sticks, they plant flowers and shit. Rich motherfuckers," I snapped.

"Boy get out yo feelings," Money said with laughter.

My stomach started to turn as I watched Pearlie put his arm around Kris and walk her to a picnic he had setup.

"Look how wack that boy is," I poked Money on the arm with my elbow. "Now, what straight nigga setup picnics for hoes,"

"That's a playa move and you don't even see it," Money said. "Now you can do one or two thangs. Let her go or go get her. Yo choice my boy,"

"Mane fuck that nigga," I said as I swung open the door.

"Cuz mad ain't it," Money yelled with laughter.

I walked over to where Pearlie and Kris was sitting and eating sandwiches like a married couple.

"Kris let me holla at you right quick," I demanded.

Kris kept eating, looking straight forward, like I wasn't standing there.

"She busy Shake," Pearlie responded.

"Kris come and holla at me, for real though," I demanded again.

"Shake, she with me, now get on down," Pearlie yelled.

I pulled my hunting knife from my side and put it to Pearlie neck as I had him in the choke hold.

"Now you gone come holla at me or not Kris," I snapped biting my lip, looking into Kris eyes with a focused stare.

"Not," Kris quickly responded.

The way Kris responded confused me. "Do she want this nigga to die," I thought.

Before I knew it, Pearlie had flipped me over his shoulder, took my knife, and had my knife pointed to my neck.

"This motherfucker know karate too," I thought. Pearlie had me pent down where I couldn't move.

"Kris get this nigga befo I kill him," I said looking at Kris with Pearlie's knee in my chest and my knife pointed to my neck.

"I got him," Money said as he tapped Pearlie on the shoulder.

"You sure. I don't want no trouble," Pearlie said.

"You straight Pearlie. I got him," Money repeated.

Pearlie allowed me to get up. I instantly tried to charge Pearlie but Money grabbed me.

"I had that nigga," I said to Money. "You lucky boy," I screamed.

Money chuckled to himself.

"You lucky or he lucky," Money asked. "And why pull a knife on the boy. You acting like Kris yo wife or something,"

"Naw that nigga disrespecting me like that," I yelled.

"How though. Thank bout what you saying right now," Money yelled. "Dude ain't did nothing to you,"

"So you taking up for that nigga now," I said as I grabbed Money arm and snatched him around.

Money threw his hands in the air and said "I ain't yo enemy my boy. I'm just calling a spade a spade,"

I didn't say nothing and started to walk back towards Money's car.

"If you wasn't my boy I woulda beat yo ass just then. You know that right," Money said.

I smacked my mouth.

"LIES," I said. "You know damn well you ain't got no hands,"

Money hit me in the face opened handily to start the usual slap boxing match between us.

"Oh, you thank you tough," I said with a smile. "I'm bout to show you what I was gonna do to yo fuck boy over there," I continued as I threw a light jab of my own.

We both stood there and showed off our best fight stance, hissing out of our mouths with every hand movement like our arms were snakes.

Money beeper started to go off.

"Wait a minute my boy," Money said as he checked his beeper. He started to walk towards his car.

"Where you going my boy," I said with confusion.

"Yo, Imma have to fuck witcha later my boy. I gotta go holla at Pops right quick. He just paged me," Money yelled cranking up his car.

"Aight. You coming back ain't it," I yelled in a defeating tone. I wanted to show Money once again I had the best hands between us. "You want me to ride witcha,"

"If you want too, but I'm coming right back," Money yelled. "Just stay put my boy,"

"You sho," I yelled.

"Yeah," Money yelled back.

"Love ya my boy," Money said as he was about to pull off.

"Love ya too my boy," I responded. "Ah you be safe on that road,"

"10.4," Money responded.

Money drove off while yelling to KO "You still ain't gone fuck nothing, ole weakass boy,"

"LIES," KO yelled back.

I laughed as I watched Money pull off, still laughing at KO.

Then everything started to move in slow motion. In a split second, I looked into the eyes of Money. Then everything made sense. I saw it on Money all along, I felt it. I saw the peace, I saw the comfort, I saw Money's makings.

I tried to yell to tell Money to look out but as soon as the words were on the tip of my tongue, everything sped up again as a 18 wheeler slammed right into the side of Money's car, sending it flying through the air.

I watched in a dazed as Money car flipped four times, throwing Money out of the car, and the car landing in Robuck Lake.

Everybody at the lake stood still in shock. My heart felt like it had dropped to the ground, like the feeling of a big drop on a rollercoaster.

I snapped out of my dazed and ran to Money, who was lying about 30 yards from where I was standing.

As I approached Money, I found him shaking all over with blood splattering from his mouth.

"My boy," I whispered as I grabbed and held him, trying to keep him alive. "My boy. Stay woke my boy,"

Money was trying to catch his breath but was choking from his blood that he was coughing up.

"Just hold on my boy. Hold on. Stay woke," I said shaking myself from fear. "Somebody help me," I screamed out loud over and over again.

Then I looked down and noticed that Money wasn't moving anymore. Money,s eyes were locked on the sky.

"Somebody help me," I whispered as I cried out, holding Money's limp body tighter. "Somebody please help me,"

"Aww Naw. Not my nigga," KO screamed as he fell to the ground screaming like a mad man.

--

"Get off me," I screamed as the paramedics tried to get Money's body from my grips but I gripped his body tighter.

"He gone Shake," somebody screamed to me from the gathering crowd. Now most of Itta Bena was at the scene.

"Fuck that," I screamed. "He ain't gone,"

"Come on Shake," KO said as he touched me on the shoulder.

"I can't mane," I cried. "I can't,"

"You got to," KO said with tears running down his face. "He gone,"

KO grabbed me as I let go of Money's lifeless body. The two of us embraced one another and cried together.

Then the anger hit me like a ton of bricks. I wanted to kill whoever was driving that 18 wheeler.

I snatched away from KO embrace.

"Where he at," I screamed. "Where the motherfucker at that hit him," I said searching through the crowd.

I finally made it to the 18 wheeler where the police was questioning the driver.

"Don't I know you," I screamed as I tried to get to the driver. The police grabbed me.

"Ah, don't I know you," I repeated, trying to get from the grips of police to get to the driver.

"I was in route to say my lasting goodbye to a friend," Jerry said to the officer. "He pulled right in front of me. I tried to put on brakes but it was too late,"

Jerry, the same guy who gave me a ride in the middle of the night from Baby Sister's house, was in route to attend King Lee's graveside burial.

"Have you been drinking sir," the officer asked.

"No sir," Jerry responded.

Jerry looked over at me and seen blood in my eyes. Jerry hated having enemies so he thought it would be a great idea to make a gesture to make things right with me.

"Let him go," Jerry pleaded. "I want to talk to Amel,"

"We can't do that sir. He is too irate right now," the police officer said to Jerry.

"You ain't got shit to say to me," I screamed. I didn't care who was around.

Then I felt a pat on my shoulder. I turned around with a mean mug.

"You better than that baby," Ms. Betty Joe said. "Just calm down,"

"I can't calm down Ms. Betty Joe. King Lee gone. Money gone. That ain't right," I cried.

Ms. Betty Joe wiped my face with her hand with a sweet and loving touch.

"I know baby but the Good Lord don't make no mistakes. Don't you put no question mark where the Good Lord put a period, you hear," Ms. Betty Joe said rubbing on my arm. "Thangs gone be alright. They gone be just fine,"

Then it donned on me. "No one gone survive"

--

I arrived at Baby Sister's house in a daze, confused and still shaken by what had transpired an hour before. I had questions for Baby Sister and desperately needed answers. I beat three hard times on the door.

"Hold on," Baby Sister yelled walking from the back. "Who is it,"

"Me," I screamed.

"Me who," Baby Sister asked.

"Amel," I said.

Baby Sister was about to open the door but didn't.

"Open yo hands," Baby Sister demanded.

"For what," I asked.

"Open yo damn hands," Baby Sister demanded.

I obliged. Baby Sister wanted to know if I was trying to pull some funny business on her. She knew I carried a knife with me at all times.

"I tried. I tried to tell ya asses, now look at what happened. See I had this feeling, this itch that told me something bad was gone happen," Baby Sister said. "I said it clear as day. I told ya,"

"Naw you said that nobody gone survive," I said. "How you expect me to take what you said and get that my boy was gonna die,"

"I just told you what was on my heart. I just relayed the message," Baby Sister said.

"Fuck yo message," I yelled as I stormed out of the porch door.

"Be careful how you talk to folks Amel," Baby Sister said in a strange voice.

"Or what? You gone get this itch to have me die too," I said as I slammed the door of the white '69 Mustang, digging off, heading back up Highway 7.

Chapter 37

I sat quietly in the empty old light blue shotgun house. My life had suddenly become indescribable and unknown. King Lee was my guider and I missed him but Money was my best friend. Money was my guy, my road dog.

The streets whispered that Money's mother, Dianne, wanted to burn Money to ashes instead of having a service for him. I heard she fainted when she heard about his death. Money was a momma's boy and as with all momma's boys, he would do anything for Dianne. I heard Money's father, Boomer, had started back drinking and doing drugs after changing his life when Money was born. They say Boomer blamed himself for Money's death.

Deep down, I wanted to honor Money in some way. I wanted to show my appreciation to him, to show my love for him.

"What better way to tell him how I feel than to write him a letter," I thought. I went to my room, got a pen and my writing pad, and started to let my feelings spill onto the paper.

I wrote:

Forever My Boy

As I write to you in this moment in time, thinking, reaching for words to fit THIS just right, day dreaming of a bright future that will never materialize, trying my best to come to terms with what's before me, trying to come to terms with the bad hand God dealt us all, that have our souls screaming with the questions, Why him? Why us? Why so young? As I write to you in this moment in time, I start to remember. Wow. There you are my boy, there they are, the memories. The memories we shared together from little boys until now in this moment in time. There they are, here before me, here before you, here before us. The memories that defined our lives, that defined our friendship, that defined our bond.

I remember how, as little boys, we would go to the baseball field every single day in the summer after NYSP, searching for honey sucker bushes, and going by the park store to get a pickled pig feet or a sour pickle to split. To be honest, I never knew how to play baseball but I told you "You know what though, I could steal bases. I'm going to ask Coach Sadell if I can play". All I wanted was to hang out and have fun with you.

I remember how we went to upward bound together, basketball camp together, slaying everybody on the court, trying our best to impress Coach Davis every chance we got. Or how we use to play basketball in the Projects in front of Cease house or play football in front of Killa Voo house.

I remember how I would walk down to your house, finding you wiring up four tweeters in each corner of either the Lincoln or the throwback Ford Boomer had given you, and wiring up the amp to your twelves in the trunk, anxious to observe the beat down it would produce. Or how we would block the City, not saying a word, listening to music, chilling, beating down the block.

I remember the two of us walking to every home high school football game in Jr. High and how excited we were at the thought of seeing Tommy Boy run a reverse for a touchdown that night in that number 44 jersey. And how we would look at each other after each touchdown Tommy Boy made and say at the same time "And he just in 10th grade". It felt like we were the only ones in the world that were paying attention to the 3 or 4 games Tommy Boy rushed for 1000 yards and like 10 touchdown before hurting his knee.

I remember the two of us rushing to the cafeteria at Sammie Beans to eat lunch in Mrs. Wayne room, waiting on Jumbo to even show his face in the food line, for me to say "There he go Money," and how you guys use to burn each other up hagging, you always telling Jumbo that he would never lay between no legs, even if you won or lost the hagging session.

I remember how you would call me out of the blue and say "What's up my boy," and I would say "My boy my boy," and instantly you would say "Now, would you tell this fool....," As always, I would laugh hard on the phone because I already knew the origins of the call. It was you and your brother Petey arguing about something of no substance, both of you guys trying to be right and prove your arguments. And when I sided with you as I normally did, you would say to Petey "Now, Thank you,". Then you would say "Aight my boy,". I would laugh and say "Aight," because I knew the argument would last another 5 hours.

I remember the most the last time that we hung out at Robuck Lake. Something in me said, "You gotta go to lake with Money" and I did. You came down to King Lee service, you scooped me at Baby Sister's house. Baby Sister told us the future before it happened but we didn't pay it no mind. You told me Baby Sister had a divine intuition about her, but I didn't listen. Then out of the blue, you started to talk about the Creator.

It's strange just thinking about it now because in our conversations leading up to that day, you had told me that you had found what you were looking for on this earth and how you were on a mission to change the world and save souls. You told me "I want to see my family again my boy,". And as we talked and talked some more, I started to notice something about you and I felt obligated to tell you about it. I said "I see peace all on you my boy," and you said. "I do have peace my boy because I found the truth. And if I die tomorrow, I'm going to be aight my boy. I ain't worried,".

As you was about to drive off to go holler at Boomer, I saw your makings written all over your face. Before you drove off, you said. " Shake," I said "What's that my boy," ...You said "I love you my boy," I said "I love you too,". Those few seconds felt like days. And just like that, you were gone, forever.

Memories my boy, good memories, are all we have now.

You know it's something to be said about a friend when you never had any ill wills against them. It's something to be said about a friend that never wanted trouble from nobody but only wanted to have fun in this life. It's something to be said about a friend that cared for his family, cared for others, and was willing to die for something he believed in. It's something to be said about a friend, that as I try to look back over all of my childhood memories, I try to find one single memory that doesn't include Money but I can't.

Even before this tragic event, on my worst days, I would sit back and reflect on our time together and whisper to myself with a smile "My Boy".

I can go on for days about the memories that we shared throughout the years. They are all special to me, you are special to me, Boomer is special to me, your family is special to me, THIS is special to me. Your influence on your family and this community will live on through your spirit for generations to come.

The two words "My Boy" represent an unspoken promise made between us many, many years ago that I will stay true to the rest of my life.

So until the next time we cross paths again, which I am confident that we will.....rest on...live on...in peace.

From one friend to another, Forever My Boy,

-Shake

--

My phone rang and lit up the dark room with light.

I looked at my phone and noticed it was an unknown number with a strange area code. I hesitated to answer, but didn't know if it was Melo calling to ask me to come get Javion.

"Hello," I said with a full fledge attitude.

"Hey," A lady said.

"Who this," I yelled.

"This Sea'Sea,"

I instantly hung up the phone. I didn't have time for Sea'Sea bullshit.

The phone rang again. I noticed it was the same number. I hit the volume button to ignore the call.

The phone rang a third time.

"WHAT MANE," I screamed into the phone.

"I know you hurting but damn," Sea'Sea snapped.

"Ain't nobody hurting, I just don't feel like going through this shit with you today aight," I yelled.

"Ain't nobody on no bullshit," Sea'Sea said. "I'm calling to see how you doing,"

"I'm aight," I snapped back.

"Damn," Sea'Sea said getting defensive. "Can't I just call to see how you doing,"

"Whatever. What's up," I asked.

"You need to talk to somebody Amel," Sea'Sea said. "I know how much Money meant to you. I know you hurting,"

"I'm straight. What's up though? That's all you calling me bout. To fake like you care bout how a nigga feeling," I yelled.

"I do care. You need to get that hurt off yo chest Amel," Sea'Sea said.

"Ain't nobody hurting. I'm straight, I keep telling you that so stop saying that," I demanded.

"Ok," Sea'Sea said.

"Ok what? What? You coming back to town now," I asked.

"How Amel," Sea'Sea asked. "I ain't got no car,"

"You ain't got no car but somehow you found yo way to Georgia," I said. "Now that my boy and yo so called partner dead, you can't find no way back here. Now ain't that something,"

"Where is this coming from," Sea'Sea asked. "What is you even talking bout,"

"You left and everything just fucked up right now," I yelled. "Can't you see that Sea'Sea,"

"Oh. So now all this shit my fault," Sea'Sea yelled.

"You motherfucking right it is," I yelled.

"How is it my fault," Sea'Sea asked.

"You left nigga," I screamed into the phone.

"You know good and got dog gone well I had to leave," Sea'Sea said.

"Fuck that," I said. "You chose to leave,"

The phone fell silent.

"Hello," I yelled.

"I'm trying," Sea'Sea said. "I'm trying to be here for you, like you was there for me when I needed you,"

"How Sea'Sea" I asked. "How in the fuck can you be here for me when you in Georgia. All that shit that I did for you and all I get is a fucking phone call. I need you here like I was there for you,"

"I can't come down there right now. I ain't got no money," Sea'Sea snapped.

I sighed out loud.

"Well walk then," I insisted.

"Walk," Sea'Sea asked.

"You know I would do it for you Sea'Sea," I said.

"Come on now Amel. Walk? Seriously," Sea'Sea said.

"See, you ain't no different than the rest of these motherfuckers out here," I said.

I heard Sea'Sea sniffing.

"What you crying for," I asked.

"Cause," Sea'Sea said.

"Cause what Sea'Sea," I asked rolling my eyes.

"I just don't like how you be doing me," Sea'Sea said with a cracking voice.

"You already know I feel right now," I yelled.

"Ok," Sea'Sea said in a mumble.

Sea'Sea held the phone for another minute.

"Hello," I yelled.

"You going to the funeral," Sea'Sea asked.

I sighed, clearly frustrated.

"He ain't having no funeral," I said.

"Why not," Sea'Sea asked.

"Call his momma and ask her," I said. "Any more questions Sea'Sea,"

"Nope. No more questions," Sea'Sea said with a sigh.

"Aight," I said hanging up the phone.

"Stupid bitch," I yelled as I threw my phone across the room. "Bitch talking bout being there for me and she in Georgia,"

Chapter 38

Darkness filled the old light blue shotgun house in the City. It seemed like everybody that I cared about was gone. King Lee, Money, Javion, Sea'Sea, even Kris had disappeared. Days slowly turned into months as I barely ate, barely took a bath, stuck in one room, numb to life, rocking back and forth, crying, trying to make sense of my life.

And then it started. I was imprisoned by my body and its movements. Mentally, I could feel my heart pump blood. I could feel every moment of my muscles. I started to twitch all over my body. It scared me. I thought I was dying. I started to think I was having a heart attack, like my body was turning against me.

Every single day, without fail, the small voice inside my head stalked me, talked to me louder than ever, feeding me thoughts, feeding me suggestions, feeding me an appetite for self-infliction never felt by me before.

I thought hard about taking my own life every minute of the day. I started to understand that the mental state of a person works differently than the physical. To stop the small voice inside my head, I had to kill it, which meant killing myself. Unlike when a person hurt a leg, that leg can be cut off and they still live. Every day, without fail, I stared at the loaded 9 millimeter I had gotten from JoJo. A couple of times, exhausted from the small voice inside my head stalking me, I put the 9 millimeter to my temple just to feel the steel against my head, to see if I would feel comfort but I didn't. A few times, I put my hunting knife to my wrists just to feel the blade, to see if I would find peace, but I didn't. For some reason, somewhere deep down, I wanted to live despite the prison of suffering.

Chapter 39

Three years passed and still till this day, they were some of the toughest years I had to deal with. I struggled to find my way without King Lee and Money. Even though I was 18, I was still a young boy in need of someone to guide me, tell me right, and keep me level.

In those three years, I mostly stayed out of the way of everybody. The old light blue shotgun house had become my kingdom and I secluded myself in it. I knew I couldn't stay hidden from life forever, but it felt good not to be bothered. Sea'Sea would hit my line sometimes with a call or text, and sometimes I answered depending on how I was feeling. Kris stayed in contact with me too. But we didn't talk like we used to. I heard from Baby Sister every now and then.

I had grown tired of the darkness in my life. I needed something to balance me out. I needed something that would take my mind away from the pain, from the small voice inside my head, from my reality. I needed to become the king of my world and not of this word. I needed freedom.

I knew exactly what would solve all of my problems.

--

As I blocked the City in the white '69 Mustang, feeling my best, being the king of my world, geeked out of my mind, taking bumps of cocaine through a straw, my phone rings.

"Come and get yo boy Boomer. He out here acting a fool," Pussy Cat said.

"Where he at," I asked.

"Over here by the park store," Pussy Cat said.

"Here I come," I said.

I turned the block from the City and started down Dr. King Drive towards the park store.

I saw Boomer stumbling in the middle of the road, screaming at cars.

Boomer looked out of his mind, like a mad man.

I checked my nose and jumped out of the car.

"You aight," I asked Boomer.

Boomer didn't say a word but kept stumbling in the middle of the road.

"Where Money at Shake," Boomer yelled.

I was speechless. I couldn't say a word.

"He gone ain't it Shake," Boomer screamed.

"Come on Boomer, lets go," I said as I grabbed Boomer by the arm. I knew Boomer didn't want any trouble with nobody. He was just going through the motions and had drunk too much whiskey. Even though it had been three years after Money's death, it was obvious that Boomer wasn't over it.

The streets whispered that Boomer had slowly drifted back to his old ways over the years but I was shocked to see Boomer like he was. Seeing him that way fucked me up.

Boomer stumbled and got in the white '69 Mustang. We started to ride towards the City in silence.

"I shouldn't have paged him," Boomer said looking out of the window. I knew those thoughts were playing in his head over and over again. "My life ain't the same no mo. That was my son, my blood,"

I could feel Boomer's pain. It was that moment I knew the hurt of a father that had lost a child that he loved unconditionally. I knew then what kind of place love could take you to when love was taken away all of a sudden.

"It ain't yo fault Boomer," I said.

"It was just a normal day just like the rest of the days," Boomer said looking out of the window, observing the stars and the moon, paying me no mind. "Got up, we talked, went to work, paged him on my break,"

I didn't say a word. I knew Boomer needed to talk through the pain to someone.

"Something in me said call, but I just still paged him for some reason. See, I shoulda listened to my first mind' Boomer said.

"You didn't know what was gone happen," I said.

"But sometimes you need to call instead of doing that other stuff," Boomer said. "Now he gone and ain't nothing I can do bout it," Boomer continued, catching himself from crying.

"Its aight Boomer," I said.

"You know Money always talked bout you and how you was a good friend to him," Boomer said.

I nodded.

"They say we gotta keep moving forward though," Boomer said. "Whatever the fuck that pose to mean,"

"We got to Boomer," I said.

Boomer didn't respond.

"You can let me out up here," Boomer said pointing to the Blue Heaven club.

--

After dropping Boomer off, I eased into the yard of the old light blue shotgun house as the moon was at its peak. I turned the lights off of the white '69 Mustang and made my way onto the porch.

I heard a silent cry coming from King Lee's rocking chair like a cat or dog would moan when it was hurt.

I moved closer.

"Javion," I said as I ran to Javion sitting in King Lee's rocking chair with a note stuck to his little head with duct tape.

I hugged him tight and took the note off his head.

"Tis thee knew me. NJoy lol," The note read.

I bald up the note and threw it in the yard. "Motherfucking JoJo. Imma kill that bitch when I see him," I thought.

"You ok," I asked Javion with concern. I could smell the stench coming from him.

Javion didn't say a word.

"Who dropped you off," I asked.

Javion continued to play the silence game. I found it kind of odd that Javion was so quiet in my presence but I didn't want to press the issue. I was just happy to have my fella around again.

"Come on in here Champ and let me take you a bath," I continued with a sense of happiness. I picked him up from the chair and took him in the house. Javion had suddenly arrived back in my life at a flip of a dime.

"You excited to be here with me, huh," I asked with a sense of pride.

Javion didn't respond.

"You ok Champ," I asked growing concerned by the second. I couldn't see Javion eyes to gauge his reaction.

I took Javion in my room and laid him down. I then went and ran him some bath water in the tin tub, and went back and grabbed Javion from the bed, laying in the same position as I had left him.

As I walked with Javion to the back room to bath, the way Javion felt in my arms was strange. It reminded me of Money's body in my arms as he was dying.

I flipped on the backroom light and looked into Javion eyes. I instantly felled to my knees.

I took out my phone with shaking hands.

"Baby Sister," I screamed.

"What's wrong," Baby Sister asked. She could tell something was wrong.

"Something wrong with Javion," I yelled.

"Where he at," Baby Sister asked.

"He right here. But he slobbing out the mouth and his eyes looking off," I yelled in fear.

"What you mean he slobbing out the mouth and eyes looking off," Baby Sister asked.

"It's like he looking up out the corner of his eyes," I yelled.

"What," Baby Sister said with concern. Suddenly she had fear in her voice. "He breathing ain't it,"

I touched his stomach.

"He breathing but struggling," I yelled.

"Do he feel hot," Baby Sister stuttered.

I touched Javion forehead.

"Naw, he feel cold," I responded.

"Here I come. Don't move him," Baby Sister said as she hung up the phone, threw on some cloths, and headed north to Itta Bena.

--

Seconds seemed like hours as I waited on Baby Sister to arrive. I made it my business not to look at Javion, it was too much for me.

I felt my phone vibrating.

"Hello," I answered.

"Where you at. I'm in Itta Bena now," Baby Sister said.

"I'm in the City," I said.

"Where bout," Baby Sister asked.

"When you come in the gate, keep straight until you see an old light blue shotgun house. The door should be unlocked," I said.

"Ok,"

--

"Lord, look at what they done did to my baby," Baby Sister said entering the back room in total shock. She moved slowly over to Javion and knelt down, touching his little face softly as tears began to flow from her eyes.

I sat back and observed.

"Who did this to this baby," Baby Sister asked embracing Javion.

"Melo and JoJo," I said.

"Melo and JoJo," Baby Sister yelled as she snatched her head around and looked at me.

I nodded. "They left a note on his head and said it was the new him,"

"Motherfuckers," Baby Sister quickly responded. "We got to get this baby to the hospital,"

--

"Ms. Rivers, can I see you for a moment," The emergency doctor at Greenwood Leflore Hospital said to Baby Sister as we were nervously waiting in the ER seating room.

Baby Sister looked at me with uncertainty, hoping for the best, but knowing deep down in her heart that the news she was about to receive would impact our lives forever.

The doctor and Baby Sister walked in another room.

"I hope he aight," I said rubbing both hands across my head.

Baby Sister returned just as fast as she left, with her head hanging to her chest.

"What's wrong with him," I asked with concern.

"He got severe trauma to the brain," Baby Sister said with a shaking voice.

"He gone be aight, right," I asked.

Baby Sister didn't respond. She started to wipe tears from her eyes.

"Baby Sister," I yelled.

Baby Sister shook her head and patted me on the leg, "Naw, he ain't gone be alright,"

Chapter 40

Though I had dropped out of school in the 9th grade, I had taken the GED and passed it. I took the ASVAB like I promised Money and joined the Navy as I told King Lee I would.

The phone alarm broke the silence of the old light blue shotgun house. I turned over and hit the volume button to snooze it. The day had finally arrived, I was leaving for the Navy. My flight was booked and my bags were packed.

Fear overcame me for some reason. Something didn't feel right.

I got up, put on my clothes, and headed south to Baby Sister's house.

"Baby Sister," I screamed as I beat on the door for the 5th time with no answer. It was unusual for Baby Sister to have her front door closed in the middle of the day. Usually the front screen door would be locked with the front door open. I dared not to walk in without getting Baby Sister's permission first.

Something wasn't sitting right with me still. Everything seemed a little bit too calm, too peaceful.

I took a leap of faith and carefully opened the front door and tip toed around the living room. I noticed how quiet the house was, like no one was at home.

Then I heard someone breathing heavy. I quickly tip toed into Melo's room where I found Javion lying in bed, sleeping.

"Javion," I thought. "Why you in here by yoself"

I noticed a packed bag on the bed. I knew then what Baby Sister's final verdict was towards taking care of Javion. She knew I was leaving today.

"That bitch," I said aloud as I looked to the sky and sighed with both hands on my head.

I observed Javion. I noticed he wasn't the innocence and pure little boy I once knew.

I couldn't figure out why Javion, so young, so promising, had been sentenced to a life of hell where he couldn't function on his own, where he had to depend on others to survive.

"You ain't gone be a burden to nobody," I cried. I knew well enough how it felt not to be wanted, how it felt to be a burden on people, how it felt to be alone.

"Go ahead," the small voice inside my head said. "You know how to free him,"

"I can't. He just a little boy," I yelled with a face filled with tears.

"Free him. Then for sure he won't be nobody burden, he will be free," The small voice inside my head said.

The tug a war of wills between me and the small voice inside my head went on for hours seemed like. I wanted Javion to be free but I didn't want him to die. But I didn't want him to go through life where he would be mistreated either. I knew if I didn't free Javion, the small voice inside my head would stalk me the rest of my life with guilt.

I looked around to see what I could use to ease Javion's pain, to set him free from this world, a world that wouldn't give a damn about him.

"I care enough to give you wings Champ," I cried. "You need to be with King Lee and Money. They gone take care of you, better than me or Baby Sister. They ain't hurting no more Javion. They free,"

I walked over to Javion and picked up a pillow that laid beside his little head. I observed him for a second as he slept peacefully. I kissed him on the forehead and said my final goodbye.

"Tell them guys I said what's up and to take good care of you," I whispered.

I reluctantly placed the pillow over Javion face.

"I can't," I pleaded with the small voice inside my head.

I stepped away from the pillow, sighed, shook my head, trying my best to convince myself that this was the right thing to do.

"Free him," the small voice inside my head demanded. "Free him,"

I stepped back to the pillow, sighed again. Deep down, I knew this was the best thing for Javion.

"I rather see you free than for somebody to throw you away," I whispered.

I started to put presser on the pillow. With every ounce of pressure that I applied to the pillow, my eyes blinked and released my deepest regrets through tears. To me, this was the hardest but most noble thing I have ever done in my life.

"No," I heard a muffle through the pillow as clear as day.

"Javion," I said confused.

I removed the pillow from his head and found him crying.

"You……..hurt……………me," Javion said with a rhythm in his voice.

Those muffled words tore me to pieces. Javion had felt my spirit, felt my love, felt my regret. Javion was telling me that he understood and that he wanted to stay with me. He felt the safest with me.

"I just want you to be free and not suffer," I said as I grabbed and hugged him tightly.

As Javion fell asleep on my lap, I sat there with my head in my hands. I had two choices before me. Leave for the Navy or stay in the City, take care of Javion, kill JoJo entire bloodline, and make Melo and others like her and JoJo suffer.

The more I thought about it, it all made sense to me. When I thought about the Navy, I felt numb inside but when I thought about finding Melo and JoJo to make them pay for what they did to Javion, I felt warm and bubbly inside.

I knew I was young and the Navy would always be there until I got old.

The choice was easy. I grabbed Javion, jumped in the white '69 Mustang and set out on my mission of finding Melo.

It didn't matter how far or how long it would take, they both were as good as dead. Only a bullet to my head would stop my vengeance against them.

Letter from Chandler Alexander

Dear Reader,

I hope this novel finds you and yours in the best of health and strength. First, let me give thanks to you from the bottom of my heart for your support in making my dream of becoming an author come true. I am at a loss for words for the support and feedback that I have received from this novel. I am truly grateful.

Author-hood for me began in the Mississippi Delta, where I was born and raised. It was those experiences and hardships growing up that shaped my perspective on life and opened my eyes to real social and economic epidemics that I am sure people have heard of but haven't really felt or lived.

From the many experiences in my life, I have developed a true understanding of who I am as an author. Simple and plain, I want to author books that gives life to the voiceless. I want to tackle social and economic issues such as poverty, mental illness, violence, education, domestic abuse, broken homes and so on through the written word. I want to leave readers with voices of reason or explanations for questions they may have had before or developed while combing through the pages of my work. Enlightenment is what I want to bring forth as an author. I want that light bulb to glow in the minds of readers from what they have learned and received from my work!

In all, writing for me is a way to help the world as I see it. No, I am not an English guru but I can honestly say with conviction that I am overly enthusiastic about writing stories that will hopefully impact a reader's life for the better. That's my passion.

Most importantly, with all of my work, I want you as reader to find your lesson. Find hope in it. Find understanding in it. Find a new perspective from it.

I humbly ask that you please share this novel and my other works with everyone that you know and give your honest assessment about it in the form of a review.

Again thank you!

With unmatched gratitude and a humble heart,

Chandler Alexander
www.chandleralexander.com

www.ingramcontent.com/pod-product-compliance
Lightning Source LLC
Chambersburg PA
CBHW021424240626
47153CB00001B/15